THE HAPPY PARTY
OF HONORABLE WOMEN

CATE QUINTARA

Water
street
press

First edition, November 2012

Cover design by Mark A. Bartman

Interior design by Typeflow

Produced in the United States of America

ISBN: 978-1-62134-033-1

Acknowledgements

"I touch the future. I teach."
—Christa McAuliffe

Everything we build, we build on the efforts of others. How long the list would be for a writer who tried to acknowledge all those who helped to create his or her work—the first ancient to sit by the fire and tell the people a tale, Gutenberg, the geniuses who built the Internet, let alone the children who wait quietly outside the study door so the writer can turn out a few more paragraphs, the husbands who take us out to dinner when we are too tired to cook after a day at our desks, the friends who believe us when we tell them we are writing a book, and don't laugh. I'd like to take this opportunity to particularly acknowledge one group of people to whom writers owe an enormous debt, rarely paid: elementary schoolteachers. Where would writers be without readers— and where would readers come from without those who actually teach us to read? Who taught you to read? Reach back through the years and remember. Why not send that most important person a note—or better yet, send a book, and it doesn't even have to be this one—to say thank you?

One more important thank you is due here, and that is to my agent, Elizabeth Trupin-Pulli. Like the very best of teachers she has opened up a world I hadn't known before I met her—and continues to be a patient, joyful and inspiring guide.

For Christy

She is a friend of mind.

She gather me, man.

The pieces I am, she gather them and

give them back to me in

all the right order.

TONI MORRISON
BELOVED

Prologue
Saturday

AT A WEDDING, THE ROLE OF THE BRIDE'S mother's best friend is usually a supporting one. It involves no official duties in any tradition the women are aware of, no common expectations outside of the ones of friendship itself, though those expectations may well be heightened by the many details and frayed nerves that must be seen to and soothed in the week immediately preceding the event. Like the mother of the groom, the bride's mother's best friend is ideally a woman who efficiently accomplishes any errands assigned to her, shows up on time, keeps her opinions to herself unless specifically solicited, and wears beige.

In any case, it's not a role that should be played with a hangover.

Deanie Morrow hears the telephone in her hotel room ring at precisely 6:42 AM on the day of the wedding. The sound it makes is a high-pitched, rough-edged, industrial jangle that Deanie has never heard before, not once in the entire week she's been in residence at the Farron House—everyone having deferred to her cell phone when they needed to dial her up—and the jangle is so abrupt and aggressive and inhumane it might have scared the pants off her except that she is already naked. She is standing in the shower, letting the steamy water work its cure on the sins and excesses of last night's rehearsal dinner. She is just lathering her hair, raising her hands slowly to her head because her armpits are sore—a phenomenon she blames on trotting out her once-incomparable dance moves at the club they all went to after the dinner, and on whoever it was who told the disc jockey to play the limbo in the first place—when the hotel phone startles her. It makes her take a slippery little hop and blink in surprise so the shampoo rinses out of her hair and right into her retinas.

"Ow, ow, owww…" Deanie's lids squeeze tight, automatically, into the sort of fierce squint that Botox should have rendered impossible. "*Fudge*," she shouts, stretching one bare arm outside the plastic curtain to grope blindly in the unfamiliar bathroom for a towel to press against her soap-stung eyes, maneuvering the fingers of her other hand in an attempt to turn off the water without scalding herself.

Fudge?

Deanie has taken it upon herself to watch her mouth all through this wedding week, in deference to the company she's been keeping—the nun, the two priests, the parents of her childhood friends; she is surprised and maybe a little pleased that she's used the euphemism now in private, too, as if she's broken a bad habit, though her staff back on the west coast would be shocked into no words at all if they heard one so sweet and chocolaty coming out of Deanie's mouth the next time she needed to blow off a little steam: *Go fudge yourself.*

Get the fudge out of here.

Fudge off.

The phone's deafening call is continuous—*brring, brring, brrrring* without the customary pause to collect itself between summonses. Deanie steps out of the tub, clutching the towel to one eye and trying tentatively to open the other, alternating between eyes, dripping suds on the carpet and the clothing and newspapers and notebooks that have exploded in the room in the course of trying to keep up with the week's hectic prenuptial itinerary. If there had been time to hang up an outfit or put the cap back on the toothpaste before collapsing on the bed at the end of the day, there had not been energy or inclination—and Deanie had instructed the housekeepers she met in the hallway each morning while jabbing at the elevator button, on the fly to whatever activity or task the bride's mother had scheduled for her, NOT to make up her room. It is a mess in there but she is pretty sure she still knows where everything is and she doesn't want someone else's sense of order confusing matters. She doesn't want to have to think about where the maid might have stashed her curling iron before she can put her hands on it and plug it back in. And she's a little embarrassed, too; she hasn't lived amid such chaos since...

Well, since the last time she spent one solid week in a hotel room. In May. In Nashville, where she traveled to give the keynote speech at the Tennessee Writers' League conference.

Now she catches the persimmon-painted toes of her right foot in the aggressively green hotel comforter that has worked its way half off of the mattress and steps on something sharp and hard hiding under a corner of it. *"Fudge,"* she shrieks at the remote control to the preposterously large hotel TV as she kicks it completely under the bed. She regrets she hasn't allowed the housekeeping staff to at least try to keep the place tidy. "I'm *coming*," she snaps as she limps toward the insistent telephone.

THE TELEPHONE IS a most chameleon-like device. Deanie remembers with fond nostalgia the heavy chunk of black plastic in her grandmother's kitchen, the pink princess model that was installed in her teenaged bedroom, the neat beige Trimline she ordered for her very first apartment—all recognizably instruments of communication no matter how unalike and cumbersome they appear next to the tiny silver gadget she now carries in her purse and that blasts the *Hallelujah* chorus when it is one of her lovers on the line.

But styles change. Grandma's black iron cook stove is not Mom's harvest gold electric range, is not the stainless steel Viking that remains in fresh-from-the-factory condition in Deanie's Napa Valley kitchen because she is hardly ever home long enough to use it. Where a telephone differs radically from other appliances of modern life is that it holds in its indifferent, fiber optic heart the power to change a life with one little ring.

At twenty-two, on one crisp December morn, Deanie answered the phone in her parents' living room to find her fiancé on the other end of the line telling her that he wouldn't be coming for Christmas and, by the way, he was canceling out on their February wedding date, too. At twenty-four she rarely answered the phone at all, letting the bill collector's messages accumulate on her answering machine while she pounded out words at forty cents a pop on her old Remington

Ten-Forty, meeting a deadline at one of the tabloids that used her stories—WOMAN BORN WITH THREE BREASTS GIVES BIRTH TO TRIPLETS. She soothed herself on payday: at least she was earning her living writing fiction, and the intermittent income allowed her to reach into her UNPAID file and write a check before the phone service was shut off. Again.

Sometimes she wondered why she bothered.

And then, at twenty-seven, she let the answering machine screen yet another call and heard her agent's voice telling her to pick up, he'd just sold her first novel.

Good news, bad news, Deanie has heard it all in tinny telephone voices, which is why that small but hyper-alert part of herself braces and prepares for a wrench to be thrown into the works whenever she hears the jingling, especially if the jingling comes at an odd, early hour. In fact—and Deanie knows this from what is now fifty-two years of experience—heartbreaking news can be announced at the most innocent time of day. In practice, a phone ringing at 6:42 AM revs up what is already Deanie's impatient nature, as if she could intimidate tragedy by being cranky.

"What the hell?"

"Well, finally," Jill Bakula, the mother of the bride, says in reply. "I thought you were never going to pick up."

"Lord, Jill, the phones at this place would make good air raid sirens. You scared the crap out of me. Why didn't you call on my cell?"

"I've *been* calling your cell. But you put it on vibrate when it went off in the church at rehearsal last night and I think you haven't put it back on regular ring."

"Really?" This subdues her. If Jill is right, she's been disconnected from her staff—her lifeline—for over twelve hours.

The books Deanie writes, while fiction, take their premises from the headlines. The last one was about a group of women friends in the suburban Midwest who respond to the critical infant mortality rate in Africa by founding a cooperative that collects and ships great quantities of that miracle elixir, breast milk, to an orphanage they adopt in Cameroon. "Your books inspire people, especially women, to realize the power even the most ordinary person has to change the world for the better," one gushing interviewer had said to her on her last book tour. It was needed validation since, in the same week, the *New York Times* had called *The Warriors of Flint, Michigan* "another four hundred pages of overblown, sentimental claptrap from the pen of America's reigning mistress of mush."

"Look at the name of the critic," Deanie's assistant, Layla, had urged when the review appeared. "It's a *man*. Men never get your books." It was the young woman's attempt at consolation and Deanie was too busy packing for the Bakula wedding in Pennsylvania to explain that both she and her readers were used to unkind reviews. Or to point out that such broad gender generalizations were the very sort of obstacles to understanding and healing that she railed about in her books.

Deanie retrieves her purse from the floor and rummages through it for the phone—for all she knows Madonna has adopted another baby and Meredith Vieira wants her via satellite right now to comment on the week of research she did in Malawi. But even as she dumps the contents of her purse on the bed, she has to ask, "Jillie, what are you calling about? Everyone's all right? Right?"

It is a reflexive reaction to her own, not-unjustified mistrust of ringing telephones and the messages they might have to deliver. But Deanie has picked up a jingling phone before and heard anguish in Jill's voice; she knows too intimately exactly what her friend would sound like if everyone she loved were not all right. And, posed as the question is, on the morning of a wedding—when surely the hairdresser is creating drama in the bride's bathroom by overdoing her up-do and the photographer is due any minute and the groomsmen are huddled in the living room catching the scores on ESPN, picking at the elaborate breakfast buffet Jill has inevitably laid out and getting confectioner's sugar all down the fronts of their black tuxedo jackets—well, it seems especially inane.

Jill sighs and Deanie can picture her throwing up her arms. "Who gets married at *noon*? I told Madeline an evening ceremony would be so much more civilized. I feel like we're all going to turn back into pumpkins if we don't get to the church by eleven-fifteen and, Dean… I could really use an extra pair of hands."

Deanie tucks the receiver under her chin and looks into the mirror over the hotel desk. She digs through her luggage looking for Advil, Tylenol, anything at all to address the aches in her head and under her arms, for the tiny bottle of Visine she is sure she cannot have forgotten to pack. The stinging in her eyes has subsided but they are rimmed red from their battle to expel the shampoo, as shot-through with blood as a vampire's. "Of course. Anything I can do, you know that. One question though. Is this going to be a quickie? That is, will I have time to come back to the hotel and change before I have to be at the church myself, or should I get dressed in my wedding finery right now?"

Deanie hears something ominous in the way Jill pauses before she answers. "You'd better get dressed."

Fudge. Forty years of friendship has taught Deanie that Jill relinquishes self-sufficiency, her control and her poise, only on her own terms. Something is going on that she doesn't want to go into over the phone. Deanie thinks fast: hair—five minutes, minimum; make-up—three minutes flat if she foregoes putting in her contacts; dress—she can waylay one of the housekeepers to set up the ironing board she's seen at the back of her room's closet and give her dress a pressing; there are precious seconds to be saved by bypassing the concierge, and she'll tip generously for the service, and these ladies owe her one after a whole week of not having to bother about changing her sheets; travel—the six miles to the Bakula house can be covered, theoretically, in twelve minutes if she presses the speed limits and doesn't get lost on the way.

"Half an hour, honey. Help is on its way."

Chapter One
Sunday

DEANIE MORROW HEARS THE MUSIC coming from 1858 Greentree Court before she has even turned off the motor of her rental car, even though all of the car's windows are rolled up tight, merry music with a beat pounding like an excited heart.

Through the house's front window she sees that the living room furniture has all been pushed up against the walls and the carpet has been rolled back and the bride and her younger brother are teaching their college friends how to polka so they won't be caught clueless on the dance floor at a Polish wedding. The kids have a recording of the "Beer Barrel Polka" spinning on an old turntable set up in a corner on the floor. An accordion is being squeezed at warp decibel level and they are laughing even louder than that, twirling each other around the room, the girls making fruitless attempts at modesty, swishing their arms over their behinds, the flying hems of their short summer skirts. They don't even notice the front door opening and Deanie walking in.

There is similar wreckage in the dining room. The long dining room table is pushed up under a window, groaning under gift boxes wrapped in sparkly papers and gossamer ribbons. The place cards that one of the bride's college friends, an art major, has been charged to calligraphy are spread out on a card table in the middle of the room. Fabric that Deanie recognizes as the floor-length curtains that usually hang at the bay window in the family room is puddled in a heap at the foot of the staircase. Through an archway, in the big, country-style kitchen, the remains of the day's buffets that Jill has been typically extravagant about—dinner, lunch, and it looks like breakfast, too— are spread all along the countertops and the dishwasher is standing open, evidence that someone has attempted to tidy up. Deanie bangs her right shin against one of the picnic coolers stacked beside the archway, keeping the overflow from the refrigerator on ice. She gives out a little groan of pain that has no chance of being heard over the kids in the living room shout-singing—"WE'VE GOT THE BLUES ON THE RUN!"—and backs up into a half a yard of potting soil mounded on the kitchen floor.

Two young men in Hawaiian shirts and baggy shorts are standing in the kitchen, pumping a keg of Michelob in the corner, refilling a pitcher for the gang in the living room. They pause, panting with exertion, goofy-drunk smiles across their pretty faces, to politely acknowledge Deanie as she shakes the potting soil from her ankles and the soles of her sandals and between her toes.

"I'm Deanie Morrow. Jill's best friend," Deanie calls across the room to introduce herself, reluctant to approach and track dirt all over the tiles. "Madeline's godmother," she adds to establish her connection to the bride herself.

"Josh," the taller of the two pretty boys calls back to her and "George," calls the other. "Friends of the groom… Grooms-men," Josh adds to establish the boys' place in the scheme of the surrounding chaos. They don't approach Deanie either, fastened as they are to their task of refreshing libations for the party in the living room. Deanie knows there are six grooms-men total, Jill has told her this much; she notices Josh's height, and the wisp of whiskers that George wears directly below his bottom lip—clues that will help her to keep the boys' names straight during the wedding week ahead.

Deanie wonders if all people her own age experience this same sense of illusion and disconnect when in the company of a group of much younger adults, this same stubborn inability to tell them apart. She reads the fan magazines, for instance— sometimes, every April when her newest book is released, she is *in* the fan magazines—and she can pick out in a wink images of Harrison Ford and Michael Douglas, real movie stars. Confronted with the new crop of Owens and Orlandos, Mischas and Minnies, she is hard-pressed to put the name to the face, to identify with certainty the Kate who is danger-ously thin from the Kate who was married to Tom Cruise. Is this because, she asks herself, these young adults are still so generically pretty and accomplished? That they've yet to either be marked by life or leave a distinguishing mark upon it?

On the other hand—to give Deanie her due—she is mark-edly moved by how distinctive her *own* young people are. Though she has never had children herself, she has taken on fierce parental pride in her friends' children—the bride,

Madeline's robust modeling career, clipped short by her acceptance at and decision to attend law school; her younger brother, Chas's dazzle as a college soccer star and how he has, in the year since graduation, translated that talent to coaching, helping the youngsters who make up his Boys Club teams to have their own shiny lives.

It is wholly within Deanie's personal mythology to believe that her own young people, Madeline and Chas, fell from a star to live among mere mortals like herself; she recognizes the disinclination to extend this generosity to other young adults as a genuine shortcoming. For a moment she thinks she will act on the impulse to enter the living room, scoop Madeline and Chas into her arms as she did when they were small, insert herself as instructor into the wild polka party—it would be a perfect way to get to know all of the kids' friends. It was, after all, for their parents' Polish wedding that Deanie herself leaned to do the dance and now she's had thirty years of practice. But the moment passes as she feels almost overcome with the urge to wrap her arms around the font and anchor of the loudness and liveliness and life in this house, her childhood friend, the kids' mother.

"Do you know where Jill is?" Deanie shouts to the two boys at the keg.

George, who is holding the pitcher under the tap while Josh pumps, nods his head in the direction of the family room, through a second archway, to Deanie's right, and she turns and sees a head of unruly black curls bobbing up and down over the back of the green plaid sofa. She waves and smiles to dismiss the boys and decides to take off her shoes before she takes the two short steps down into the family room and makes her way around the couch.

"No, now, don't you feel bad," Jill is saying into the receiver of a cordless telephone. She makes a check mark on one of the pads of yellow legal paper on the coffee table in front of her, scribbles "2 chicken" next to the name she's checked. "I don't want you to feel bad, I'm sure your RSVP card is just lost somewhere in the disaster on my desk. It's just, you know, *caterers…*" She rolls her eyes, saying the word as if she has been forced to curse. "I have to give a final count to the caterer in the morning."

Through some quirk of acoustics, the music coming from the living room is muted down in the family room—maybe it is the thick red shag carpeting absorbing the tuba's bleat—but still Jill has got a finger jammed in her free ear so she can hear over the party at the other end of the house. When she looks up and sees Deanie standing in front of her she is immediately on her feet, speaking in quick clips to her caller—"Well, thank you. Got to run. Lots of details to see to. See you at the church!"—and she has Deanie in her arms even before she presses the "End" button.

"Ohmigod!"

"Ohmigod!"

They hug hard and long, Deanie's face tangled in her friend's halo of kiwi-scented curls, Jill's nose pressed into Deanie's neck where Chanel perfume doesn't quite mask the fatigue of a day of plane travel. They hug and rock together and then hold each other at arm's length so they can peer into each other's faces and squeal like the little girls they once were together.

"Ohmigod, you look so good!" Jill cries.

"So do you!" Deanie answers, truthfully. When Jill and Deanie look at each other they don't see middle age, encroaching crow's feet or thinning lips; they see dewy teenagers who have yet to wince under a syringe of Botox or lower the hem of a skirt in prudent consideration of an aging knee or sweat through a hot flash. They see each other's energy, each other's spirit, each other animated with the wisdom that accumulates with years of living and is nevertheless trembling with optimism. Enthusisam. Cheer, unsullied and guileless.

"I thought you were going to be here in time for dinner! I was starting to wonder if I should worry."

"I would have been here in time to eat, but my plane was delayed in San Francisco, and there was a mix up with the rental car in Philadelphia. And I got lost on the way to your house…"

Jill still lives in Lenapi, Pennsylvania, the town where the women met as seventh grade girls and grew up. But Jill lives in a development tucked within the rolling hills on the outskirts of town, built long after Deanie had left for college, New York City, several interludes of several years each in Italy, the final sanctuary she found in the vineyards of the Napa Valley. Jill and her family have lived in the same house in the "new" development for going on seventeen years and Deanie has never been able to remember the directions clearly enough to drive directly there when she comes for a visit: the curve of Hemlock Lane turning into Willow Way and snaking off into a cul-de-sac that is decidedly NOT Greentree Court unless Deanie is very careful about the street signs, or someone has thought to cut back the lush suburban shrubbery that overtakes them every spring.

Even then there is the challenge of determining just which little Tudor belongs to the Bakulas, squinting at the numbers painted on the curbs to find the right driveway. Deanie had been crawling around the cul-de-sac like she was casing the joint when she noticed the creamy tulle draped abundantly around the entrance of number 1858, the bundles of pale purple paper lilacs that held the fabric back at either side of the front door, the two silver cardboard bells over it that announced there was a bride-to-be living within, a wedding taking place, joy in this house.

And then she had heard the music. The merry music had perked her ears at the very moment the automatic timer lights decided that dusk had become evening. The Bakula house had glowed and vibrated unmistakably before her.

"What's up with rental car agencies these days?" Deanie asks, still clutching her friend, forearm-to-forearm. "I ordered a compact car. I very specifically told Layla to ask for the smallest model they've got when she made the reservation, because I don't want to use up more than my share of precious gasoline, but when I get to the counter in Philly the clerk informs me, all chirpy, that I've been 'upgraded,' at no additional cost, and she wants me to be all 'thank you, thank you!' Like I can't smell the scam: nobody wants to pay for precious gasoline these days and so everybody is requesting small cars, and SUVs are all they've got left on the lot. I argued with her for twenty minutes."

"What's up these days with people not RSVP-ing to wedding invitations? I've got a list of twenty calls I have to make before I meet with the caterer tomorrow because people are too lazy to drop a pre-addressed, pre-stamped envelope in the mailbox."

"You win," Deanie says and the women clutch each other one more time, squeal their way into one more familiar, comforting embrace, and then Deanie gasps for a drink. "White wine, beer, whatever you've got that's cold and alcoholic."

"Mojitos," Jill informs her, untangling herself from her friend's arms. "I've been waiting until you got here to have my first one, which is what really annoyed me about you being so late." Jill moves to the kitchen and starts to rearrange the plates and platters on the counters so she'll have room to squeeze limes and muddle their puckery juice with mint and sugar and rum. "Do you want a sandwich? When was the last time you ate?"

"San Francisco." Deanie follows Jill up into the kitchen, shouting again so she'll be heard over "The Sneaky Pete Polka." "I had some sushi at this unlikely good place right at the airport. I'll just pick." She rolls up a slice of pastrami from one of the deli trays on the counter and bites into it, uses the portion that remains in her fingers to gesture around the kitchen. "So, I get the coolers and the card table and the rest of the disarray. Why the potting soil?"

"Lovers' herbs," Jill shouts back. "Rosemary for fidelity, and I don't remember what the thyme and basil stand for. Shakespeare laid it all out, Madeline tells me—said with a smirk, no less. 'You're a librarian, Mom, for crying out loud, you've read every book on the shelves in that place. I can't believe you don't know this.' The one thing my legal-eagle daughter gets from the one English Lit class she ever took and she's holding it over my head. Anyway, we're potting lovers' herbs in these really cute terra cotta cherubs for centerpieces at the rehearsal dinner."

Deanie nods and accepts the tall, acrylic glass of Mojito that Jill hands to her. "Are we going out on the deck?" she shouts.

"Unless you like competing with Verne Meisner and the Wisconsin Polka Kings."

JILL CLICKS ON the deck lights as they go out the sliding glass door in the family room. Floodlights illuminate the pool. Jill and Chuck Bakula bought this house because of the pool, when Chuck's doctor told them that swimming was the best exercise he could do for rehab after the accident. Chuck, a former soccer star himself, had never really taken to any activity that took him off dry land, but the pool had been taken over every summer since by the couple's two children and all of their little friends. "Best investment in keeping track of the kids we ever made." Strings of small, orange Chinese lanterns hung from a wooden trellis light up seating areas around the pool—three large picnic tables with benches and a dozen lounge chairs are scattered around, mismatched furniture acquired as the family and the circle around them grew.

Deanie closes the door behind her and the dance party inside is instantly muffled. She pauses for a moment to listen to the crickets talking in the night, and to take in the view from Jill's deck. A view like this, overlooking the nightlights of Lenapi, was impossible when the women were girls, unless they hiked up into the undeveloped hillsides, a thing they would never have dared to do in the dark. The view encompasses all of Lenapi, anchored by the strip of globed streetlights through the distant downtown, making the town look large and impressive and, at the same time, compressed into a glowing repository of memory, as if a person could hold it in the palm of her hand. Deanie looks into the light-dotted density before her and then sinks her travel-weary body gratefully into the thick cushions of one of the lounge chairs.

The women take satisfied sips of their frosty drinks. It is a longstanding joke between them that Jill missed her calling by taking up books instead of bartending as a profession; the Mojitos are delicious. At last Deanie speaks. "All right.

Catch me up," she says and, leaning toward the chair where Jill has taken a seat, adds, "and then put me to work." Jill is frequently and accurately described as ultra-organized and uber-efficient but, no matter how serenely she's checking off items on her to-do list, one look around the Bakula household and anyone can tell there is plenty left to do.

"No, Deanie," Jill protests, "this is your vacation."

Jill has been one of Deanie's best friends ever since the summer night in 1967 when three twelve-year-old girls were taken into police custody for breaking into the new wing of the Lenapi town library while it was still under construction and climbing the scaffolding to its roof. It was an event that had put the fear of God into at least two of them and that began, improbably, a friendship that each of them would find essential for the rest of their whole lives.

Jill was a Kuznicki back then—she married Chuck Bakula the year after their college graduations—and the extended Kuznicki-Bakula clan, though small by even modern standards and certainly by Catholic ones, was as close-knit as any Deanie had knowledge of. Through a friendship that has now spanned forty years, Deanie—as well as the third member of their girlish triad, Trick Danforth Kiley—has been taken into the clan's big heart as one of its own, expected to attend births and deaths, baptisms and First Communions and graduations and Madeline's Sweet Sixteen party and Jill's parents' fiftieth anniversary dinner and now this wedding as unquestioningly as if the blood shared among them amounts to much more than the few drops the twelve-year-olds had stabbed their fingers to swap on the roof of the town's library, before the police showed up.

But the Kuznicki-Bakula clan is also, within its small circle, maddeningly self-sufficient, not to mention too thoroughly polite to impose on their friends without good cause. Forty years and counting and this ritual of consideration still irritates the hell out of Deanie: "Don't you dare play the good hostess with me, Jill Bakula. I didn't come to Lenapi an entire week early only to be an attendee at the pre-wedding festivities—the bridal shower and the bachelorette party and the rehearsal dinner. I intend to be a functional part of getting my goddaughter down the aisle."

Jill stifles a smile. And, then, almost as instantly, she frowns. Jill knows that her house is the place that Deanie conjures when she thinks of "going home." Beautiful, flamboyant Deanie, in all of her successful, peripatetic life has never had a family of her own. Ever. Even her parents, when they were alive, never really made a place for their only child in their crowded, sun-kissed lives. Every one of the Bakulas is quick to check himself and draw Deanie in a little closer whenever she gets sensitive or insecure about the place they have made for her. "If that's the way you feel," Jill says in reply, and Deanie lets out a satisfied, indignant little grunt to close the matter.

The women fall silent then, drinking in rum and the contentment of being in one another's company. Six months separate them from their last visit with each other and still there is no rush to talk now that the initial squealing is over. They have spent too many long nights lying on the grass in one or another's back yard, listening to the ancestors of tonight's crickets sing their summer songs, dreaming and plotting, questioning and composing answers to whatever circumstances of life were immediately confronting them to feel any urgency now. Now, both of them are home.

Yet, within the depth and duration of their happy silence, there is a hard subject waiting to be brought up, some suitable answers to be composed for questions that have been plaguing their phone conversations for months.

But they will get to that.

Only, not just yet.

Not yet.

"So," DEANIE ASKS lazily, after a while, "what are Madeline's colors?" She feels that she's been deficient in not knowing this very basic information, and she's been thinking that she wants to go to Kelly's Candy and Floral down on Main Street and order bags of gumdrops and gummi bears and candied almonds in Madeline's bridal colors to give as favors at the shower. She likes the notion of presenting Madeline with an extravagant display of sugar as a metaphor for the sweet life that she is wishing for her.

"I can't tell you."

Deanie turns her head and cocks it toward Jill. "What do you mean you can't tell me?"

Jill shrugs. "Madeline's orders and, frankly, I'm not sure what she's finally settled on."

"Oh, come on, how can the mother of the bride not know a thing like that?"

"Cream colored tablecloths and napkins. White flowers. That's what I know." Jill tilts her Mojito glass until an ice cube falls into her mouth, and she crunches it.

"Well…" Deanie shakes her head. "What color are the bridesmaids wearing?"

"Dunno," Jill says innocently, and truthfully, and then she looks over at Deanie, the tiniest bit of alarm in her eyes. "You did get my message, didn't you? Madeline wants you and me and all of us old girls in little black dresses. You did bring a black dress?"

"Of course I did, and when have you ever known me not to have a black dress on hand anyway? I think Madeline's request that we all wear black is tasteful, and sophisticated— and bearing that in mind I am going to choose to assume she's not going to put her bridesmaids in god-awful orange Quiana."

"It was *coral*. And those dresses were very much in style in 1978."

"I rest my case."

After another few minutes of silence, while Jill pouts, Deanie speaks again. "Which of the pretty boys is for me?"

Jill chokes on the piece of ice she's chewing, sits up and spits it into her hand. "Deanie Morrow, don't you dare take any of the groomsmen to bed."

"Give me one good reason to break with tradition, please."

"Those are my soon-to-be son-in-law's friends!"

"And your point is?"

Jill pelts her with the melting ice cube and when she stops laughing she says, "You know, Rob Tedesco is going to be at the wedding. He's coming in on Friday. Chuck is just all over the idea that our whole wedding party is going to be at our daughter's wedding, too. Rob's single again now, and Chuck says he still asks after you."

Deanie grins. "Of course he does," she says, and makes Jill groan.

They chuckle, in counterpoint to the concert of crickets. And then Deanie whispers, "Jillie?"

"Yes?"

"You ready to talk about Trick?"

Jill sighs, a soft little snort that says she doesn't know where to begin.

"Are you still mad at her, then?"

"Furious," Jill confirms. "Aren't you?"

Deanie doesn't know. Anger enters into it, but she's more frightened than she is pissed off. "Is she staying on her meds this time? Is she keeping her appointments with her therapist?"

Jill purses her lips and expels air forcefully and pointedly— "*Pffft*"—a sound of thorough disgust. "She says she is."

Deanie nods. "You wouldn't be so mad at her if you didn't love her so much."

This comment brings Jill to a posture of rigid attention, a hard effect to achieve, sunk as she is into the downy cushions of the poolside recliner, but Jill pulls it off. "I'm going to tell you what: if you still lived around here, and you were the one who got the telephone call every time she made some new mess, that wouldn't be so easy for you to say. How hard is it to remember to take a couple of little pills every day? I am so tired of sitting next to her on a hospital bed or in a police station and hearing her say, 'But, Jillie, I *felt* fine. I thought I could do all right without the drugs this time, I was feeling really strong, but… I'm sorry. I'm so, so sorry. Does everyone know what I did? Did you tell Deanie?' You know she isn't here tonight because she didn't want to see you? She says facing you is going to be the hardest part."

"Well, that's just Trick being dramatic…"

"I know that. I know that! She's using you as her excuse this time. If she doesn't pull herself together and get to this wedding it's going to break Madeline's heart and then I really will never forgive her."

There is more to say. There are forty years of words to say. There are a hundred million words that have been said and shouted and cried and muttered and laughed and whispered among three little girls who rode their bikes together around one small Pennsylvania town and had sleepovers at each other's houses and took turns tickling each other's arms before they fell asleep and painted each other's toenails tomato red and made crank calls to the boys they really liked on pink princess telephones and Deanie and Jill want to recall every one of the words so maybe they can follow the story of how they got to this place, this dangerous place of being fifty-two years old—a place that means such different things to all three of them. Jill has raised a world-class family, and Deanie has achieved worldwide fame, and Trick has flailed around the world, more or less, depending on whether she's downed her Lithium on any given day, and she has never once gotten it right.

This time, though, this last time, six months ago, Trick had not wrecked her car and punched the police officer who showed up at the scene, or fallen down a staircase and dislocated her shoulder, or maxed out her credit cards or painted her entire kitchen purple or even picked up a phone at two AM and kept either Jill or Deanie on the line until both the night and the mania had passed. This time Trick had drawn herself a hot bath and climbed into the tub and slashed her wrists with her manicure scissors.

Then she had telephoned Jill.

By the time Deanie's staff had tracked her down in Africa and made arrangements for her to fly back to the States, Jill had Trick sedated and safely tucked in a hospital bed. She'd telephoned Trick's two grown sons, who were living in Texas, and told them to fly home, and she'd scrubbed the blood out of the grout in Trick's bathroom tiles so the boys wouldn't be horrified when they got there.

She had also called the radio station where Trick had been employed selling air time, to lie to them so Trick wouldn't lose this job, too: "Trick has had a family emergency, she will need to take a leave of several weeks, I think she'll be able to be back to work sometime the week of the seventeenth..."

She'd found out that Trick had been fired nearly two weeks earlier.

For ordering four cases of champagne and inviting all of her clients to a "live broadcast-slash-open house" that she hadn't bothered to tell anyone else at the station about, the idea having just occurred to her that morning, as she was listening to the station on the way into work; the station manager was still apoplectic when he told Jill about it ten days later.

Initially, Jill had directed her fury at the radio station people, people too hard-hearted to reach out a helping hand to a fellow employee who was clearly falling off the edge. Only later, after she'd managed Trick's affairs as efficiently and artfully as she always did when Trick couldn't manage them herself, did Jill decide that the person she was really mad at was Trick.

"She didn't even tell me she'd been fired. I should have known something was up because she wasn't returning any of my calls. When she avoids my calls, I should know by now, it's because something has triggered the depression. I should know that!

"But I never thought she would do this. Of all of the stupid, selfish things she's done at either extreme of her illness, and all of the warnings about bipolars nursing suicidal thoughts, I never thought...

"Deanie, the looks on her boys' faces when I picked them up at the airport! It broke my heart to see their faces, these sweet young men, and so desperate. How could a mother do a thing that makes her children have to look the way that those boys looked!"

Recalling the desperation on the faces of Trick's sons would plunge Jill into tears for weeks afterward. Now, six months later, her anger at Trick's betrayal has gelled into something harder, and less vulnerable.

"But," Deanie asks gently, "she's stayed on her meds for six months now, hasn't she? That's the longest she's ever been stabilized."

"Yes, it is." Jill fans her fingers to acknowledge that, as far as she knows, this is true. "And what kind of rose-colored, Pollyanna-world are you living in that makes you think she's not going to go waltzing down Crazy Lane again any day now?"

"Jill!"

Jill drops her face into her hands. She shakes her head, hard. "I can't believe I said that."

Jill's contrition makes Deanie feel protective of her. "It's the stress of the wedding talking, honey. That's all."

Jill laughs into her fingers, an abrupt snort that is as derisive as it is defeated. "You and I," she says to Deanie, "are either the most patient people in the world, or two of the greatest enablers in all of history."

THERE IS MORE to say—much more—but there is also Madeline, long legs and shining hair flying, leaving the sliding door standing open wide behind her so the crazy-happy notes of the accordion follow her out onto the deck. There is Madeline lunging for Deanie and shrieking, "I knew it was you, Auntie Dean! George just told me some hot older babe walked into the kitchen while he was refilling the beer pitcher and I

knew it had to be you! How was your trip? Please don't say
you are too tired from your trip, you have to come in here
and show my friends how to polka. Mom"—Madeline leans
over Deanie to plant a kiss firmly on the top of Jill's head—
"has been no help whatsoever in the dance department, what
with having her panties all in a knot about the final count for
the caterers, so you have to." Now Madeline is pulling Deanie
by the arm. "You *have* to."

There is Jill muttering that she's got nineteen more calls
to make to people too inconsiderate to RSVP to a wedding
invitation, and about an hour left in the day until it is no longer decent to make telephone calls—Jill waving Deanie off
with Madeline, and there is whirling around the bare hardwood floor in the living room with pretty boys and girls all
loose and daring on beer.

There is Chas, shy as he was as a baby boy and every bit
as tow-headed, leading Deanie around the dance floor once,
and twice, and ten times before he stops, panting, in front
of a young woman who is collapsed on the sofa, and intro-
duces her as his girlfriend, Allison. Allison's a writer, too, he
tells Deanie—or, she wants to be; she's just had a short story
accepted for publication in her university's literary magazine.
Chas's girlfriend is a tiny young woman with an out-sized
smile, clearly overcome at meeting this famous author, even if
she has known the identity of Chas's Auntie Dean for months.
Chas tells her now that Deanie is the person responsible for
any taste he's got for literature—"Sure, Mom is a librarian,
I'm not saying we didn't have access to books or encouragement to read, but nothing got me onto it like Auntie Dean
reading *The Stinky Cheese Man* to me at night before bed.
She did all the voices. Do the Little Red Hen, Dean—Ally,
this is going to crack you up…" Deanie attempts to invoke

the high-pitched Southern hysteria she remembers inflicting on the Little Red Hen, but she has not had as much beer to drink as the kids so, even though they laugh, she thinks she hasn't really pulled it off.

And there is then, because they are all hot and sweating from dancing, a break, Madeline removing the needle from the old 33 LP and one of the boys, a beefy boy with no neck and a football-shaped head whose utter lack of rhythm has made him unable to find any sort of satisfaction out on the dance floor, absolutely shudders with relief. There is cleaning up the kitchen—wrapping the perishables and finding places for them in the picnic coolers and stacking the dishwasher, which Deanie does while the kids kick the keg and two of the boys roll it out of the kitchen, to the garage, and bring in a fresh one and ice it down and tap it so it's ready to go the next day.

There is Chuck at last arriving home, hopping over to Deanie to put his arms around her in welcome, his still-lush mane of blond hair bouncing as he approaches, his silver braces still out in the car as he never uses them around the house—he is as steady on the one leg he's got left since the car accident as most other people are on the two God started them out with. He's been at dinner with potential philanthropists, wooing their donations to Lenapi's small but thriving satellite campus to the state university where he is the athletic director, and he announces now, with great cheer, that he is officially done with work obligations for the duration of the wedding week and someone needs to draw him a beer. "Holy shit," he says when Chas tells him that his is the first pint from the second keg. "You guys kicked a whole keg already? Without me? I guess someone will have to make a run to the distributor's tomorrow for another back-up." Josh takes it upon himself to remind their host that the original keg was tapped three whole days ago, last Friday afternoon and, anyway, it was only a quarter keg to start with.

There is Jill, quietly entering her kitchen where everyone is now gathered, sipping the last of their beers and lifting the Saran Wrap from a tray of cookies for a late evening nosh. Jill coming up beside Deanie, laying her carefully checked and neatly aligned yellow legal pads on the counter and her head on Deanie's shoulder, whispering, "I got through to everyone I had to call. And I'm better now. Let's go see Trick in the morning. First thing after the caterer." There is Jill smiling when Deanie answers her, touching her dark curls with her fingertips, "Yes. Let's."

There is, finally, confession—all the pretty boys and girls admitting, one after the other, that they are too sleepy, too tired, *too drunk* to drive back to the Farron House, and Chas declaring that they should all just stay over at the Bakulas'—"Lots of room right here." Plenty of sofas, and sleeping bags stored out in the garage to spread on the floors, and bunk beds in his room, and one of the girls can stay with Madeline in her room since Adam, the groom, isn't due to arrive until Tuesday, and there is Chuck taking exception to his son's presumption, the groom is damned well going to stay at the Farron House, too, until after the wedding, and there is Jill, her head still resting on Deanie's shoulder so Deanie feels her forehead tense, the subtle muscular contraction that indicates discomposure, a surrendering of self-possession, the beginnings of panic at the idea of waking up and having to step over bodies splayed in every room of her house as she tries to ready her notes for the caterer, steady herself to see Trick...

"I can take you all back to the hotel," Deanie tells the kids.

Jill lifts her head from Deanie's shoulder. "How are you going to do that?" she asks, counting the number of people who must be transported, the thinnest film of accusation coating her words. "There are eleven people who have to get back to the hotel and you spent twenty minutes fighting with the Hertz clerk to give you a compact car."

"I didn't," Deanie tells her, "say that I won the argument."

Chapter Two
1967

THE LENAPI LENDING LIBRARY—A NAME exploited for its comic potential by genera-tions of third graders daring their younger schoolmates to twist their tongues around it; "Go on, say it three times in a row, *fast*"—was the real, true name of the public library in the town of Lenapi, Pennsylvania. It was housed in one of the Victorian mansions on Clearview Avenue, a street so named because the lumber barons who'd founded Lenapi and built their big houses along the town's then-highest peak had a clear view down to the Schuylkill River and the logs that floated on its steady currents to their sawmills on the river's banks.

By 1967, Lenapi, Pennsylvania was a prosperous, pretty little mill town tucked into the lush green of the northeast's rolling hills. Most of the mansions on Clearview Avenue were

still single-family homes, like the one Deanie rattled around
in with her parents. Only a few had, at that time, been taken
over as offices for doctors or lawyers, and these were mostly
toward the eastern end of town, near to the Courthouse and
the post office and the commercial district that was located on
Front Street where it intersected with Clearview, down along
the river's bank where hardware stores and dress shops and
a Woolworth's that was a whole half a block long had long
ago replaced the sawmills. The grand, gilded Farron House,
at the corner of Front and Clearview, was just beginning to
be shabby, to ripen for the jaws of the 1970s urban renewal
programs that would tear out its Victorian soul, replacing its
marble tiles with aggressively green indoor/outdoor carpeting and its plaster frescos with sheet paneling.

The road that continued up the mountain, behind Clearview, was still unpaved and ground had not yet been broken
for the new hospital the town fathers were planning to build
up there. The explosive growth of the state university system
that would turn Lenapi State Teachers College into one of
that system's most successful satellite campuses, clear the rest
of the mountain behind Clearview and throw the decorous
old Victorians into the shadows of new classroom buildings
and dormitories and a cafeteria-slash-student union, had not
yet happened. The thought that a residential development of
mock Tudor mini-mansions might be just the thing to locate
beyond the new hospital and campus buildings had not yet
occurred to anyone.

In 1967, mills belched smoke far to the west, in a hollow
the next valley over so their stacks were barely visible from
town and the smell from them barely noticeable except to
those who lived in the frame houses in the First Ward, at the
foot of Lenapi; the closings of these mills that would make

the state university's expansion so meaningful to the town's economy and cause a seismic shift in the make up of the population of Lenapi—from blue collar to college professor— were still nearly a decade away.

The Lenapi Lending Library, however, had been at home in its Victorian mansion since 1898, when the spinster who'd lived in it had died and willed it to the town with the stipulation that it be turned into a public library. But by 1967 it was determined, by the same progressive town fathers who were at the forefront of the fundraising effort for the new hospital, that the library's collection of books had sorely outgrown its original space.

The spinster had kept luxurious gardens. The double doors of a solarium-nee-periodical reading room at the side of the mansion led to a quarter acre of box hedges that formally bound, in precise quarters, a rose garden, a cutting garden, an herb garden and a vegetable patch. Surrounding these cultivated beds were stone pathways leading to a wrought iron bench beneath a stand of lilac trees, or to a gingerbread gazebo—comfortable nooks and niches designed for leisure— and all of this was surrounded by eight-foot high walls of moss-covered red brick. For nearly seventy years these gardens had been maintained for public use by a group of women volunteers. In 1928 this group—the grandmothers of 1967's crop of volunteers—had formalized itself as the LPGA, the Library Public Garden Association. Over the years, the LPGA had expanded its original mission. Not only did it maintain the library gardens, but the women conducted summer classes in the gazebo in how to grow and dry culinary herbs for gastronomically adventurous housewives, and they taught the sophomore high school home ec girls how to can by helping them to process the garden's always bountiful harvest of tomatoes each fall and stocked church kitchen pantries with the output. They hosted the annual D.A.R. Fourth Grade Patriotic Poetry Contest awards tea under the fragrant, spring-blooming lilacs.

It was these gardens the town fathers determined to sacrifice to the library's expansion.

The summer of 1967 was hot. The slate sidewalks and asphalt streets soaked up and hoarded the sun so children actually had to wear shoes. Dust that was kicked down into town by the grading of the new road up behind Clearview caused homemakers to keep their windows closed at night and those who had air conditioners to actually turn them on.

By mid-September, however, the dust had settled into Indian summer and three twelve-year-old girls pedaled their bikes barefoot on their way down Clearview to the Woolworth's that anchored the downtown for Tulip Sundaes. Their route took them past the Lenapi Lending Library, and there they stopped.

The demolition of the Public Gardens had been duly mourned in the pages of the Lenapi Morning Star-Sentinel and construction of the new wing was nearly complete. The LPGA found a role for themselves in the transition—choosing the perennials to be planted around the yellow brick exterior of the new wing as well as unpacking the cartons of new books that were arriving daily, all needing to be entered into the card catalog, embossed with the library's stamp, placed in order of author upon miles of new shelving, and all of this before the building was officially opened by the mayor on the second Saturday of January in the new year, 1968.

A construction site is a naturally interesting place for children, but when it is also the site of demolished memories it can be a place that pisses them off, though they are unlikely to be able to articulate exactly why they are angry, and this is the reason the three girls stopped in front of the new library.

Deanna Jane Morrow, a name she'd shortened immediately upon entering the seventh grade to the preferred Deanie, and Jill Ruth Kuznicki, who was sometimes called J.R. within her immediate family circle, and Fredericka Kaye Danforth, who let it be known that her three big brothers always called her "Trick" and that she would like everyone else to use the name, too, had met just weeks before. Yanked out of the safety of small neighborhood elementary schools, where skill sets and reading levels and social comportment had long ago established the pecking order, they'd been thrown into the brave, new world of high school where they were mixed up with kids from every other elementary in town. The girls were at the very beginnings of the scramble to launch the new identities that would follow them for the next six years.

Deanie and Jill and Trick had been thrown into the accelerated reading and math program along with sixteen other girls and seven boys. The girls, through sheer number, had more varied opportunity for choice in new friendship, but Deanie and Jill made the effort to laugh along with Trick at the cadaverous old Latin teacher, Mr. Abramson, they drew for homeroom when he tried to make moldy jokes about the sort of ridiculous nicknames he'd heard in all his years in education—"Trick" being, he proclaimed, among the more outré. Trick had been less mortified at being singled out for scrutiny because Deanie and Jill had joined her in derision when Mr. Abramson went on about how Fredericka was a perfectly lovely, old-fashioned name and it was a shame to put it aside for a made-up moniker as silly as Trick.

"Choose the labels you wish for yourselves carefully now, ladies and gentlemen," he said. Addressing Trick directly, he added, "Think of what you will want to be known as, girl, when you are a fifty-year-old woman."

Deanie had leaned into Trick and whispered, "When you're a fifty-year-old woman that old fart will be dead," causing the three of them to break into giggles so ultimately uncontainable that Mr. Abramson exiled them to the principal's office for the rest of the period.

This was a common blot among them now, the stigma of this exile—not a basis for a best friendship, but it was something—and they started meeting at a common point, in front of Woolworth's, to finish riding their bikes the rest of the way to school in the mornings or to spend their Saturdays together.

This Saturday morning the three almost-teenaged girls stood barefoot astride their bikes in front of the new, mustard yellow wing of the library. The mustard yellow section of the building was still fenced off from the red brick of the spinster's mansion, so the girls couldn't get too close to it, but it was the old part of the library that was of interest to them anyway.

The old children's room had been just inside the main entrance to the spinster's Victorian, off to the right, her old parlor, the first and most important place in the house. It was a big room, aligned perfectly east to be bright with natural light streaming in the bay window where a kid could curl up on a pillow to read, and where groups were gathered for storytelling hour on Saturday mornings. It was the only room that many of the children knew even existed until they took the mandatory fifth-grade class trip and were ushered by the ladies of the LPGA into the lesser rooms in back to learn how to use the card catalog and periodical library and be given a walking tour of the gardens to which they were now considered mature enough to have unchaperoned entrée. The new children's room was going to be located on a whole floor of the new wing and there were promises that the room would be furnished with lush carpet and lots of beanbag chairs and have double the selection of books as the old one.

The three girls were unmoved by such promises—they were outgrowing the children's room anyway; Dickens and Orwell were on this year's reading list—but they were overcome, speechless, when they threw down their bikes to peer in the bay window and saw how dark it was in there, at midday, and how desolate with the shelves stripped bare of books. The room was slated to be renamed "The Pennsylvania Room," a place to house state maps and books on local history as well as what was left of the spinster's original bequest of books, a leather-bound set of Shakespeare's plays and first editions of authors who had been her contemporaries, those items that had not been sold off to pay for the new wing, and these were to be kept in locked metal cabinets placed in the corner from which the children's diminutive drinking fountain had already been removed.

The sight of the stripped room filled the little girls with some ungraspable sense of insecurity, sad and exciting at the same time, a wrenching of their novice hearts that was likely tighter and more tense because of all the talk they heard from the grown-ups about the new hospital, how the one in which they'd been born was out-of-date, even dangerous to its patients considering all of the modern equipment that it lacked; they'd even heard Trick's mother refer to it as a "rat trap."

Deanie was the first of the girls to speak. Her mother and father were older than most of her peers' parents, professors at Lenapi State and unenthusiastic about activities like Girl Scouts or swim team that might have intrigued Deanie had they shown any inclination at all to get her to meetings or to practice. Deanie's primary physical activity was riding her bike down the Lenapi mountain and deep into unfamiliar neighborhoods until she got gloriously lost in an exotic maze of streets, so lost she didn't even see it getting dark until she got scared that she would never find her way back home and knocked on strangers' doors to ask to use their phones to call her dad to come pick her up.

The other thing that Deanie did was read books. Oh, Deanie read books! She had long ago got through the assigned *Oliver Twist* and, rather than make her read it twice, the teacher had started her on *Great Expectations*, although no one was required to read that until freshman year. Because she'd spent so much time with books and, accordingly, so much time at the Lenapi Lending Library, it might be expected that Deanie would be the one most bitter about being displaced from the old children's room.

But Deanie was an optimistic child, and a dreamy one, her long blond hair falling unnoticed over her eyes unless it got in the way of a page she was reading, in which case she'd grab up the whole length of it and tie it in a knot and fling it over her shoulder. She looked up at the new wing, up the expanse of all five stories of it, the tallest building ever in Lenapi and built on its highest peak, too, and she said, "I bet you can see forever from up there on the roof. If we could get up on that roof, I bet we'd see the whole town, down the river to maybe even the next town. Wouldn't it be a thing to see as far as that? I bet no one's ever seen the town from a spot that high up before."

"Well, *perch*," Jill said, crooking her finger and holding it up as if she were waiting for a bird to alight upon it, a thing she did to you if she thought you'd said something bird-brained. "The roofers have been up on the roof. They've seen the whole town from that high up."

Jill was the tallest of the trio of little girls, thin in a willowy way as opposed to thin in a skinny way, which was how Deanie was often described. She loved to dance, and she was good at it. The girls had spent the early afternoon at Jill's house, watching "American Bandstand," Jill grooving all over the screened-in back porch, which was where the Bakulas kept their TV during the warm summer months, gangly Deanie and tiny, plump Trick trying to follow the way Jill waved her arm or flipped her back or rocked up and down on her bent knees and made her black curls bounce all over her shoulders. Deanie and Trick got it so wrong they all ended up in a giggling pile on the brown-and-gold-plaid Colonial sofa, Jill complaining, "You two are so *spastic*," which only made them all giggle more breathlessly. Trick laughed so hard she started to cough and, untangling herself from their pile, got up to perform a *really* spastic version of the Swim, sticking out her butt and crossing her eyes so Jill and Deanie shrieked and Trick didn't stop until Mrs. Kuznicki entered the room, at which point she froze.

They all froze.

Which made Jill start to laugh again. But all Trick did was pull in her butt and stand up straight, and Deanie watched, fascinated, as Mrs. Kuznicki set up three TV trays and put a plate down on each one of them. On each plate was a ham sandwich, cut diagonally, Fritos corn chips in between the triangles and pitted black olives garnishing the toothpicks that held the sandwich halves in place.

It worried Mrs. Kuznicki that her daughter's friends were staring at her, as if there were something wrong about her, perhaps her skirt was tucked up in the back in her underwear or she had mustard in her hair. She patted at herself and said, "There's milk or iced tea in the refrigerator, I'll let you get your own drinks. No soda, Jill, girls, you had nine among you last night and that's more than enough for the whole weekend." Then she went to the bathroom to check her skirt and her hair in the mirror.

"Does your mom make you lunch every Saturday?" Deanie waited to ask until Mrs. Kuznicki left the room.

Jill shrugged. "Every day."

"Wow. You mean she packs your lunch?" This from Trick.

Jill shrugged again, unsure if she should be embarrassed, if it was babyish to have your mother pack your lunch. "Doesn't yours?"

Food made Deanie's mother sick. Even going to the grocery store made her nauseous. Deanie and her dad ate out almost every night.

When Trick was hungry she swiped dimes from her mother's purse and went to the Superette for an ice cream sandwich or Fritos and a Coke.

Jill's favorite thing to do, besides dance, was to eat out at restaurants, especially the fancy steakhouse where Deanie said her father took her a couple of times a week, and she adored ice cream sandwiches and Coca-Cola, which were rationed around her house like the butter and sugar their history teacher told about in World War II stories. She was envious of her friends and sorry for them, she didn't know which. She thought it would be kind to say, "Big deal, I get a ham sandwich every day. Ham or turkey. It's so booooooring," and then she felt crappy, saying something so mean about her mother, especially as there *was* variety—a meatloaf sandwich at least once a week in her lunch bag, and always tuna fish on Fridays.

·

Now, SEEING HOW Deanie's face had sort of crumpled up when she realized that she *was* being stupid to say no one had ever seen the town from the new library roof when any idiot, really, could have figured out about the roofers, Jill added, kindly, "Anyway, none of us are probably ever going to get up on the roof. It's probably too dangerous. Probably only the workmen are the only people who are ever going to be allowed up that high."

"Let's do it!"

Deanie and Jill turned to Trick.

"Really"—Trick was shouting—"probably you're right, they'd never let us up on the roof, but what if we don't ask? What if we just go?" An idea was forming and Trick's enthusiasm for it was startling to her new girlfriends. "Now will be the best time to do it, too, before it's finished and they get all the doors and locks and stuff put together. We need to do it now. Tonight!"

"Are you crazy?" Jill put her hands on her hips, like she was asking a serious question.

"I don't know." Trick eyed the site critically. Then she said, "Let's see," and she ran over to the gate of the chain link fence around the new mustard yellow wing, looked around once in each direction and, caution to the wind, flung it open so it rattled on its hinges.

"It's open! It's not locked! Ha, ha, ha!" Trick cackled as she ran back fleetly, on her tiptoes, toward Deanie and Jill.

"You *are* crazy," Jill said, but in a whisper, so scandalized that it took her several seconds to scramble back to her bike and follow Deanie and Trick, who were already pedaling away.

"Dare you, dare you, dare you!" Trick chanted under her breath when they got to Woolworth's, flushed and sweating, while they waited in their window booth for the waitress to bring them their vanilla ice cream and strawberry sauce. "Dare you, dare you, dare you," she repeated and then she hummed and jiggled her feet as the other two girls mulled over the challenge.

Trick had the tiniest, most nervous feet in the world, Deanie and Jill had decided, jiggling and swinging and kicking, and these restless appendages were shod, when they were shod at all, in brown suede moccasins with an inch of fringe around the ankles so there was often an accompanying sound to their motion, a soft and insistent *thack, thack, thack*. And the moccasins weren't the only coveted item in Trick's wardrobe. She owned hip hugger jeans with bottoms so long and belled a person wouldn't have been able to see her feet at all if she hadn't acquired the habit of jiggling them. She wore loose tops in brilliant patterns, their gauzy fabrics still smelling of India. Sometimes she popped an enormous white felt cowboy hat, its brim surrounded by red-brown hawk feathers, on top of her ashy blond head. Trick was a good head shorter and a full year behind losing her baby fat than either of her two new friends, but she dressed like a real teenager, according to girls who were still in matching shorts and top sets, and Deanie and Jill were reluctant to say no-I-won't-do-it in response to her dare, to be left out or labeled a chicken or a coward or a wet blanket by the coolest girl in seventh grade.

BREAKING IN WAS as surprisingly easy as Trick had promised it would be.

The girls contrived to spend the night at Jill's—Deanie's house was closer to the library but at the Kuznicki house the girls were always put to bed for sleepovers in sleeping bags on the screened-in porch, at ground level, and sneaking out the back door after Jill's parents had gone to bed was a snap.

They left their bikes parked in the backyard, placating Mrs. Kuznicki with promises until she forgot she'd wanted them to put the bikes in the garage for the night, so their getaway was swift and soundless. The alleys were deserted at two-thirty in the morning, a little scary, but they ran into no one as they huffed up the hills.

Trick had swiped the flashlight Jill's mother kept in a kitchen drawer and brought that with her. She carried it in the pouch of her hooded jacket—an item of clothing all three of the girls wore over their pajama shorts because the temperature had dropped as night had fallen—but the moon was newly full and bright and they didn't need artificial light.

The gate to the chain link fence was still standing open when they got to the construction site. They hid their bikes in the mountain laurel bushes under the bay window of the old children's room and walked in.

A sheet of heavy plastic hung over the frame where the double entry doors were to be installed. Trick pushed it aside and held the flap open for Deanie and Jill and then she followed them into what would be a walkway connecting the two buildings when its walls were completed. The scaffolding up the side of the new yellow brick was no more difficult to scale than the monkey bars at the playground. Deanie's foot landed on a dead bird when she hoisted herself over the roof wall, but Trick was right there beside her, clapping a hand over her mouth. "Jeez, shut up, you want the whole town to know we're up here?" That was the only glitch.

The girls walked to the edge of the roof and looked at the town of Lenapi spread out below them—the floodlights trained on the Farron House rooftop sign, and the streetlights that made a ribbon of the downtown strip, and the headlights of cars snaking away from a shift change at the mills and slowly turning into driveways up and down the hills. Lights that looked as if they belonged in a football stadium filtered the smoke from the stacks over in the next valley, making it glow a ghostly blue, and porch lights, living rooms lamps and television screens flickered within a surprising number of houses. "I didn't think so many people would still be awake," Jill whispered.

"Come on, it's three o'clock on a Sunday morning. Probably a lot of people are still up celebrating Saturday night," Trick said dismissively. And then she reached into the pouch of her hooded jacket and drew out a can of Budweiser beer she had stashed in there with the flashlight. "My mom had it in the refrigerator." She shrugged, to make it seem as if having a beer in her hand was no big deal. "Watch your trap, I'm afraid I'll fall in there and get lost," she added, to get Jill to pull her jaw from where it had fallen on her chest and close her mouth. She popped the top on the beer and slurped at the foam that spurted out of the hole. Then she broke the pop-top in two, inserting the curled tab back into the can and putting the circular portion on her finger, like it was a ring.

"My mom told me never to do that," Jill told her, indicating the tab Trick had dropped back into the beer. "She says never to do that because you could swallow it," Jill insisted, as if this were the strongest objection she could make to the three of them having a can of beer with them up on the roof.

"Yeah, well, my mom says that it's a better thing to stick the tab back in the can than to litter with it. You want me just to drop it here and leave it on the roof?"

"I… I don't know," Jill stammered, trying to figure out where the logic lay between their mothers' advice and Trick, who was holding the can out to her.

"Take a drink."

"I don't like beer."

"How do you know, did you ever even have any?"

"A sip of my dad's Iron City."

"Iron *Shitty*. Take a drink of this, you'll like this kind."

But none of them liked the beer. "Probably it's not so good because it got warm on the way here," Trick explained. "Beer has to be ice cold to be any good," she said, but even she abandoned it, her enthusiasm for the adventure gone as suddenly as the warm Budweiser she was pouring out on the rooftop. She crumpled the can in her fist and replaced it in her pouch for the return trip, so she wouldn't leave it as litter.

Deanie turned away from the view, toward her friends. "I guess we've seen all there is to see now."

"Let's just go." Jill shivered. "It's getting cold."

Later on it would occur to each of them that if they'd done just that—if they'd just *gone*—they might not have gotten caught.

But Trick had one more idea left in her, a wild inspiration that came to her as immediately as she jammed her hands sullenly into her pouch, accidentally slicing the inside of her right middle finger with the rough edge of the pop-top she was wearing like a ring. "Fuck, owww," she shouted, caught herself being too loud, added in a bright whisper, "Hey, I know, let's be blood sisters!"

Before Deanie or Jill could respond, Trick had the bloody pop-top ring off her finger and was handing it to Deanie, explaining the rest of her new plan: "We have secrets now, the three of us. We broke into the library. We drank beer together…"

"We didn't really drink beer. We just sort of sipped on it."

"We *tried beer together*, Jill, for God's sake. That's a secret. And if you're blood sisters, you can never tell your secrets to another living soul."

Deanie accepted the pop-top gingerly. She knew she was supposed to use it to slice her own finger open and she was unsure she wanted to and she felt bad about that; there was something desperate about the way Trick was talking, something unsafe and exciting.

"Oh, come on! If we don't do something big and sort of, you know, *permanent* up here, then why did we even bother to come? Climbing up here will just be a big old waste."

"Climbing up on the library roof wasn't big enough?"

Trick moved close, right up in Deanie's face. "Being blood sisters is bigger."

Deanie thought she might start to cry. There was an urgency about the way Trick was going on that made it seem like something was really on the line.

"Do it fast." Trick spoke low but quickly. "If you cut real fast it doesn't hurt as much."

"Oh, and how come you know that?" Deanie snapped back because she couldn't do it fast. She couldn't just slice into her own skin with abandon. She set the rough edge of the ring on the pad of her left forefinger and pressed into it.

"You have to do it harder," Trick told her, disgusted, so Deanie closed her fist around the ring and clenched it. In the same instant the metal broke skin, bringing tears to her eyes and filling her with relief, Trick turned to Jill to insist, "Now you."

Jill had been watching Deanie silently as she made herself bleed. She held the ring now, watching her friends squeeze their fingers to keep their blood flowing.

"If you don't get a move on we're going to dry up before you get it done," Trick complained, and still Jill hesitated. "Then I'll do it for you," Trick said and made a quick move toward Jill.

"No!"

"Shhhh! Shut up. Jeez, it's just a little cut on your finger—like you never got a little cut before. I've never seen such a little pansy."

"Really, it doesn't hurt very much once it's done," Deanie offered.

"I'm not doing it with that," Jill said, throwing the ring back at them. Littering. Then she stuck her finger in her mouth and bit on a hangnail, drawing thin, transparent strips of skin away from the cuticle until there was enough of her blood flowing that she could become a blood sister, too.

Trick instructed them to press their fingers together, smear each other's hands with blood. Seal their secrets.

"*Now* can we go?" Jill begged.

"Sure," Trick said, satisfied.

Fingers throbbing, goose bumps on bare legs, shivering so that Jill worried she was shaking too hard to safely climb back down, they headed toward the scaffolding. Trick hoisted her leg over the side of the roof first, and felt for the crosshatched metal platform to drop down onto it, and then Deanie dropped beside her, and then Jill. And then they heard the smooth whoop of a siren begin, breaking the night, an unusual sound at any time of the day in Lenapi. Trick and Deanie continued making their way down to the next level of the scaffolding, but Jill froze in place.

"Whenever you hear a siren, you're supposed to stop and say a *Hail Mary*," Jill explained. "A siren comes from an ambulance, or a fire truck, and it means someone is hurt and needs your prayers."

Trick, whose loose ties to the Lutheran church were based on her mother having married her father in one thirteen years ago, shook her head and smirked, and even Deanie, who was being raised in the church of organized-religion-is-a-bunch-of-hooey-but-never-make-fun-of-someone-else's-convictions, tossed her head with disbelief, but Jill continued to stand still and pray, Trick and Deanie thought, and they waited for her, sighing loudly, engrossed in their impatience, unaware that Jill had got an inkling that the whoop of the siren was not attached to some random, anonymous hurt. It was meant for them.

THE GIRLS NEVER found out what it was that got them caught—had a neighbor seen a shadow, or heard Deanie yelp when she landed on the dead bird? They never found out because, frankly, they were too afraid to ask. They were at the Lenapi Police Barracks, lined up in a row on hard folding chairs against the wall of a small, plain, cold, ugly room furnished only with hard chairs like these, all lined up against its four puke green walls. A nice policeman had brought them rough, red wool blankets to wrap around themselves, because they were so cold Jill's teeth were chattering, but with that act of kindness the nice policeman left the ugly room and another one came in, followed by Mrs. Kuznicki, and it was all down hill from there.

How did you get on the roof?

Where did you get the beer?

Whose idea was this?

Jill was crying—sobbing and actually blubbering, "I'm sorry, I'm sorry, I'm so sorry," her teeth still snapping together every once in a while, not with chill now but with fear, her chin tucked as far down her chest as she could get it. She was wiping her streaming nose on the red wool blanket, a thing Deanie was surprised that neither of the grown-ups objected to.

Deanie slumped in her hard chair, watching Jill blow her nose and the policeman tap his left foot and finger the butt of the gun mounted on his right hip, and Mrs. Kuznicki pace as if this event were a dream, a scenario she was reading about come to life, horrible but far too provocative to turn away from. Deanie had never before seen grown-ups so angry, or so interested in her.

Trick was the only one of the girls who was sitting up straight and tall. Her feet were moving so relentlessly they were rattling against the legs of the chair but she had her chin stuck out, right back into the face of the policeman who kept bending down toward her, making a sort of swooping motion at her face, his eyes in slits, growling, "Whose idea was this?"

Trick's mother was divorced from her father, as she had been divorced from her first husband. Both husbands were mystery men in that neither of them lived any longer in Lenapi and no one, not even Trick, ever saw them anymore. But Trick's mother and her first husband had had three sons together before their divorce, Trick's older, half-brothers, though she claimed them entirely.

Within the first few days the girls had known each other, Trick had taken her two new friends to her mother's little turquoise-colored house in the First Ward—warning them to jump over the rotted board on the front porch steps on the way in—to show them pictures of the boys, teenagers with girlish eyelashes and high cheekbones and sullen pouts in five-and-dime frames on the dusty pink living room wall. Jill and Deanie understood why Trick wanted to show them the photos—her brothers were beautiful, boys a girl could worship from afar though even to the young girls the photos already looked suspiciously old. Her brothers, Trick confessed, were in their twenties now, the oldest actually going on thirty, and they all lived out west, in Texas, and when Trick talked to one or the other of them, which was at least every Christmas Day, they promised her that when she got to be old enough she could come out there and live with them, too.

The oldest one—going on thirty—had even sent Trick that white felt cowboy hat for her tenth birthday, a gesture Trick had accepted as a seal on the promise.

This was Trick's myth of the Wild West, and her new friends believed it for her, so they blinked and frowned when the mean policeman growled, "Just like your brothers, aren't you?" into Trick's face.

"This is getting us nowhere," Mrs. Kuznicki said to the mean policeman, sounding a little mean herself, as if she'd decided the girls weren't willfully holding back information, only too scared to speak up.

"I have a deal for you," Mrs. Kuznicki whispered conspiratorially, and crooked her finger to draw the policeman to her. "There was no damage done, no vandalism. We found one crumpled, empty beer can on them, but they appear to be terribly sober—not exactly evidence of a wild drinking spree. Let me take them home tonight, and next weekend I'll put them to work in the library. I'm a member of the LPGA and we've got a thousand books that need to be unpacked, have card pockets glued into them, and be shelved in the new wing. I promise you they won't have a free Saturday until after Christmas."

Jill stopped her caterwauling instantly. Trick frowned in confusion, no longer certain that she should continue trying to look defiant. Deanie actually smiled—it was a delightful punishment to each of them.

"How about it?" Mrs. Kuznicki asked the cop.

The cop shook his head and rested his hand on the grip of his sidearm while he thought. "They're all yours," he said at last and, when he did, Mrs. Kuznicki cut her eyes at the girls, in case any of them was going to be senseless enough to do something like let out a cheer.

"I AM GOING to tell your parents, you know," Mrs. Kuznicki said when they were all outside, the girls shivering again under the red blankets that the kind policeman had told them it would be all right to keep until the next day. Mrs. Kuznicki's threat didn't matter to Jill, of course, her own mother being the one who was making it; she was resigned that both of her parents were going to know about this incident and the worst was already over for her. Deanie just nodded, conjuring a dream of what her mother and dad would say in response to Mrs. Kuznicki's news of the crime and the punishment that had been devised—"Oh, all right then," she imagined. Trick stuck her jaw out. "Go ahead," she said. *Dare you, dare you, dare you.*

The girls' reactions infuriated Mrs. Kuznicki. A sharp woman normally, the thing she missed was the girls' wonder as they watched her with her puff of blond hair, her teensy

little wrists no bigger around than their own, and her stringy
little legs, picking up their bikes and tossing them into the
back of her station wagon single-handedly, like she was a
stevedore.

"You terrible, terrible little girls!" Mrs. Kuznicki turned
toward them to scold, making them take a step away from her,
wondering if now that the bikes were loaded she was going to
turn her dreadful, manly strength against them, but she just
shook her tiny fists and kicked a stringy leg out behind her,
slamming the wagon gate shut with her foot. "You could have
gotten hurt! You could have fallen! Five stories you could have
fallen! Drinking beer on the roof of a five story building—
what were you thinking? You weren't thinking! Well, here's
something to think about now: you will never do a thing this
stupid again! You will never again make me come down to the
police station at three-thirty in the morning to pick you up!
And don't you think I don't know whose idea this was, either.
I know, the police know, we all know!" Mrs. Kuznicki glared
then, at Trick, and as she glared she kicked back again, like a
mule, several times, aiming for the wagon's gate and missing
it every time, furious with Trick even as she realized that her
outburst was unfair; the other two were just as bird-brained.

Mrs. Kuznicki put her hands over her face, like she was
embarrassed about trying to kick the gate and missing it. She
stood like that for a moment and the girls took the opportunity to look at each other, wide-eyed. Jill shrugged at them;
she didn't know what was coming next either.

Mrs. Kuznicki took her hands away from her face. "Don't,"
she said in a tone so unearthly calm it was more frightening to the girls than her shouting at them, "don't you think
for one minute that you get to be proud of yourselves for
not tattling on each other. You may think that what you're

doing is sticking together, but all you're really doing is hiding the blame. Is that how you want to go through life? Hiding blame? Doing bad things you have to share blame for? How about doing something good and sharing *credit*? How about that? That would be a much better use of your loyalty."

Mrs. Kuznicki said these things so calmly but purposefully that a little bit of spit flew out of her mouth, and then she seemed to run completely out of steam.

"Get in the car," she ordered and the girls scurried—there was no other word for it, they scurried like scared mice to obey, crowding each other into the back seat.

Mrs. Kuznicki came around the front of the car, pausing once to hold on to the hood ornament and steady herself on the way, and then she walked to the driver's side door and got in.

"I *am* going to tell your parents," she repeated as she started the engine.

"Except," she muttered, turning around and resting her right arm across the back of the front seats, looking not at the girls but for non-existent traffic behind her, pulling out of the parking space, "there's no reason to do it right now. No sense getting everyone up and exercised in the middle of the night."

Then she looked directly at Jill, though she still seemed to be muttering mostly to herself. "You're just lucky the mill is so busy, extra half-shifts and double shifts and your father volunteering again for a double, how much overtime does that man think we need to live on? Your father should be the one down here driving you home from the police station."

Chapter Three
Monday

5 DAYS, 3 HOURS, 9 MINUTES
UNTIL THE WEDDING

THE SUV, WHICH DEANIE HAD SPENT TWENTY minutes at the Hertz rental counter trying to worm her way out of, is proving to be very handy. Chas helps Deanie roll the new back-up keg out of its back doors and, then, before Jill can whisk her away on the day's other errands, she asks Chas to load in a ladder. She chooses both hedge clippers so heavy she has to squat a little bit to lift them and stem cutters—she's not sure which tool she'll need for her task; probably both—and drives herself back around the Greentree Court cul-de-sac to where its signpost is hidden behind a gorgeous, overgrown display of pink climbing roses that have used it as a trellis.

The development where Jill lives, Shady Pines, is laid out like a misbegotten maze and too many people—deliverymen

as well as wedding guests—have to find their way to the
Bakula house this week for the roses to stand. Deanie sets up
the ladder in the triangle of manicured grass that hosts the
signpost and pulls on Jill's leather gardening gloves against
thorns.

It's not yet nine o'clock, but the day is already hot, the
sun gearing up to steam, the famous Northeastern humidity.
Deanie breaks a sweat even before she hoists the hedge clippers and takes her first step up the ladder. She's got several of
the larger branches lopped off, and is arranging the remaining ones around the cross that announces the intersection of
Greentree Court and Willow Way, deciding to prune more
modestly from this point with the stem cutters, when she
hears a car approaching slowly from behind her, it's wheels
crunching to a stop on the hot asphalt, the whirr of a window being lowered.

"Girl. Hey, you, girl up on the ladder there!"

The summons is loud and so abrasive that for a moment
Deanie can't believe it's being directed at her.

"Stop what you're doing there, girl, or I'll call the police."

When Deanie twists around on the ladder she sees a black
Lincoln Town Car, circa late 1970s, a little worse for the years
but all in all kept proudly, shining. From the passenger window an ancient man is thrusting a bony finger in her direction,
still moving his mouth in the aftermath of his threat, as if the
effort of speaking with such passion has hurt his jaw. From
the driver's side of the car a stout women in her mid-thirties is slipping out from behind the wheel, hurrying around
the front of the car, waving her hands defensively and calling out, "I didn't know he was going to do that when he told
me to stop. I thought he just wanted to watch what you were
doing; really, I'm so sorry."

Deanie thinks now, watching the stout woman approach, that this encounter has a chance of being a reasonable one after all and she descends the ladder, pulling off Jill's gloves.

"Sherry Platt"—the woman extends a plump, diamond-ringed hand—"number sixteen twenty-five"—she points at the Tudor on the corner, the wellspring of the magnificent pink roses. "I'm supposed to keep them trimmed back myself but it's hard to find the time. I'm bringing my great-grandfather for a visit, he gets a little agitated in new surroundings, not like he hasn't been here before, he's been here a lot, sometimes he remembers and sometimes he doesn't…"

"Deanie Morrow." Deanie takes the woman's hand and shakes it, to spare her the pain of further explanation.

"Wait a minute. Wait just a minute—Deanie Morrow?"

"Yes," Deanie confirms.

"The writer?"

"Yes."

"I love your books! I'm in the middle of *The Warriors of Flint, Michigan* right now!"

"I'm visiting friends at eighteen fifty-eight, in town for their daughter's wedding."

"The Bakulas? I'm going to be there, too! Jill called me just last night because one of us misplaced my RSVP, but she didn't tell me a celebrity was on the guest list! I mean, I knew you were originally from Lenapi, but… I can't believe I ran into Deanie Morrow trimming my very own roses!"

The women might have continued like that, punctuating all they are finding in common with exclamation points, but the ancient, agitated man in the black Lincoln recovers himself. "Vandalism is a crime, girl. The police will want to know about this!"

"Oh, hush, Paw-Paw," Sherry calls to him, "this lady is saving me the trouble of trimming back those old roses myself." She turns back to Deanie. "The Homeowners' Association hasn't made their annual stink yet about the sign being overgrown, so I didn't think to get around to it"—she winks, as if the two of them are conspirators—"I've been too busy reading your book! Hey, if I go get it, will you sign it for me?"

"Of course, I'd be honored," Deanie replies, and Sherry leaves right that very second to go to get the book, ducking behind and through the roses, toward a back gate Deanie hadn't noticed amid all of the shrubbery, the black Lincoln idling in the street and Paw-Paw glaring.

"Hi!" Deanie waves to him, unsure of how to handle their awkward aloneness, wondering why in hell Sherry wouldn't have at least pulled the car into the driveway beyond the rose bush and Deanie's SUV and turned it off. "Hi," she says again and approaches the car, "you're visiting with your great-granddaughter for the day. How nice." Deanie has the fleeting thought that what she is doing may be dangerous, provoking a person who is already annoyed and may not be in complete control of his faculties, but it would be rude to simply return to her pruning while Sherry's in the house searching for her book. "Hey," she says, and comes up short at the car's window, now that she's got a good look at its passenger.

Paw-Paw is a skeleton. His dark blue sweat pants and bright green cardigan lay on his limbs as if all the layers between flesh and bone have been recalled. The fingernails that tip his large fingers are ridged and brownish and remarkably long and they have been filed, disturbingly, into perfect ovals. The sacks under his eyes are so heavy they expose the soft red membrane under his eyeballs. Deanie thinks she would recognize that face anywhere. "Mr. Abramson!"

She leans into the window. "Mr. Abramson, it's Deanie Morrow. I'm sure you don't remember me, you've had so many students over the years, but I had you for seventh-grade homeroom. And you taught me Latin freshman and sopho-more years."

Deanie is genuinely delighted with the encounter, calcu-lating with some amazement how many years her old Latin teacher must have racked up by now, and then Mr. Abramson speaks. "I know exactly who you are, girl. A big-shot author now, isn't that what you think of yourself? Friends with that other one, calls herself 'Trick.'" He spits out the name as if it's a sneeze. "'Trick.' Heard she's been holed up in that rat trap she calls a house ever since she failed at doing herself in. A complete failure, that's what that girl is. Always knew that one would come to a bad end, name like that."

"One hundred and two years old," Jill says, softly, as if she is in awe of the accomplishment.

"I don't know why he isn't… Isn't…"

"Isn't what?" Jill and Deanie are in the coffee shop at the Farron House, a pink-and-white room that is trying hard to look like someone's dream of an old-time soda fountain. They're drinking the caterer's complimentary coffee, wait-ing for the saleswoman to appear so they can give her the final count, and go over a few details about the wedding day decorations Jill wants in the hotel's ballroom. Jill chooses a croissant from the pastry tray the caterer has sent to their table, and Deanie picks at a throbbing puncture on her left forefinger where a thorn slipped through a hole in the seam of the gardening glove. "You don't know why Mr. Abramson isn't…" Jill prompts, "nice? When was he ever that?"

"Dead," Deanie answers. "I don't know why he isn't *dead*."

"He's a one-hundred-and-two-year-old retired Latin teacher, how much deader do you want him? We were his last class, remember? The school stopped offering Latin after that year. Why are you so worked up?"

"Because it's unnatural for a person to remember with such vehemence someone who passed through his life four decades ago. And because it's Trick. What did Trick ever do to him? Did you hear what I told you he said about her?"

Jill has been putting raspberry jam on her croissant and she stops now. Lays it down on the small pink plate in front of her and pushes the plate away. She dusts crumbs from her fingertips on the pink napkin in her lap. "Do you wonder if you're so upset about what Mr. Abramson said because you're worried it's true? That Trick finally has made some bad end for herself?"

It occurs to Deanie that she would be lying if she spit out what is on the tip of her tongue right now, which is, *No*. Not in a million years.

JILL IS STALLING at the dry cleaner's. An old classmate, one of Deanie's high school crushes, Ty Gugino, owns the place now and he emerges from the steam and clatter in the back of the shop when Jill calls out from the reception area, "Ty! Oh, Ty, someone's here and I think you're going to want to say hello to her!"

"Deanie!" Ty recognizes her immediately and stretches out his arms to hug her hello.

"How are you?" Deanie asks, hugging him back.

"Oh, you know," Ty says, an open-ended answer so Deanie can make her own assessment.

Ty has morphed from a high school center court hunk into his father. The resemblance is striking—the change startling: where steel blue nylon basketball short-shorts once hung insolently below rippling abdominals is the basketball itself; where chestnut hair so fashionably long and genetically unmanageable once formed sausage curls that bounced around Ty's face as he swaggered down high school halls is… Nothing. Nothing but the smooth shine of Ty's scalp.

But Deanie has run into Ty before, on other trips to Lenapi; his appearance is shocking to her only as a rude reminder that she herself must continue to do anything and everything necessary not to turn into her own parents— her dangerously elegant mother, Jane Morrow, whose heart stopped at fifty-eight, the last of her organs to give up, to tire of trying to sustain life on a lettuce leaf smeared with French's mustard and washed down with tap water-diluted chardonnay. Nor must she turn into the gruff but loveable Witt Morrow who flattened himself in a midnight tumble over the rail of the second-story landing of the family's rambling Victorian when he was just sixty-one, an inadvertent, Drambuie-induced dive after a wrong turn on the way to the bathroom, doing himself in when all he'd wanted to do was have a pee.

"It's good to see you, Ty. Really, how are you? What's up?"

Ty's pause makes Deanie glance at Jill, blink in some confusion, wonder if she should have been warned about something; Deanie doesn't know until this moment that Ty's oldest daughter is in the army and stationed in Iraq. Ty looks away from them as he speaks of his first born, as if that will keep them from seeing his eyes getting wet. It's almost unbearable for Deanie to hear him comfort them and himself with the words: "Third goddamn tour, but she's safe. Safer than most. She speaks Arabic. She's an interpreter. She's not in the line of fire."

Jill offers her prayers for the girl, and Deanie makes a quick second, and Ty accepts—an exchange that is as heartfelt as it is helpless, and rapid, none of them willing to dwell on the unspeakable. It's a relief when Ty changes the subject. "What have you got for me today, Jill?"

"Curtains." Jill spills the contents of a green plastic lawn bag on Ty's counter, and a rambling explanation follows: "You know Madeline is getting married this weekend? Well, her new in-laws are not from Lenapi. Rather than having them take their pre-ceremony family photos at the hotel, I've offered our family room. Our family's going to use the front living room for our pictures, to keep the bride and groom from seeing each other until they get to the church, I think that will work"—she looks to Deanie; she's got the good sense to be uncomfortable about the very different immediate future her daughter's got from Ty's and, still, the curtains haven't been to the cleaner's in three years. "Ty, I just couldn't have them taking wedding pictures in front of dusty curtains. Can you have them ready by Thursday? So I'll have time to hang them back up?"

Ty is assuring her that he will, of course, for *her*, have the curtains ready on Thursday morning, and that's when the door to his reception area squeaks open and Heidi Jean Welkins walks in.

Heidi Jean, as no one who attended the 1973 Lenapi High School senior prom will ever forget, was first runner-up for prom queen; so great was her faith in her stations as head cheerleader, offspring of Lenapi's most successful contractor, and Miss Junior Aluminum Products 1972 that she fled the stage, sobbing, when Amy Tanner's name was announced instead of hers. She'd rushed to her custom-colored, baby blue Trans-Am, locked its doors behind her, and refused to come out to participate in the Court's ritual promenade around the festive gymnasium, confounding her escort until he decided there was humor about the situation and took his turn around the gym solo, cart-wheeling and hand-walking and mugging so there was little doubt that someone had indeed spiked his punch.

Heidi Jean, whose head now bobbles atop a body starved so even Jane Morrow would have approved, and whose skin is so tanning-booth crispy an old-time Bain de Soleil model would have paled in comparison, flashes neon-bright tooth veneers to the little cluster of her old classmates, but she doesn't say a word.

Heidi Jean, as even Deanie knows, has been making local news for over a year now—since she got caught sleeping with her husband's best friend, a man whose wife Heidi Jean had claimed as her *own* best friend, two couples who had marched at the apex of Lenapi society in lockstep for twenty-six years, until the wrong two of them got into bed together. Heidi Jean's appearance now chokes the conversation so even she can't recover it gracefully.

"Congratulations!" Jill's bellow startles all of them. "I heard you and Dave just got married to each other! Well, congratulations!"

It's a moment of awkward celebration, Jill's acknowledgement of the elephant in the room, yet what else was to be done?

"Thank you!" Heidi Jean accepts the good wishes as if this second marriage of hers hasn't made everybody's life a little more difficult—the pro at the country club scrambling diplomatically to coordinate tee times for Heidi Jean's former

spouse and her current one so they are at least several hours
apart; the women of the LPGA (the gardeners, not the golf-
ers) severed into separate camps to feud over which of their
members—Heidi Jean or her former best friend—will be wel-
comed back into their ranks; Jill and Deanie and Ty glancing
at the squeaky reception door, worried that now would be
just the time Murphy would expect that the former spouse
or the former best friend waltz through it, too.

Deanie's head is spinning with the effort it takes to exist
peaceably in a small town when the door does squeak again,
and admits Loretta Bastioni.

Lo is one of the few people who, Deanie thinks it can
honestly be said, hasn't changed a bit since they were all kids.
Lo's hair has always been cropped short as a little boy's, and
her voice has been as full of gravel since they first heard it
on the first day of seventh grade, and she has always been so
plump she's never been able to quite reach her arms around
herself—all the more reason to marvel that she stands each
night behind the grill at Bastioni's Tavern, as her father and
grandfather and great-grandfather did before her, turning
out some hundred and fifty-odd meals a night, breaking a
sweat but never her rhythm, each piece of meat grill-marked
with military precision, each bowl of macaroni perfectly *al
dente*, and every plate passed through her hot window right
on schedule if not a few minutes ahead of it. Save for a prep
cook four hours on weekend afternoons, Lo manages this
nightly feat alone, though she has succumbed to the pain in
her over-sized, over-used knees enough to hire a helper whenever she has a banquet on top of her regular customer load,
as she will this Friday night, when she cooks for the Bakula
rehearsal dinner.

Deanie is relieved to see Lo at Ty's dry cleaning shop. Perhaps the conversation will turn now from the war in Iraq and wrecked marriages to Friday's menu, Friday's count, any blessed thing Jill might have to discuss with Lo about preparations for Friday night.

Instead, before any one of them can even greet her, Lo tosses a canvas sack of fresh linen napkins over one shoulder and points at Heidi Jean with the forefinger of her opposite hand. "Don't you be coming to the restaurant tonight, Heidi Jean. Your ex-husband has a reservation and I can't take the tension any more whenever you two show up on the same night."

"I COULD SHAKE you." Deanie's teeth are clenched as she speaks so the words come out in a wet hiss, but she isn't mad so much as she is ghoulishly amused by the impromptu reunion at the dry cleaner's.

Jill aims her key ring at her minivan to unlock its doors and slides into the driver's seat, unflappable and still in a hurry. "Get in the car," she scolds, and absolutely squeals the tires pulling out of Ty's parking lot. They are half a block away, halfway through the long red light at Front and Clearview before Jill leans her head against the steering wheel and starts to laugh. "'Don't you be coming to the restaurant tonight, Heidi Jean.' Oh, my God, Dean, did you see the look on her face?"

"Whose? Heidi Jean's or Lo's? And did you happen to get a look at poor Ty?"

"I'm so sorry. Who would have known that parade was going to happen, or that Lo is so solidly in the camp that

thinks all this is Heidi Jean's fault? I really did just have to
drop off those curtains."

Deanie nods. "Of course you did," she says though she
knows, however necessary the errand, prolonging it with a
visit with Ty was a ruse—like their laughter now is a ruse—
buying time and any lightheartedness they can squeeze from
the moments before they descend to the foot of Lenapi, to the
little frame house in the First Ward where Trick has, by all
accounts, barricaded herself for the past six months.

"She *never* goes out?" Deanie asks as the light turns green,
a signal to proceed soberly to their destination.

"Chuck's seen her once"—Jill's shoulders drop—"buying
cigarettes at the convenience store on Vesper Street. Other
than that... Look, I had to put my foot down. I wasn't her
personal delivery service. I thought it would force her to come
back out into the world if I stopped running her errands for
her."

Instead, as Jill has discovered, and related to Deanie,
Trick's sons now take turns coming up from Texas every other
month, stocking Trick's house with foodstuffs and toilet paper
and cartons of Merit Ultra Lights. While Trick was still in
the hospital, Jill had facilitated the complicated paperwork
for both unemployment and disability for Trick and, though
there were payouts from both of the insurances, neither benefit was permanent; every other month one of Trick's boys
slips her a little cash in addition to the groceries he brings.

"When all of this first went down, I told her I would loan
her as much money as she thought she needed to get back on
her feet," Jill says now. "Chuck and I would have been happy
to do that. All she had to do was come out of that house at
least once a day. And I wasn't pressing her to get a job. Go out
and take a walk was all I asked of her, volunteer somewhere. I

wasn't pressing her to get a job if she wasn't ready to do that, but she's highly functional when she takes her pills. Why should those boys have to provide for her? They need to be building their own lives..." Jill has been helpless in the face of Trick's stubborn commitment to her seclusion, and now she thinks of another source of potential irritation: "Don't you even think about offering her money, Deanie, the time that money alone could help her has passed. At least until she takes some initiative."

"Like, *asking* for it?"

"That would, actually, be a very good start."

"Oh, yeah. Tough love. I get it."

"Don't mock me," Jill says as they approach Trick's street.

As THEY HAVE so many times before, Jill and Deanie pull up in front of the little turquoise house on Clay Street, off Vesper, the property Trick has either lived in or rented out to tenants all of her life, the place that has been her safe house since her mother willed it to her nearly thirty years ago.

Jill reminds Deanie about the broken board on the front porch steps, a repair that has been attended to several times over the decades and has never seemed to take—"I'm not doing it again until she lets me have those gutters replaced, that's what's causing that board to keep rotting out," Chuck said the last time he'd hammered in a new one—and then she knocks on Trick's front door.

Trick's house needs to be repainted in the worst way, neglect that's not unusual in this neighborhood, once an enclave of mill workers, tidy, proud houses settled on neat patches of green grass, framed by flowerbeds and pots of geraniums on the wide front porches. Now these streets are given over to housing for the students at the satellite campus, whole blocks of houses that have been used hard by their young, temporary residents. Bed sheets spray-painted with Greek affiliations fly from second story windows; third-hand sofas abandoned in the May exodus from campus sit, waterlogged from last week's rains, on front lawns; cardboard and duct tape seal a window shattered in a graduation revel gone a little too wild. A lonely silver beer keg lays on its belly in a gravel driveway, the retrieval of its deposit not worth the trouble for some kid anxious to get out of town for summer break. Even now, during summer break, music throbs from the rooms of students staying on for the June session, competing cacophonies of discontent to ears accustomed to Leonard Cohen and James Taylor.

Loggins and Messina.

"'I've seen brighter days...' Remember, we used to call it 'music to commit suicide to,'" Deanie whispers.

"You wanna diss like you got a trick up your sleeve? Fuck spittin' you would need my permission just to breathe..."

"When did it become mandatory to cuss on every other cut of a record?'

"They're not called records anymore."

WHEN THERE IS no answer to a second, and then a third knock on the front door, Jill pushes it open; walking into this house unannounced is not a thing either of the women consider remarkable—they've been in and out of this house of their own volition nearly all of their lives. Trick grew up in it. She and her first husband lived here, with her mother. By the time her mother died, Trick and Dominic were on their way to splitting up, and into a knock-down-drag-out fight for custody of their boys. Trick lost and stayed on at home. Alone. During her second and third marriages she'd moved into homes owned by her new husbands and, in between, there had always been the little turquoise house on Clay Street, as long as Trick timed her divorces to coincide with semester breaks and student turnover.

The abused exterior of Trick's house—the outline of her last tenant's Tau Kappa Epsilon letters still evident on the wall by the front door where the paint has faded around them—fixes the house comfortably within its uneasy land-scape; inside is evidence more particular to Trick's personal disease. The kitchen is still bright purple. Its tiles are cracked or missing altogether, the result of having installed tiles meant for countertops on a floor, which Trick had insisted upon over the objections of the salesman at the hardware store— she'd fallen in love with their cobalt color, and couldn't wait for a special order of the same hue in a floor-grade tile to be shipped in—then spent that same entire manic night glu-ing them into place. The first one had cracked the very next morning, when Trick stepped into the kitchen in her stilet-tos, on her way to whatever job she had at the moment; the damage had discouraged her from ever getting around to grouting them.

The banister hangs away from the steps to the second floor at a dangerous angle.

"When did *that* happen?" Deanie asks, fanning at the air, stale and hazy blue with Merit miasma.

Jill shakes her head. "A paramedic fell into it the night I called them to come take Trick to the hospital. She swears it was the paramedic's fault but I think it had to have already been loose. It's us, Trick—Deanie and me," Jill calls. "Please, come on down." To Deanie, she adds, "Can you at least try to not look horrified? If she sees you looking at her like that it'll upset her. It would upset me."

TRICK APPEARS AT the top of the stairs, looking down on her two friends who have turned their faces upward to greet her. Her hair is long, past her shoulders, parted in the middle as they had all worn their hair when they were girls, more ashy gray now than ashy blond, and the texture is all wrong. It's stiff, and thin, and teased at the crown and lacquered all over to create an illusion of volume; Trick has made some effort for this meeting, effort that is heartbreaking given the whittled frame underneath her brittle hair, her sunken eyes and bloated cheeks.

She's got on a pretty, gauzy top in peacock green, and fresh jeans, and a pair of beaded stiletto sandals. She's wearing makeup, too, some lipstick and a little mascara though her eyes are outlined enough with trepidation; she's making only tentative eye contact, as if Jill's gaze, or Deanie's, is too hot to hold. She keeps tugging at the long sleeves of her top, pulling them further down over the silk scarves she's got wrapped around her wrists—not because she is hiding bandages, her wounds have healed well; she just can't bear that anyone might catch a glimpse of even the scars. She is tapping the toe of her right foot furiously; the beads on the sandals make a soft, insistent *tack, tack, tack.*

"Oh, for heaven's sake, Trick, it's just us," Deanie says at last. "It's just *us,*" she says, which makes Trick smile and start slowly down the stairs, as if grace and forgiveness are things that must be approached cautiously.

Chapter Four

1970

37 YEARS, 7 MONTHS, 3 DAYS, 18 HOURS,
26 MINUTES UNTIL THE WEDDING

*T*HE BOYS WERE DUE TO ARRIVE IN LESS THAN an hour. "I don't know what tablecloth you're talking about!" Jill hollered from the dining room where she had every drawer in the pine hutch hanging open, ransacking it for linens. She was so anxious about the evening ahead that Deanie and Trick, who were in the Kuznicki kitchen, could hear her stamp her foot.

Mrs. Kuznicki, who had just mopped egg white froth from the bodice of Deanie's Dutch blue corduroy jumper, and tied one of her own full floral aprons around each of the girls to prevent further wardrobe disaster, surveyed her kitchen. She was looking around less to spot any uncleanliness than to assure herself that nothing the girls were cooking was about to boil over or catch fire, or explode.

She called back to Jill, "I'm coming, J.R. A little patience, please."

"Just, Mom, I want to get the table set so I can finish getting dressed, and I have to pee, and *can you get this baby out of here?*" Jill cried, tugging doilies roughly from her little sister's chubby fists and making Beth let out a piercing wail of indignation. "I knew as soon as that little monster started to walk she'd be nothing but trouble," Jill added, trying to squeeze the doilies back into their proper drawer without making the effort to refold them.

"Don't call your little sister a monster," Mrs. Kuznicki sighed, as if she'd reminded her older daughter about this a thousand times. "Give me those"—she took the doilies from the drawer and laid them out, one by one on the dining table—"for heaven's sake, if you just shove them back in the drawer in a bunch like that they'll have to be pressed again before I can use them, and you'll be the one doing the pressing this time, Jill Ruth. Here." She preempted Jill's protest that there wasn't time to be neat about the silly old doilies by reaching into the hutch's top drawer and handing out a yellow lace tablecloth.

"This one?" Jill asked. "Really? The good one?'

"Of course the good one," Mrs. Kuznicki replied. "It's your first dinner party. We have to do it up right."

THE GIRLS HAD decided to cook dinner for their boyfriends. Jill invited Stu Jenner, the middle-weight state championship wrestler she'd been grappling with on the sofa in her parents' screened-in back porch for three months. Deanie invited Ty Gugino, the dreamy star of the basketball team, even though at the few dances they'd gone to together since they'd been going steady—two weeks, exactly, tonight—he'd draped himself over her so thoroughly all night long, leaning all of his lean, tall weight on her for so many hours her shoulders hurt by the time he took her home, she thought she was going to have to break up with him before he ended up breaking her. Trick had invited Dominic Ferrara, who was not exactly, *officially* her boyfriend, as these things went, but who seemed to make a point of coming over to stand nearest to her all winter long, after the twice-weekly basketball games, while the rest of the team did as their coach required—humbly, if perfunctorily, thanking the cheerleaders for their support, win or lose. "I'm just going to ask him," Trick declared when Deanie and Jill got the idea to give the dinner party. "Who else could I ask, anyway? You guys wouldn't have a party if I didn't have anyone to ask, would you? Jeez."

Dominic, too shy to say "yes" outright, had looked back at Trick's desk and nodded his head in agreement when Trick passed him a note the next day in American History and, so, now, pork chops were stuffed with Mrs. Kuznicki's special mixture of bread cubes and celery salt and milk, and there was a green bean casserole ready to go in the oven, and Deanie was punching russet potatoes with a fork in preparation for baking and Trick was icing a chocolate layer cake with Mrs. Kuznicki's famous fudge frosting, and Jill was setting her parents' dining room table with the good tablecloth and china and flatware. Mrs. Kuznicki even pulled six of the hobnail milk glass goblets down from their perch on the very top shelf of the hutch and rinsed the dust off of them and offered them to Jill for her pretty place settings.

"Thanks, Mom," Jill told her, as if this were just too much to have hoped for.

In response, Mrs. Kuznicki smiled and repeated her warnings about the evening's beverages: "There's a whole new case of soda in the closet. I want to see at least half of it still there when I get back."

That was the most remarkable of all the terribly thrilling things about the evening that lay ahead: Mr. and Mrs. Kuznicki had agreed to take baby Beth and go out. For two and a half whole hours. They would go to Sal Turk's place, have pizza and hoagies and let Beth drop nickels into the tabletop jukebox—which Beth thought of as a sort of enthralling piggybank; she hadn't yet made the connection between the nickels and the tunes they bought. Later, after they ate, Mr. Kuznicki would take Beth, over Mrs. Kuznicki's mild objections, into the arcade in the back room and hold her up in his arms while she whiled away a few quarters trying to play one of the pinball machines. The three Kuznickis would be at Turk's, if the girls needed to call, but if no call was forthcoming they would not be back home until nine o'clock.

Jill's awful gratitude to her mother for the lace tablecloth and the good goblets was tempered by her desire to get her parents and the monster out the door; "Thank you, Mom. Thank you for everything. Now, can you please hurry Dad up? You can't be here when the boys get here, it'll spoil everything."

"I'll be sure to tell your father just that," Mrs. Kuznicki said, picking Beth up and carrying her toward the stairs. "I've got a wet diaper to deal with, and my own dress to change, and then I'll see what's keeping Dad. I hope you're not going to hop around like that in front of your company. I know you're excited, but you shouldn't be so obvious about it in front of the boys…"

"Mom"—Jill clenched her teeth and whispered—"I have to *pee*. Dad's been in the bathroom for half an hour."

In the kitchen there was debate about the sodas. "We're only allowed to have two apiece," Jill reported. Again.

"We know, we know"—Trick shook her head impatiently—"your mother's got a bug up her ass about soda pop, doesn't she?"

"She's worried it will rot my teeth," Jill answered. "Anyway, here's what I'm thinking. We can fill the goblets with lots of ice and serve the sodas from the kitchen. That way one can will fill almost three glasses every time. And the boys won't see it's the BiRite stuff." Beyond the rationing, there was disappointment that Mrs. Kuznicki had insisted on buying the supermarket brand of cola even for an evening as important as this one. "What do you think? Serve from the kitchen?"

"Serve from the kitchen. Yes. Definitely," Deanie agreed.

"Pork chops in the oven at six o'clock," Jill continued, jostling her weight back and forth from one foot to the other. "That'll give us about half an hour after the guys get here for hors d'oeuvres"—she looked at Trick who was now slicing cheddar cheese and laying strips of it lengthwise on rectangular crackers, topping each with a circle of green cocktail olive—"and we have to remember to turn the oven down to three-fifty when the casserole goes in at six-fifteen…"

"Your mom made a list," Deanie reminded her, pointing to the fridge where a detail of the cooking schedule was tacked with a magnet in the shape of an unearthly big blue daisy.

"Oh, and when we're done with the oven, before we serve dinner, we have to remember to…"

"...TURN THE OVEN OFF," Deanie and Trick joined her to chorus.

Trick crossed her eyes at Jill, and would have crooked a finger at her except her hands were full of cheddar cheese. "*Perch.* Go to the bathroom. You look like you're in pain."

Jill was leaning over from the waist, pressing her fists into her crotch. "The flowers?"

"I'm gonna do them right now," Deanie told her. Mrs. Morrow's contribution to the girls' hostessing debut was a basket full of fall flowers she'd culled from her lush cutting garden. Mrs. Kuznicki had provided Deanie with a tall, amber glass vase in which to arrange them and Deanie started to fill it now with cold water. "Go get dressed, Jill. Everything's under control in here. For God's sake, go pee."

"Jeez," Trick said when Jill left the room, "it's like she thinks if everything's not just exactly perfect Stu Jenner's not going to ask her to marry him or something."

"We're fifteen," Deanie offered. "Nobody's marrying anybody any time too soon." And then she added, "Candles."

"What about candles?"

"Jill was going to ask her mother if we could have candles for the table. Did she?"

"Dunno," Trick said. She held up the plate of cheese and crackers to show her arrangement off to Deanie, popping the last leftover rounds of olive into her mouth and licking her fingers. "I'll go ask her."

"Yoo hoo, candles?" Trick called as she moved toward the stairs, stopping in the dining room to strip off Mrs. Kuznicki's flowered apron and drape it over one of the chairs.

"And music," Deanie called from the kitchen. "What music are we going to have on the record player when the guys get here, and not Carole King. I love Carole King as much as anyone but it's just too embarrassing, sitting there next to a boy and Carole's going, 'Will you still love me to-mo-OO-row.'"

"And music," Trick amended, ascending.

"What?" she heard Mrs. Kuznicki call out from the baby's room.

"Candles and music," Trick called, a bit louder. "I need to ask Jill about candles and music."

"And rolls!" Deanie was shouting now, a note of urgency entering her voice, as if she had suddenly caught some of Jill's anxiety. "Mrs. Kuznicki didn't write a time down on the list for when the rolls go in the oven!"

"Yeah, yeah," Trick muttered. "Like we can't figure out when to put dinner rolls in the oven. Read the package," she shouted back down the stairs, swinging, as was her habit, on the post at the top, pivoting in the narrow hallway in the direction of Jill's room.

"What?"

"READ THE PACKAGE, DEAN!" As she shouted, Trick noticed that the door to the Kuznicki bathroom—which was down the other end of the hallway from Jill's room so it just caught the corner of her eye as she swung around the post—was closed. "Candles and music and rolls," she chanted as she made a quick turn to swing herself in the opposite direction, gripped the bathroom doorknob and twisted it.

"What?" she head Jill ask.

Later, Trick would insist that if she hadn't already started to lean into the opening bathroom door, to throw her weight behind her stiffened arm—if she hadn't already started to giggle to herself and the word, "Boo!" wasn't so far out of her mind it was already in her mouth, she might have realized that Jill's voice was coming from behind her.

"Good Jesus Lord Christ!" Mr. Kuznicki cried, rising in the instant and with the same furious speed lowering his newspaper so it covered the critical area between the trousers around his ankles and the hairy chest that Trick truly regretted getting a glimpse of.

Chapter Five
Monday

THERE ARE TWO WOKS ON JILL'S STOVE, PEA-nut oil heating to a smoke in one and coconut milk coming to a boil in the other. Shredded canary yellow mango, thin strips of Christmas red pepper, and shiny green, shelled sweet peas are mounded in individual ceramic bowls on the counter. Madeline, who is orchestrating this Thai feast, has Jill slicing chicken breasts, and Deanie deveining shrimp, and her grandmother frying tofu for the Pad Thai.

"Exactly what *is* tofu?" Mrs. Kuznicki asks, curious, not exactly wary. "I don't believe I've ever had it before."

Mrs. Kuznicki is seventy-six years old. She's still got her puff of blond hair, and her wrists are still as small around as a twelve-year-old's, but she has made an effort to put on a few pounds with the years so her face still looks full, her

skin smooth over the bit of extra weight. Still, in her effort
to gain a little weight, she hasn't given up walking several
miles every day so her posture is as erect and her movements
as fluid as any of the younger women in the kitchen. If Jill
is worried about her own graceful aging, as she is from time
to time, she thinks of her mother and takes heart, attribut-
ing a portion of Mrs. Kuznicki's grace to genes and a portion
to maintenance and a big portion to attitude and she slaps a
smile back on her face.

"It's made from beans, Gram. It's just beans."

"Oh," Mrs. Kuznicki says. "Well, I like beans."

Jill's younger sister, Beth, is less enthusiastic. "With everything we have to do this week, I don't know why we're going
to all this trouble for a dinner for just us. It's just us old girls,
we should have ordered in a pizza or something, Mad. We've
got a lot of work to do tonight."

The work at hand is folding the wedding programs, hot
off the printer's press, putting the pages in order and punching holes in them and lacing them together with creamy satin
ribbon. It's a project Beth says she's going to start on as soon
as she finishes laying out the McDonald's Happy Meal she's
brought along for Cara, her five-year-old daughter.

"No," Madeline says, her tone leaving no room for argument. "I want you to wait until we're done with dinner and
we can do it all together, like an assembly line. I've got it all
figured out."

"Bossy bride," Beth shoots back.

"Bossy like mommy," Cara observes and everyone but Beth
laughs.

Where did Beth come from? It's a question Jill and Deanie
and Trick have been asking themselves since they were fourteen years old. Beyond the obvious—that Beth was the

longed-for culmination of Mr. and Mrs. Kuznicki's long-held desire for a second child, or Jill's own adolescent reaction to a new baby in the house, any of the conventional resentments a teenager might have in response to acquiring a sibling after so long solo in her parents' spotlight—the question is a legitimate one.

Where Mrs. Kuznicki and her daughter Jill are willowy women, their small, long bones just skimmed with flesh, Beth is broad and buxom, her hips filling out her low-cut jeans and her bosom spilling out of her halter top in a way designed to cultivate catcalls. She's dyed the black curls that she, like Jill, inherited from their father, to a shade of blonde to rival her mother's and she piles the curls on top of her head with the help of rhinestone bobby pins and other sparkling clips so they float in a just-out-of-bed tangle around her face. And, where Jill and her mother temper their Polish passion with judiciousness, Beth is imperious, apologizes for nothing she says, and cusses like a truck driver. If Beth had been born in the wild west, Deanie has often thought, she would have grown up to be a saloon girl; if a movie were ever made about the Kuznicki family, Beth would have to be played by Bette Midler.

"You don't talk about your mother like that," Beth warns Cara, who lowers her eyes, slipping a smile back at her Auntie Jill as she sticks another French fry into her mouth.

"Whose glasses need to be refilled?" Mary Golinski asks, to distract Beth and save them all.

On the island counter, off to the side of where the ingredients for the Thai food are being measured out in individual bowls, are three pitchers of colorful sour fruit slushes—lemon, green apple, and raspberry. The slushes are meant to be spooned into champagne flutes, depending on the flavor one wants, and topped off with chilled sparkling wine—Andre's because, as Jill says, why waste good champagne when it's going to end up tasting like sour apple anyway? Jill, of course, has concocted this delicious, girly drink bar, but the evening's self-appointed bartender is Mary Golinski, Madeline's favorite professor from Villanova, where she did her undergraduate work.

Deanie has met Mary Golinski before—at Madeline's graduation, and at several other Kuznicki-Bakula family functions over the last few years—but she has never before spent the time with her, in such a small group, that might have allowed the women to know each other. Before this evening, Deanie thought of Mary Golinski only as another body orbiting the Kuznicki-Bakula universe, a vivacious but plain—even dowdy—woman who teaches chemistry and has remained single into her sixties because, probably, she is a lesbian. Come to find out, as she refills Deanie's glass with the lemon slush, Mary Golinski is a nun.

"Get out," Deanie responds to this information.

"No, really," Mary assures her.

When Deanie and Trick were twelve and first dragged along to Sunday Mass at St. Boniface with the Kuznicki family, whenever the three little girls had a sleepover at Jill's house on a Saturday night, more than a dozen Sisters of the Immaculate Heart lined up in two orderly rows in the very front two pews of the church. Their black habits were voluminous, giant rosaries clacking where they hung from waistbands, their faces and necks shielded by wimples and their bosoms draped in fabric so thoroughly starched Deanie had at first thought the bibs were made of cardboard. Back then, every little Rust Belt town had its own parade of these pious women called to do God's work, which was mostly being a part of the teaching staff at a parish grade school.

Lenapi had, in fact, two such parish schools, one at St. Boniface's, the Polish church, and one at St. Cecilia's, the Irish one. The Italians, who had never had as much of a presence in Lenapi as they did in other small Northeastern towns along the old railroad lines, divided their loyalties between the churches, the parishes competing for members until the bishop succumbed to the see's dwindling finances, and both churches' dwindling memberships, and closed St. Cecilia's in the late 1980s. St. Cecilia's had been the smaller of the two churches, torn down now to make way for new student housing, though in the intervening years a resurgence in church attendance had the consolidated congregation of St. Boniface contemplating the need for a larger building.

Though there had been a renaissance in the number of parishioners, no such rejuvenation had happened to the numbers of women and men who heard a calling to the religious life. Where fourteen Sisters of the Immaculate Heart had once called St. Boniface home, and another ten St. Cecelia's, lay teachers now staffed the sole remaining Catholic school and a single nun rotated her time among four such schools in three adjacent counties. This nun, Sister Hubert, was not a teacher, but part of the administration. She did not live in a convent but kept a small, private apartment in each county in which she worked. She dressed plainly—even dowdily— in sensible shoes and knee-length skirts and cardigans, but she had her hair styled short and curly every few months at a salon, and smelled of citrus and lilac, good talc being one of the indulgences she allowed herself. Deanie had met Sister Hubert at Jill's family gatherings, *knew* that Sister Hubert, for all her lack of a black veil and nuclear rosary beads, was a nun; she doesn't know why the revelation about Mary Golinski should surprise her. Perhaps it is Mary's skillful and enthusiastic bartending that throws her. Deanie begins to nurture a small idea for including a character based on Mary Golinski in her next book and resolves to spend some time in the next week getting to know this intriguing woman a little better.

"All right, everyone out of my way now," Madeline announces when all of the ingredients for dinner have been portioned in their bowls—saucers of fish sauce and chopped garlic and green curry paste and a chiffonade of fresh basil leaves and Trick's contribution, ground peanuts, which she brings to Madeline in an enormous stone mortar and offers up as silently as she's managed everything else she's done this evening.

"Thai food," Madeline tells them, "has got to be cooked very quickly, and I have to work everything at the same time, so just stand over there"—she points to the area on the other side of the island—"watch you don't step in the potting soil and get your plates ready because this is the kind of food that needs to be eaten as soon as it's done."

That Trick is among the gathered women is something of an act of will; Jill's.

Trick had come down her stairs that morning slowly and steadily, as if the broken banister were superfluous anyway, but the descent was not stately; she'd kept her shoulders hunched forward, and her eyes on the toes of her sandals, clicking and picking her way. At the last step she'd sighed and swung on the post at the bottom of the banister so heedlessly that its creaking alarmed her friends, swinging into Deanie's waiting arms. Their embrace was so long and hard that eventually they opened up their arms and Deanie waved Jill inside. Both Deanie and Jill felt Trick's fingers curling into fists, clutching the backs of their blouses for dear life.

"It's so good to see you," Deanie said, when she could find words. "To see you looking so good."

"That's just because the last time you saw me I was in a hospital bed and I'd just lost a couple of quarts of blood. Of course I look better now. It doesn't count."

Trick spoke abruptly, and then she laughed and neither Deanie nor Jill knew what to make of that; each of them had felt her own eyes filling, her soul welling up and spilling over with gratitude that all three of them were together, still standing. Alive. Trick's attempt at a joke cut them off at the knees, as if she thought she was undeserving of their tears. Or was bored with the whole idea of crying.

"Get your purse." Jill responded so quickly that both Trick and Deanie frowned at her. "You remember your purse, it's that thing you carry with you when you leave the house? It holds your wallet, your sunglasses, your keys. Get your purse, Trick, we've got a whole afternoon of errands ahead of us and you're coming along."

Deanie drew in a deep breath. Trick had been known to dig in her sharp heels with much less provocation and Jill was absolutely manhandling her.

Trick's eyes flashed at Jill, and her shoulders unfolded, as if she herself were taking in a full breath for the first time in six months. Then, just as suddenly, she expelled every bit of air and sighed—"Fine."

She looked around for a moment, as if she had misplaced the purse she was supposed to retrieve, and then she moved to the kitchen where a brown leather satchel was sitting on the counter. The items littered around the satchel—common items like wallet and keys, as well as a crumpled pack of

Merits and a couple of prescription bottles and some loose change and three or four books of matches, each with a match or two left inside—she scooped up and tossed inside.

Trick followed Deanie wordlessly to Jill's van and assumed for herself the back seat, the lesser place. She rode along to the appointment at Kelly's Candy and Floral where Jill approved the sample Kelly had made of the wedding day centerpieces, an extravagant topiary built of white roses, and where Deanie ordered bridal shower favors, white candied almonds and white gumdrops and ribbon candy as hard and clear as ice striped with frost. Trick rode along to the dressmaker's where Jill had her final fitting in the black silk faille sheath she'd chosen as her mother-of-the-bride dress. She rode along to the gift shop to pick up the crystal champagne flutes that Jill had had engraved with the bride and groom's entwined initials. At each stop Trick climbed out of the back seat when Jill pressed her key chain to slide open the van's side door, accompanying the party but not part of it, only nodding quietly to questions about the height of a topiary, the length of a hem, an appropriate quantity of ribbon candy, nodding less to express her opinion but in wonder that someone would consider that she had one. She was especially reticent around Kelly, wandering the candy aisles or peering in the flower cooler as if to study every nugget, every twig, avoiding even greeting Kelly, as if the incident that severed their friendship had happened last week instead of almost thirty years ago.

The whole exercise of the afternoon was unsettling to Deanie. It couldn't be that Jill was used to this—the ease of shaming their fiery Trick into obedience; she worried that Jill was just as surprised by Trick's vacant compliance as she was, but not at all disturbed by it—rather, Jill seemed relieved. Deanie wondered if it could be the new drugs Trick was on that were responsible for her being, among other things, so damnably pliable.

Even Beth likes the food—she pronounces Madeline's Yum Mamuang and Kaeng Khiao Wan Kai "fucking yummy" and stuffs more bites into her mouth as the other grown-ups at the table wince. Even Cara, after being coaxed into a bite of Pad Thai, pushes her Chicken McNuggets aside.

After the meal, the dirty dishes seem to disappear in minutes, what with seven experienced women handling the chore—even the little woman-in-progress, keen to emulate her elders, picks up empty bowls and used silverware from the table and carries them carefully to the sink and offers them to Mary Golinski to be rinsed and put into the dishwasher. Jill folds the tablecloth and takes it to the deck to shake out crumbs, and Madeline brings the boxes of wedding programs and spools of ribbon and several scissors and stacks them on top of the now-bare kitchen table. She shoos her aunt's hand away from the printed pages. "Have a seat, Auntie Beth."

"We're never going to get this done in one night if you don't let us get started," Beth complains, but Madeline only raises her eyebrows and, slowly and carefully, lifts the lid from the top box. Inside are six already-assembled copies of the wedding program. These Madeline hands around to the women at the table, and then she retreats to the dining room.

"She had these printed up in Lancaster," Jill says, sighing the name of the town where her daughter now practices law and lives in an old brownstone that she and her groom purchased a year ago and are now in the process of remodeling. "As if there isn't a printer in Lenapi who could have done the job, and probably for less. I haven't even had a chance to proof it for typos." She scans the list of musical selections, Scripture readings, spellings of the names of the two priests who will

be conducting the ceremony, saying each letter of their con-
sonant-laden last names out loud to make sure every one is
in its place: "G...R...U...S...Z...C...Z...Y...N...S...K...I..."
She seems satisfied with the rightness of the words, as well as
the simple, elegant font Madeline has chosen for them, and
then she turns to the final page of the program, and she gasps.

"Madeline? What do you mean by this?"

Madeline returns from the dining room, from which she
has retrieved seven oblong boxes from the gift table. The
boxes are wrapped in matching silver paper, tied with small
satin bows, and Madeline sets them on the kitchen tabletop.

The rest of the women, curious now with Jill's breathless
question, lean over the table to see what page she's looking at, flutter their own copies quickly to the same one, flip
them open to the same remarkable text. Beth gasps in her
turn. Mary responds by clapping a hand over her heart.
Mrs. Kuznicki inhales the words, "Oh, dear." Deanie has to
read the words on the page twice before she looks up at Madeline with her mouth hanging open. Trick reads the words
last but her eyes have no trouble catching up with the wonder that is already welling in everyone else's.

THE BRIDAL PARTY

Matron of Honor, Mrs. Jill Kuznicki Bakula, Mother of
the Bride

Attendants

Mrs. Marilyn Achinbach Kuznicki, Grandmother of the
Bride

Mrs. Elizabeth Kuznicki Vanatter, Aunt of the Bride

Ms. Deanie Morrow, Godmother of the Bride

Mrs. Fredericka Danforth Kiley, Godmother of the Bride

Sr. Mary Golinski, IHM, Friend of the Bride

"Anyone can pick out four or six or eight of her girlfriends, put them in matching dresses and call it a bridal party," Madeline says, suddenly shy, and enormously happy, her grin about to come off her face, her twin dimples deepening and reaching upwards toward the corners of her crinkled eyes. "I·want my party to be more than that. I want to honor the women who raised me."

TRICK IS THE first to recover her voice. "I'm glad you skipped my middle two married names. 'Fredericka Danforth Ferrara Williamson Kiley.' It'd be like having Elizabeth Taylor on your wedding program."

Trick's words, like the first ones she'd spoken at her house that morning to Deanie and Jill, are again abrupt, inappropriate, as if she is determined to avoid sentiment. Tears. Her words are jarring, and not the least because they are very nearly the only ones she has spoken all evening long. Still, they do nothing to dilute the emotion of the others who are standing, one by one, confused, weeping and laughing and hugging Madeline and taking her face in their hands to kiss her cheeks, demurring and murmuring disbelief and throwing over composure for delight.

"Maddie, are you sure?" Mrs. Kuznicki asks. "I'm seventy-six years old, I'll make an awfully funny-looking bridesmaid. It's not too late to have the programs reprinted if you want to change your mind."

"Oh, Gram." Madeline takes her tiny, tough little grandmother in her arms. "You and Pop have been married for fifty-four years. Can you think of a better example for me to follow down the aisle?"

Mrs. Kuznicki doesn't respond because she is speechless. Trick slips, without one more word, out to the deck for another cigarette.

SIX OF THE oblong boxes contain pashmina shawls. Deanie and Jill and Mary and Beth and Mrs. Kuznicki unwrap their packages and hold the soft cashmere to their cheeks, coo appropriately at the pale lavender color, untangle the long, knotted fringe with their fingers and drape the shawls over their shoulders. These are the items of clothing that, worn over the black dresses Madeline has requested, will mark them as members of the bridal party on Saturday.

"Lavender..." Jill chuckles at the color Madeline has chosen for her wedding, "I should have known." From the time Madeline was four and could request it, her bedroom has been painted some shade of pale purple. She has selected dresses in various shades of violet to celebrate nearly every important occasion in her life. The fabric that she chose to upholster the sofa and club chair in the small living room of her new brownstone swirls with lilacs in full bloom.

"And, for you..." Madeline hands the last of the boxes to Cara. Inside of it is a lavender slip and a billowing overdress made of sparkling, sheer white organza.

"Mad!" Cara shrieks, tearing the tissue paper away, holding up the slip in one hand and the overdress to her chest with the other. "It's so pretty!"

"A pretty dress for a pretty girl." Madeline kneels on the floor so she is eye-level with her little cousin. "Will you be my flower girl, Cara?" she asks.

"Oh, yes!" Cara agrees, flinging her arms and the dress around Madeline.

Beth steps up behind them. "Well, now, you're just going to wrinkle it all to hell," she says, and pries the organza out of Cara's fist. "You just give this dress to me and leave it alone until Saturday. Jesus, if you keep bunching it up like that I'll be at the ironing board all week, and if any of you encourage her to dress up and model it for you, you'll be the ones doing the pressing."

Chapter Six
1971

*T*HEY WERE HUDDLED IN THE VESTIBULE OF St. Boniface's—Deanie in the dotted Swiss dress her parents had brought her from their last trip into New York, and Jill in her Easter outfit, a splashy floral with an orange brocade vest, and Trick in a god-awful mint green tent with long, lace sleeves that her soon-to-be mother-in-law had given her as a gift.

"I look like a big green beach ball."

Neither Deanie nor Jill had the heart to confirm what Trick knew to be true. They were only in their sixteenth years but they had the good sense to lie, the compassion to step into the roles the day required of them. Jill handed Deanie the nosegay she was clutching so she would have both hands free to adjust the lace puff at the back of Trick's matching pillbox hat. "You only have to wear it until the ceremony's over. Then we can all change into more comfortable clothes for the reception."

Trick kicked at the radiator at the side of the double doors to the church's center aisle—*tink, tink, tink* against the cross-hatched metal cover—and peered through the stained glass side panel. Dominic Ferrara was already at the altar, waiting for her, a small, nervous smile on his lips and his father's hand on his shoulder. His long arms were hunched forward, his hands over his crotch, like he was protecting his dick; Trick had the fleeting thought that if he'd been more protective of it six months ago they wouldn't be in this mess now, but she didn't say it out loud. "At least the shoes are cool, huh?"

Deanie and Jill looked at Trick's tiny feet. The shoes were mint green, too, sandals with a dozen knotted leather straps to hold them in place and the highest, most slender heels any of them had yet to wear.

"Don't they make me look tall? I'm never going to wear flats again."

Privately—separately—Deanie and Jill thought the shoes were ridiculous. They might have worked for Trick a month ago, before she made her pregnancy public, the announcement setting the halls of Lenapi High buzzing with sibilant whispers and seeming to release Trick's midsection in the course of a single day—that morning she'd been just another teenager sashaying to class and by the afternoon she was waddling from room to room, dropping off text books for courses she would no long be taking, saying goodbyes, promising the few teachers who expressed concern that she'd start to work on her GED right after the baby was born.

Until that day even Deanie and Jill, who'd been parties to the secret of the very first missed period, hadn't really let themselves believe that Trick was in trouble. She and Dominic had tip-toed around each other after twice-weekly basketball games for two, long, frustrating years without so much as getting up the nerve to speak; it was another two weeks after the dinner party that had finally brought them together before Dominic got up the nerve to hold Trick's hand and another whole week after that for him to give her a kiss; the idea that the two of them had gone from first kiss to all the way in a matter of days just didn't seem plausible.

"My mother is going to kill me," Jill had said the day Trick dropped out of high school, after she and Deanie had turned down a ride with Trick and Dominic in his Carmengia—skipping the opportunity to crush together in the compartment behind the couple in the two bucket seats—and were walking home from school, just the two of them. "My mother is going to be beyond pissed off."

"Why would *your* mother be upset?"

"*Perch*"—Jill crooked her finger—"because if one of my best friends turns up pregnant, my mother is going to wonder if I'm doing the same sorts of things."

Which Jill, rather notoriously, was not, and she took a fair amount of abuse for it, too—after she broke up with Stu Jenner, notes of unproven authorship were shoved through the vents in her locker: "COCKTEASE."

Mrs. Kuznicki had indeed grilled both Jill and Deanie when they broke the news to her that evening before supper—sweeping Deanie into her inquisition because, after so many years, she knew the Morrows wouldn't have a single useful thing to say to the girl about how to avoid ending up having to drop out of high school herself. But Mrs. Kuznicki was there now, in the church. Third row back, on the left. Wearing a smart spring suit and a small flowered hat and an

expression on her face so brittle that the girls almost wished
she had declined Trick's invitation.

"WHOA," TRICK SAID, trying to catch herself on the door handle. The vestibule was dark, lit only by what little midday sun
could penetrate both the day's rain and the dense stained glass,
so Deanie almost didn't see Trick lose her balance, stumble
back from the radiator, but she felt the spike of Trick's sharp
heel land on the toe of her own white patent leather platform
and she was able to grab Trick around her substantial middle
and set her back upright.

"You're gonna think this is stupid, but..." Trick said,
straightening her tent, "you know what keeps going through
my mind? That I'm not going to graduate with you guys. I'm
not going to be in your class anymore. What happens if, you
know, in ten years, we're not friends anymore?"—Jill made a
motion, a crook of her finger to indicate that she was going to
speak and Trick cut her off, hissing into the hollow echo of the
vestibule—"Listen! What happens if we're not friends anymore,
and not even classmates, because then I won't get invited to the
class reunions and I'll never get to see you guys again."

"Trick"—she finally let Jill speak—"we'll always be friends.
We're blood sisters," Jill laughed.

"And, you know," Deanie added, holding a shoe in one
hand and with the other staunching the blood on her middle toe where Trick's spike had gouged out a chunk of skin,
"Dominic's in our class. He'll get invited to the class reunions.
Wives always go to those things with their husbands."

THE MUSIC STARTED, *Processional of Joy*—Dominic's parents had sprung for an organist—and Trick clutched her nosegay and straightened up as tall as she could make herself. She knew she had no choice about waddling into the church but she wanted not to wobble. The girls could see Mrs. Danforth down in the first pew rise, leading the seven other people in the church to their feet for the bride's entrance. When Trick had told her that she was pregnant, Mrs. Danforth had replied by sighing and saying to her, "Well, it's only the good girls who get caught," and Trick still hadn't figured out exactly what she'd meant. Now Mrs. Danforth was fast to her feet, wanting to get the wedding underway so she'd have as much time as possible to enjoy the reception the groom's parents were giving in their backyard before she had to report to the Farron House, where she worked overnights at the front desk.

The plan was for Deanie and Jill to walk together down St. Boniface's wide center aisle—Trick had decided not to distinguish a Maid of Honor but to give them both equal billing—with Trick to follow. Deanie and Jill took their places and, from behind them, heard Trick say, "I don't think I can do this."

Deanie and Jill turned.

Jill spoke slowly. "If you don't want to get married," she said, "you don't have to. There are other ways out of this mess. My mom even said so."

"No," Trick told her. "I meant I don't think I can get down the aisle in these shoes."

"Oh." This from Deanie.

"Ahh…" Jill nodded, understanding. "Take them off."

Even the idea made Trick stagger again. "Barefoot and pregnant?" she snickered, groping for Deanie's arm to steady herself.

Jill shook her curls, using the toe of a foot to peel off one of her own shoes, and then the other. Deanie, who was already holding one of her platforms in her hand, smiled as she kicked off the other one.

"Really?" Trick asked.

"Church wants us to wear hats. I've never heard anything about foot gear."

Without the crazy stilettos, Trick's dress looked nearly floor-length. She wiggled her toes and, unable to get a view of her own, eyed her friends' stocking feet. "Don't you feel silly?"

"Yes," Deanie agreed. And then she laughed and took one of Trick's arms, and Jill took the other, and together they proceeded.

Chapter Seven
Tuesday

*I*T'S A LITTLE AFTER EIGHT AM. THE REST OF THE Bakula house is quiet, Chuck and Chas and Madeline still bedded down, each asleep in their own rooms, sheets pulled up over shoulders, the only covering required on this brilliant, sunlit early morning. Jill has been up for hours.

She checked on each member of her family when she awoke—Chuck snoring softly, his blond head resting half on her pillow and half on his own, a film of summer sweat on his forehead where she kissed him, lightly, so he wouldn't stir.

She went to their bathroom and slipped into a pair of cotton pajamas that were hanging on the back of the door, brushed her teeth and splashed water on her face and laid out Chuck's morning portion of pain killers in a shallow dish, which she left by his side of the bed with a fresh glass of

water. Through trial and error it had become clear, over the
years, that when Chuck was able to take his meds first thing,
before even any slight activity, the nerves that sent messages
to his phantom leg were less restless, the pain they rousted
awake each morning more bearable; it was part of Jill's morning ritual now, this dish with a hummingbird painted in its
shallow bowl and this glass of cold water by Chuck's bedside,
and in the fifteen or sixteen years that she'd been performing
it Chuck had never once failed to acknowledge his gratitude
for a kindness that was, to him, sustaining in the most fun-
damental sense of the word.

Jill checked on Chas, home now for the wedding week in
his old bedroom, surrounded by soccer trophies and other
mementos of his boyhood—boutonnières from dances he
couldn't remember attending but that his sister had insisted
on drying for him, the signed cast from when he broke his
arm the summer before eighth grade, the disco ball he'd
swiped as a souvenir from his fraternity house. Jill moved into
the room and drew the blinds at his windows, a nighttime
task for which Chas had never developed a habit no matter
how he complained each morning about a harsh awaken-
ing, the sun in his eyes. "Draw his blinds before you go to
bed," Jill had advised Allison after she and Chas had been a
couple for a few months, because she had decided she really
liked this girl.

She checked on Madeline, her arms flung over her head,
her lavender nightgown bunched around her waist, a smile on
her face even in sleep. The mementos in Madeline's childhood
room—the dried corsages and stuffed animals and Mardi
Gras beads hanging in colorful loops from her dresser mirror—were only a backdrop now, things to hang other things
upon, the blue satin garter Beth had bought for the bride and

the string of pearls Adam had given her as a wedding gift and the pale ivory gown that hung on the closet door, pinned into a cardboard form to keep its shape, sheathed in plastic to protect it from dust until the day it was worn.

Jill tiptoed down the steps to put up an urn of coffee—provisions for all of the people who would be a part of the day ahead—and to brew a quick cup just for herself in the French press she used when she wasn't expecting an army to descend. She thought that today, among all the days of her life, was going to be one of the very last in which she would experience a morning quite like this one, waking and being able to look in on each member of her family asleep in a bed that she had made up for them. She thought she ought to be sad about that, the loss of her children to their own lives, and she was sad, but only through the first half of her cup of coffee. As she sat in her kitchen, in the light that Chas thought of as harsh and she thought of as cleansing, starting on her second half, the satisfactions of her life overwhelmed the sorrows. She had made mistakes; there had been tragedy. But, also, somehow, she'd come to this morning, this splendid hour, this season with its own ripening, juicy fruit.

She glanced at the potting soil mounded on her kitchen floor.

By a little after eight, Jill has the flats of rosemary for fidelity and basil for protection and thyme for eternity transplanted into two dozen terra cotta cherubs. The cherubs are lined up on one of the picnic tables on the deck. She is standing in her cotton pajamas and bare feet with a garden hose, lifting a gentle spray over the herbs. She is wearing a pair of sunglasses to protect her eyes from the glint and glow of the sun that is growing stronger, it seems, each moment; it is going to be another hot day. She wishes, thoughtlessly, for a bit of cooling rain, and then amends herself quickly, "But not on Saturday, OK? Let's not have rain on Saturday if You can help it."

Still, it is so early, and already so hot.

Impulsively Jill turns the hose on herself, the gentle spray cooling her from the top down, her black curls, her upturned face, her shoulders and breasts and belly, a baptism for the second half of her life that will begin this weekend, on her first child's wedding day.

MARY GOLINSKI WAKES on the sofa bed in the living room of her friend's small apartment. The Bishop authorized this apartment for Hubert, a place to live during the week or so every month that she is in Lenapi working at the St. Boniface elementary school—three rooms on the second floor of one of the Victorians on Clearview Street that have been carved into rental units. But Hubert is going to be at Sacred Heart in Tioga County all week long; she won't be coming in for the wedding until late Friday night, will probably even miss the rehearsal dinner. Mary has the apartment all to herself.

Sleeping past eight o'clock is an indulgence Mary rarely allows herself. But she got back late from last night's Thai feast, and she had drunk a good deal of champagne while she was there; hadn't God provided sleep as a way for the body He created to rejuvenate itself? Also, she has promised Father Cielinksi, the Bakulas' parish priest, that she will serve as his Eucharistic minister at the Mass he says every Tuesday at eleven at the Lenapi Home for Assisted Living; it's not as if she's missing a day of church altogether.

Also, Hubert isn't here to tiptoe around until Mary wakes and *tsk, tsk, tsk* her upon a late rising.

Mary swings her feet out of the sofa bed and into a pair of flip-flops waiting on the floor. Hubert's apartment is small, but charming, the suite of rooms that made up the nursery when the Victorians were calling the house a home; there's a window seat tucked under a tri-panel, leaded glass window in the sitting room, overlooking the back gardens, and a sweet little nook for dining adjacent to where a tidy kitchenette has been installed. But the apartment is new, a recent accommodation of Hubert's overloaded schedule, all the driving she has to do every month as principal of four of the region's parochial schools, and it is still not fully furnished. Hubert has not yet placed a rug anywhere near the sofa bed and the hardwood floors are chilly even on this summer morning. Mary sends up a prayer of gratitude that even after so much champagne she thought to put the flip-flops so close to the bed before she went to sleep. Then she lowers herself—first one knee and then the other, the one that gives her trouble— to the floor for a more formal session with God.

Our Fathers, Hail Marys—a whole rosary later Mary takes a few moments for personal intentions and, this morning, a few of them rather amuse her. She's been asked to be a *bridesmaid* for heaven's sake!

Mary's life has been filled with blessings—forty-seven years in service to the Lord, her post at Villanova. Her dedication to teaching, spiked as it is with a spirited sense of humor, has earned her regard and affection within her chosen community. The professional honors that accompany a distinguished career, Mary accepts those humbly, and she accepts her students' professional victories with substantially more enthusiasm. When a former student returns to visit her, or sends her a letter or an e-mail to catch Mary up on the trajectory of her life, these she brings into her heart as her true

rewards. Mary never has any idea what might await her when
she opens her door to a new freshman class, the lives and stories she might be drawn into as she helps to shape a new crop
of young people into formidable adults. She couldn't have
imagined the day she opened the door to young Madeline
Bakula that she was on the threshold of a cherished—and
enlightening—new friendship.

Until that day Mary had prayed along—as most Catholics
will pray along—for an increase in vocations to the religious
life, entreating God to call more young men and women to
lives as priests and nuns. It had been an automatic prayer,
based on the direction of whatever priest was serving Mass
and her own fond recollections of the women she had once
lived amongst, the gaggle of young girls who'd been novices
with her in 1961, the bustling convent she'd been a part of
in her earliest days as a religious. It was her personal sorrow
that being a part of any convent, bustling with the activity
of other people or not, was no longer an option. The health
of the community she'd entered in her girlhood was no longer robust and, therefore, she thought of herself as unwell.

Then Madeline had come to her, eighteen years old and
confused, like a great many of them were at that age, about
the path she was supposed to walk. But what Madeline was
confused about was that she might have a calling of her own,
the voice in her head that was only a whisper, and a weak
one, but nonetheless nagging enough that she thought she
ought to talk through the idea with someone who would
know about such things.

Mary had been horrified.

Now, kneeling on Hubert's chilly hardwood floor, four
days before the girl's wedding, she fully understood why. Nostalgia for a way of life, however fond, did not mean that it was

not or should not be over. The days of keen young women submitting themselves to the authority of the Church's priests and bishops were gone, and good for that, and no matter that entering a convent had been the right personal submission for Mary Golinski in 1961. Had young women continued to enter the convent in numbers anywhere near approaching those of Mary's youth, the roles that all women were allowed to play in the Church would surely not have evolved. There would be no women ushers, no women reading from the pulpit. No women demanding of the recalcitrant Vatican that they be given leadership positions as their faith and the good minds that God gave them provided the competence to take on. And Father Cielinksi would have no Eucharistic minister today at his eleven o'clock Mass.

Mary had shepherded Madeline through her confusion— the involuntary reaction of nearly all girls raised in practicing Catholic homes that they want to enter a convent and which most of them outgrow by the time they are twelve. Over the course of many months, over the tea that Mary brewed and the pastries that Madeline brought to Mary's kitchen to share, Mary had done more than help to clarify a path for that rare student still caught up by her faith in a by-gone way of life. She had opened up her own life to scrutiny. To the solitude of it, the aloneness. The loneliness she would not have Madeline endure. In the process she'd cemented a friendship with a remarkable young woman, a young woman Mary believed to be a wonder. A brave and open-hearted angel.

Mary Golinski has no idea what the Bishop will say when he hears what Madeline has asked of her this time. He is a sweet old man, older even than Mary is old, and he's adamant about few things anymore, mostly that he will eat nothing that either swims or flies so Mary makes him a nice pot roast when he comes to visit. She imagines they'll have a good laugh and wonder together if there is precedent for a sixty-eight-year-old nun being asked to be a bridesmaid.

Mary has been kneeling on the chilly floors for a good long while and she thinks to stretch her knees—first the good one and then the other—and she wonders at all of it.

MARILYN KUZNICKI STOPS for a quart of milk and a carton of eggs on her way home from seven o'clock Mass. More often than not her husband, Vic, goes to daily service with her, but she didn't even try to wake him this morning.

Last night, while all of the women were at Jill's house enjoying Madeline's Thai feast—*tofu*; that's the other thing Marilyn wants to scout around for in the grocery store, so she can make those delicious noodles for Vic—while all the old girls were enjoying their Thai party, Vic and Chuck had entertained the kids' friends at the neighborhood fire hall with pitchers of beer and a rigorous dart tournament. The kids had a terrific time, or so they told Marilyn when they arrived back at the Kuznicki house at one-thirty this morning, while Vic made them all coffee and cut them thick slices of the chocolate cake Marilyn had in the refrigerator. *Vic* had a terrific time at the fire hall; he hadn't stayed up that late in years.

Marilyn had ruffled his hair when she woke at six this morning; he didn't stir, didn't even snort or snore and turn over like some disgruntled angel when she tried to rouse him, as was his habit now that they were retired and he had no obligation to rise and provide, and Marilyn was happy to let him sleep in.

Still, as she wheels her cart around BiRite Foods, down the dairy aisle where a helpful clerk has told her she'll find the tofu in the cooler, just past the cottage cheese section, she's impatient to get home and sit down over coffee with Vic and tell him what happened to *her* last night.

Each time she thinks about Madeline's remarkable desire to make her bridal party of a bunch of old ladies, Marilyn gets caught in a breathless collision of emotion: pride so filling it is almost like eating chocolate cake—to have a granddaughter so sensible and sensitive that she wants to follow Marilyn's marital example!—and *excitement*. Thorough, overwhelming, unnerving excitement of the sort she believes she hasn't felt since Beth was in labor with the last grandchild, Cara. Yet the joy of birth doesn't quite match the character of the current reason for eager anticipation; there is an element of silliness, of vanity, that accompanies Marilyn now around the supermarket as she thinks about being a bridesmaid, and she relishes it. She chuckles softly to herself, ducking her head low over the cottage cheese to search for tofu, so no one will see her foolish grin.

She can't wait to see Vic's face—see the pride there when she tells him what Madeline has done. She knows that he's going to object to the plan for the bridal party when he first hears of it; it's an unconventional plan and it will take him a moment or two, as it took her, to be delighted. But, after a moment or two, Vic will laugh. He'll shake his head and laugh and put his arms around Marilyn and tell her that she'll be the most beautiful bridesmaid in the bunch. Marilyn can't wait for that. In the meantime, she picks out a package of firm-texture, organic tofu and savors her secret.

ALL BETH WANTS in the world is Cara in the family room, planted in front of the TV, at peace with a bowl of Cheerios and Spongebob Squarepants.

Instead, there is nearly a tantrum when Beth tells Cara, *No*. No, she can't model her flower girl dress for her father before he goes to work. "No, Cara, Sweetie, no, please go eat your breakfast," Beth says and the child's tears start to well, the little body goes rigid, the head tilts backward in preparation for the wail of protest, and then Terry intervenes. "Why not, Beth? I'll bet you look like a fairy princess in that dress, Cara. C'mon, Beth, let her try it on so I can see."

And, so, in between ironing Terry's work shirt, and scrambling him some eggs, and shooing the cat off the counter and packing a couple of ham sandwiches in a brown paper bag for Terry to eat at lunch because, as a field inspector for the DEP he spends most of his time on the road checking betanapthalamine levels in gas station monitoring wells and he hates the food at the one little diner in the town where he is assigned for the day, and yanking on a pair of stockings so she won't be late for her own job and then tearing them off because they are making her legs sweat, and checking her e-mail because her boss told her yesterday before he left the office that he'd let her know first thing in the morning if he needed her to stop by the courthouse on her way in today to pick up the papers on the Jackson bankruptcy, and scrambling some eggs for herself because she is so hungry her stomach is cramping and eggs are pure protein and won't hurt her efforts to fit into the sleek black satin dress on Saturday rather than the crepe one with the gathered waist that is her back-up plan and writing a note to Cara's babysitter about not giving her too much sugar, again, and about making an effort to be on time for once dropping her off at afternoon kindergarten—"No later than 1:15, PLEASE!!!"—and pinning up her curls with several mint green rhinestone clips because it is clear she isn't going to have time to wash her hair again today—in among all of these activities Beth helps Cara strip off her Dora the Explorer pajamas and climb carefully into the organza flower girl confection.

Cara, who is still stifling indignant little sobs, happy to be getting her way but unsure of how kindly disposed she is toward her mother at the moment, twirls and twirls and twirls for her father, making the skirt swirl around her. "See?" she asks him. "See how it blows around when I dance?"

"If you think that's something, watch what it does when I do this," Terry tells her, picking her up under her armpits and starting to spin her, round and round, faster and faster, raising her high above his head and then lowering his arms so her bare feet, toes wiggling, nearly touch the floor before he raises her high again, giggling and shrieking, the dress flying, the light-as-air fabric supple as the fins of an angelfish, as the wings of an angel.

Beth watches this and, nodding to herself, takes a seat on one of the stools at the kitchen counter. To hell with the betanapthalamine and the Jackson bankruptcy. She'll go barelegged into the office if she has to and Terry can damned well pull into a McDonald's for lunch if he doesn't like the food at that diner so much; she's not going to miss a second of this.

DEANIE COVERS HER head with a pillow. Her travel alarm is chirping—8:15! 8:15! 8:15!—and all she can think is that, for her, it is really 5:15! 5:15! 5:15!

She got an early start yesterday and put in a full day on jet-lagged, east coast time; last night Jill said to be at the house "first thing" this morning—Jill wants to get the herbs potted into the cherubs before she has to start cooking for the shower later this afternoon—but surely "first thing" can't mean before nine o'clock again. Jill is, after all, merciful.

Deanie buries her head in the hotel pillowcase. She complains frequently about the amount of travel that is required to do her job—travel from city to city, country to country, continent to continent to do research, give speeches, sign books for her fans—but, truth be told, while she really does despise all the hours she logs in planes, she loves new places, new people, and new hotel rooms.

And every hotel room is new. It doesn't matter how old the hotel *building* might be, the sheets and towels are fresh, and the bathroom sparkling, all the tiny bottles of shampoo and lotion still full and sealed, and the pillows are plump, waiting only for her own head, an oasis of aloneness where no housekeeper will chide her for being untidy, like Mrs. Beech does back home; no typist will bang on the door because there are pages due at the publisher and Deanie's handwritten notes in the margins of the draft are once again illegible; no lover will claim, however temporarily, more than his fair share of the bed.

Deanie stretches her arms and legs luxuriously, one to each corner of the mattress, tenses her muscles and draws in her breath and holds it for one, two, three seconds before she exhales, relaxes, reaches an arm out to quiet the travel alarm and then burrows her head more deeply into the pillows to relish the solitude.

The added bonus of travel, according to Deanie, is waking up in a part of the world where California, and her staff there, is still asleep. Playing musical chairs with time zones might wreak a bit of havoc with her circadian rhythms, but upon waking, if she isn't waking in Pacific Standard Time, there is a vacuum of an hour or two from which responsibility has been sucked—no deadlines to race toward, payrolls to meet, people to look after.

This, Deanie thinks, is a point that no one, least of all Jill or Trick, really gets: she *likes* living alone. It suits her. She was a dreamy child and she is a dreamy adult, lucky enough to have found some talent for doing work that pays her to dream things up. She was fortunate to have been abandoned by her youthful fiancé—she's not had to prove that she is either very good, like Jill, or very bad, like Trick, at marriage. She's blessed with the children of friends to whom she can be devoted, drawing them to her to play, off with them on larks and thoroughly spoiling them along the way, offering perspectives and advice their parents found subversive but the kids thrived upon—letting Chas drive around the private roads on her Napa Valley property from the time he was twelve, and showing fifteen-year-old Madeline how to unroll a condom over a cucumber, against the day when she would eventually need to know how to unroll one over a more critical object.

And this brings up another point that, Deanie decides, everyone overlooks: she may be single, but she does not really live alone. There are always guests in her house, friends and children and lovers, and when there are not guests there is staff, typing her pages and coordinating her schedule and screening her calls and, where there is not staff, there is Mrs. Beech, tut-tutting about outfits that should be hung in closets, not draped over the backs of chairs, and lost toothpaste caps.

"I adore hotels," Deanie confesses, aloud, and rolls over on the big, soft Farron House bed, deciding to give herself another hour before rising. Another hour in the vacuum from which all care has been sucked clean.

It hadn't always been so appealing at the Farron House. The old Victorian had not always been an oasis.

In the 1970s, the Farron House had been "renovated"— a word that was applied loosely even at the time to what was going on at the hotel—sheet paneling to hide crumbling horsehair plaster and indoor/outdoor carpeting to camouflage missing marble floor tiles. The newly-ugly Farron House had stayed in business for three very practical reasons: the owners filled the ballroom with all of the fifth-year class reunions and frat dances that no other hall in town would take, wary as they were of the damage young drunks can cause, but the management of the Farron House thought it was easy enough to hose vomit out of indoor/outdoor carpeting; they sold thirty-five cent drafts and hired a rock band every Saturday night, packing the bar with college students and never carding one of them; there was no other hotel in Lenapi.

Deanie had stayed there once in the mid 1990s and, on her last day, when Jill picked her up to take her back to the airport, Deanie had said, "I think I have fleas."

"Fleece? Oh, I hope you do, honey; it's January."

"*Fleas.*" Deanie had scratched at her stomach, lifting her pullover to show Jill the red skin there. "I think the Farron House has fleas."

When she'd returned to Greentree Court, Jill had stripped down in the mud room, washed the clothing she'd been wearing, showered in the tiny stall she and Chuck had put in for the kids to use when they came in from the pool, and bombed her car with the insecticide she'd bought on the way home.

When Deanie got back to Napa, she'd picked up her telephone and called Hazel Frank.

"Haze, are you still looking for a project?"

"Every day, Dean."

Hazel had been a sous chef at the renowned Napa Valley restaurant, The French Laundry, before she married into one of the county's most famous wine families. She had had three children before she realized that her husband's only interest in either matrimony or fatherhood was to placate his mother, a jug-wine dowager—and the dowager's only interest in a daughter-in-law or the grandchildren that resulted, in this case, from having one, was the preservation of the esteemed family name. After the divorce, Hazel's husband didn't fight the lump-sum settlement she asked for. He gave it willingly and then fled with his latest boy toy for the life he'd always longed for in the south of France—and Napa was no longer big enough for Hazel and her mother-in-law. Hazel had the money and the motivation to take her children and go anywhere; Deanie proposed Lenapi, Pennsylvania.

"You're kidding, right?" Hazel had answered.

"Just fly back with me when I go in March. The Farron is a beautiful old building, gone to seed, yes, but still loveable. Just take a look at it."

"I don't know, winters…. My blood has thinned, being out west in the warm for so many years."

"Oh, who do you think you're talking to? You're from Connecticut, Hazel, a little east coast girl like me, hardy stock. And your kids will love the snow! And great schools, and no mother-in-law… I'm buying our plane tickets, so put the dates on your calendar."

From their first tour through the old hotel, Deanie knew that Hazel was hooked. She peeled back the damp, green carpet and ran her hand lovingly over the marble beneath. She pounded on the dry wall that was sealing off the front staircase and asked the Lenapi building code officer who was taking them on the tour what it would take to bring the grand, mahogany gem back up to code. She smiled when she saw the musicians' balconies in the old ballroom, and actually clapped her hands when she saw the size of the kitchens.

A year later, back in Lenapi for the grand opening, Deanie was stunned when Hazel's youngest daughter, Christiane, a four-year-old in a bright yellow dress to match the bright yellow walls in the sunny main dining room, rushed to Deanie and threw her arms around her knees in welcome. "I didn't think Chris would remember me," Deanie marveled.

"She doesn't. She does that to everybody, really strangely friendly. She's going to be a worrisome teenager. Anyway, what do you think?" Hazel asked, opening her arms to encompass all of the enchantment she'd returned to the Lenapi landmark.

"It's beautiful. It's just perfect, Haze," Deanie cooed. Hazel led her through the main restaurant's yellow dining room to the kitchens, now floor-to-ceiling, brand-new, spotless stainless steel. She led her back out of the kitchens, to the ballroom, it's creamy fresco walls restored and its tall, arched windows outlined in the palest robin's egg blue. She led her through a small but efficient waiter's pantry to the hotel coffee shop.

"Well?" Hazel asked.

"Well! Well…" Deanie nodded. "It's certainly pink in here."

"It's supposed to be pink—an old-fashioned-ice-cream-shop theme."

Deanie continued to nod.

"Deanie Morrow, be honest with me."

"OK. I think it's a little hokey."

Hazel laughed and poked a finger in Deanie's ribs like she was trying to tickle her. "It's not hokey, honey. It's *homey.* Fresh baked pastries every morning, banana splits in footed glass boats and, for dinner, the best chicken-and-waffles in the whole chicken-and-waffle eating state, and only six ninety-five if you get here in time for the Early Bird Special."

Deanie cocked her head to get a good look at her friend. "You really love it here, don't you?"

"Deanie," Hazel said, "I love this town. I love the people. I am in love with this old hotel. If you never do another nice thing for anybody else, your karma will still be all right because you earned your angel wings when you hooked me up with Lenapi."

As it turned out, Deanie was more angelic than even Hazel had imagined. Hazel discovered, in her years at the Farron, that she really didn't like being a chef anymore—and she resented every hour the administration of the hotel part of the business took her away from her children; what Hazel had liked was the renovation itself—finding ways to preserve historic architecture while complying with modern building codes; planning menus and configuring restaurant kitchens that could produce them most effectively; choosing unconventional and charming color schemes—the pink coffee shop was packed with customers on opening day and every day after that. Three years after Hazel bought the dilapidated Farron House for under three hundred thousand dollars, she sold an historic treasure with a healthy P&L for sixteen million. Then she set herself up as a restaurant consultant with a specialty in historic preservation; restaurants and inns and bed & breakfasts fashioned by Hazel Frank Historic Hospitality from thoughtfully restored buildings had been popping up ever since all over the northeast, and into the mid-Atlantic region too.

Deanie cuddles herself into the downy pillows in her Farron House bed, stretches her legs under the satiny sheets, dozing, not sleeping, reveling in her hour of freedom, pleased with herself for her part in making this hotel viable again. She doesn't approve of the pink coffee shop, or the over-sized television sets Hazel installed in the guest rooms, but the beds here at the Farron House are more than just flea-free now. Now they are fine.

She decides to get up and open the curtains at her room's window, let the morning sun flood in over the bed so she can bask in it like a cat. She blinks in the first light, until her eyes adjust. On her way back to the bed she sees the lavender pashmina shawl laying over an arm of the wingback chair near the desk, where she draped it when she got in from last night's Thai feast. She lays her hands on its softness, which is irresistible, and she gathers it up and draws it around her shoulders and takes it back to bed with her.

She doesn't want to wrinkle the shawl—she knows she can't lie here too long with it wrapped around her like a receiving blanket in the lap of luxury—but it is a most extraordinary thing to spend a few moments of a rare unhampered hour surrounded by evidence of the good things you have helped to create.

Trick stands at her kitchen sink, holding on to the rim of it for support until the coffee is finished brewing and she can drink a cup to bolster herself. She can drink only decaf these days but there is still some part of her that doesn't turn on until the familiar aroma fills her nose and she scalds her tongue on the first too-hot sip. She's gathered her prescription bottles and laid out her morning pills in a saucer by the coffee pot; there are a few pills she's supposed to take on an empty stomach but trying to swallow anything before she has had her coffee will make her gag. Drinking a cup of coffee before she takes her pills hasn't inhibited their efficacy for six months.

She's been stable for six months.

She reaches for the pack of Merits on the window ledge, shakes one free. Puts it in her mouth and lights up. The cigarettes are her one remaining vice—she even drank last night's syrupy-sweet fruit slushes diluted with club soda instead of champagne; the cigarettes are all she has left, except sleep. Unless sleep doesn't qualify as a vice—she really doesn't know anymore; is it a vice if you have no control over it? If the pills that keep you sane do so by knocking you out for sixteen hours a day?

"You just haven't come up with the right combination yet," Nicky said to her the last time he was up from Texas. Last month. "You need to tell your doctor to change up your prescriptions again."

"Yeah, yeah."

The problem with changing up prescriptions is that you don't know what new horror is waiting for you inside a new bottle, what new side effect is coming to get you: weight loss or weight gain; hair loss or excessive hair growth in places no one wants a tuft of the stuff; blurry vision or headaches that make you want to claw your eyes out of your head; bloating and a supply of gas that puts you right up there with Kuwait. As side effects go, sleeping isn't so bad and Trick is reluctant to trade it in for something worse.

Trick is aware, of course, that some day she will have to wake up. Her sons can't keep taking time off and taking turns running up to Lenapi. She misses her grandkids; the boys have never said it outright, but she knows they haven't yet brought any of the grandkids with them to visit her because their wives object to the kids being around a crazy person. Jill long ago lost patience with her.

Jill. Perfect, capable, organized, admirable, prissy, judgmental Jill.

Who is probably at this very moment feeding Deanie instructions about how to manage their flakey friend Trick while Dean's in town on her little visit.

Distant, dreamy Deanie up there on the television screen at least once a week talking about women, strong women, loving women, *warrior* women, for Christ's sake, women who have the power to save the world and she can't even save one of her best friends. Which is probably why she's so mouthy about saving everyone else.

Let either of them try to function for a few days with a broken brain and see how competent or empowering they are then.

It feels good to get mad at Deanie and Jill. Not because they deserve anger so much but because it is the one sensation that's penetrated the chemical haze Trick's been in for six months, so she nurtures it: Jill the tight ass and Deanie with her head up her butt.

Trick looks at her coffeepot. Some day she is going to treat herself to a machine with a stop-drip feature so every morning doesn't include a dilemma: wait for the pot to finish brewing or make a mess trying to shove a cup under the drip to catch the flow so you can suck down the first lukewarm dribbles.

Trick decides she can't deal with coffee all over the counter this morning and sucks on her cigarette to ease the anxious wait. To ease her anger at Deanie and Jill for their whole, damned happy lives.

She isn't really mad at either of them. She just wants their lives, Jill's or Deanie's, it doesn't matter which. And it's not the pretty houses or the bright careers or the exotic travel or the fabulous kids she craves, she has fabulous kids of her own, for one thing—in spite of everything, because their father took them away from everything bad, including her, when they were still little boys, the kids have turned out fabulous. What she wants that Deanie and Jill have is their confidence... the confidence that when they wake up every day they don't have to gag down a handful of pills before they can be sure they won't do anything stupid. They don't have to buffer any brain receptors in order not to be bad. They don't have to choose between sleeping for sixteen hours a day or having mustaches growing out of their noses.

Trick hears her bare foot slapping spastically against the broken floor tiles before she feels it. *Thap, thap, thap, thap, thap, thap, thap.* What is taking the coffee so goddamned long?

She has to pee again. It's one of the side effects she's decided she can live with—frequent urination—but going to the bathroom right now means going all the way back upstairs, and Madeline's lavender shawl is hanging there, over the post at the top of the staircase.

The arrogance of that kid, springing a command performance like this on a sick person!

Trick shakes her head.

She isn't really mad at Madeline either.

She just needs her cup of coffee and another cigarette and then she'll be able to think clearly. And then she won't be mad at anyone.

Maybe she'll even be able to feel honored about being chosen as a member of Madeline's wedding party, like all the rest of them feel.

She doesn't know why Madeline's announcement should make her feel so irritated. Madeline's just a kid with a charmed life; it's the rest of them who should know better. Should know she is in no condition to have her emotions yanked around like this. She can't even go out in public without being forced—being bullied into it by Jill, or running out of cigarettes—and these people want her to be a wedding sideshow!

How is she supposed to go out in public and do that? She can't even speak when she's with people.

Or, she *can* speak, but whenever she does she says the wrong thing, something she knows is off-the-wall the instant it is out of her mouth, before anyone even looks at her like she has three heads. She might as well just keep it shut. She might as well not even try to explain that being included in Madeline's wedding party is like being given a new reason to live and, after all, after all she has been through in the last six months, she knows she has to live— she accepts that—but she is not yet ready to have another reason to do it. Her boys won't even let her see her own grandkids, her own little babies who, in spite of everything, in spite of having a crazy person for a grandmother, have turned out to be angels and she aches for them; how dare these people shove another opportunity to fail at loving someone in her face?

Trick yanks the pot out from under the spout. Her hands are shaking as she fills a cup. Coffee floods onto the counter and she doesn't care. She puts the pot back on the burner to catch what it can of the remaining brew.

She'll have her coffee, and then she'll take her pills, and another day will begin.

She'll have to wake up for one of them—one of the days coming—but she doesn't want to dwell on that this morning. She just wants her decaf.

Chapter Eight
1977

TRICK HAD HER TWO SONS IN TOW—NICKY, born two and a half months after her hasty wedding to Dominic Ferrara, and Cole, born eleven months after that because, as Trick explained, neither she nor Dom fully understood that it was only a *probability* that a girl couldn't get pregnant again while she was still breastfeeding. The boys were now five and six years old, sweet kids who weren't much trouble—who seemed, in fact, preternaturally inclined not to cause trouble, as if they were concerned that their presence was trouble enough. Their big eyes took in everything in the exotic Morrow living room—the Afghani rugs on the floor and the pre-Columbian stone figures on the bookshelves and the vaguely erotic canvases on the walls. The vases of the fresh cut flowers on every flat surface that

Mrs. Morrow couldn't do without and that gave the room a funereal scent. Their eyes took it all in but they didn't move to touch a thing. They went obediently with Mrs. Morrow into her kitchen when she offered them a piece of the chocolate cake Mrs. Kuznicki had brought over that morning. There was nothing unusual about Mrs. Kuznicki delivering a cake to a grieving neighbor; Mrs. Morrow's willingness to serve it was an indication of how befuddled she was by the current circumstances in the Morrow household.

Jill had arrived earlier in the morning. Unencumbered yet by children and blessed to work under a head librarian at the Lending Library who was sympathetic to the crisis underway, Jill had gotten there fifteen minutes after Mr. Morrow's summons, kicked off her pumps and was already sprawled with Deanie on her bed when Trick arrived to join them.

"He just called, out of the blue, to say that he wasn't coming to Lenapi for Christmas?" Trick demanded.

"Oh, screw Christmas," Jill snapped back at her. "He called off the wedding."

Deanie lay still on her bed, face down, in the hollow formed by her two friends on either side of her. It was the same spot she'd lain in since she'd hung up the phone in her parents' living room, run upstairs and flung herself at the bed. She'd been mumbling into the mattress—"Call Jill and Trick," at her father and "Tell Mrs. Kuznicki thank you," when her mother had knocked on her bedroom door to announce the arrival of the chocolate cake; the spot on the comforter directly under Deanie's mouth was wet with spittle, but not with tears. Deanie had sobbed when she first hit the bed, moments after her fiancé's telephone call, but she had stopped that soon after Jill had arrived and the tears were nothing more now than salty stains on the satin beneath her.

In Jill's presence, the wild, immediate grief that had demanded tears gave way to humiliation. It was not that Deanie was embarrassed in front of Jill about the turn of events, but that Jill's entry into her bedroom had triggered thoughts of all the calls that would have to be made to invited guests, all the wedding gifts already delivered that would have to be returned.

Deposits that would have to be forfeited to the caterer and the florist.

The white silk dress hanging in her closet that she wanted to shred with her bare hands. "The son of a bitch," Deanie mumbled into the comforter.

"Anger is good," Jill prodded. "Go ahead, Deanie, get really mad. Let it all out."

But all Deanie had managed to do was follow her mercurial, swirling, cycling emotions to a new layer of anguish—disbelief. Was her fiancé only joking about canceling the wedding? Was he only setting her up for some elaborate surprise? Hal McKinley was a jokester, no question about that; hadn't he, just this past summer, pretended to forget her birthday, suggesting penitently that the two of them go out to her favorite pizza place on Bleecker Street that Wednesday night to make up for his neglect, only for Deanie to find that he'd arranged for her to be surprised by all of their friends gathered there. Not just their New York friends either—Jill and Trick, too. He'd gotten Jill and Trick to New York in the middle of the week for her—paid for their round-trip bus tickets and made a personal call to Dominic to convince him that just because he and Trick wanted to get divorced that was no reason to punish Deanie; couldn't Dom stay with the boys for one lousy night so Trick could come to the party? Maybe Hal was joking around now, too.

"Deanie," Jill said gently, "if this is a practical joke, it's a bad one. You'd have to think twice about wanting to marry a guy who would play such a mean joke."

But Deanie's cycle had gotten stuck on this—disbelief— and was still there when Trick arrived. "Maybe it's all just a big, bad joke." Trick and Jill lifted their heads from the bed and peered at each other over the motionless body of their friend. "Ooooooh"—Deanie let out a long, dry wail—"and what if it's not? What am I going to tell people?" Jill shrugged at Trick to indicate that this was how it was going, rolling from one state of despair into another without warning and back again.

"You're not going to have to tell people anything," Trick said. "They're going to figure out all on their own that Hal McKinley is a rat."

Jill's eyebrows shot to the top of her forehead when Trick spoke. "Don't you think we should let her get through this in her own way? We don't have to be mean to her too," she scolded, but Deanie had lifted her head, so Jill stopped talking.

"Oh, my God," Deanie mumbled, but not into the comforter. She eased her arms out from under her chest, where they'd been crossed for nearly an hour, and shook out her right hand that had fallen asleep. "Oh, my God," Deanie repeated and sat up.

"What?" Jill asked warily as she and Trick arranged themselves into sitting positions, too.

"Is Hal a rat?"

Jill and Trick looked at each other, avoiding Deanie's pleading gaze.

Jill nodded. "I guess you'd have to say that he his, if he could do a thing like this to you."

Trick was more direct. "I sort of always thought he was."

Jill crossed her eyes and puckered her mouth at Trick, then quickly brought her features back to neutral when she saw Deanie look her way, but Deanie had caught her.

"It's all right, Jill," Deanie said. "I've wondered about that myself. You know, that there could be a few rodent-ish things about him."

"Like the way, last Super Bowl, we all got together and he only brought enough beer for himself?" Trick was quick to offer.

"A lousy six pack of Heineken, and he didn't even offer to share," Jill agreed, her indignation about the incident overriding her concern for kindness.

"Like how, when the three of us go out together, you have to get up seventeen times all evening long and call him and check in," Trick continued. "Even when Dom's alone with the kids he doesn't make me do that."

"That is way out of line," Jill confirmed. "Or, how about your last birthday, he was all bragging about how he paid for our trip to New York. Like we couldn't buy our own *bus* tickets…" She let her voice trail off, afraid that she'd gone too far; even as the words were coming out of her mouth she was pretty sure Trick couldn't have managed the fare.

In fact, over the last six years, there was a lot that Trick hadn't been able to manage—she didn't have the money or she didn't have the time, caring for her boys during the day and working overnights as a maid at the Farron House so her husband could finish high school, and then college at the Lenapi campus. Studying for her GED when she had a free half an hour, which wasn't often, so the high school equivalency was five years in the getting.

In the last years—with both Deanie and Jill at colleges far from Lenapi, absorbed by classes and rock concerts and being courted by college boys like Chuck and Hal—Trick had faded to the periphery, an obligatory visit when they were home on break, a restless glass of Coke and some cooing over how fast the boys were growing until they could get out of the chaotic turquoise house and back to their own lives.

Chuck had even once asked Jill, when they were first dating, where she'd met Trick and how they had gotten to be friends, as if there had always been gaping differences in their destinies and he couldn't figure out why Jill had ever attempted to bridge them. Jill had shrugged—she and Trick and Deanie had been best friends for eight years at that point and it had never before occurred to her to consider that some people might think longevity was all that was needed to sustain these things.

Trick started bouncing now on Deanie's bed. "How about: Hal can only get off if you're doing it doggie-style?" she shouted, horrifying Jill in case Mrs. Morrow might overhear, exploding the tension in the room as Deanie fell face forward, laughing into the satin comforter. "I mean, how weirdo is that, there's only one position he can come in, and you don't even like it so much? There's something really weirdo about that."

Deanie giggled into the satin until she made Trick and Jill laugh, too, and tears came to her eyes, and then she sat up and wiped her cheeks with her fingers.

Jill sat up too, watching Deanie's face and wondering if they had all now gone too far. Trick fell on her back, expelling a loud sigh, sated, and Jill flicked her hand, rapping Trick on top of the head.

"Stop it, Jill. Deanie laughed first."

"I did," Deanie agreed.

They were quiet then, even Trick at rest, listening to each other breathe.

"You should have told me what you really thought about Hal before this," Deanie said softly.

Jill nodded, but she said, "How can you just tell your best friend that you don't like her fiancé?"

Trick propped her head up in her hand. She spoke slowly. "I'm glad I have my kids. I can't imagine not having my boys. But I know you two didn't really think getting married to Dom was a good idea." She let her head fall back on to the mattress. "We can finally afford for Dom to move out and get his own place. Go see lawyers about a divorce." Trick's left foot rattling against the bedpost was the only sound in the room. "I'm going to be divorced before either of you are even married."

There suddenly didn't seem to be enough air in the room for Jill. "Trick, if, if either Deanie or I had thought you and Dom shouldn't get married, we would have... We... You shouldn't say things like that, you have two kids."

"Blood sisters have no secrets," Trick reminded her. She sat up and reached irritably for her purse, the pack of cigarettes inside of it, the abalone shell Deanie kept on the second shelf of the night table for her to use as an ashtray. She moved deliberately, daring Jill to object to her lighting up, the whole time her foot *thunk, thunk, thunking* against the post.

"Then I have to tell you something," Deanie said. "I think I have a secret. I'm upset about Hal calling off the wedding. I'm hurt and I'm mad, and it makes me sick to think about having to call everyone and tell them it's cancelled. But really, deep down? I think I didn't just get dumped..." Deanie shook her head in wonder. "I think I escaped."

Trick hooted and waved her still unlit Merit in Deanie's face. "Then take that big old fat diamond off of your finger and we'll mail it back to Hal right now with a note that says 'Good riddance.'"

"Oh, no." Deanie covered the ring protectively with her other hand. "If this ring is going anywhere it's going to my father to reimburse him for what he laid out for the caterer and the hall and the stupid white dress and everything else we won't be needing anymore."

Chapter Nine
Tuesday

THERE IS A BRIDE ON THE FRONT OF THE INVI-tation—a squiggly stick-figure bride, strictly representational, with a few slashes at the top of her head to connote a veil and a martini glass in her hand. The figure is drawn in black on glossy white paper and the only color is the dot of green olive in her glass. Underneath it reads:

Madeline Bakula has got her man,
And so we've got a shower planned.
Come show her that you're elated,
And help us get her inebriated.

"THIS IS ADORABLE," Deanie says.

Jill is at the stove, stirring a pot of what looks like pale yellow kindergarten paste—Swiss cheese and white wine and all-purpose flour. When the mixture has thickened, she will drop it in teaspoonfuls onto parchment paper and bake them in the oven until they are crunchy round crisps. She's got three other hors d'oeuvres in various stages of construction around the kitchen; Deanie is squirting salmon mousse onto puff pastry rounds Jill's fashioned from a tube of Pillsbury croissant dough. "Yes, well, my mother didn't think it was so adorable when she got her invitation. 'People throw a kitchen shower for a bride, or even a lingerie shower. But a *bar* shower?'"

Inside the invitation are the where and when of the party—the Bakula house, six p.m. tonight—and a list of the event's hostesses, a group of Madeline's college girlfriends who are due to arrive at any moment to help Jill with the food and finish turning the deck into a bridal wonderland. Already there are yards of tiny white Christmas lights wrapped around the trellis and over the fence, and there are silver Mylar streamers and helium balloons to come.

Also inside of the invitation are specific instructions as to an appropriate gift for the shower: "Help Mad and Adam stock their bar! Bring a bottle and any barware they'll need to make your favorite drink! Don't forget to include the recipe!"

"Well, anyway, *I* think the whole idea is darling," Deanie says, laying the invitation aside and resuming her task with the pastry bag of salmon mousse. "What do you get people who've already bought a house together and have been living in it for almost a year? It's unlikely they need measuring spoons. I think a bar shower is a fine idea, and the invitation is a hoot."

"One of the girls drew it herself. She was an art major."

"Just really clever." Deanie chuckles. "'...get her inebriated.'"

Jill looks up from her stirring. "You haven't seen the invitation before? I know I gave the girls your address over a month ago."

Deanie sighs, caught red-handed. She is reluctant to admit to Jill that she hardly ever sees her own mail. Layla goes through it, culling requests for book jacket blurbs from ones for speaking engagements. Separating fan mail by category and answering with appropriate gratitude and a form letter. Separating out manuscripts from would-be writers who hope their work will engage Deanie so she'll recommend them to her agent, slipping them back in the mail, unopened, with a cover letter that explains Deanie's "No Read" policy and wishes them luck. Making a list of the items Deanie needs to take action on and presenting it to her on a clipboard. Madeline's shower invitation actually came to Deanie's desk listed under requests for personal appearances.

"But I do know what I got her for a gift," Deanie insists. "I told Layla myself what to buy for her—a bottle of Grey Goose vodka and a jar of anchovy-stuffed olives and a martini shaker."

"Dirty martinis. You're still drinking those?" Jill laughs. "All right, all right, I have a secret, too."

"OK." Deanie pauses and tastes some of the salmon mousse that's squirted itself onto her finger. It really is very good.

"I haven't read your new book yet."

"But…"—Deanie's still got her finger in her mouth when she starts to talk. "Jillie, you called me as soon as it came out. You said you liked it."

"No. No, what I said was, 'You've done it again, Dean.' And you thought I meant you'd written another wonderful book, which I'm sure you have and which is what I wanted you to think but, technically, all I really did was acknowledge that you had, indeed, written another book, period."

Deanie nods. "What do you call that again? 'A Catholic lie?' True to the facts if not the spirit."

"It all started with that nun in the fourth grade. Sister Ambrosia. She convinced me it was perfectly acceptable to tell a telephone caller my mother wasn't at home, even if Mom was standing right next to me. Sister Ambrosia said it wasn't technically a lie because your real meaning was that your mother wasn't at home for *whoever it was on the phone*. Deanie, your book is four hundred pages long, and with all of the wedding stuff going on, and it's only been out for two months… If it's any consolation, I haven't read anything else either. My assistant is even doing all the spring purchasing for the library so I can concentrate on the wedding. I haven't read an entire book that isn't about wedding ceremonies since March."

"You are so going to get a quiz on *The Warriors of Flint, Michigan* exactly one week after all of this is over."

"And you are so going to get a hangover if you drink dirty martinis all night long tonight."

"You know I don't drink like that," Deanie mumbles. "*Witt* drank like that. I haven't had a hangover since nineteen eighty-two."

Jill turns the heat off under the pot of kindergarten paste. "Listen, speaking of things we all don't do anymore… We have got to do something about Trick's hair."

Salmon mousse splats from Deanie's pastry bag.

"No, Deanie, I've thought about this. Hear me out. Maybe one of the things that's holding back Trick's recovery, that keeps her locked in that house, is that she looks terrible. It would be easy enough to fix her hair. You know, just a little something to make her feel pretty. And my parents are treating us all to the day spa tomorrow anyway so it wouldn't even cost her anything. I could just schedule an appointment for Trick to have her hair done…"

"You can't just tell a person her hair looks like hell."

Jill stops with a teaspoon of the cheese paste in midair, on it's way to the parchment paper. "Trick isn't just a person. She's our blood sister."

"Oh, will you stop that? We're fifty-two years old…"

"And we're still complete cowards. Plain, old cowards if we can't master our own discomfort about speaking the truth to help a friend."

"Jeez, Jill…" Deanie winces.

"I know, I know. So, here's the plan: you and I are going to get our hair done tomorrow, too. Cut and colored, and don't tell me your guy in California did yours just before you left to come here, I can see he did. But this way, if we all get our hair done, then getting *her* hair done will just be part of the process to Trick. I use Mona all the time, and she's great, and I promise you she won't fudge your hair all up. For Trick? Are you in?"

Deanie rolls her eyes and another turd of salmon mousse drops from the bag onto the counter. "For Trick. Sure."

"Good. Now we just need to find out if she's got a black dress ready. You know, one she really likes and not just any old thing, something that makes her feel smashing…"

IT HAS SOMEHOW become Deanie's job to chauffeur Trick. Not that Trick doesn't drive, or doesn't have a car—a 1996 Sunbird sits in her driveway layered with dust and bird droppings, a lavish dandelion growing behind its left rear wheel, but it still runs. Trick's boys fished the keys from the ashtray where Trick dropped them right before she went upstairs last December to kill herself, and one of the chores they attend to on their monthly pilgrimages is starting it up.

No, the point of picking Trick up and driving her wherever she needs to be is to make sure she gets where she is supposed to go. Actually shows up. To make certain she won't sleep through everything going on this week.

Trick is wide awake, however, when Deanie arrives at her house at 5:15. She's got on a yellow sundress, and the same spiked sandals she wore yesterday, and an assortment of thick plastic bangle bracelets up and down each arm to hide her scars. Her hair is tied up in a ponytail. She's sitting on the front porch swing, rocking herself gently, holding a cellophane-wrapped basket in her lap.

"I got here early, in case you needed to stop by the liquor store for a shower present, but I see you've already got one."

"Of course I do. I walked downtown this afternoon. I'm not totally incapable."

"No, of course you're not, honey. Of course not, nobody said that." Deanie takes the place next to Trick on the swing while she reassures her. Trick's defense of her competence makes Deanie feel sad, and tender, and reluctant to approach the subjects Jill has asked her to bring up. "So, what did you get her?" Deanie points to Trick's basket.

Trick shrugs. "Back in the day, when I was drinking, I liked everything so it was hard to pick a favorite." In the basket is a bottle of Jack Daniels and two shot glasses. "It's an all right present. Isn't it?"

"Sure. Certainly." A breeze picks up, rippling the cellophane and cooling the rocking women. Deanie turns her face into it. "Feels good."

"Does." Trick's got her eyes closed and her chin lifted to catch the coolness on her neck and chest.

"Trick? It's good you're not drinking."

Trick nods. "And no one even had to tell me not to. Not one of my doctors said anything about it, which I have to think is a gross oversight. I've got a whole pharmacy worth of pills in me every day and I'm afraid if I add alcohol to the mix I might combust."

Deanie opens her eyes and looks at Trick and sees that she is grinning.

"Yep," Trick continues, sensing Deanie is looking at her, "and I've got every one of the pills in me tonight, and a smile on my face as evidence of my cheerful attitude. The chances of me saying something you'll have to be ashamed of are greatly reduced."

Deanie nearly jumps. "No one is ashamed of you, Trick."

Trick opens her eyes and looks as directly at Deanie as she has looked at anyone since December. "Dean, I've got no job, a rotting house, gray hair that seems to be falling out of my head strand-by-strand no matter what I do to it, two friends and two sons who are all rapidly losing patience with me, and a brain that doesn't work without chemical intervention. Not least of all, unlike you two lucky bitches who are now both gracefully on the other side of menopause, I'm still getting my period and I have it right now and the cramps are killing me. I have regrets by the bucketful, but I have to be a part of a wedding party. Act cheerful and happy so I won't bring anybody down during the celebration. The least you can do is let me speak the truth. Don't try to deny those few things I really do know to be true."

Deanie smiles. She can't help herself. In Trick's succinct and realistic summary of her circumstances she sees her friend as sturdy as she's seen her since... Since Deanie doesn't know when.

"We can do something about your hair. At the day spa tomorrow."

Trick shakes her head. "That's one pre-wedding event I'll be sitting out. I can't afford it."

"Mr. and Mrs. Kuznicki are treating."

Trick snorts. "Sort of a 'Treat for Trick.'"

Deanie laughs. "No, all of us. They're treating all of us."

"Really?"

"Yes!"

"Hot damn."

MADELINE GREETS TRICK, and then Deanie, with a hug when they walk in the front door of the Bakula house. "They won't let me go in the back of the house until exactly six o'clock," Madeline says. "A surprise, they say, so I'm cooling my jets in here."

Madeline nods her head in the direction of the living room where the carpet is still rolled up and the furniture is still pushed back and there are what appear to be several hundred CDs spread out on the floor in front of the stereo cabinet.

"Jazz trio for the cocktail hour, chamber music quartet for dinner music, and a disc jockey coming for when we can finally let loose and party and you can't leave those guys on their own or you don't know what you'll get. Adam says I'm being obsessive about the play list but I really don't want to dance to 'Paradise By the Dashboard Light' at my wedding reception."

Trick is nodding, covering the cellophane basket with her arms in case the Jack Daniels will give away any part of the surprise waiting in the back of the house. "Well, I'm not the bride, so I think I'll just go see what's cooking in the rest of the house right now."

Deanie starts to leave with her, but Madeline catches her arm. "Can I talk to you for a minute, Auntie Dean?" she asks when Trick is out of earshot.

"Sure. What's up?"

"Mom and Dad's thirtieth anniversary, next month."

"Thirty years?" Deanie winces. "I guess the numbers get away from me. But I wouldn't forget the day."

"I didn't think you would. No, Chas and I need your help with our present. I know I should have checked with you sooner..."

"What do you need? Am I coming back to Pennsylvania again for another party?"

"No, no, you've got to be in Napa. You know how Mom and Dad both love to cook, so Chas and I got them a weekend pasta-making course at the Culinary Institute out there—Greystone, where they've wanted to take a class for forever—and reservations at the B&B on the Beringer Estate. But if they go to California and you're not there, Mom will think the whole trip is a waste."

"Oh, you clever kids! What a marvelous present! Of course!" Deanie is on her cell phone with Layla, telling her to clear her schedule for the second weekend in July, but she can't answer when Layla asks her why because Jill walks into the living room.

"Dean, got a minute? As soon as you're done?" Jill mouths, gesturing to the back of the house.

"Ahh, yep. Layla, I'll call you back in a few..."

"What did you tell Kelly when you called this afternoon to change the candies you ordered from white to purple?"

Jill whispers when Deanie hangs up, as she clutches Deanie's arm and hurries her through the kitchen and out to the deck.

"That I wanted purple candy," Deanie says. "Or violet, anything she had that was lavender."

"Uh-huh."

"Why? You're hurting my arm."

Jill stops short just outside the sliding glass door so Deanie can see for herself.

There are the white Christmas lights, turned on but they won't be really effective until after dusk. After that, Deanie can see, they will be brilliant. They will be shining through clouds of tulle wrapped so lavishly around the trellises it seems the deck is part of heaven, reflecting off Mylar streamers and shiny, pearly white helium balloons blowing and bobbing in the breeze. They will illuminate the picnic table where the girls have set out the hors d'oeuvres and the makings for Kir Royales, the drink du jour, and another picnic table that is burdened with gaily wrapped packages for Madeline, and a third picnic table that is a candy store.

In addition to the white candies Deanie originally ordered, and the purple candied almonds and gumdrops and ribbon candy that she revised the order for this afternoon, there are lavender almonds and gum drops and ribbon candy. Violet almonds and gumdrops and ribbons. Gummi bears the color of peonies. Rock candy the color of amethysts. Sugar sticks the color of eggplants. Pale purple M&M's that must have been left over from Easter. Each sort of candy is in one of its own giant lidded glass candy vases, making a rather professional-looking display, tiered as they are on bricks the girls have hidden under more clouds of tulle. It is garish, of course, an obscene wet sugar dream, but in the way that Disneyland is over the top, loaded with possibilities for sweetness.

"Auntie Dean!" One of Madeline's friends sees Deanie and gasps the name that all of the kids, following Madeline and Chas's example, have taken to calling her. "The candy is way cool! Thank you for doing this! We were all about blown away when the delivery truck showed up!"

Trick, who has been adjusting a bit of tulle over a still-exposed brick, looks up and around her and at Deanie and breathes, "It's just magical out here. It just looks magical out here, doesn't it?"

"Is this what you ordered?" Jill asks, finally releasing Deanie's arm.

Deanie smiles back at Trick, at the magical smile on her face. "Yep," she says. "This is exactly what I ordered."

Chapter Ten
1978

THE GIRLS WERE LYING ON THE GRASS IN THE Kuznicki's backyard. They didn't know it, of course, but it was the last time for a long time they'd meet quite like this, prone on a patch of cooling green under a starry, summer sky. After tonight, after Jill married Chuck Bakula tomorrow evening, something would shift. Even after Trick's two children, and Deanie's move away from Lenapi into her own apartment in New York City, they all recognized this wedding as the first proper event of their adult lives.

"We have to grow up now, you know," Trick even said. Out loud. It was a theme she'd been on for a couple of months, ever since Dominic had brought the boys up from Texas to visit her over Mother's Day.

The visit, one long weekend in May, had been hard on Trick. She hadn't seen her boys in nearly a year, and they'd grown. Nicky, seven, had lost his baby face and was a real little boy now; Dominic had cut the curls on Cole's head that Trick had nurtured for four years because he'd started kindergarten and Dom didn't want the other kids making fun of him. The boys themselves were shy around Trick, awkward, and had to be told to give her a hug or a kiss, otherwise keeping their arms around Dom's waist and legs. Trick wanted to take them out for pizza, alone, just the three of them, and the boys had to be urged to go.

"It's what I get for letting their father take them to Texas," Trick had cried, later, when she'd told Jill and Deanie about the weekend.

"You didn't *let* Dominic take the boys, you fought like hell to keep them," Jill reminded her.

Trick waved the comment away. "I fought until Dom said he'd tell the judge about me getting the boys up and out of bed so I could go out and get cigarettes. I mean, what did he want me to do? Leave them alone in the house? Dom had already moved out, and I knew I was going to be awake all night, and I needed to get cigarettes! You know, I still don't sleep at night. It's like I'm still used to working overnights at the Farron. I think that job permanently screwed with my sleep patterns.

"Anyway, I let him take the boys because I didn't want him telling the judge things that could mean I'd never get them back. And because he was taking them to Texas, down there with my brothers and I knew my brothers would get Dom a good job on the oil lines, and they'd all take good care of Nick and Cole and… *Because*, you know?"

But Jill and Deanie didn't know. Didn't know why Trick didn't just go down to live in Texas, too; she'd always wanted to. Didn't know why she wouldn't go back to court and try to get custody again now that so much time had passed, and she'd held the same job for nearly the whole time the boys had been gone, and she'd inherited the house from her mother in the meantime and had a stable place of her own for the boys to live.

"I *will* get them back," Trick promised Jill and Deanie and herself. "But not until I've grown up a little more."

Growing up meant, to Trick, being more than an assistant flower arranger at the shop Kelly Yocum had opened up down on Front Street. She'd been accepted to the Lenapi State campus. She was going to start in the fall on a degree in elementary education, a teaching certificate—not her dream but a way to a decent paying job with benefits. No judge would deny her custody of her own boys once she had a job teaching other people's children. Dom, with his degree in business administration—a degree he'd been able to get only because Trick had changed sheets and scrubbed toilets at the Farron—his fast rise though the management ranks at the muckety-muck oil company and his fat pay check could kiss her ass once she was on the payroll of the Lenapi Unified School District.

"Four years is a long time to wait to get your kids back," Jill ventured tentatively.

Trick nodded. "That's why I'm taking a heavy course load, so I can finish in two and a half. I mean, I don't sleep anyway, like I told you. Why not put the time to good use? Now I just need to find a job where I can work overnights again, by September."

As it turned out, Trick needed to find herself a new job much sooner than September. Kelly had fired her earlier in the evening, right before the rehearsal dinner.

"But, she's supposed to be your friend!" Jill was outraged. "And the flowers you made for my dinner were beautiful! How can she fire you when you just did such a beautiful job for her? Trick, if the wedding wasn't tomorrow I'd call her and cancel the flowers and go to someone else, I swear."

"No! Don't do that," Trick told her quickly. "Don't, you don't want to screw up your wedding because Kelly Yocum is being a jerk. Don't say anything to her about me, you don't need to start a fight with the florist on your wedding day."

"*Pffft*," Jill replied.

The truth was, while Jill was looking forward to the flowers, and to walking up the aisle at St. Boniface in her pretty dress, behind her two dearest friends in their coral gowns— and while she was certainly looking forward to the party at the Elks Hall after the ceremony—all she really wanted to do was to marry Chuck Bakula. "We should have just eloped," she teased her mother every time Mrs. Kuznicki presented her with another wedding chore, keeping a file of the RSVPs or choosing which tuxes the groom and his ushers were going to wear or making a chart of the seating arrangements for the dinner. Deanie and Trick would laugh and Mrs. Kuznicki would narrow her eyes at them, warning them not to give Jill ideas. But, however Jill teased or complained, her work on the wedding was as organized and timely as the work she did at the Lenapi Lending Library, afforded the same attention to detail that had gotten her noticed by the board of trustees and promoted only six months after she'd been hired.

The wedding to Chuck Bakula had been in the works for four years—from the night Jill had met him their sophomore year at Temple, and slept with him impulsively, overcome by her attraction to the blond campus soccer god, on their first date. She was sure when she woke up in the bed in his dorm room the next morning, his roommate snoring in the bunk above them, he'd do something humiliating to her, like ask her what her name was. Instead, as Jill was preparing to sneak out of the room to try to convince herself that she really wasn't a slut, Chuck wrapped them both up tight in his scratchy gray wool army blanket and told her that he was in love.

"Yeah?" Jill had asked. "With whom?'

 He'd laughed. "You."

"Are not."

"I am," he'd replied, twisting his head to look down at her.

"Stop it."

"You don't believe me?" Chuck had asked, sitting up in the bed and, in the process, unwrapping them both from the wool blanket and, not gently, bumping his head on the upper bunk, making his roommate snore and roll over.

"No. I don't. How many girls have you tried that with, anyway?" Jill had grabbed at the blanket, shivering, wanting something to cover herself in case the roommate heard all the noise and woke up and peered over the side of his bunk to see what was going on. She was shivering with cold, and with anger, the problem being that all during their date the previous evening—all the while they had been walking through Philadelphia and waiting in line at the movies, and sharing a bag of popcorn while Mia Farrow and Robert Redford fell in love on the big screen in front of them, she had thought she could be in love, too. All the while that it took for them to walk back to campus, Chuck's calloused little finger hooked casually through her own, talking about things guys usually didn't go on about—how he hoped to coach kids someday, and how he thought sports helped to mold kids and keep them out of trouble, they had sure helped him get his head on straight after his parents' divorce—she had been sure of it. This morning, naked in his dorm bunk, it was as if he knew her certainty and was making fun of it. "Look, you know, don't be an asshole."

"You don't get it, do you?" Chuck had asked her, but he didn't wait for a reply. He'd scrambled over Jill, out of the bunk and onto his feet, whipping the army blanket over his shoulders as if it were a cloak. Jill scrambled herself, to draw the sheet they'd kicked down to the end of the bed over her own shoulders as Chuck poked a forefinger into his sleeping roommate's backside. "Rob?'

"What?" Rob had snapped at him. "That hurt, man."

"I'm in love," Chuck told him.

"Fucking good for you," Rob had said and jerked his own blankets more tightly around himself.

"What do you think you're doing?" Jill gasped.

But Chuck didn't answer her. He went for the door and stepped out into the hall. He paused, breathless, and turned to her. "I'm about to make a major fool out of myself so if you don't think you could ever be in love with me you'd better stop me," and then, with no pause to give Jill a chance to do any such thing, he shouted, "I'M IN LOVE!"

"Who the hell cares?" came the answer from a room far down the hall.

"Ohmigod, it's seven AM. On a Saturday." Jill ducked her head under the sheet.

"I'M IN LOVE WITH JILL KUZNICKI!" Chuck thundered down the hall and ran back to the bed, slamming the door behind him before the indignant answering chorus could start in earnest, ducking back into the bunk with Jill and laughing—as Jill later reported to her friends—like a lunatic. "*Now* do you believe me?" he'd asked her.

Rob Tedesco had lowered his head over the bunk and glared at the two of them. "If I tell you *I* believe you, will you knock it the fuck off?"

From that point on it was only a matter of formalities. Purchasing an engagement ring that Jill wore around her neck and under her sweaters so no one else but Deanie and Trick—certainly not her mother—would know that she was only nineteen and had already agreed to marry someone. Processing applications and pulling strings to get Chuck hired at the Lenapi campus, preferably in the athletic department, a cause in which Mr. and Mrs. Morrow were enlisted even though throughout their long tenures there neither of them had ever attended an athletic event of any kind. Breaking the news to Jill's parents.

"Married is forever." Vic Kuznicki spoke for both himself and his wife, practical people unwilling to put a deposit down on a wedding dress the very second after Chuck's hiring at the Lenapi campus had been confirmed to them in writing, the way these crazy kids were asking them to. Not after the fiasco with Deanie's cancelled wedding just the year before still fresh in their minds. "You're only twenty-two years old, for crying out loud."

"We'll be twenty-three when we get married, if we do it next summer like we want to," Jill retorted. "Dad, we've known each other for almost four years. It's not like we're in our sophomore year and eloping or something."

"Don't you even say that word…"

"Twenty-three," Mr. Kuznicki had huffed, cutting off his wife. "You don't know what you want from life when you're twenty-three. Hell, I'm forty-nine and sometimes I don't know what I want. If you can tell me, right now, what it is you want from life and it sounds anywhere near like something reasonable, we can continue this conversation, OK? All right? Let's have it, man." He'd turned to challenge Chuck. "What is it you want?"

When Jill and Chuck reported this conversation to Deanie and Trick a couple of nights later, over pizza and a pitcher of Bud at Sal Turk's place, Chuck said it had taken everything in him not to blurt out, "A hot chick who screws my brains out on the first date," and made himself choke, he started laughing so hard.

Jill hit him on the back of his head.

"You slept together on your first date!" Trick crowed gleefully. "You never told us that part!"

"Shut up." Jill reached across the table to swat at Trick, too.

"So, really, what'd you say to them to get them to let you have the wedding?" Deanie prompted.

"Well"—Chuck grew very serious—"I thought about listing goals, you know? Get promoted to head soccer coach, win the state championship. Then I thought the goals ought to be more Jill-specific, like I want to eventually earn at least thirty thousand dollars a year so I can support your daughter in style, or I want at least two kids, or someday I want my family to be able to live in one of those new houses they're building in that ritzy new development up in the hills behind the hospital. You know, tell him my wildest dreams…"

"Just tell them what you finally said," Jill scolded him. To Deanie and Trick she added, "Wait until you hear what he said. It was really good."

"Which *was*?" Trick kicked him under the table.

"Which *was*"—Chuck paused dramatically and Trick kicked him again—"'Maybe I haven't figured out everything

I want in life, but I've figured out what I don't want. I don't want to live a day of it without your daughter.'"

TRICK PLUCKED ANOTHER blade of grass from the Kuznicki's backyard. "That is still the most romantic thing I think anyone I actually know personally has ever said," she breathed. She spoke wistfully but she was plucking blades of grass out by their roots with restless fingers and her foot was going a mile a minute over the same square inch of Vic Kuznicki's lawn; the girls knew she was uneasy about something, and Jill thought it was a wonder her dad wasn't leaning out of a window to yell at them about messing up his perfect grass. "Don't mess up the most special day of your whole life with the most romantic guy any of us know by worrying about Kelly firing me. Don't say anything to her. I need you to promise."

There was a pause before Jill spoke, so both Deanie and Trick knew she was rolling her eyes. "Fine, then."

"Fine."

"*Fine.*"

"Fin*er.*"

"We should probably go," Deanie said to stop them. "Jill's getting married tomorrow. Don't you have to go to bed and get your beauty rest or something?"

"Nope. I'm getting married in the evening, remember? I planned it that way so we could stay up late. It's my last night ever as a single person, so don't go, huh?"

"*Fine*," Trick laughed.

"Good," Jill said, and she sat up, shifting position easily, unlike the subject she was about to change. "Look, I was thinking, Trick, maybe you ought to go back to the Farron House, pick up your old overnight shift if that's the time of day you want to work while you're going through college. There was an ad in this week's Star-Sentinel, they need someone."

"*Pffft*"—Trick imitated Jill's exasperation. "Go back to work at that old fleabag? I've got an application in to be the night manager at the new convenience store on Vesper Street when it opens next month. The pay is just as good, and there's only one toilet I'll have to clean."

"You know what? Don't say the Farron is a fleabag," Jill told her. "My future mother-in-law is sleeping there right now. Don't say that."

Chapter Eleven
Wednesday

THE NAME OF LENAPI'S DAY SPA IS AMALIA Rose, after the owner's daughter. The girl is now fifteen and not as unconditionally delighted as she was when she was seven about having her name plastered in twenty-two inch letters on the side of a bright pink Italianate mansion on Clearview Street. The teenage Amalia Rose is decidedly not as enthusiastic about being asked to help her mother out at the spa on weekends and over the summers as she was when she was ten. She tilts the office chair dangerously onto its two back casters, bored, waiting for the women in front of the counter to choose among the services on the menu.

"Gram, you really ought to get one of their Milk 'N Honey Hydrating Facials. I've had one here before and they make your skin so…"

"Soft as a baby's behind, I'll bet," Mrs. Kuznicki finishes for her granddaughter.

Amalia Rose is not Marilyn Kuznicki's style. In fact, until today, she'd never set foot in the place. But she and Vic Kuznicki had wanted to give Madeline a present—a party, some part of her wedding that she would never forget; Jill and Chuck wouldn't let them pay for a thing so one morning, lying in bed after making love and before getting up to go to seven o'clock daily Mass, they had hatched a scheme to surprise Madeline with a day at Amalia Rose for her and all of her bridesmaids. Madeline was always going on about the great massage she'd gotten in Lancaster, or the place in Philly she drove to especially to get what she swore were the best pedicures in the state. Even Vic thought the idea was practical enough after Marilyn explained to him that Madeline and her girlfriends were assuredly going to do a lot of pre-wedding primping anyway; Mrs. Kuznicki had reserved the spa for the day for a private party long before she knew she was going to be a bridesmaid herself.

"Everybody can relax now, the booze has arrived!" Beth's voice booms as she throws open the front door and enters the salon carrying a cardboard case with a little cut out handle in each hand. "Six packs for champagne," she says, raising her arms to show off the clever packaging. "This is my idea of a brilliant innovation."

"Holy Mary, Mother of God, Beth, it's ten o'clock in the morning."

"It's OK, Mom. We're going to mix it with orange juice, so it'll be healthy."

Amalia Rose is laid out on either side of a wide entry hall—hairstyling stations lining the Victorian's old parlor to the right, and manicure tables and two pedicure thrones with built-in footbaths in the one on the left. The second floor bedrooms, accessible to the public via the house's grand staircase or a chairlift mounted against its mahogany wainscoting, had been transformed with tables for massages and facials and a variety of other services Marilyn is again looking at on the menu and puzzling over. The décor is fussy with chintz curtains and cushions, white wicker furniture and enormous pots of tropical plants so lush and well made they look remarkably real, but the rooms are large and high-ceilinged, scrupulously clean and bright with sunshine.

Today, in the parlor on the left, the manicure tables have been pushed a little closer together to accommodate a buffet under the two front windows. Urns of coffee—regular and decaf—little pitchers of cream and large ones of fruit juices, and a three-tiered tray of pastries from the Farron House's bakery sit on the skirted table. Amalia Rose has the presence of mind to get up and go help Beth make room in the tub she's set up for the carafes of juices and screw a couple bottles of the champagne down into the ice.

"All right, maybe not a facial then, Gram. How about a pedicure?"

"No, no"—if she looked closely, Madeline would have seen her grandmother squint for a second, as if she was warding off pain—"I don't want anyone touching my feet."

"THE MARVELS OF modern technology," Deanie says to Chuck. "Thank you."

Layla had telephoned this morning at what was a torturous early hour in California to tell her FOX wanted her for a segment they were doing at eight-seventeen, a panel discussion about the morality of charity that begins at home. "That is," Layla informed her, "they want to beat you up for advocating aid outside of America's borders. You know, if people just refused to engage in jingoistic debate, if enough people just refused to do their shows when they come up with silly subjects…"

"Then all their viewers would ever hear is one side. You gotta light a spark before you can expect a fire. Go back to bed, Layla; I've got it covered."

Deanie had telephoned Jill. Chuck, as he'd promised, had hustled up a couple of Lenapi's communications majors to open the campus's television studio and send a feed to New York.

"You don't look bloody," Chuck says when the interview is over. He's joking but he'd watched the performance and he is now scrutinizing Deanie's face for signs of wear and tear.

"I'm fine"—Deanie laughs to show him she means it—"my skin is good and thick and, anyway, I thought I got in a couple of good shots. Made a few nice points."

Chuck nods. "You did. You did."

"Guys, thank you," Deanie calls to the two kids who are powering down the equipment in the studio and locking it back up.

"Naw, it was exciting. Thank *you*, Miz Morrow," one of them calls back. His Southern accent is so thick Deanie doesn't know whether he's being politically correct or just polite.

"*Deanie*. Call me Deanie. See you fellows next time around?"

"Sure thing, Ma'am," the Southern boy says.

"Our pleasure," the other one assures her.

"*Ma'am?*" Deanie is walking down the narrow stairs outside of the studio in front of Chuck. He's moving slowly, one silver brace on one step at a time, and Deanie matches the pace of her descent to his. "I wanted to tell him to go 'Ma'am' his mother, I've got boyfriends younger than he is."

"And his mother probably is, too," Chuck laughs.

"Is...?"

"Younger than you."

"You know something, you little prick? One good kick and that crutch would be right out from under you."

Chuck heaves his shoulders and sighs. "Yes, but then you'd have to pick me up, and I'm heavy, and you'd feel bad, and you'd be even later getting to the spa than you already are..."

"Hey."

"Hey?"

"Hey, you really are moving kinda slow today, Uncle Joe. You OK?"

Chuck positions a crutch on the next step and leans into it. "Madeline was a little wired last night. After you all left she decided it was a great time for the two of us to practice our father-daughter dance. We're dancing to 'The Way You Look Tonight,' did you know?"

"I did."

"It's gratifying, the moves you can still make on one good leg and a crutch, but my shoulder is killing me this morning—don't tell Madeline. Or Jill, for crying out loud, she'll have me plastered with Ben-Gay and I hate the smell of that shit. I'll be fine; my skin is thick, too." He takes the last step and Deanie holds out her arms to steady him as he transfers both crutches to one hand and pushes open the door for her.

"Maybe not as thick as yours…" he adds as they walk through the parking lot. "I'd rather deal with anything else than a FOX News bottle blonde first thing in the morning." Chuck unlocks the passenger door to his station wagon for Deanie and then tosses his crutches into the back seat before he hops around to the driver's side. "Yes, sir, you're one tough cookie, *Ma'am*. You, and Jill, too. Tough cookies." He is joking, but he is also shaking his head with admiration, mentioning Jill and then having to take a moment with himself, that look spreading across his handsome face, wondering how he got so damned lucky.

"That's why I always liked you," Deanie says when Chuck has recovered himself, gotten in the car and started the engine.

"I didn't know you *always* liked me. And here I worked so hard to impress Jill's friends."

"From the day I met you, Charles Bakula, I liked you and I knew you were the right guy for Jill. It couldn't have been clearer to me."

Chuck looks over at her now, a little confused. "It's nice you're telling me this thirty years later."

Deanie sighs. "Just acknowledging that I appreciate your continuing conviction that you married up."

JILL BUSTLES IN the door of the spa waving her yellow legal pads. "I'm sorry I'm late, I was on the phone with Father. Madeline, you can't have birdseed either."

The substance that will be thrown at the newlyweds as they emerge from the church after the ceremony has become more than a bit of an issue. Father Cielinksi won't allow rice, as that is a blatant waste of food. He won't allow rose petals because they make the slate sidewalks in front of the church slippery, hazardous to ladies in high heels, or anyone else in a hurry.

"Why won't he let me have birdseed?"

"Because when the birds fly down to eat it they shit all over the church steps. He says to ask you, 'What about bubbles?'"

"No, I already told you. My friend who got married last year had bubbles and they broke all over her dress. The whole reception she had these big old soap stains..."

Jill holds up a hand. "Do you want to debate this now, Madeline, or do you want to get your legs waxed?"

Marilyn Kuznicki thinks her granddaughter looks for all the world as if she's three years old again, has never conferred with a judge in chambers in her life or had the wherewithal to go out and buy herself a house, not the way she is sticking out her bottom lip like that and pouting at her mother. "Legs waxed."

"All right then, Amalia Rose?" The teenager, who'd retrieved another bag of ice from the kitchen and is still packing it around the extra bottles of Beth's champagne, scoots behind the reception desk. Jill extracts a loose sheet of paper from her legal pad, the spa's buck slip upon which their menu is printed.

Banana Masque Toning Facial

Avocado Seed Deep Cleansing Facial

Milk 'N Honey Hydrating Facial

Peppermint Refreshing Facial

"Looks good enough to eat," Marilyn says.

Next to each menu item Jill has written the name or names of the women who have requested the service, and the times at which she's scheduled them to have it, based upon the number of operators she was told would be available and all coordinated with slots for other services that the individual has indicated she would like to receive. "Mom," Jill says, "I've got you down for a French manicure and a lymphatic drainage massage…" Before Mrs. Kuznicki can object, Jill adds, "Don't argue with me. Go, go on now, your massage starts in five minutes and you have to get changed. Beth, is the champagne chilled? Father Cielinksi, I love him, but he could drive anyone to drink."

"SHE'S MAD AT me anyway." Madeline takes the fully satisfying, surreptitious puff on a cigarette that she allows herself on the rare occasions when she is around someone who still actually smokes full time. She had flown out to the patio area behind Amalia Rose when she saw Trick through a window, lighting up.

"Why is she mad at you?" Trick takes the Merit back from Madeline. She hasn't yet been inside the spa.

"Adam got into town late last night so, after the shower, I sneaked out of the house to go stay with him at the Farron."

"Madeline"—Trick takes a drag on her cigarette—"you and Adam live together. I'm pretty sure your mother's figured out you're sleeping together, too."

Madeline fans her hand in front of her face, as if the wind from her fingers will do something to prevent the smell of smoke from settling into her blouse, her hair. "No, it's not that, of course. I made Dad practice our father-daughter dance after you all left and then, after *that*, after he went up to bed, that's when I left and I guess I woke him on my way out. Mom said it took him an hour to get back to sleep, and he is kind of dragging around today, like he's really tired. That's what she's mad about."

Trick nods. She's not sure what to say. Waking up some-one who takes Methadone before he goes to bed—Madeline must have been awfully loud getting out of the house and Trick can't imagine that. Madeline letting doors slam in the middle of the night? Not with all of that inculcated Kuznicki courtesy.

The sort of inbred, overweening courtesy that had prompted Madeline to drag her brand new boyfriend, Adam Osic, all the way in from Lancaster one weekend when Deanie was visiting in Lenapi to introduce him to her mother's friends. She'd made spaghetti and meatballs that night—comfort food, in case it took that little something extra to make everyone feel at ease together—and sat them all around her parents' dining room table, Jill and Chuck and Madeline on one side, Adam plunked down right between Deanie and Trick.

Adam—Trick had to give the boy credit—was game. He'd been amusing when he told them how he and Madeline had met, something about a mix up with their class schedules the first day of law school that wasn't inherently entertaining; he'd been attentive, turning from one dinner partner to the other, giving each equal time and keeping both of their wine glasses filled; he'd been earnest when he spoke about his plans to be a trial lawyer after graduation—"We get a bum rap, trial lawyers do, but without us, who protects people from corporate greed? What's to stop an industry from putting toxic chemicals in our drinking water if there's no one to stand up for the little guy who gets bladder cancer from it? Or what's to stop them from manufacturing inferior products that they *know* are inferior if no one's going to do something when one of their customers is injured? Someone has to say,

'Hey, this is against the law, and you did it anyway and now you have to pay the piper.' Or they have to say, 'Maybe it's not against the law but it should be. You knew for ten years that your chemicals caused bladder cancer and you hid the evidence and kept dumping them anyway. That's just as bad.' Or, actually, it's worse."

Adam was sincerely interested—or he made himself look as if he were—in the story after story after story Madeline was telling at the table about growing up with *three* women scrutinizing and analyzing her every move so that if her Mom didn't catch her at one thing or another, the other two had Jill's back and, consequently, Madeline never got away with a damned thing. He commiserated, but not to the point that it might cause offense, with Chuck when Chuck leaned over the table and stage-whispered, "It's OK, you'll get used to it, the women in this family"—and he'd made two large circles with his arms to encompass every woman at the table—"love to brag on each other."

"Once," Madeline continued, pointedly ignoring her father and taking another big gulp of wine, "Mom and I had this really ugly fight. I was maybe fourteen and I couldn't tell you what the fight was about now if you tortured me for the information, but it ended with me screaming at her, 'I don't want to live in this house any more! It's unbearable. You're unbearable! I'm going to go to Italy to live with Auntie Dean!" She turned to Adam, bumping her wine glass so some of the cab sloshed out onto the tablecloth. "Dean was living in Italy at the time," she said, "so, so…"—she laughed, verbally vamping while she mopped at the cab with her napkin—"so Mom screams back at me, 'Fine! You want to go live with Auntie Dean? I'll help you pack!'

"I go up to my room and I'm stomping around, royally pissed off, you understand, and when I stop stomping for just a minute, I hear Mom all the way from downstairs and she's shouting things like, 'I really will send her to you. I am so fed up with her adolescent arrogance, I'll put her on a plane to you tonight, don't tempt me, Deanie.' Of course, I don't think Mom knows I'm listening, so when she shouts, 'Get down here to the kitchen right this minute, Madeline Bakula, your aunt wants to talk to you,' it scares the bejezus out of me.

"I go stomping down the stairs, ready to take them both up on the offer to expatriate myself, and Mom throws…"

"Mad, don't exaggerate, I don't recall that I…"

"No, Mom, you *did*. Oh, but you did! You *threw* the phone at me!" Madeline looked around the table as if repetition alone would prove her claim's veracity—"She *throws* the phone at me and, by this point I'm so mad I'm crying, right? I'm on the phone sobbing to Dean, 'My mom's so mean' and 'My mom doesn't understand,' and Dean's just listening, you know, until I pull myself together a little bit and then, when I do, you know what she says?"

Of course, everyone at the table save maybe Adam knew what Deanie had said, but Madeline had worked herself so deeply into her story that she was looking at all of them expectantly.

"She says, 'You're always welcome at my home, Mad. Wherever that is. Always. And right now I think your mother *is* being unreasonable. But you'd better really think about how you want this fight to end because your Mom's about to buy you a ticket and from three thousand miles my bet is that you're going to start missing her awfully quick.'"

Madeline sat back in her chair, reaching for her wine glass again even though she looked thoroughly sated. "I mean, come on, *Auntie Dean* says Mom's being unreasonable? That means *I'm right*. I can live with my mother as long as I know that sometimes I'm right." She smiled at Jill, who was laughing too hard to object. "Auntie Dean," Madeline said to everyone, and then zeroed in on Adam so he'd pay particular attention to what she was going to say, "is my hero."

Sweet, funny, thoughtful Madeline, Trick thinks, whose courtesy failed her just that one time: Trick had waited all night long for a story about herself. Not just a story in which she'd had a part, but a story in which she was the main part. And it didn't come so when she went home she was still thinking about it. Still trying, herself, to think of a story in which she was the hero.

And it didn't come because there wasn't one.

"One more drag." Madeline wiggles her two smoking fingers at Trick and Trick hands over the cigarette.

"Hurry up," Trick tells her. "If your mother sees you smoking my cigarette she's going to be mad at both of us."

ALLISON IS DRIVING slowly down Clearview, looking for a big pink Italianate mansion. "You can't miss it," Jill had said. *Famous last words*, Allison thinks.

When Allison accepted Mrs. Kuznicki's invitation last night at the shower, to join the bridal party this morning at the spa, Jill had said, "Oh, good. Then, Ally, why don't you pick up Mary on the way? She doesn't know her way around Lenapi." So now Allison, who doesn't know her way around Lenapi either, is crawling down Clearview with a nun in her passenger seat.

Allison is not Catholic. Allison has been raised Presbyterian and she's fairly certain she's not that anymore either. She doesn't know what she is. She is under the impression that a person doesn't have to be Catholic to get inside the Kuznicki-Bakula family phenomenon; Trick isn't, and Deanie doesn't appear to be, and Chas even told her outright that his Auntie Beth's husband, Terry, is a Methodist. Still, she has fallen in love with Catholic Boy and the least she can do is have a cordial conversation with Sister Mary Golinski on their way to the day spa. The least she can do is talk to the woman and she will, she thinks, if she can stop stumbling over the thought: what is a nun doing going to a day spa? Somehow Milk 'N Honey Hydrating Facials do not fit with old women in voluminous black robes and their vows of poverty, chastity, and obedience.

Of course, Mary Golinski isn't wearing anything black. Allison steals a look at her passenger. She's got on a navy blue skirt, and a pretty flowered blouse, and a baby blue cotton cardigan tossed over her shoulders. She could be any conservatively dressed older woman in the world. Betty Ford! *That's who Mary Golinski looks like*, Allison thinks. *Only maybe a little bit younger*. It has been driving her crazy for two days trying to figure that out. Mary Golinski is a nun who looks like Betty Ford, and tends bar with the enthusiasm of Tom Cruise in *Cocktail*—and she is pro-choice.

That last bit of information really blew Allison's mind. She had always just assumed that all Catholics—or, at least, a Catholic *nun*, for Christ's sake—would be anti-choice. But last night, when she and Mary and Madeline were sitting at one of the picnic tables together, picking at these almighty good cheese crisp things Mrs. Bakula had made, Madeline started to tell them about the newest pro bono case she'd taken on, and the strategy she was devising for her unwittingly pregnant fifteen-year-old plaintiff. Allison had been stunned when Mary Golinski had clapped her hands and said, "Madeline! That's brilliant! Now, I know I'm a scientist, not an attorney, but—I think I'm right about this—this isn't the only type of case where your logic is applicable. What of girls other than your client who have gotten pregnant? What of the young fathers of those babies? What of the kids who've contracted STDs?"

Madeline had nodded in agreement. "It is a good case, I know. What worries me most about taking it on is that I'm too young to do it. That people won't take me seriously because of my age. I was thinking I'd try to enlist one of the older partners at the firm to present the actual argument."

"Madeline!" Mary said, shocked. "Sarah Weddington was twenty-six when she argued Roe v. Wade before the Supreme Court. I get goose pimples when I think of all you can accomplish if you're thinking this originally at only twenty-four. You'll do no such thing, give this case away. This is your baby!"

The nun's enthusiasm made Allison's head swim so she could no longer follow the threads that tied Madeline's strategy together. Mary, sensing her confusion and understanding its root, had laid her hand on top of Allison's and said, "'To know what you prefer, instead of humbly saying "Amen" to what the whole world tells you you ought to prefer, is to have kept your soul alive.'" She'd squeezed Allison's fingers and added, "Robert Louis Stevenson..."—and then turned back to finish the conversation with Madeline.

Now Mary Golinski reaches over and puts her hand on top of Allison's where it is resting on the gearshift. "That has got to be it," she laughs and points to the hot pink house a block ahead of them.

"Oh! My gosh, it is pink."

"Jill said we couldn't miss it."

"Jill was right," Allison agrees.

Jill meets them as Allison pulls her VW Bug in behind Amalia Rose, shooing Madeline and Trick inside on her way, breaking up their tête-à-tête on the patio overlooking the parking lot and walking purposefully toward Allison's car.

"Good morning, good morning," Jill calls to greet them. "I was hoping you'd be right along. Allison,"—she kisses the girl's cheek—"thank you for joining us today, we're going to have so much more fun because you're here…"

Thank you for joining us? Allison thinks. *OK, a) you don't turn down your prospective in-laws when they invite you anywhere and, b) I wouldn't miss this for anything in the world.* "Thank you for including me."

"…I have an eleven-thirty manicure scheduled for you, honey, and a one o'clock sea salt scrub. Just go on inside and pour yourself a cup of coffee while you wait, and there are some awesome apricot tarts on the buffet… And champagne. Pour yourself some champagne… Mary!" By this time Jill has worked her way around Allison's car, to the low-slung door out of which Mary is struggling to climb. She kisses the nun, too, and says, "We've got to hurry you on inside, your massage starts in five minutes and you'll never guess, one of the masseuses here is trained in Feldenkrais, do you know what that is? It's a bodywork technique and I think it's just going to do wonders for your knees…"

Allison watches as the two women walk through the patio area into the day spa. Jill's got her arm around Mary's waist. As they pass Trick, who is just now stubbing out her Merit, Jill pauses to look askance, just for the most fleeting moment, at the butt in Trick's hand. "We have got to stop you from doing that," Allison hears Jill say. "I can't stand it that anyone

I love is still hurting themselves, smoking," she adds as she puts her other arm around Trick's waist and hustles both of her friends inside.

Allison watches and she thinks, *Thank you, thank you for including me in this phenomenal family. Even if they are Catholic.*

DEANIE ARRIVES AT the spa, kisses Chuck on the cheek and thanks him once again for making the broadcast this morning possible before she climbs out of his station wagon. Inside, Beth greets her with a mimosa and the warning that Jill is running a tight ship. "She's got you scheduled for an eleven o'clock pedicure so you'd better pick out your color and get over there and get your feet in the water." Beth points toward the two pedicure stations that look like thrones for airline pilots: seats deeply upholstered in yellow-tan Naugahyde set on top of two-foot-tall faux marble platforms.

Deanie lets her shoulders sag. "I have never understood the purpose of those contraptions, except to make a person feel conspicuous about having her feet handled by a stranger."

"Have a couple of these"—Beth raises her own glass of orange juice and champagne—"you won't care how conspicuous you look."

"You've had a couple, I see," she laughs at Beth.

"Hey"—Beth pokes at her—"this is the first weekday I've taken off work in about three years that I'm not using to take Cara to a doctor's appointment or something. The kid's with the sitter and Mama's gonna play."

Deanie walks over to the rack of colorful little polish bottles, picking up one and holding it up to the sunlight coming through the parlor's windows and frowning at it before putting it back and picking up another. She is debating between "Cardinal Sin Red" and "Persimmon Pudding" when Jill walks by with an arm around Mary Golinski and reaches out her other arm to catch the sleeve of Deanie's blouse and pull her along.

"I've got a pedicure in three minutes—and Beth says you're being a Nazi about staying on schedule…"

Jill gives her head a little shake to indicate that she's going to ignore Deanie for a moment. "Mary, this is Brianna, the Feldenkrais person. Brianna, Mary Golinski," she says and takes her arm from around Mary's waist, turning her over to the masseuse and gathering up Deanie in her place. "Before any of us do anything, we've got a hair consultation."

Jill ushers Deanie and Trick into Amalia Rose's hairstyling room where Mona is waiting for them. Mona has been fashioning Jill's black curls into some semblance of order for over twenty-five years. Mona has cut Chuck's hair, too, for almost twenty, ever since the accident when she came to the hospital one day to visit Jill—Jill hadn't left the hospital grounds for three weeks and Chuck was still in a coma so no one who visited really thought they were doing it for his benefit.

Jill had led Mona into Chuck's hospital room where he lay, Christ-like, serene, on a high white bed, his limbs spread out to receive the tubes that fed him drugs and fluids, accommodating the monitoring lines that attached to his chest and his fingertips. He was naked save for the sheet draped over his loins, for his privacy, and to conceal from general view the site of the amputation that was otherwise unbandaged. Chuck was still being taken to the operating room every other day to have any flesh that might have become infected scraped away and the surgeons needed easy access to the wound.

Pictures that Madeline and Chas had drawn were taped on
the walls and on the ceiling over Chuck's head; an audio loop
of his kids singing and talking to him played on a Fischer-
Price tape recorder on the table by his head.

Chuck's doctor had instructed Mona, as he'd instructed
everyone Jill led into this sanctuary, to touch Chuck while
she was in there. "Just put your hand on his arm, or his foot.
It'll help him be aware that you're here. And it will transfer
your life energy to him and help make him stronger." Mona
had looked at the doctor as if he were from the Planet La-Di-
Dah. "There's a reason healing is referred to as the 'laying on
of hands,'" the doctor had responded.

When Mona entered Chuck's room, however, she found
that it was very nearly impossible to keep her hands off him
anyway. The rise and fall of his chest, breathing, was as
peaceful a sign of hope as Mona had ever witnessed. Hope,
present and persistent. His one foot, bare and turned out at
the ankle, moved her with its sweet vulnerability. His head,
such a handsome, good head, now swollen to nearly twice its
size, compelled her. She moved to his side and touched her
fingers to his brow, petting it lightly and stroking the pale,
wheat-colored bangs out of his eyes.

Jill stayed at the foot of the bed, her own hand resting
on her husband's ankle, the position she habitually took up
when other people came into the room to visit with him, in
consideration of the fact that she was always in here visiting
with him, brushing his hair and whispering in his ear, and
she thought he'd probably like to hear someone's else's voice
for a change.

"His hair has gotten really long," Mona said.

"Please don't talk like he can't hear you," Jill asked her.
"Just talk to him."

Mona nodded, and turned to look at Chuck while she spoke. "Your hair's a mess, buddy. I've got my scissors in my purse. Mind if I take off a couple of inches?"

Mona, the barber shop saint—as Chuck referred to her after he regained consciousness; Jill's two tow-headed kids couldn't remember ever having their hair cut by anyone but Saint Mona—has been working for Amalia Rose's mother for twenty-five years, before there was an Amalia Rose, when the hair salon had been located in one little room in a Vesper Street storefront, and she still looks about sixteen years old. Her hair is dyed black at the roots and white at the tips and is spiked all over her head, and she wears a black leather Harley vest over a wife beater t-shirt and a quarter mile of the thinnest black leather strops wound up and down her forearms and around her throat.

Deanie and Jill can see Trick, who has again tied silk scarves around her own wrists for that day's trip out into the world, looking at Mona's strops as if they are giving her ideas.

"You"—Mona points at Deanie and walks over to pull at her blond bob—"get honey highlights. Your color is too flat, it needs some highlights to give it a little life and you"—she waves at Jill as if she is dismissing her—"get the usual. You're going to have to start coming in every three weeks if your gray keeps coming in at the rate it is. And you"—she walks over to Trick and gathers up the complicated colors of straw on her head, running her hands through the hair, separating individual strands of it to rub them between her fingertips and gauge their health. "The first thing you get is olive oil."

"Olive oil?" Trick looks warily at Jill and Deanie for help.

"I could call it something fancy—an 'Italian Hot Oil Treatment,' how's that?—and charge you an arm and a leg for it. But all I'm really gonna do is put warm olive oil on your head, like from the grocery store? You're hair is thirsty for oil and olive oil is what it wants, it'll make your hair smooth again and, I don't know why it does this, but it promotes new growth. You'll see. Get in the chair, I'm gonna put the oil on your hair before I do anyone else, so it's got a good couple of hours to sink into the shaft."

"Hey!" Beth leans in the archway that opens to the room from the reception area. "Mona, you want a mimosa? I'll bring one over to you?"

"No, thanks," Mona says, flourishing a plastic cape so it floats down over Trick, and she fastens it behind Trick's neck. "I never drink while I'm operating." She opens up the cabinet under her styling table and withdraws a bottle of Bertolli and turns it upside down so it glugs into a small crock-pot on her stand.

Deanie leans toward Trick and says into her ear, "At least she's going to be sober while she does this to you."

"Thank God." Trick rolls her eyes and then she closes them, waiting for the salad dressing Mona seems to be concocting to be slathered on her head.

Chapter Twelve
1978

DEANIE WOKE UP AT THE FARRON House, in Rob Tedesco's bed. She had a blinding headache but she knew it was not a hangover; she hadn't drunk that much at the wedding, had had time for only a few Tom Collins's between polkas, and she was sure she had sweated out those few ounces of alcohol while she was on the dance floor.

No, she had a headache because she was dehydrated. Because she'd polkaed—and, consequently, sweated—so lavishly. And because she'd cried.

It was actively humiliating to recall in the light of day the way her tears had flowed.

They had started when she saw Vic Kuznicki standing in the vestibule at Saint Boniface about sixty seconds before

Jill's wedding was scheduled to begin. Rob Tedesco had just ushered Mrs. Kuznicki to her seat in the front pew. Chords of the processional music were starting to waft through the dense, stained-glass doors. She and Trick were fussing over Jill's veil, the train of her dress. Little Beth was standing with them holding the basket of orange and yellow rose petals she was to scatter down the aisle before the bride and chanting, "I hate orange. Orange is a stupid color. Do you know that nothing rhymes with orange? Porange, jorange. Zorange..."

"It's *coral*," Jill snapped at her little sister. "Now shut up."

"Don't be testy, it's your wedding day," Deanie had laughed, and looked up, and seen Mr. Kuznicki standing there in the vestibule with them, four feet and light years away, his tuxedo crisp and his spine erect, as if that, too, had been starched, his eyes two round, smooth river stones glistening at the bottom of a pool of tears. He had one of his hands resting over his heart.

"That's exactly the expression he had on his face the day when we were kids and I surprised him in the bathroom," Trick leaned over to whisper. "Like there's a train coming and he knows he won't be able to get out of the way."

Trick had laughed but Deanie thought she'd never before seen Mr. Kuznicki look so serious, and so vulnerable. And handsome.

She had started to cry then, and she had continued to cry all the way down the aisle. Cried the whole time she stood on the altar next to Jill—cried so hard that at one point Mrs. Kuznicki got up from her front pew and walked up to the altar rail and leaned over it and stuffed a tissue into the vise grip Deanie had on her bouquet of orange and yellow roses. Cried her way through the reception—on and off—before dinner when the priest asked them all to bow their heads and lend their prayers as he blessed the newlyweds, and when Mrs. Kuznicki told her that she had learned to polka so well she might as well be Polish, and she cried so passionately that she could barely get through her toast. Cried when Chuck used his teeth to remove Jill's garter, and when Beth caught Jill's bouquet, and she cried so incessantly that when Jill had changed into her powder blue travel suit and was about to get into the car with her new husband to leave on her honeymoon, she stopped and shook Deanie by the shoulders and asked, "You gonna be OK?"

Cried, not sobbed. That was an important distinction; there had been no heaving or wailing—thank God for small mercies—only a steady stream of salt water running down Deanie's face, ruining her make up. She laid now on the far side of Rob Tedesco's bed, facing the hotel room wall, and tried to open her mouth but she was so dehydrated it hurt and her lips made a loud and disgusting smacking sound which she knew Rob Tedesco heard because she felt him turn over and sit up and get out of bed. "Shit," she thought.

She couldn't imagine what had possessed Rob to take her up on her overtures—how badly did a guy have to want to get laid to take up with the bridesmaid who wept every time someone crossed his eyes at her? But even in the confusion of her crying jag, the light-headed haze that resulted because there was no longer any fluid left in her brainpan for the cells to swim around in and connect with one another and gurgle up some common sense, she knew why she'd wanted to go back to the hotel room with him.

Escape.

Kelly Yocum had come to the Elks Hall to arrange the flowers for Jill's reception in the late afternoon, and Ty Gugino had arrived to deliver the dinner napkins Mrs. Kuznicki had

ordered from his father at the same time, and Kelly had told
Ty. Lo Bastioni had arrived to set up the dinner buffet and Ty
had offered to help her carry in the heavy pans of prime rib
and while they were juggling one of the pans of beef through
a side door that wouldn't lock open, Ty told Lo. Heidi Jean
Welkins got to the reception hall early, because she hated
hanging around outside a church after a wedding, chilling
out while the bridal party had their pictures taken when there
was a perfectly good open bar waiting at the reception hall,
and Lo had changed into the spiffy white chef's jacket she
wore when she carved at banquets, and while she was sharpening her knife, back and forth on a whetstone, Lo told Heidi
Jean. During one of the lulls in Deanie's crying fit, while she
was in a stall in the ladies' room trying to hold up the skirt
of her orange gown at the same time that she was trying to
pee while not actually sitting down on the Elks' toilet seat,
Heidi Jean Welkins, who relished a good morsel of juicy gos-
sip, told Deanie:

"Kelly was just driving home from having dinner at Sal
Turk's place last night and she saw the lights on in her shop.
It kind of scared her because she thought she'd locked up
after she loaded up the van and sent Trick off to deliver
the flowers for the rehearsal dinner. She said she about died
when she saw the inside of her shop—it was so bad that, at
first, she thought for sure she got robbed. Ribbons were all
wound off their spools all over the floor, her whole stock of
Styrofoam cubes were all sawed up in little bits, and hun-
dreds of dollars worth of flowers were laying out all over
the tables, not in vases, not in water, chopped up and laid
on the tables and left to die. But she hadn't been robbed
because all the money was right in the register where it
should have been."

"Oh, my God, Heidi Jean, that's terrible. What happened?" Deanie called out from her stall.

"Trick decided she didn't like the flower arrangements Kelly made for the rehearsal dinner and went back and made all new ones."

"What!"

"You heard me. Sort of lets you know why Dom got custody of the kids, doesn't it? I heard she got the kids up from bed one night and took them out with her so she could get cigarettes and then just left them in the car when she got home. Forgot about them. Dom found them there when he came to pick them up the next morning, all the windows rolled up tight, diapers soaked, screaming in their car seats, and Trick in the house sound asleep on the kitchen floor and—get this—a chocolate cake burning in the oven."

"That's not true, Heidi Jean."

"That's just what I heard. You go ask Kelly yourself, she'll tell you what Trick did; there's something wrong with that girl."

Deanie didn't know what to do. She heard the crisp click of a lipstick top being snapped back on its tube and she saw, through the crack in the stall door, Heidi Jean look in the mirror and touch a finger to her mouth to wipe away a stray smear of it and shrug and smile at herself before leaving the ladies' room.

Deanie didn't know what to do, so she spit. On the floor of the stall. *Like a fishwife*, she thought. She thought that if she wasn't locked in a toilet stall with her dress up around her waist and her pantyhose down around her knees she would have spit on Heidi Jean.

She couldn't talk to Jill about what Heidi Jean had said and spoil her wedding day. She wouldn't be able to talk to

Jill until ten days later when she got back from her honey-moon. And she didn't have the courage to push through the crowd on the dance floor and find Trick and ask her herself what the hell was going on. So she continued to cry, because at least now she had a reason, and at the end of the evening, when Rob Tedesco seemed amenable, she went back with him to his hotel room and got laid.

"Here." She felt Rob crawl back into the bed and lean over her. He dangled a glass of water in front of her face.

"Oh." Deanie twisted herself around and into a sitting position. "Thank you." Crying, sweating, spitting—the water was delicious. "Ummm," Deanie mumbled, catching some of it that was dribbling down her chin with her palm, "it's really good. I was really thirsty."

"Yeah, you were," Rob said, taking the empty glass from her. "You want more?"

"No." Deanie shook her head. She was relieved to see that in the light of day, standing there in his boxer shorts, Rob was still as cute as she'd thought he was the night before. And she was glad that he seemed to be a nice guy, getting the water for her and all. "I better get dressed and go home. I mean, it's morning, and even *my* parents are going to start wondering where I am sooner or later."

Rob nodded. He put the glass down on the table by the bed. "So," he said, "you want to go downstairs and have breakfast or something first, before you go?"

Deanie cocked her head up at him. She said, "I was supposed to get married last year."

"Oh. Yeah?"

"My fiancé dumped me about six weeks before our wedding day."

"Wow. Bummer."

"Yeah."

"Yeah. Is that why you were, like, a basket case last night?"

"No. I don't think so. I'm way over Hal McKinley. But I am sort of off the whole relationship thing. At least for now."

"OK."

"OK."

Rob was nodding furiously by that point. "OK. But I'm just asking if you want to go have eggs."

Deanie laughed. "Eggs?"

"Eggs."

"Could I have pancakes?"

"Whatever."

"OK."

"Yeah? OK."

"I'm gonna get dressed then."

"Me, too," Rob said, and pointed his thumb over his shoulder to indicate that he was going to go put his clothes on in the bathroom.

"OK." Deanie turned and put her feet on the floor and saw her bridesmaid's dress flung over a chair in the corner of the room. "Oops."

Rob leaned out of the bathroom door. "What?"

"You got an extra pair of sweatpants, and maybe a tee shirt? If not, I'm going to have to go have pancakes in an orange evening gown."

Chapter Thirteen
Wednesday

2 DAYS, 13 HOURS, 44 MINUTES
UNTIL THE WEDDING

"I HOPE MY GUY IN CALIFORNIA CAN RECREATE THIS COLOR."

"Isn't Mona the best?"

"I love her. I'm freaking in love with her. I'm going to have to fly back once a month so she can do this for me all the time."

Deanie's bob, which she has had colored to match her teenage yellow ever since the first subtle yellow gray began to appear at her temples—at about the same time that she decided the length was making her maturing face look gaunt and had the last fourteen inches lopped off—is now layered with blond, honey and flax and a glint of metallic gold so it seems to shimmer when she moves. Jill's dark corkscrew curls, which have been known to stand straight up and willy-nilly upon her head like a band of frightened soldiers, are calmed now, at ease—"*ruly*," Jill jokes.

"And the massages!" Deanie marvels.

"I know! Mary told me her knees haven't been so pain-free in years. And my mom already booked her next one. *My mom.*"

The women are silent with the thought, the depth of the pleasure that tough and practical Mrs. Kuznicki must have felt to have scheduled another massage for herself.

"I never think of my mom as needing anything," Jill says. "I would never have thought to get her a massage."

"Well, then," Deanie tells her, "it's a good thing she was sort of forced into it. Now you know."

"Yeah," Jill replies dreamily, gazing up at the night sky, the endless expanse of stars that has always made her feel a little frightened, a little insignificant, and wonders for a rare and humbling moment about all that she does not know.

None of them, Jill or Deanie or Trick, could have said how it happened, or when the decision was made to do it, but they are, all of them, lying on their backs in the Bakula backyard. It occurs to none of them that it has been thirty years since they last assumed these positions, side-by-side on green grass on a summer night. Deanie is at one end, her right hand gently trailing over Jill's upturned left forearm. Jill is in the middle, her right hand making lazy circles on the inside of Trick's left elbow. Trick is on what they have always called "the good end"—the end of the tickling chain where there is no pleasure to give, only to receive. Trick is using her right hand not to pluck at the grass and denude the lawn, as was her habit when they were girls and she was on the good end. Instead she is running her fingers through her hair, slowly, seducing herself into believing that its silky texture belongs to her head. Even her feet are still. Even Trick is at peace.

"By the way," Deanie asks softy, "have you figured out what to do instead of rice or whatever when Madeline and Adam exit the church?"

"Nope," Jill sighs.

Deanie grins up into the stars. "I have."

"What?"

"I think I don't want to tell you. Will you trust me on this?"

"I will." Jill shrugs as best she can without dislodging her forearm from under Deanie's fingers or disrupting the patterns she is making inside Trick's elbow. "Father Cielinksi, that's another story."

"I promise you he won't be able to object."

"Fine," Jill says.

"Fine," Trick echoes, but she is referring to her fine, silky, miraculous hair.

"Hmmm," Jill moans with pleasure as Deanie makes swirls at her wrist. Then she groans.

"What? You don't like?"

"I *love*. No, I was just thinking, I have to go into the office tomorrow."

"I thought you had the whole week off."

"I do. It's just a couple of hours. For the LPGA board meeting."

"The LPGA? They have board meetings? That the head librarian has to attend? What do they even do these days?"

Jill laughs, and even Trick chuckles. "Raise about a hundred thousand dollars a year for the library's endowment. They're our main fundraising arm. They've even started to admit a carefully chosen man or two to join the organization. You're way out of the loop, Dean."

"Hmmm," Deanie grunts. "Whadda ya know. Hey"—she props herself up on her elbows—"I think it's my turn on the good end."

Trick speaks, emphatically: "Not for two more minutes."

"Really now?"

"I'm keeping track in my head."

"You know what I think?" Jill asks. "I think I'm hungry. There's a whole tin of leftover cheese crisps I'd love to have in my hand right about now."

Deanie flops back onto the grass. "There's also Sal Turk's place."

"Yummm…"

"I could go for a good hoagie. I don't get good hoagies in California."

"Mayonnaise just dripping out the sides, and Italian dressing, and cold cuts loaded with trans fats…"

"They don't know how to make a good hoagie in California."

"Let's go to Turk's. Trick? You up for Turk's?"

"Hmmm…"

The women agree. But they don't move. They lay with their eyes closed under the stars, under each other's ministering fingers, on the cool green grass.

"We should go," Jill murmurs. "I'm really hungry."

"We should," Trick says. "It's getting late. I could fall asleep out here."

"We should," Deanie confirms. "But I want my turn on the good end first."

Chapter Fourteen

1982

LEGEND HAD IT THAT ON THE WEDNESDAY night before Thanksgiving, in the year 1982, Deanie Morrow and Chuck Bakula sat in Marilyn Kuznicki's kitchen and consumed an entire liter of tequila. This was not true. It was a 750. Still, it was the reason, a quarter century later, that Deanie could not even hear the name Jose Cuervo without a sour taste rising at the back of her throat, flinching at the memories of retching and of the room spinning and of referring to Mr. Kuznicki as "Honey." To his face.

"Even I knew you'd gone way past your limit," Chuck claimed, "when I saw you wrap your arms around Mr. Kuznicki and tell him, 'Gonna need help up the stairs, honey. And maybe you can put a receptacle by the bed 'cause I think I'm gonna be sick.'"

Jill's brainstorm was to have a "Mexican Thanksgiving" that year. Most of the family thought that just meant she'd be serving Margaritas before dinner.

Thanksgiving dinner was traditionally held at the Kuznicki house. In those days, when Jill and Chuck were still renting a tiny Father-Son-Holy Ghost in the First Ward, it was the only house that had a dining room big enough to hold all of them. Mrs. Kuznicki, the hostess, had looked over the shopping list Jill had presented to her. She realized they were in for a grander culinary adventure than anyone had bargained for, but gamely drove an hour and ten minutes out of her way to a grocery store that she knew to be stocked with a larger selection of exotica than BiRite, and she purchased the tomatillos and Poblano peppers, the cilantro and corn husks Jill had requested.

Jill had arrived at her mother's house late Wednesday morning; she wanted to make the salsas a day ahead of the party. While she was unpacking the box she'd brought from the State Store, the bottles of tequila and jugs of Margarita mix, and cooing over the produce she was pulling out of Mrs. Kuznicki's shopping bags and organizing it on the counters and rinsing cilantro in a colander and laying out the fruit on a cutting board, she miscarried.

"She was about seven weeks along this time," Chuck told Deanie before he licked the salt off the back of his hand, sucked on his lemon, threw back his first shot of Jose Cuervo. "She said she was far enough along to feel safe telling people. She wanted to make us all a really memorable feast, and then she was going to make the announcement over dessert. She was going to make flan."

Two previous pregnancies had ended at two and four weeks, respectively; Jill wanted to make sure that this one was going to take before she went public with it, sympathy having proved to be more than she could handle on top of loss, so even her mother didn't know yet. Didn't know why Jill was standing in front of the cutting board with tears running down her face—thought it was from dicing onions, but saw that all Jill had been doing was peeling the husks off the tomatillos—saw Jill drop one of the round green fruits and grab hold of the edge of the counter just as it hit the floor—saw Jill's shoulders fold, her lower back retract like she was taking a blow, her knees soften as if she might have to kneel.

Mrs. Kuznicki gripped Jill under her arms. "Let's go to the porch and lay you down on the sofa," she said, but Jill shook her head. "Your bedroom? A doctor? Do you want me to call a doctor?"

Jill's body was limp but she shook her head so hard some of her tears spattered on her mother. "It hurts so much," she whimpered.

Jill was letting her mother hold her up by the armpits, weight Mrs. Kuznicki had to brace herself to bear. "How pregnant were you, Jill? Tell me because I think I should call your doctor."

Jill heaved and released a single, long, soft, pitiful sound.

"Jill, at least tell me what hurts so I can decide if I should call for an ambulance. Cramps? Cramps like you've had before when this happened? Answer me, Jill Ruth, where does it hurt?"

"My heart," Jill cried. She started to sob and with each shudder she grew wetter between her legs. Life leaking away. "My heart is breaking."

IT WAS MRS. Kuznicki's tradition that every year, while her clan was gathered around her Thanksgiving table, after the formal prayer but before the turkey was carved, they would go around the table and each person would tell what they were thankful for. These personal gratitudes were always honest, and often honestly funny—little Beth offering that she was glad her mother had agreed to stop packing tuna fish for her lunch on Fridays because she hated tuna fish, or Jill praising the doctor who'd cured Chuck's snoring so she could sleep through the whole night again without being woken by her husband imitating a semi trying to parallel park. Irreverence was tolerated, even encouraged, so long as one was sincere.

Deanie had worked on what she wanted to say that year on the train from New York to Philadelphia: "This year I'm thankful that last year I took a two-year lease on my apartment as I really couldn't have managed another rent increase. And I'm thankful that I got a three-cent-per-word increase at the *Star* because it does add up and it covers the payment I have to make every month on my new IBM Selectric, since I retired the Remington Ten-Forty in July. And I'm thankful that I now have the best new typewriter on the market because I'll be using it a lot—to make corrections on the manuscript of my novel. I JUST SOLD MY FIRST BOOK!"

There would be a great deal of squealing around the table, Deanie knew, after she made that announcement, Jill leaping up to throw her arms around her, and Trick whooping or banging on the table or something, and then Mrs. Kuznicki saying how proud she was, how she always knew Deanie would make her dream come true, and then Mr. Kuznicki, or Chuck, or both of them raising their glasses of whatever Jill had mixed up for them all to drink and offering a toast.

Then, when the hubbub had died down, Deanie would say something more. She would add to the list of things that she was grateful for. She would say how thankful she was that she had a place to come to give thanks and share happiness. She would tell Mr. and Mrs. Kuznicki how much she appreciated that they had made her a part of their family. Especially this year.

Deanie's mother had died several months before her book was sold. She'd told her father about the sale, of course; at least four times. She hadn't yet been able to catch Witt when he was sober and tell him so he'd remember it. She supposed that by the time they were all gathered around the Kuznicki dining table, Witt would have had enough of Jill's concoction du jour that he wouldn't remember it then either. Which was fine by Deanie because then he also wouldn't remember Deanie claiming the Kuznickis as family, or figure out that he was a part of the festivities only because Mrs. Kuznicki insisted upon it.

"You got through to your father?" Chuck asked as he cut fresh lemon slices and tipped the Jose Cuervo bottle into their shot glassed for the second round.

"Yeah," Deanie answered. "But I'm going to have to tell him again tomorrow, and phrase it differently. I told him 'Thanksgiving has been cancelled this year,' and I think he thinks there's something going on with the national holiday, not just ours."

"Trick? Did you get through to Trick?"

Deanie shook her head.

"Don't you think you better do that before we have too much more to drink? I'll do it if you really don't want to, but we'd better get it over with."

CHUCK HAD TOLD Deanie about the miscarriage as soon as he'd picked her up at the train station. It explained why he'd been forty-five minutes late and why no one was picking up at the Bakula house when Deanie called from the depot to find out why. "You mind driving back?" he'd asked, and looked at her with eyes that were brimming over with tears, cheeks that were flushed, lips that were trembling. It was a moment of intimacy that Deanie could never have envisioned sharing with her best friend's husband; she was grateful when he'd handed over the keys and, overwhelmed with the day's unexpected toll, fallen into a fitful sleep in the passenger seat that lasted the whole way to Lenapi.

At the Kuznicki house, where Chuck had instructed her to drive, Deanie left her bags in the back of Chuck's car when Mrs. Kuznicki met them in the driveway and said, "Deanie, she's been waiting for you. Go up right away."

Jill was in her childhood bedroom, propped up on three pillows and tucked under the blue-and-white checkered bedspread she'd had since they were teenagers. The furniture in the room was the same—the blond wood set that her parents had used when they were first married and handed down to their eldest daughter when they were able to afford their pine four-poster—but Deanie was grateful that the accessories, Jill's pink ballerina jewelry box and the Lenapi High pom-poms and the collection of troll dolls, had been changed out in the last years for items more appropriate to the guest room it now was.

"Hey."

"Hey."

"Do you feel like talking?"

Jill had shrugged.

"Can I sit here?"

Jill wiggled but didn't really move over, and still there was room at the edge of the bed for Deanie to perch.

"I'll call my dad and tell him that he and I are having dinner at Bastioni's tomorrow night. You know. I don't think you want a whole bunch of people around."

Jill nodded and sniffed and wiped her nose with the wad of tissues she was clutching in her right hand. "Call Trick, too."

"Sure. Nobody else has called her yet?"

Jill shook her head.

Deanie reached for the pink princess phone on the bedside table. "I'll tell her to get right over here..."

"No."

"OK."

"I mean"—Jill looked at the ceiling, the walls, the edge of the blue-and-white checkered bedspread where it was beginning to fray, everywhere but at Deanie—"I mean, I just can't handle Trick tonight, all right?"

Jill and Deanie knew everything about Trick now—why she'd lost her boys and why she'd gotten fired from the flower shop. That she'd gotten fired from the Farron House so many years earlier, too, something about deciding the dust ruffles in all of the rooms needed to be washed and stripping them from all of the beds, delaying check-in time the next day by a good two hours for twenty-three pissed off guest with reservations.

They also knew that she rode the battered old banana bike she'd had since they were all twelve to classes at the Lenapi campus, subsisting on Velveeta cheese and saltines while pulling all-nighters to finish her teaching degree in just three years. Then, immediately after these three, hard, admirable years were over, after Trick had graduated, the school district had refused to hire her. They cited, among the other unsavory documents they had in her application file, transcripts from her custody case. Deanie and Jill knew that one night in October, just a few weeks ago, Trick had taken a block of canning paraffin and ridden her banana bike to the house of the judge who'd heard the case and written, in beautifully detailed letters worthy of an ancient monk illustrating a sacred book, "Go to hell," and Fuck you," and "Eat shit and die" all over his first floor windows. She was now doing twenty hours of community service in penance.

"You never know what she's going to do," Jill explained, "and I don't need to worry about that tonight. Tonight I just want a little peace, all right?"

"Oh, hell," Trick said when Deanie told her the party the next day had been called off. She continued before Deanie could explain the reason for the cancellation: "And I had a really good thing to say this year, too, when Mrs. Kuznicki asked us what we were thankful for."

"Yeah?" Deanie sighed. She could hear the urgency in Trick's voice that signaled she was on the brink of one of those things you never knew she was going to do. She decided to wait until the next day, or the day after that, to tell Trick about the miscarriage. "And what was it you were going to say?"

"I'm manic-depressive," Trick said brightly.

Deanie hung her head. She gripped the telephone receiver in one hand and a hank of her hair in the other. "What is that supposed to mean, Trick?"

"It means we now have an explanation for all of the crazy things I do. Do you get it?" Trick giggled. "I'm a nut!"

Deanie was torn between saying, "Oh, Trick, of course you're not," and "So, what? We've known that for years," so she didn't say anything.

"See, what happened is, besides doing community service for decorating Judge Paulsen's windows, I had to agree to psychiatric testing in order not to do jail time…"

"We didn't know that. They were going to put you in jail?'

"I think it was just for overnight but, yeah, unless I agreed to these tests, and it turns out I flunked 'em! Or, at least enough of them for the doctor to figure out what's wrong with me. Dean, there's something wrong with me! And now that they know what it is, they *can fix it*. No more acting crazy, no more I-can't-sleep-at-night-so-I-think-I'll take-the-refrigerator-apart..."

"You took your refrigerator apart?"

"I was having trouble defrosting it. But no more! A couple of little pills every morning and I'm as predictable as Judge Paulsen himself. I start treatment right after the holiday. First thing Monday morning I see the doctor and—presto!—I'm as boring as you or Jill. Do you get it? After all these years, I get to be normal, too!"

DEANIE HUNG UP the phone in the Kuznicki kitchen and turned back to Chuck, who was laying out the lemon slices for their next shot. "I don't even want to know," he said when Deanie started to speak. "Dismantling her refrigerator? Going to *jail*? I just can't hear about it tonight, Deanie."

Deanie nodded and took a good look around the Kuznicki kitchen—the tomatillos in a cornflower blue bowl, stripped of their husks; the pile of diced plum tomatoes bleeding on a cutting board and the cilantro wilting in a colander in the sink—food that even practical Mrs. Kuznicki hadn't bothered to put away because no one was going to eat it now anyway. She looked at the hobnail milk glass goblets washed and sparkling and draining on the sideboard—eleven in all, for the Kuznicki's and their guests—that would simply be dried now and put back on their shelf on top of the pine hutch. She glanced away, into the dining room, but everywhere in there was memory, too. On the dining room wall there was an arrangement of photos of Jill and Chuck's wedding, the happy couple in gown and tux in formal portrait surrounded by candids taken at the reception. One of the candids was of Deanie in her orange dress. It was taken during one of the brief interludes when she wasn't actively weeping. She and Chuck are dancing, the polka, their heads thrown back, mouths open with laughter, and Chuck is swinging her with such abandon that her legs are at a ninety degree angle to the dance floor, her dyed-to-match shoes flying in the air about a foot and a half behind her feet. Jill is standing in the background, her eyes crinkled with delighted disbelief, pointing at the flying shoes with the same hand that is holding up the train of her wedding dress. It was a moment that could never have been staged, captured on film by some quick-witted guest with a disposable camera; it was abandon and delight and joy frozen forever in time.

"Did I teach you to dance like that?" Jill had asked a moment or two later, when Deanie had joined her, barefoot, at the head table. "You are *incomparable*—lost your shoes and didn't miss a beat when Chuck put you back down on the floor. *We* are incomparable," Jill had laughed, fueled by equal parts wedding day expectation and champagne. "We are going to have incomparable lives, wait and see." She had thrown up her arms, open to the world, and wore a smile so big it had to have hurt. "Just you wait and see!"

"Make mine a double," Deanie said to Chuck, who was measuring out two more portions of the tequila.

"Really?"

"Double it up, double down, twice as nice, do it, Chuck. Let's get ripped."

LATER, AFTER MRS. Kuznicki had come downstairs to tell her husband that Jill had finally sobbed herself to sleep and now she was going to go to bed, too, and after Vic Kuznicki had wedged Beth off of his lap and into his arms and carried her up to bed, he came into the kitchen. "Marilyn made up the trundle bed in Beth's room for you," he said to Deanie, and then he pointed at Chuck. "You, on the sofa in the living room. No arguments, I don't want either of you driving anywhere tonight."

Chuck, not quite drunk enough to be belligerent but wounded and ready to find a target for his pain, announced, "My wife just lost our third baby tonight, Vic. I think I'm man enough to figure out I shouldn't drive all on my own."

Deanie, in drunken response to the wide-eyed look of pain in Mr. Kuznicki's river-stone eyes—with the wild, alcohol-induced notion that it would diffuse or distract, or even soothe both men if she inserted herself aggressively into the conversation at just that moment—threw her arms around Mr. Kuznicki and said, "Gonna need help up the stairs, honey. And maybe you can put a receptacle by the bed 'cause I think I'm gonna be sick."

Chuck's mouth had dropped open. Even before the words were completely out of her mouth Deanie knew that recalling them would make her burn with mortification for years. She struggled to regain her balance and extract herself from Mr. Kuznicki's hold and assume a posture of some little sobriety.

"Nope," Mr. Kuznicki said, holding on to her, "you're done for the night. Only you gotta be quiet going upstairs because Beth is already asleep. There's a trash can in her room we can put by the bed..."

"Mr. Kuznicki... I'm so... Sorry."

"I'll be back down to get you settled in a minute," Mr. Kuznicki said to Chuck.

"Vic," Chuck stammered, "I didn't mean to be... Mean. You lost, too. We all lost. What I said... That was just a crappy, selfish thing to say. Maybe a person who's that selfish doesn't deserve to be a father..."

"Hey!" Vic Kuznicki snapped at his son-in-law to snap him out of it. He spoke so abruptly it jarred Deanie's head off his shoulder where she'd decided to rest it on the way up to the trundle bed.

"You listen to me, both of you," he said, and with such insistence that Deanie lifted her head to look at him. "Tomorrow is the day we count our blessings." His eyes were bigger and wetter than Deanie had ever seen them, even on Jill's wedding day. "You two are going to be too sick tomorrow to appreciate it, but this family has blessings to count!" Deanie was so rapt in Mr. Kuznicki's words that she was having trouble staying on her feet; Mr. Kuznicki hitched her up a little more over his shoulder. "I don't want to hear talk like that from you," he said to Chuck. "And I don't want to hear anyone say that we are 'canceling Thanksgiving' one more time. This is not going to be remembered as the year we cancelled Thanksgiving!" he ordered.

The command issued, however, he didn't quite know what else to say. He pointed around the room, jamming his finger at nothing in particular, and at everything, and then he muttered, 'C'mon, *honey*," and maneuvered Deanie up the stairs.

Chapter Fifteen
Thursday

2 DAYS, 2 HOURS, 6 MINUTES
UNTIL THE WEDDING

*D*EANIE IS SWEATING. SHE'S GOT THE treadmill set at a speed of four and a half miles an hour, at an uphill grade of eight, and she's been on it for twenty-six minutes. She takes the towel from around her neck and swabs at her forehead, her chest, the drips that are falling off the hair at the back of her neck and running down between her shoulder blades. "Sorry, Layla," she pants into the headphone she's got inserted into her right ear. "What were you saying?"

It's seven AM. on the west coast and Layla, though she was the one who initiated the phone call, is still groggy, still waiting for the barista at Starbucks to hand her her first mocha latte of the day. "I was saying that I'm totally overwhelmed," Layla answers. "You need to know what's going on out here."

Unlike Layla, Deanie has been awake and alert and pouring herself into the day for hours. It started early this morning with a phone call from Jill, a problem with orchestrating transportation—Madeline needing the station wagon for her errands, and Chuck not being able to drive Mad's stick shift, of course, and no one wanting to take Chas's twenty-seven-year-old Beamer because the air conditioning didn't work. Deanie picked up Jill at seven forty-five to drop her off at the Lending Library, where her office was on the top floor of the five-story mustard yellow addition. "Want to come up a minute and see the view?" Jill had asked.

Deanie was parked in Jill's space, designated with a metal sign: RESERVED – Library Staff – HEAD LIBRARIAN ONLY. "Aren't you a muckety-muck," Deanie teased.

"The board did it when they found out that sometimes the closest parking place I could find was all the way down on Front Street. They were going to put my name on it, you know, instead of 'Head Librarian,' but I put my foot down."

"Why in the world? I think your name *should* be on it."

Jill shook her head. "And what happens when I retire? They'd just have to go to the expense of a new sign."

"Oh, come on, how expensive can those signs be?" Deanie held out her hand, palm up, to gesture at the object, and then she turned to Jill. "Are you thinking about retiring?"

Jill shrugged. "My kids are both through college. We own our house, my daughter's wedding is paid for. I'll have thirty-two years in on my next job anniversary. We celebrate those here, you know, job anniversaries. Cake and coffee. Any excuse to have cake," she laughed, but Deanie just sat in the driver's seat shaking her head. "What?'

"I think," Deanie said, "that the years pass differently for people like me, who don't have kids. We don't have that day-to-day measure of time going by, the kid learning to walk, or going off on her first day of school."

"What are you talking about? You've been in on every major rite of passage in my kids' lives. Madeline still wears that heart pin you sent her when she got her first period. And, if you look, you'll see the note you sent with it—'Dear Madeline, Welcome to womanhood! It's a hard, crazy, beautiful place!'—tucked into the mirror in her bedroom."

"Then why do I get thrown by things like you and Chuck having your thirtieth anniversary? Why do the numbers always shock me?"

Jill reached over and hugged Deanie's arm. "Because time really does fly when you're having fun?"

THE VIEW FROM Jill's office is expansive, a plate of glass in front of her desk overlooking Lenapi down to the river, the river drawing itself inexorably downstream, like time.

"If I'd known you were going to get moody about it, I wouldn't have said anything about retiring."

"But"—Deanie turned from the window—"I thought you loved it here. I thought you loved what you do?"

"I do, Dean…" Jill might have given Deanie a more complete answer but there was a knock on her door, three ladies of the LPGA bustling in to make copies of the morning's agenda on Jill's machine, and asking Jill for the depreciation schedule the accountant had sent over, and telling her that her mother had arrived for the meeting and was setting out the cake in the conference room—a chocolate cake, Marilyn Kuznicki's famous chocolate layer cake with fudge frosting!

"Your mother's still a member of the LPGA?"

"And still making the same damned cake."

"I love that cake. I want a piece."

"I want a piece, too. Except I can never decide whether to eat it or just rub it directly on my saggy ass."

The view from the conference room, down the hall from Jill's office and on the opposite side of the building, is of the library's parking lot, a few spare trees left on the abutting mountainside, the road beyond to the new, modern hospital of their childhood which is now in need of renovation and competing this year with the library for available community funds.

"Beyond upgrading the computers in the Learning Lab in the children's room, and replacing the roof on the old wing... Well, what other capital expenditures do we have this year, Tammy?"

"Our operating budget is covered, for that matter..."

"Jill has suggested we expand the Reading Challenge to the eighth and ninth grades..."

"But, still, Brenda, I don't like the idea of jockeying with the hospital for United Way funds... I *want* them to have a new MRI machine."

So went the pre-meeting conversation among the eleven women and one man standing in the library's conference room, spreading folders on the table, taking off their jackets and hanging them on the backs of chairs, pouring themselves cups of coffee and licking Mrs. Kuznicki's fudge frosting off of their fingers.

"What's the Reading Challenge?" Deanie leans into Mrs. Kuznicki to ask.

"Something Jill cooked up a couple of year ago, for the fifth and sixth graders. For every book a teacher certifies that a student has read, the kid earns a dollar coupon to spend at the arcade at Sal Turk's. Sal subsidizes it but, still, it's an expense. One little girl alone cost us a hundred and twenty-five dollars last year."

"Yes, but what a wonderful idea to get kids to read. How much will it cost to expand the program this year? It's really just a *wonderful* idea."

"I think it's outright bribery."

"Do not tell your mother I'm giving you this," Deanie said later, to Jill, as she wrote out a check to cover the estimate on the costs of expanding the Reading Challenge in the coming year. "I don't think she approves of the whole scheme."

"I know she doesn't."

"Well, then." Deanie ripped the check out of her wallet. "Mum's the word to Mom."

"Dean?"

"Ummm?"

"One of the compensations of time passing is that you get to do things like this. You couldn't have written out a check like this for the library thirty years ago."

"I'll tell that to my saggy ass."

DEANIE LEFT THE library and turned on to Front Street, into the parking space directly in front of Kelly Yocum's florist shop. Downtown Lenapi was quiet at this early hour. A young woman was using a squeegee to wipe down the windows in front of the video rental store before the sun was out in full force and would streak her efforts and, on the sunny side of the street, the owner of the men's haberdashery was already rolling down his striped awning to preserve the cool inside of his shop. The walkers were out—a man with a Dalmatian on a short leash, and a woman with a Shih Tzu running circles around her feet like a hyperactive dust mop, and another woman with iPod ear buds in each ear and neon orange nylon shorts was stopped at the corner, jogging in place to her private serenade until the light turned in her favor. A lone car pulled into the drive-thru at the bank.

A "CLOSED" sign hung in the door in front of Kelly's shop, but Deanie could see a light on at the back of the store and Kelly at one of the long worktables bent over a ledger. Deanie knocked on the door and waved when Kelly looked up.

"I'm sorry to bother you off-hours," Deanie said—she was due to pick up Trick later in the morning and didn't want to subject any of them to another awkward interview by bringing Trick along—"but I need to place an order and have it here in time for the wedding, so I thought I'd better get to you as early as possible."

"No problem," Kelly told her, holding the door open until Deanie was inside the shop and then locking it up again behind her. "I open in half an hour anyway. What can I do for you?"

"Well, not flowers, and not candy either this time— although I have to tell you, Kelly, the candy you sent for the shower was a real hit."

"Good, good. I'm glad. You said to send over anything I had that was purple and I was surprised to find that I had so much."

"No more surprised than anyone else," Deanie replied. "What I need today may be a little harder to lay our hands on. I can describe what I want and, then, I was thinking maybe I could help you go through some of your suppliers catalogs until we find just what I'm looking for. I'm sure other florists have used them as accents, or embellishments, in their arrangements, maybe even you have, I don't think my idea can be *that* original. That is, I'm sure somebody makes these things I want. See, what I'm looking for is…"

Twenty minutes later, Deanie was back in her car, smiling, her surprise on its way and Kelly's promise in hand to package it up prettily and deliver it to St. Boniface early on Saturday morning along with the altar flowers. She sat at the long stop light at Vesper Street punching the scan button on the rental car's radio, trying to find a station that was playing some music she actually recognized, when the frenetic opening chords of "The Song Remains The Same" stopped her. *Houses of the Holy*. She remembered that Ty Gugino used to lean on her, hard, at high school dances and whisper-sing in her ear, "Lady, you got the love I need. Maybe more than enough… Oh, darlin', darlin', darlin' walk a while with me…" Ty had not had one of the world's great tenors, but even so she remembered his crooning to her as the first wildly romantic gesture she'd ever experienced. She remembered how this particular album had become the defining music of her youthful fantasies.

"The song remains the same," she sang along with Robert Plant now, with enough gusto that she was glad all of the car's windows were rolled up. It was comforting to note how fresh this music still sounded in her ears, how true Robert Plant's plaintive voice still rang, how well the album had held up over the years.

Or, maybe, the music still sounded fresh only because she hadn't heard it in… What? She hadn't listened with any sort of intention to *Houses of the Holy* in probably twenty years.

Maybe Led Zeppelin sounded so good in her ears because it was what she knew, Plant's bluesy warble and Page's genius guitar licks and the confounded bridges having laid down neural connections in her brain, and the connections triggered

now were pleasant only because they were familiar. Nostalgic. Evocative in the way that the tunes her mother had first
heard on the Lucky Strike Hit Parade made her grow wist-
ful unto her dying day.

Deanie punched a finger at the radio on the dashboard—
Led Zep was suddenly much too frenetic for her—and drove
back to the Farron House in silence.

TWO OF THE first floor rooms at the Farron House had been
converted in the last year into a gym—an amenity that
guests had long been hinting was overdue—and Deanie
wanted to work off a little of Jill's excessive buffets, the Italian-with-everything she'd had at last night's hoagie orgy,
Mrs. Kuznicki's chocolate cake.

Jimmy Page's frenzy.

The gym was open 24/7 and free of charge to guests of the
hotel. It was open as well as to residents of the local community for a twenty-five-dollar-a-month pass card. Deanie waited
at the front desk for the clerk to finish checking out a guest
so she could ask for her free daily pass.

The lobby, done now in brilliant emerald against black
marble, bore no resemblance at all to the Farron House
of her youth, the moldy indoor/outdoor carpeting and
the buckling sheet paneling and the funky smell of the
old place, but the old switchboard behind the front desk
remained. Unused now, it was a curiosity, a relic, an
antique like the pier glass mirror just inside the front doors
or the hand-turned balusters in the sweeping staircase. Still,
Deanie's memory flashed to stopping by the Farron House
as a teenager with Trick, so Trick could get some spending money or, as she put it, "Make a withdrawal from the

First Bank of Kaye Danforth." She flashed on Mrs. Danforth behind the old front desk, before it was this marble one, her head wrapped in the operator's headset, holding up a hand, palm out, to shush the girls while she talked to a hotel guest, connected him to his party by plugging one of the burgundy-wrapped wires into what always seemed like a random little hole—the mysteries of the switchboard which, for Mrs. Danforth, unraveled into working knowledge.

Deanie shook her head to clear it. If she didn't stop thinking about the new irritation, time passing, then, like a rash you didn't know was there until it spread over your whole body, she was afraid she would start to actually itch.

"Deanie Morrow!"

Deanie turned cautiously. Writers' fans were, on the whole, not given to accosting their celebrities, although one time a woman did shove a piece of paper and a pen under a toilet stall for Deanie's autograph. A greeting this enthusiastic made her wary.

"Hazel Frank!" Deanie returned her old friend's embrace as readily as it was offered. "I thought you were in North Carolina converting some old barn into an art gallery. If I'd have known you were going to be in town I would have called!"

"No, no"—Hazel waved a manicured hand to dismiss Deanie's protest. "I'm only back in town for one day. *Architectural Digest* is doing a piece about me and, of course, I had to include my first renovation. I'm just in to supervise the photography."

"I'll bet the new owner is beside himself. *Architectural Digest*, huh? Fancy."

Hazel agreed. "It's the kind of reward I've always heard comes to people who take a risk and dive into doing what they're passionate about. Whaddaya know? It's true! You have time for a quick cup of coffee? The photo crew isn't due for another few minutes."

"Yeah, yeah. Absolutely."

Hazel led her into the bright yellow dining room, which didn't open to the public until lunchtime, but a waitress setting the tables with fresh linens and silver for the noon crowd was happy to supply the old owner and her guest with a silver pot of freshly brewed French roast.

"So," Hazel said, pouring for both of them, "I read *The Warriors of Flint, Michigan*—very good, very good, and the critic from the *Times* should burn in hell."

"From your lips to God's ear." Deanie raised her china cup and clinked it with Hazel's. "So, then, you know what's going on with me. How are *you*!"

"Well, let's see. Chris will be starting her second year at Penn in the fall…"

"No! Really? Where have I been?"

"…a-huh, and my ex-husband was mentioned in the *Times* recently, too, front page…"

"Now, see, I missed that. Why?"

"…because he and his partner flew in all the way from France, out to your neck of the woods, just so they could get married in San Francisco with all of the rest of gay America…"

"A-huh."

"…and…" Here Hazel paused, as if what was going to come out of her mouth next was simply too shocking to utter without some sort of preface.

"And?"

"Eduardo and I are celebrating our tenth anniversary together next month," Hazel whispered, and then drained her cup of French roast.

Deanie sat back in her yellow upholstered dining chair. "Well," was all she could manage to say before the waitress returned to their table with a summons for Hazel—the photographer was ready to start shooting. She watched Hazel rise, straighten her dark blue pencil skirt, arrange a lock of hair that had fallen into her eyes. "Has it really been ten years?"

"I know—can you beat that?"

Deanie smiled. "Not even going to try, Hazel. Not even sure I *want* to try."

So DEANIE IS on the treadmill in the gym at the Farron House, combating time mile by mile, step by step, on the phone with her twenty-something assistant who is complaining there isn't enough of it. There isn't enough time.

"You need to know what's going on out here," Layla says, sounding as adamant as anyone can while they are slurping the foam off the top of a mocha latté. "The new typist is pregnant, going to pop any day now and I don't know if she'll be able to finish your latest manuscript before she does, which is almost beside the point as she can't read your handwriting and I'm spending so much time interpreting for her I might as well be typing it myself, which I couldn't have done yesterday even if I'd had the time because Mrs. Beech ran over my computer cords with the vacuum cleaner and by the time the computer guy came out and got them fixed there were a hundred and four new e-mails, ten of them from your PR guy—and why didn't you tell me Suzzie was retiring and the firm was assigning some new asshole to you? He wants you to start posting daily to your blog and he sent over about eight different drafts of things to post and they're all crap and I don't think it's my place to tell him so, so I just e-mailed him back and told him you're on vacation. And that you write your own blog anyway—sorry if that was snotty—and, another thing, when has any director who's ever filmed one of your books ever sent you a scene breakdown and asked you to approve shooting locations? And, get this, he's casting next week and wants to know if you want to take a look at the audition tapes with him and, look, I know it's all very good when a director deigns to ask the writer's opinion but, I don't know, should I e-mail all of this stuff he's sent to you? I mean, I looked at your e-mail. *You* haven't looked at your e-mail all week."

"Is that all?"

Layla takes a breath, as if she'd deflated now that she'd got all of the bad news out of her system. "We're going to need to buy a new vacuum cleaner."

"Hire an assistant."

Layla is quiet for a moment, thinking. "But, *I'm* your assistant."

"Hire one for yourself, Layla. Someone for, what do you think, six weeks? A couple of months? Just as long as you need to get through this crunch. Call a temp agency this morning to send some people over for you to interview, or see if Luke over in Suzzie's office knows someone. The manuscript is the first priority. I'll be home on Monday, so e-mail the director back and tell him I'll look at the scene breakdown and location notes on Tuesday morning. Go ahead and schedule a time for me to go see the audition tapes, whenever it's convenient for him next week, and thank him *profusely* because it is a very big deal that he's asking for my opinion. Then schedule a meeting with this new PR person and tell him, meantime, not to fuck with one word on my web site without my approval. See if you can get Suzzie at this meeting, too.

The new guard can't come in without a proper debriefing from the old one, right? And, for heaven's sake, cut Mrs. Beech a check so she can go get a new vacuum cleaner."

"Sheesh," Deanie mutters, pulling the phone out of her ear and sticking a finger in, wiggling it to dislodge the shrillness Layla seems to have deposited there, and she stops only when she sees a man enter the gym, the only other person who's come to work out the whole time she's been in the room.

"Hey!" he calls out to her.

Deanie doesn't have her contacts in, so she can't see his face clearly, but she knows the voice. "Hey, Mr. Kuznicki," she calls back as her eyes come into focus. "Father of the bride!"

It strikes both of them, like a splash of water in the face, as soon as the words are out of her mouth. It stops both of them in their tracks, which is inconvenient as Deanie is still on the treadmill.

"*Grandfather* of the bride," Mr. Kuznicki corrects, laughing when he sees that Deanie has managed to stumble back onto her machine, and he climbs onto the elliptical.

Chapter Sixteen
1984

24 YEARS, 18 DAYS, 1 HOUR,
37 MINUTES UNTIL THE WEDDING

HERE WAS, PLANTED IN THE KUZNICKI'S front lawn, a three-foot tall, bright pink stork with a face drawn to look like Groucho Marx. It was holding a cigar in one anthropomorphic wing and, in the other, a placard that spelled out: "IT'S A GIRL!"

"To be perfectly fair, he did put one in Jill and Chuck's yard, too," Mrs. Kuznicki told Deanie when she greeted her at the door.

"So, you're liking this being-a-grandfather-thing then, Mr. Kuznicki?" Deanie laughed.

"I'll tell you what, Deanie, it's better than..." He didn't finish the sentence, only winked and rolled his big black eyes and wiggled his eyebrows up and down at Mrs. Kuznicki and tapped the imaginary cigar he was holding up to his mouth.

"Vic!" Mrs. Kuznicki swatted, backhanded, at the paunch she'd been nagging him to go to the gym and deal with, and her neck and ears turned a brighter pink than the stork.

"All these years and I can still make her blush," Mr. Kuznicki bragged.

"Ohhh," Deanie groaned. "He's really liking this just a little too much, isn't he?" she asked, already on her way up the Kuznicki's staircase. Madeline Elizabeth Deanna Fredericka Bakula was four days old and Deanie couldn't wait to meet her.

"Go right on up," Mrs. Kuznicki said.

Jill was laying in bed, propped up on a mound of pillows, the blue-and-white checkered bedspread drawn up to her chest, her legs splayed and sticking out from either side of it, propped up at the knees with more pillows.

"That's attractive," Deanie said when she entered.

"Shhhh," Jill warned as she lifted her face to receive Deanie's kiss and pointed at the bassinette on the other side of the room, under the windows. There would be no squealing at this reunion; a child was sleeping. They were four people now.

"I'm doing her toes," Trick said, to explain Jill's cumbersome position, while she reached up to give Deanie her own kiss. Indeed, Trick was sitting at Jill's right side, Jill's foot in her hand, carefully dabbing frosted pink at the tip of each fat toe.

Deanie's last visit to Lenapi had been over a month ago, and she was shocked then to see how Jill's small frame was adapting to her pregnancy. Jill had grown round, of course, but not just her belly. Her arms, her ankles, her neck were bloated. Her fingers were so swollen she was wearing her wedding band and engagement ring on a chain around her neck. Even her head looked fat and full of fluid. Deanie couldn't find words that might express her concern and yet also be in any way diplomatic—had Trick ever looked like that when she was pregnant? Deanie searched her memory, and her face gave her away. "I look like a pig on a spit," Jill had shot at her, "and you would, too, if you'd just spent eight months lying in a bed."

Doctor's orders. A leave of absence from the library. A move into the Kuznicki house and her childhood bedroom because she couldn't be left alone all day while Chuck was at work. Deanie coming in from New York for long weekends to help out. Beth having a total change of heart about being saddled with an older sister and catering breakfast in bed every morning. Mr. Kuznicki refusing overtime for the duration, so he could spend his evenings in his daughter's company, reading her to sleep—"We agreed on James Mitchner, and we made it through about everything he ever wrote," Mr. Kuznicki reported proudly. Trick spelling Mr. and Mrs. Kuznicki for a few hours after she got off work in the afternoons, before Chuck got home from soccer practice.

Trick. For the last year and a half it was as if Jill and Deanie had had to get to know a whole new person. As if Trick had had a karmic makeover. She was still brash, and often louder than necessary, but at the end of an evening she'd yawn and announce that she was going home, to bed, to sleep; and then she did. She went to work every day, on time, as a secretary in the administration department at the Lenapi campus where she commanded the largest salary she'd ever thought she'd earn, and benefits on top of that, and co-workers who cut flowers from their gardens to put on her desk and asked her to go to the movies with them on Thursday nights and set her up on dates with their brothers and sons. She flew to Texas one weekend every six weeks, like clockwork, to see her boys—and her boys could never wait for her to arrive. She still wore stilettos, but the feet inside of them were serene.

"Grab a foot," Trick said, tossing Deanie a bottle of base coat. "I haven't even started on the other one yet."

Deanie caught the bottle in the air. "Not until I at least see the baby," she replied.

"Don't wake her."

"I'm not going to wake her, Jill, I'm going to *look* at her."

Not that there was much to look at. A tiny head, bald, Deanie presumed, under a pale pink skullcap-sort-of hat. A body hidden beneath the square of knitted blanket. Slits about where eyes ought to be. Two flaps of skin flaring, drawing in breath, and another two, pinker, a mouth, twitching slightly, even in sleep, like a guppy. A baby. Six and one half pounds of longed-for, suffered-for, miraculous beauty and, ultimately, after a few seconds, if you couldn't pick it up and hold it and play with it, not much else.

And then Deanie caught its scent. Not baby powder or A&D Ointment or sour milk. Some scent distinct from those prosaic aromas, something beneath them, and above them, and she stooped lower over the bassinette and sucked in through her own flaring nostrils to get more of it, and it was gone. Whatever the sweet scent was under and above the others, Deanie had lost it, or couldn't pick it out again—wait. There it was! A tease, but the first whiff hadn't been a fluke. Where was it coming from? The baby's mouth? Her pores? Deanie bent still lower and inhaled again.

"What are you doing?" Jill asked.

Deanie straightened up.

She looked down at Madeline.

At a little, tiny person who smelled—new. A *new person*. The thought was abrupt—a whole, entire new person—though she'd joked just as often as Jill or Trick had in the days since the birth that now they were four girls altogether. But that joking had gone on over the phone. The enormity of having a new person in their midst made Deanie reel.

What am I doing? I'm falling in love, she thought.

She turned away so she could wipe her tears; since Jill's wedding, she'd taken a lot of abuse for her ability to cry at the drop of a hat, but she couldn't help herself. This new person was bending her heart all out of shape.

And then, suddenly—she almost let out an audible gasp— she wasn't crying for Madeline alone but for Trick's boys, old loves, babies she hadn't fallen in love with, not like this, because, because… Because she'd been too careless and busy to let love like this take hold of her, too young to be bowled over by any potential other than her own. *Both* she and Jill had been too careless, but not Trick—who'd had to hold this enormous love up all by herself—and she'd had to let it go, too, to Texas, of all places, and Deanie suddenly understood what breaking in two felt like and how admirable Trick was for being able to get up every single morning and go to work and paint somebody's toenails and have any heart left to love anybody else, let alone somebody else's baby who was right there in front of her. A baby no one was going to take away. Ever. From any of them.

"Get with the program, Dean." Trick motioned at the bottle of base coat. "We have to be at the church in an hour and a half, and these toes need to dry, and Jill still has to get dressed, and…"

"I have to feed Madeline again."

"And Jill has to feed Madeline and… Aw, jeez, will you look at her? The faucet's on."

Deanie staggered over to Jill's bed to sit down.

"Is that what you're wearing to the church?" Trick asked when she saw Deanie wipe her leaky eyes on her sleeve.

Deanie had been on a train since five o'clock that morning. Her denim skirt and cotton blouse were rumpled, tear-spattered, and inappropriate anyway for a baptism. "No. I have a dress in the car."

"Well, get cracking on the other five toes over there so you can change into it and we can get this show on the road."

So Deanie painted. And drank the cup of coffee and ate the toast that Mrs. Kuznicki brought up to her. And went downstairs to retrieve her garment bag and lug it up to Jill's childhood room and change into a fresh shift. And started when she heard the sound, like a cat's cry, and watched Trick reach into the bassinette and bundle Madeline into her arms to bring her to Jill. Jill shifted herself on her mound of pillows before she accepted Madeline into her lap, unbuttoned a flap of her nightgown and then another flap of a large, stark white, industrial-looking bra, and fitted Madeline's twitching guppy mouth onto her left breast and stilled the mewing.

"Did you finish your new book?" Jill asked when she'd got Madeline settled at her lunch, as if there were anything of interest in the room or the house or the world other than that miniscule motion, the slow, steady, slurping grace of Madeline's lower jaw.

"Ahh, yep."

"Finally!" Jill laughed. "We have that to celebrate today, too."

It was Deanie's second book that Jill was asking after and she'd turned in the final manuscript just the week before, almost a year overdue. "I'm told your second book is the hardest," Deanie said. "At least that's the justification I jollied myself along with every time I had to make another excuse for another delay." The truth was, at twenty-nine, Deanie felt as if she'd shot her wad, told her story and had nothing left to say. In consequence, the second book was a long time coming out of her and, at the finish, thin and, Deanie suspected, just within her editor's minimum acceptable standards, just good enough to move the editor to sigh and shrug and not drop the option.

Now, in the moment of watching Trick tenderly hand Madeline over to Jill to feed, she felt swollen with stories, things to say—sagas!—the burdens and joys of life as she was witnessing it.

In order to keep herself from getting up and searching for pen and paper to start a saga in that very instant she said, "And, Trick, *you*. You look so good, and happy, and that's another thing we have to celebrate."

Trick smiled, shy and sly, and took Madeline from Jill and expertly turned her over one arm to burp her. It was on the tip of her tongue to say, "Better living through chemistry," and shrug, but she didn't. She watched Jill button up her bra and struggle to get out of the bed, pulling herself up at the last with a grip on Deanie's reaching hand. "I've never felt as good and happy before in my entire life," she answered instead. She itemized: "I'm seeing my boys regularly, and I have a job that makes me feel useful. I'm not dragged up and down or split in two by things I can't control—raging thoughts and a wild heartbeat that makes me feel as if I'm not moving, if I'm not doing something, then I might die. I feel so good and happy, you guys, listen—I think I'm even going to be able to get off of all of the pills pretty soon."

Madeline let out a belch so long and thorough Deanie wondered how it had ever fit into her little body and Trick lifted her over a shoulder, on the way back to the bassinette to change her diaper and dress her in the Kuznicki family's ivory satin baptismal gown.

"Really, Trick? That's wonderful news."

"Is that the way it works, Trick?" Jill asked. She was stepping out of her nightgown, standing there in the industrial-strength bra and a pair of graying bloomers. "You take the pills until you get back into balance, and then you don't need them anymore?"

Trick deposited Madeline's Huggie in a trashcan next to the bassinette. "I'm not exactly sure. I mean, no one's said as much to me, but that's the point of taking medicine, isn't it? To make you well? Well, I feel well. I'm thinking the medicine has worked."

"Ohhh!" Jill stretches luxuriously. "It feels so good to be able to get out of that freaking bed!"

"I'll bet it does," Deanie agreed, laughing at the language Jill felt compelled to use in making this important point, trying not to look at her sad underwear, or the alarming expanses of flesh it failed to accommodate. "When do you think you'll be able to go home?"

Jill answered as she shimmied a blue paisley jumper over her head and shoved her feet into a pair of leather flip-flops. "As soon as I can pick up the baby by myself without feeling as if my stitches are going to give. Another few days at most."

"Your dad is going to be devastated when you leave."

"I know. But one's man's sorrow is another man's happiness, or something like that. Chuck has had it up to his ears with living like a bachelor."

"Here," Trick said, "one of you has got to help me." She was holding Madeline up under the baby's armpits, the long ivory satin underskirt of the baptismal gown tucked in Trick's fingers so it wouldn't fall from around the baby's pudgy waist. "Was this made for an infant? Look how big the waist is on this thing."

"It was made for my dad," Jill corrected. "He was a big baby. Can you safety pin it?"

"You have a pin?"

Jill poked around in the drawers of her old dresser, rooting through the extra linens and old thermal underwear her mother now stored in there and that no one had thought to remove during Jill's long confinement in the room.

"Jill?"

"I'll find one, Trick, give me a minute."

"No. Your dress, not the baby's."

Deanie saw Jill stiffen, stop her search. She stayed bent over an open drawer while she spoke. "What about my dress? What are you going to say that's going to make me feel worse about it? It's a size twenty, OK? And it's the only thing I have that fits."

"So," Trick said, carefully, Deanie looking on silently at the awful paisley thing that was clinging so completely to Jill's unaccustomed curves the paisley pattern was distorted. "So, we need to make it fit a little better. You need a little structure under that thing. A pair of pantyhose?"

Jill stood up slowly, holding her right forearm under her belly, and with no more than a second to gather her courage, looked at herself full on in the mirror over the dresser.

"I know it's warm out today," Trick added kindly, "but I always found that pantyhose gave my belly that little bit of extra support it needed right after I had my boys."

Jill sighed. Deeply. "There's a pair of maternity tights my mom got me, in my suitcase somewhere. I've never worn them before."

"That's because you haven't been getting out much. Deanie?" Trick crooked her head at the open suitcase on the floor by the bassinette and Deanie dropped to her knees to find the hosiery. Trick laid Madeline back down in the bassinette, turned her over and gathered the underskirt in neat folds at Madeline's back, ready to fasten it as soon as Jill found her a safety pin. And Mrs. Kuznicki knocked on the door to ask if she could come in and take some pictures of the two god-mothers dressing the baby. And Mr. Kuznicki followed her into the room and took the baby from Trick, all slippery in her satin gown, and sat on the bed to coo at her, turned dis-creetly away from Jill on the other side of the bed wiggling her legs into the tights and muttering, "I don't know why we bothered about painting my toes then."

"Which of you godmothers is going to hold the baby at the font?" Mr. Kuznicki asked. "Have you two arm wrestled over that yet?"

Deanie and Trick were not, officially, "godmothers." They weren't Catholic so the best title they could claim was "Chris-tian Witness," and that only as long as Madeline had someone else who actually *was* Catholic to stand up for her, too—a single role that was being filled by both of the women's coun-terparts, the godfathers, Chuck's distant cousin, Mark Bakula, and his college roommate, Rob Tedesco. It was tradition, or custom at any rate, Deanie and Trick were told now, that a woman hold the baby during the course of the actual baptis-mal ceremony itself.

"You hold her," Deanie said quickly to Trick.

"Why?" Trick laughed. "Are you afraid to hold her, Dean? You haven't asked to hold her yet. You held my boys and you always did it fine."

"I'm not afraid to hold her." Deanie held out her arms indignantly to take possession from her grandfather. "See?" she asked, cuddling the tiny, contented thing, catching that heady scent again and letting it waft into her nose like perfume. She wasn't afraid of holding Madeline; she was afraid if she held her during the baptismal ceremony itself that she wouldn't be able to tamp down the urge she was feeling even now, which was to hold her in the palms of her hands, lift her high, up to her face and higher. She was afraid that while the four of them were up there around the font renouncing Satan on behalf of this baby she would do some awful pagan thing and lift her up high, over her head, presenting her aloft to God and the congregation and the world.

Chapter Seventeen
Thursday

*D*EANIE PULLS TO A STOP IN FRONT OF Trick's house on Clay Street, to pick her up for the bachelorette party, and spontaneously performs an act she considers intrusive and arrogant when it is not absolutely necessary: she beeps her horn.

Witt and Jane Morrow may have failed utterly to connect with their offspring on a conventionally parental level—Deanie cannot remember a single instance in which one of them helped her with her homework or expressed interest in her extracurricular activities or afforded her advice—but they did manage to impart their prejudices. The boyfriend who beeped his horn is long forgotten but the memory of Witt thundering down the front steps of the old Victorian to rage at the hapless youth who tried to

alert Deanie that he was there to pick her up for their date
with three quick blasts is burned in her brain: car horns
were warning devices, to be used when an idiot driver tried
to pull out in front of you, cut you off or otherwise endan-
ger your vehicle or the passengers it contained; they were
not instruments of social communication. Deanie remembers that Jane kept her in the house while Witt dismissed
the date, hissing with her own outrage, asking Deanie if
she really wanted to go out with a boy whose utter lack of
upbringing were laid so bare.

Yet, here is Trick, on her front porch, dressed in a fiery red,
short satin robe, a brilliant chiffon scarf tied at each wrist,
rocking aimlessly on the swing, restless bare feet skimming
off the porch boards with each back and forth, propelling
herself, and Deanie lays on her horn.

"Hey," Trick shouts when Deanie beeps, happy to know
her friend has arrived and indifferent to the method in which
the information is conveyed—she had never witnessed placid
Witt inflamed—and Deanie is oddly comforted by her calling out. Deanie has arrived early, in case Trick is still asleep,
or needs some help to get ready for the party, but she is in
no mood for Trick to dig in her sharp little heels and declare
that she is not going to do this thing that is expected of her—
not without Jill there to bully her into compliance—and it
seems she does not have to be.

"Hey, good, good, I was hoping you'd be here soon," Trick
continues as Deanie steps over the hole where the step ought
to be and pulls herself onto the porch. "I want to show you
the dress I'm thinking about wearing to the wedding. We
have time, right?"

"We have time."

"Good, good," Trick mutters as she pads toward the house, holds the screen door open for Deanie, motions her to follow her up the stairs.

THERE ARE FOUR bedrooms upstairs at Trick's house, three small rooms off a narrow hallway and one larger room at the very end of it that was once her mother's. The three smaller rooms are nearly empty—one holds a twin bed and a wood laminate dresser; another contains several dented commercial dress racks laden with garments, some of them Trick's mother's old stuff, Deanie can tell by the cut of the clothing and because these racks were Mrs. Danforth's clever solution to the house's lack of any real closet space; the third is consumed by a green metal desk so massive Deanie cannot imagine how Trick got it up the stairs and through the door. "My boys," Trick tells her. "I told them I wanted an office so Nick brought the desk up on one trip and Cole and a couple of the neighbor kids moved it in the next time he came."

Trick's house is spotless—even at the worst of her disease she has always been a neat freak, spending much of her mania in scrubbing and polishing, the aroma of Pine-Sol and Lysol Toilet Scrub mingling with but not quite masking that of the Merits—but their footsteps echo on the bare wooden floors and the house feels hollow, cold on even this warm June evening, these small rooms too big for Trick's life.

Trick leads Deanie to Kaye Danforth's old room, the master bedroom, where half a dozen black dresses are laid out neatly on the crisply made bed and across a tufted green armchair.

"I was thinking of this one," Trick says. She picks up a linen dress with a full circle, tea-length skirt and a thin, yellow leather belt with a gold buckle. "It's the only one that really fits right right now. But it was my mom's. Is it too... You know? Old-fashioned?"

"No, no, honey. These days that's called vintage. Try it on."

Trick slips out of her red robe and into the Donna-Reed-headed-to-a-dinner-party dress. She is stunning in it, especially when she slips on a pair of her trademark heels, yellow leather platforms with little cutouts at the toe. "The shoes were Mom's, too. I remember she bought them especially for this dress. They're a little tight, but I can still walk all right in them. See?" Trick takes a quick turn around the room, and then she turns her back to Deanie. "And I thought about these..." Deanie can see her unwrapping the scarves from her wrists and fastening in their place two big yellow fabric daisies on grosgrain ribbon. "Well?" Trick turns and waves the flowers. "I made them from the hat Mom used to wear with this outfit. I'm not going to wear a hat, after all." Trick smiles, pleased with herself. "What do you think?"

Deanie nods. Catches herself. For all of the courage one or another of them has screwed up over the years to say exactly what was on her mind about a major life decision, why was it always matters of appearance that made them step lightly? Why did it feel less shocking to have your girlfriends tell you they thought your fiancé was a rat than it did to hear one of them offer a brand new mother the perfectly reasonable advice that she ought to put on a pair of maternity pantyhose? If they couldn't be honest with each other about these relatively minor things they would have no credibility when it came to the larger issues.

Still, Deanie knew, it was Trick who rarely wanted for that kind of courage. Trick who matter-of-factly spoke up about the maternity tights. Trick who needed honesty now, if only to refresh her better judgment.

But—God, oh God!—why did the honesty have to include the damned scars on her wrists? The evidence of despair that Trick was trying so hard to keep hidden? And why did it have to come from Deanie alone, without Jill here to back her up!

"Trick?"

"Dean?'

"The flowers don't work."

"Oh. Well"—Trick turns back to the bed, stripping off the daisies and reaching for two thick, gold, circa-1985 slave cuffs—"I have these, too. What about these…"

Before Trick can slip the cuffs around her wrists, Deanie says, "No. Not those either. Trick, turn around."

Trick drops the jewelry on the bed and folds her hands across her stomach. But she stays where she is.

"Really, Trick. Turn around and show them to me. You can't wrap up your wrists for the rest of your life. Someone's going to see the scars sooner or later. Get it over with. Show me."

Trick doesn't move.

Deanie waits.

And waits.

And, then, slowly, like the tiny dancer in a music box, Trick spins on her yellow heels, hugging her arms close to her for another moment before she opens them, cautiously, so not to lose her balance. She keeps her elbows tucked at her waist and holds her hands out toward Deanie, like she is waiting for her to slap on handcuffs.

Deanie breathes and takes the three steps that will bring her near enough to Trick to take the offered hands in her own. Trick flinches, as if she is going to pull away, but Deanie holds tight and Trick only closes her eyes and turns her head to one side.

Deanie is relieved to see that what Trick has been hiding are no more than two thin white lines at the base of each palm, pale skin raised a bit from the surrounding flesh, tiny lines no more than a couple of millimeters wide.

"There was a plastic surgeon on call at the hospital the night that this happened. No"—Trick gulps for air—"*the night I did this.* Jill asked for a plastic surgeon to stitch me and there was one on call..."

Deanie looks at the ghostly lines on her friend's arms and, more to heal than to hide them, places her thumbs over top of them and presses there, hard, until Trick turns her head and looks her in the eye.

"I hate these scars as much as you do," Deanie says. "I hate them! They are... *unnecessary* scars for you to have to carry, but now they're yours. Like Chuck's leg, or the Cesarean scar Jill's got across her belly, or any of the various marks I've got all over me—the burn mark on my left leg from crashing that motorcycle when I was nineteen or the dent in my right boob where I had that cyst removed. Scars are what we get for living and the point is, *you're living.* You claimed what you did, now claim the marks that go with it and live with them. The trick, dearest, dearest Trick, is to live with the scars, and all the sadness and joy and stupidity they represent, and to know that however you are marked, you are still loved."

Trick tries to draw her hands away.

"Beloved," Deanie insists, holding tighter.

"Stop it." Trick tries a quick jerk to free her arms.

"You stop it," Deanie says, holding on. "Be loved, Trick. Because you are."

Trick stops fighting. She sighs, looks away, less convinced of anything than resigned, Deanie thinks. But that will do for now.

POCKETS. DEEP, IN-SEAM pockets on either side of the cotton wrap dress Trick puts on to go to the bachelorette party. Her arms disappear into the pockets almost to her elbows and that's where she keeps them, letting Deanie open the door to Sal Turk's place for her.

Sal Turk's has been a Lenapi institution for as long as Deanie can remember, and longer than that: Mrs. Kuznicki, who also grew up in Lenapi, has told them all stories of her own girlhood, eating Sal's hoagies and going to Saturday night dances in his back room which was known then as The Teen Canteen. By the '60s and '70s, when Deanie and Jill and Trick were regulars in Sal's back room, he'd changed the décor to include black lights and flocked psychedelic posters and renamed the space The Crystal Ship. Across the years it's also been known as Disco Haven, The Fire, The Pit, and even, for a brief, notorious few weeks, The Midnight Blood Club, capitalizing on a fad for Goth that was short-lived because it creeped Sal out. Sal's attractions have been more consistent than its décor—a live band, cheap cover, free sodas, and a long row of once-latest, now-classic pinball machines against its back wall.

Sal, himself, has remained remarkably consistent across the eras as well—the same old, grouchy bald guy in a spattered white chef's apron and Phillies' ball cap, shoving pizzas around in his ovens with the same wooden paddle he arms himself with whenever he sniffs out a kid with contraband, alcohol, marijuana, and he's got a sense for the harder drugs, too—in short, a nose that several generations of parents, if not some of their offspring, applaud.

Tonight Sal sits in a booth at the front of his shop as Deanie and Trick walk into his place. They've heard he's turned over most of the cooking to the students he employs for this purpose from the Lenapi campus. They've heard that he no longer goes flying into the back room with his pizza paddle over his head when the aroma of burning weed mingles in his twitching nose with that of other herbs.

"Hey, Sal," Deanie says when she passes his table, and he grunts at her. He has never been able to remember the names of the kids who pass through his place, and he is even less adept these days. They'd heard that Sal has recently put the business on the market, but so far there have been no takers, no one who wants to take on a pizza-and-pinball palace where the owner has spent every night of the last sixty years slapping cold meat onto warm buns for the family crowd and policing the teenagers who are drawn to the back room like ducks to water on Saturday nights. Deanie is almost glad of that—that the old place, it seems, will go when Sal himself checks out. Sal's place without Sal would be like one of those reruns of *All in the Family* after Edith is dead. There are eras that are better ended than artificially sustained.

Though, she thinks, she'll miss the hoagies terribly.

The lights in Sal's back room are dim, necessarily—back here it's either a full force of overhead fluorescent tubes or romantic shadows on the dance floor, one or the other. Sal's place doesn't have a liquor license, so Beth and Mary Golinski are in one corner of the dance floor uncorking the Chianti Jill has brought in for the party. "Italian food, Italian wine," Beth says as one of Sal's cooks wheels in an eight-foot Italian-with-everything and trays of Sicilian pizza slices on a three-tiered metal cart, and she pours a plastic cup full for Deanie.

In the opposite corner is a life-sized cardboard cutout of a Chippendale's dancer in an immodest pose. "'Pin the Dick on the Dancer,'" Beth whispers, and then giggles. Madeline's friend, the art major, thought up the game and made the decidedly well-designed playing pieces—the blow-up, and photos of a dozen out-sized penises mounted on card stock, thumbtacks stuck painfully through their bases; she did this presumably before she knew that a nun and a grandmother were going to be participating in the event and everyone is studiously avoiding the game corner.

Allison is lighting what seems like a hundred tea candles in votive holders on the tables clustered in the middle of the dance floor, and the voices of Sheryl Crow, Aretha Franklin, Pink, Janis Joplin, Liz Phair, The Dixie Chicks, and Ani DiFranco spill in random rotation from the surrounding speakers. "Madeline said she didn't care what the music was, as long as it was all girls," Beth advises.

Deanie sips her wine and nods in time with *Me and Bobby McGee*.

"Everyone's got their toenails painted!" Another of Madeline's girlfriends, not the art major, is standing next to Deanie, peering through the dim light at her toes and Trick's, exclaiming as if she's scandalized by the pedicures.

"A fairly common practice, painting one's toes," Deanie offers reasonably.

The girl shakes her head. "Xenoestrogens," she says.

"I'll bite," Deanie answers.

"Petrochemical compounds, by-products in the processing of petroleum that have a potent hormone-like effect on the human body. They're extremely toxic: central nervous system damage and oxygen deprivation. Long-term exposure can cause brain swelling, headaches, short-term memory loss. Irritability, anxiety, loss of coordination. Depression. They're used to manufacture nail polish."

"Is that true?' Trick leans past Deanie to ask.

"Every word. And more," the girl replies, wiggling her own pristine, polish-free toes.

"So"—Deanie looks down at her pretty, persimmon paint—"doing your toes is now a health hazard?'

"A *big* hazard," the girl says, and then she grins, "for the moment." She points across the room at another of the girls Deanie doesn't know, a magnificently freckled young woman whose pink dress sets off brilliant red hair. "That's Angie. She and I are working on a formula for a Xenoestrogen-free polish. We haven't got it right yet—right now the polish takes forever to dry, and it chips too easily—but when we do, the first hormone-free nail polish line will be on the market. My name's Rachel." She holds out her hand for Deanie to shake, and then for Trick, and Deanie has to poke Trick to take Rachel's hand because she is absorbed in studying the bright orange-yellow color poking out of the open tops of her stiletto sandals. And because she doesn't want to take her hands out of her pockets.

"Ladies, ladies!" Angie is clapping her hands and waving her arms to get the attention of the two dozen women milling around in Sal's back room. "Grab yourselves a plate of this delicious food and top off your wine and gather around, we've got a game to play!" She shouts over Aretha wailing, "R-E-S-P-E-C-T!" and adds, "Can someone turn down the music so we can hear each other?"

A game? Deanie eyes the cardboard Chippendale dancer with suspicion, but Angie is gesturing them all to take seats at the cluster of tables. "The game we're going to play is called 'Tattle on Madeline,'" she says, to Deanie's great relief, as the music fades into the background. Madeline, who has been obediently claiming a place at the table, stops suddenly and is about to protest, but Angie puts her hand on Madeline's shoulder and pushes her into a chair. "I'll start, so you'll get an idea of how to play. OK. Where did Madeline get her first kiss from Adam?"

"Flyers' game!" Rachel shouts.

"Skybox," another of Madeline's friends embellishes.

"Way too easy," Allison complains, though this is news to every one of the old girls.

"All right, then"—Angie grins wickedly—"where did Madeline get her first kiss ever?'

There is silence in the room, even from Madeline who is looking around and trying to figure out to whom exactly among those in attendance she has confided this secret.

"Right in this room," Jill answers and Madeline's eyes grow wide with surprise. "What? Did you think I didn't notice your lip gloss was gone and your eyes were glazed over when Billy Shampasky brought you home from that dance in seventh grade?"

"Billy Shampasky!" It's one of Madeline's high school friends who is shouting out. "*Billy Shampasky*? You never told me that!"

"That's because Billy Shampasky was a nerd and I didn't want anyone to know," Madeline laughs. "And my eyes were not 'glazed over,' Mom."

"Billy Shampasky! Billy Shampasky!" The girls take up the chant and the high school friend adds details: "The smartest guy in the whole class, always wore a white t-shirt under his shirts and buttoned the top button, and he had a crew cut and mustache in the eighth grade!"

"He did not have a mustache!" Madeline leaps up to defend herself. "He just had early puberty and no one had taught him how to shave yet!"

"Early puberty!" Beth squeals. "*Early puberty!*"

"OK, OK," Jill stands up and raises her hands to quiet everyone. "I have one. How old was Madeline when she wrecked the family car?"

Deanie and Trick, Beth and Mrs. Kuznicki, and Madeline herself hold their tongues, knowing the answer and not wanting to stomp on Jill's punch line.

For a few moments Madeline's friends remain speechless, eyeing each other for clues, until Jill provides the answer: "Four."

Jill and Chuck were living then in the first house they'd bought together, one half of a two-story duplex down the block from Jill's parents. There was a detached garage behind the house, at the end of a steep driveway. The garage, inconvenient to the house, was used mostly for storage, with a small, comfortable space inside set aside as Madeline's playhouse—the child-sized refrigerator and stove and tables and chairs and doll beds she employed while playing at Mommy. Jill and Chuck parked their vehicle at the curb in front of the house. Except on the day that Madeline wrecked the family's tan-and-brown Plymouth Duster.

Chuck had picked up a roll of the wire fencing Jill wanted him to put around her tomato patch, to keep out neighborhood rabbits, and Chuck had driven the Duster up the driveway so he could unload the wire more easily, nearer to the garden. He'd decided to eat dinner before he installed the fencing. He came into the kitchen and kissed Jill hello, hoisted his baby son out of his highchair and flung him in the air a few times, asked where Madeline was. "In her playhouse," Jill said at just the same moment that both of them saw the Duster's brown top go flying backwards outside the kitchen window and heard Madeline shrieking, "MOMMMMMMY!"

In the thirty seconds it had taken Chuck to park the car, enter the house, and rescue Chas from the highchair, Madeline had come out of her playhouse, climbed into the Duster's front seat, turned the engine on, adjusted the radio station until she found a tune she liked, and climbed into the back to buckle her doll in Chas's baby seat. In her climb to the back, her foot hit the gearshift, throwing it into reverse.

For an instant, the car only crept backwards—an inch or two. Then it's back wheels hit the point in the asphalt where the steepest part of the downgrade began and the car wheeled itself away, fast and free, picking up speed as it zigzagged down the driveway, clipping one neighbor's parked blue Ford pick-up and cutting off another who was on her way home from the grocery store as it careened across the street. The woman driving home with her groceries slammed on her brakes, upsetting a carton of eggs all over her dashboard but avoiding a more serious collision. The Duster bumped over the curb on the other side of the street, over the lawn of the people who lived in the house across the way, through the peony bushes planted on either side of their front walk, into their front porch, bringing the gingerbread railing crashing down onto the Duster's brown vinyl roof and bringing the Duster itself to a grinding halt.

Jill was the first to get to the car, Chuck a couple of paces behind her because, although he was the more athletic of the two, he was running with Chas in his arms. The back window had shattered when it clipped the neighbor's Ford and Jill dove through it, extracting her hysterical daughter, screaming *Hail Mary*'s at the top of her lungs and holding Madeline so tightly the child was struggling for air.

"She's bleeding," Chuck shouted as he caught up. "Look to see where she's bleeding, Jill, for crying out loud!"

His cries prompted Jill to release her grip on Madeline and inspect the child for injury, anything broken, the source of the blood that was beginning to be copious, dripping into the peonies, a source she didn't find until Madeline was nearly naked and hanging upside down in Jill's arms, a gash that ran the entire width of one baby butt cheek where it had caught, in the course of the wild ride downhill, on a loose end of the wire fencing.

As Jill tells the story to the women in Sal's back room, Marilyn Kuznicki crosses herself, the sign of her quiet acknowledgement that the outcome of Madeline's first driving experience could have been a great deal worse, though they are all laughing about it now. They are laughing at Jill's willingness to be the butt of the joke—the utter loss of self-possession she's owning up to—and at Madeline who is standing up and threatening to bare the scar she's got that proves every word Jill has said is true.

"We believe you! Everyone believes you," Mrs. Kuznicki urges as Madeline inches her skirt up her thigh. "Really, now, keep your clothes on, Maddie, or you're going to make me think you're too young and immature to get married at all!"

Jill fixes a grin on her mother. "Like you thought that Chuck and I were too young to get married?"

"Oh, Jill, I never... I don't recall ever objecting to..."

"No, Mom"—Jill is full out laughing now as her mother fumbles—"you *did*. Oh, but you did..."

By MIDNIGHT THERE are only dregs left in the Chianti bottles. Madeline and Jill are on the dance floor, swinging lazily together as Judy Collins promises, "I'll Be Seeing You." Jill, Deanie notes, even with an excessive amount of the grape in her system, and without even really trying, is still the most graceful dancer. Beth and Mrs. Kuznicki are at the far end of the room, at the pinball machines, Beth instructing her mother in the subtleties of play so, every so often, Judy Collins's clean, aching soprano is punctuated by Mrs. Kuznicki's racking up a few more points. Trick is looking on, listening intently to the conversation Mary Golinski is having with Angie and Rachel. "Sister," Deanie overhears Angie saying, "those are all solutions that might work, and it would have taken Rachel and me months to think of them. Listen, I have a proposition for you: be on our team. Angie was a bio major, and I was business admin—we need a real chemist to work with us. Help us get this nail polish formula to work and we'll cut you in for a third."

A few of Madeline's friends have already said goodbye and headed back to their homes, or to the hotel for the night. A small group is over in the far corner playing the art major's game—now that Mrs. Kuznicki and Mary Golinski are suitably distracted—blindfolded and spinning and howling over each new near-miss with a cardboard penis. Deanie edges herself off her seat so she can get her toe under the seat of a nearby chair, drag it closer, prop her feet up on it. Allison is with her at the table, pouring the last of one of the bottles of wine into their plastic cups.

"I have to say," Deanie tells Allison, "this is the first bachelorette party I've ever been to that didn't involve shots and strippers."

"Really? Mrs. Bakula had strippers?"

Deanie looks across the table, at Allison's sparkling eyes, her amusement. It is, indeed, Deanie thinks, somehow easier to imagine Jill throwing back lemon drops than it is to imagine her stuffing dollar bills into a leopard print jockstrap, which she also did. "*A* stripper. One. There was only one stripper, Allison."

Allison nods. Tries not to laugh. Puts a hand over her mouth, which does not conceal her dancing eyes. "Listen, listen," Allison says, changing the subject so she'll be able to take another sip of her wine without snorting it back out through her nose, "I've been meaning to ask you something, and I'm only going to ask because Mrs. Bakula said I should, otherwise I never would, I'm sure you get asked to do this sort of thing all the time…"

Allison has recovered her composure, driven the image of Mrs. Bakula cavorting with a live Chippendale dancer out of her mind, and still she can't seem to simply ask her question, so Deanie puts her out of her misery: "Will I read some of the stuff you've written?"

Allison is suddenly somber. "Yeah."

Deanie has a strict policy about this sort of thing. She never reads anyone's manuscripts prior to publication unless she'd been asked to supply a blurb for a jacket cover—and then only for a very few favorite authors and/or select writer-friends. Deanie, in fact, gets irritated by such requests and not because the *reading* is such an imposition on her time, but penning the notes back to hopeful writers, finding diplomatic words to balance encouragement for their effort with realism about their talent, is a god-awful drain. She says now, "Sure."

"Really?"

"Do you have something you can drop by my room tonight?"

"You bet I do!"

Before Allison can squeal with delight, as Deanie winces to see that is indeed what she is gearing up to do, Beth is squealing across the length of Sal's back room, "Thirty thousand points! Mom just hit thirty thousand points!"

Madeline and Jill stop mid-dance step. Trick tears herself away from the riveting conversation about toenail polish and stands up to go look at the pinball machine Mrs. Kuznicki has been playing on. Even the girls playing pin-the-penis look over and one of them calls out, "No way."

"Way!" Beth answers, clapping her hands and hugging her mother around the neck at the same time. "My mom is a pinball wizard!" she shrieks.

Mrs. Kuznicki loosens Beth's grip and ducks her head out from under her arms. "Oh, nonsense," she says, but her grin is ear-to-ear.

Chapter Eighteen
1988

MADELINE WAS MAKING HER WAY DOWN the stairs, not bumping with laughing abandon down each step on her rear end as if the staircase were an amusement park ride, as she was given to doing before she wrecked the Duster. She was making her way in bare feet, one step at a time, sideways, holding on to the spindles with both small hands, easing her way as if she were not a sturdy four-year-old but a child much newer to walking, favoring the leg attached to her uninjured buttock, mewing softly—"Mama?"

Deanie picked up Madeline to soothe her. "Shhhh," she breathed into the little girl's hair, "Mama and I are in the kitchen. Do you want to come in the kitchen with us?" Madeline nodded into Deanie's neck. Even as she spoke, her words muffled in Madeline's hair so she could inhale the child's heavenly scent, Deanie saw Chuck leaning over the rail at the top of the stairs.

"Are you trying to wake the whole house?" Chuck asked.

Chuck was wearing only boxer shorts, and his thick blonde hair stuck up at odd, spiked angles, and he squinted his eyes to peer through sleep into the light coming from below. "What time is it? Did you two stay out all night?"

"It's only one-thirty," Deanie advised him. "We left the party early. It's still going on but we're home. Go back to bed."

Chuck nodded that he was happy to do just that and was starting on his way when he heard the cranky moan from Chas's room, the indignant "ahh-haaaa," of a little boy beginning to wake, disoriented, alone in the dark. "Could you two have made more noise?'

"I'll get him," Jill snapped, hurrying out of the kitchen where she'd been putting up a pot of coffee, followed by the scent of brewing French roast. She made her way up the stairs. "It's only one-thirty," she told her husband as she met him on the second floor landing. "One-thirty isn't too late to come home from the only fifteen-year class reunion you'll ever have." She swatted Chuck on his backside as she passed him. "I spent eighteen months in bed, a year and a half of my life lying flat on my back, and you bitch about having to baby-sit for one lousy night," she mumbled as she entered Chas's room to retrieve him. "Go back to bed," she told Chuck sharply when she'd gathered the two-year-old, on her way back to the first floor, and he obeyed.

Chas was asleep again before Jill's foot touched the bottom step. He sprawled across his mother's lap as she sat at the kitchen table, his head turned into a shoulder just above her breast, one arm curled up around her neck and the other dangling limp by her hip, breathing in and out in satisfied slumber, light summer sweat moistening the curls at the back of his neck. Jill reached her free arm for a sip from her cup. "You know, really, would it have killed him to go lay down with the baby until he went back to sleep?"

Deanie was sitting with Madeline curled carefully in her lap, the injured bottom half propped up via a bent knee, a habit Madeline had acquired since the accident that made her look like a lopsided tree frog. Madeline was curling a piece of Deanie's long hair around one of her fingers, smoothing it against the ruffle down the front of Deanie's evening blouse, pulling the ends of it through a button hole. "You're awfully grouchy tonight, Mrs. Bakula," Deanie said. "Especially considering that Stu Jenner showed up at the reunion with a date who was wearing fingerless lace gloves, a gold lamé corset, and a belt that spelled out 'Boy Toy.'"

Jill could barely contain her hoot, stifling herself only for the sake of the sleeping boy. Even Madeline looked over at her, the start of a smile on her kittenish face. "Can you believe a grown woman in that get-up?'

Deanie reached for her own cup of coffee. "Isn't the whole 'Boy Toy' thing over anyway?"

"You know," Jill said, "you don't go to these sorts of events with the intention of being nasty. You go to see old friends, remember…catch up. Have an evening out with your girlfriends. Why do some people hand you the opportunity to mock them?"

"And why is it so delicious when the person who is so easily mocked is the girlfriend of the boy who tormented you the whole last two years of school?"

"Ohmigod," Jill squealed loud enough that Chas wiggled his head and pinched the fingers lying up against Jill's neck.

"Cocktease!" she laughed even though Madeline was sitting on Deanie's lap, wide awake and paying attention to every word.

Partly to distract Madeline—an inquisitive child who, to Deanie's horror, piped up, "What does 'cocktease' mean?"— and partly because Jill clearly needed more coffee to sober her up, Deanie stood and hoisted Madeline onto her hip, gripping her carefully under her uninjured bottom half, to pour them both another cup. "I think you're grouchy because Trick wouldn't go to the reunion with us."

Trick's behavior over the last three or four years had baffled both of them, not just Jill. Trick herself understood this well enough. After announcing with great bravado that she was going off her meds, declaring her confidence in her cure, she was well enough to feel terrible remorse when she lost her job at the Lenapi campus for calling in sick for six straight weeks, and to resume her pharmaceutical regime with contrition. She was well enough to find another job—typesetting classifieds at the Lenapi Morning Star-Sentinel—and fall in love with one of the pressmen, and get married to him, and she was well enough to feel the sting of betrayal, desertion, life's futility when neither her brothers nor her children made the effort to come north and participate in the little wedding Jill threw for her in the Bakula backyard. She was well enough to decide that if her own boys didn't want to give her away, what was really the use of being well at all? She was well enough to be anguished that, in her fury at her sons' absence at her wedding, she'd destroyed every photograph she had of them, slashed at their baby pictures with a scissors and lit the school photos that Dom had sent her over the years on fire with her Bic. As for her brothers, she'd torn the five-and-dime frames off the dusty pink wall in her mother's old living room and shredded their pretty faces with her bare hands.

Trick was well enough to concede that she wouldn't want
to be married to someone who could destroy her own children's baby pictures either. To understand why the managing
editor of the newspaper thought it best if she "took some time
off." To know that surviving her second divorce and securing another job would require full control of her emotional
range and check herself into the hospital to seek treatment
once again. Well enough to feel sorrow when the doctor who
was so successfully treating her retired and referred her to a
colleague, a man to whom Trick took an immediate and not
incredible dislike, and to decide insanity was a better option
than suffering the new doctor's weekly condescension. Well
enough to get her job back at the newspaper, and to hold it
for nearly five straight months while she sought out a new
doctor who could provide her with both the chemicals that
kept her composed and the reason to remain so, and to feel
despair when this person could not be found, and to quit her
job when she felt herself tipping over the brink again, about to
do harm to the business, alienate the managing editor who'd
been kind enough to risk providing her with work—twice—
and she was well enough to be sickened with herself when she
awoke in the hospital room in Dallas where she'd landed after
she'd flown to Texas unannounced and put her arm through
a plate glass window on the first floor of her oldest brother's
apartment trying to break in when she arrived and discovered no one was home.

She was well enough to feel brutalized when she looked
up to see her oldest brother entering her hospital room, to
cling to Deanie's hand on one side of the bed and Jill's on
the other even while she wished them away from the room,
away from whatever humiliating thing her brother was going
to say to her, the big, beautiful bully who stood over her and

ordered, "Don't come here anymore, Trick. You think it's good for Nicky or Cole when you pull shit like this? The only thing they can count on from you is you acting crazy, so why don't you just not let 'em have to count on you at all? Let your friends take you home. It's not good for anyone for you to be here."

She was never really well enough.

Trick's behavior baffled even Trick.

It would continue to bedevil all of them through time—Trick's third marriage and subsequent third divorce, a steady succession of jobs each less and less demanding of the skills Trick could indeed command when fully harnessed to her abilities, each new beginning attended with solemn promises to get right with her brothers, make it up to her boys, not let her friends down: stay on her meds, stay-on-her-meds, stayonhermeds. These were promises she did not break so much as she was simply incapable of keeping. New beginnings dotted her horizon, always, when she turned her back to the chaos she left in her wake, turned to the sun with fresh resolve, but she never truly released her regrets, only stored them up for the next and the next and the next time the bright sun made her blink. Chaos. She lived in chaos.

Except when she lived in moments of stunning calm and clarity.

She'd had such a moment just that evening, when Deanie and Jill arrived at the turquoise house to pick her up to go to their fifteenth-year high school reunion.

They'd found her upstairs, sitting on the edge of her bed in her mother's old room. She was dressed in a worn, checkered flannel bathrobe, her bare feet swaying and worrying the dust ruffle, her ashy blonde hair hanging in a sheet over her shoulders, still damp from the shower.

"Get a move on. Cocktail hour starts at six and we don't want to be late," Jill had directed her, before she'd realized that something was really the matter.

Trick, who'd been staring into her own lap, her fingers nervous with a thread of loose whip stitching on the bathrobe's sash, looked up at Jill. Over at Deanie. "I'm not going with you."

"Trick," Jill said impatiently.

"No. I'm not." Trick turned her attention back to the sash in her lap even as Jill took up the place beside her on the bed and Deanie moved in front of her and slumped against the dresser.

"Come on." Jill put her hands over Trick's fingers. "It's a night out with your girlfriends, and how often do we get to do that anymore? With Deanie living so far away? How often does Chuck volunteer to keep the kids while I go out to a party?"

Trick let Jill's hand remain on hers. She smiled. She said, "Do you know why people go to class reunions?"

Jill and Deanie looked stumped for a minute.

"To see old friends. To remember," Deanie offered.

"To catch up," Trick told them. "To find out what people have been doing with their lives since graduation spit us out into the world. What in the world can I tell people I've been doing?"

Trick's eyes, when she turned them up again to Jill and Deanie, were wide, searching and sad, but immaculately dry. Her mouth was turned down, not in bitterness but resignation. Her feet were still, suddenly, resting one beside the other on the bare floor, the toes turned up slightly, as if she were digging her heels into the hardwood. "I'm not going, and don't plead with me and don't try to bully me into changing my

mind because I'm not going to. And, no, God, I don't want
to *talk about it.* If you love me the way you always say you do,
you'll understand why I don't want to go to the goddamned
class reunion so there's nothing to talk about anyway. I'm
not going and you might as well leave now because all you're
going to accomplish by staying is to make yourselves late."

"*GROUCHY?*" JILL ASKED. She spoke in a whisper, but one
with such vehemence that Chas's arm dropped from around
her neck and he curled it under himself, between his chest
and Jill's.

Deanie was standing at the sink, replacing the pot on
the hot plate of the coffeemaker. Madeline's legs, which had
been dangling at Deanie's side, in deference to the wound
in her behind and any extraneous motion that would make
her stitches pull, lifted now and wrapped themselves around
Deanie's waist. She pulled her arms in close and buried her
head under Deanie's chin. Deanie bent her own head until
her lips were pressed into Madeline's golden hair, her nose
engulfed in the curls.

"I'm not grouchy about Trick," Jill said when everyone had
braced themselves. "I'm fed up with her, and I'm worried as
hell about her and, to be perfectly honest, however petty it
sounds, I'm annoyed with her for putting a damper on the
evening tonight. I'm sitting in the Elks Hall, trying to take
some satisfaction that my high school nemesis is dating a
thirty-two-year-old Madonna-wannabe and all I keep thinking about is my friend sitting on the edge of her bed in that
sad flannel robe *in pain.*

"Grouchy? That's the least of it, Deanie, and I'd think
you'd know better."

Deanie nodded, slowly, into Madeline's bright, warm curls. Madeline stretched her neck, offering Deanie more of the comforting, heavenly, ordinary aroma of childhood. By four, Madeline was entirely accustomed to Deanie wanting a whiff of her. She wiggled the top of her head into Deanie's nose now as if it were a great game, and she giggled when Deanie squeezed her around the shoulders and started to make little snorting noises all over the top of her head.

Jill rolled her eyes. "Oh, for God's sake," she snapped, "will you stop smelling my children? You're going to give them complexes."

Chapter Nineteen
Friday

*T*HE LAST FULL DAY BEFORE THE WEDDING. Deanie has anticipated that it will be one of frenzied activity, but when she enters 1858 Greentree Court in the morning, at a little past nine-thirty, she finds the Bakula household filled with unhurried people.

Deanie enters through the garage, where she's backed in her SUV to make it easier to unload the fresh keg she's just picked up from the distributor. Chas and most of the grooms-men—she doesn't take time for an exact count of the young, nearly naked men floating in the pool—are cooling their bachelor-party hangovers in the deep end. She calls to them about the keg and hears groans in response, one lone voice vowing to never touch another drop of beer, but she sees two of them splash over the sides of their rafts to attend to the Michelob.

At one of the picnic tables, under the shade of a large orange and yellow striped umbrella, Mary Golinski is gathered with Angie and Rachel, their heads bent together, their language one that goes right over Deanie's head—"styrene" and "stearalkonium hectorite" and "bensophenone-1." Mary is saying something about trying to suspend the fingernail polish pigment in a solvent that solidifies rather than evaporates because it's the solvent that's responsible for the Xenoestrogens.

Deanie knows Trick is nearby before she sees her—a Merit is streaming smoke from an abalone shell on the deck outside the family room. Inside the room, Trick is standing barefoot on a ladder, feeding the floor-length curtains back onto their rods and hanging them back over the bay window.

"What are you doing here? You told me not to pick you up until noon."

Trick smiles. "I woke up early, so I walked."

"You *walked*?"

"It's good exercise."

"It's six miles."

Trick shrugs, and she eyes her toes while she wiggles them so Deanie will look down at her feet.

"Oh, your pedicure!" Deanie mourns when she sees there is no pink polish on Trick's animated toes. "What happened?"

"I took it off. 'Irritability, anxiety, depression.' I need all of the advantages I can get these days *not* to feel those things. So I nixed the pink. 'Nix the pink.' That's my new motto until those girls out on the deck build a better nail polish."

Beth is in the kitchen, at the table, clipping Madeline and Adam's wedding announcement out of a dozen copies of the Lenapi Morning Star-Sentinel.

"Oh, let me see," Deanie says.

The Lenapi newspaper is thin every day of the week, committed as it is to strictly local news—town council meetings, reports of Kiwanian activity, the high schools sports scores—and on Fridays it seems as if it is published solely to contain write-ups about the weddings that will occur over the weekend. "*Bakula – Osic Wedding,*" Deanie reads on page two.

"Madeline Elizabeth Deanna Fredericka Bakula, daughter of Mr. and Mrs. Charles Bakula of this city will wed Adam Richard Osic, son of Mr. and Mrs. Michael Osic of Philadelphia, in a noon ceremony at St. Boniface Roman Catholic Church tomorrow. The bride, a member of the 2002 class of Lenapi High School and a graduate of Villanova College and The University of Pennsylvania School of Law, will be attended by..."

"You want a copy?" Beth asks. "I think I got enough for everyone, plus one for me to decoupage."

"Sure," Deanie says, tucking her copy in the purse she lays down on the seat of a kitchen chair and moving toward the counter, where the great coffee urn is perched, pouring herself a cup. She pinches a chunk of watermelon from the fruit salad on Jill's breakfast buffet.

In the dining room—Deanie can see through the archway—one of Madeline's friends, the art major, is seated at the card table, concentrated on calligraphy, individual place cards spread out around her so the thick ink she is using will dry evenly. An ironing board is set up behind her and Mrs. Kuznicki is standing over it, smoothing the wrinkles from a tablecloth printed with cheerful, over-sized bright red apples. "I don't like you sitting under there while I'm working," Mrs. Kuznicki says to Cara, who is posed, cross-legged like a yogi, under the tent of the tablecloth. "The iron could fall and hit you on the head. Come on, Cara, get out from under there." When Cara doesn't obey, Mrs. Kuznicki calls— "Vic!"—as if there has already been an accident.

"Yes?" Mr. Kuznicki hustles in from the direction of the living room.

"Why don't you take Cara to McDonald's for French toast? You'd like that, wouldn't you, Cara?"

"No," Cara replies adamantly.

"Well, come on with me anyway," Mr. Kuznicki says, reaching beneath the cloth for his granddaughter, struggling to pick her up because, while she is not resisting him, she is refusing to uncross her legs, going out with a grudge.

"I want to stay at Auntie Jill's house!" she insists, and Deanie can understand why. There is an atmosphere here of both expectation and peace, anticipation of celebration and a celebration already begun, a quiet security surrounding the mundane activities of these purposeful people and Deanie thinks it must be a feeling even more intense to a child who knows that it is her family that has created this well being.

"We don't have to go to McDonald's if you don't want to," Vic concedes, hoisting Cara onto his hip. "Come with me into the living room and watch everyone dancing then," he tells her.

In the living room, Mr. Kuznicki sits on a sofa and plants Cara in his lap. The sofa, still shoved up against a wall, also holds another man, a fellow with close-cropped gray hair in a polo shirt and khaki shorts, nodding impatiently as Frank Sinatra croons, "I will get a glow just thinking *uuuuv* you, just the way you look tonight…" The man has about him the air of uncontained energy of someone who'd much rather be out on the lawn throwing around a football, whacking a golf ball, doing anything that isn't constrained by four walls.

"Deanie, have you met Adam's dad yet?" Mr. Kuznicki asks.

The man jumps up and extends his hand to Deanie so quickly she feels herself stunned with his relief at having something—anything—else to do. "Mike Osic, glad to meet you, I hear you're one of Jill's good friends."

"Nice to meet you, too, Mike," Deanie says to him, but her attention is drawn to the dancers in the middle of the living room floor. Chuck is leading Madeline in moves that are just uncomplicated enough for him to execute and—as Adam will lead his mother to the dance floor halfway through this very song at the reception tomorrow—he is twirling her now in an exaggerated spin of the sort he would never inflict on her at the formal event.

Adam's mother, Cecilia Osic, is dressed as sportily as her husband, a youthful forty-six, and she gives back Adam's tomfoolery as good as he is giving it to her, stepping behind him, wrapping her arms around his waist as she goes, holding him tightly by his hands so he has to turn with her, coming out of the spin cleverly so they are facing each other again and Adam is confused as to how they got back into these positions. "Take that," she tells him as Adam groans. "A little too much for the groom's hangover?" Cecilia taunts.

"The groom had better not be hung over," Madeline says over Chuck's shoulder.

"I'm not," Adam is quick to insist. "I'm not," he lies.

"Right," Madeline answers, because she knows better.

"Do you know where Allison is?" Deanie asks Mr. Kuznicki. Allison seems to be the only one missing from the menagerie, except for Jill who is, Deanie imagines, among all of them, in high-gear with final wedding preparations; Deanie would just as soon wait until she's finished with her coffee to run into Jill.

"Jill sent Allison to Bastioni's. To deliver the pots of herbs for the tables tonight. I think." Mr. Kuznicki replies.

"Then she's picking up the cold cut trays from the deli for lunch today," Mrs. Kuznicki adds from the dining room. "She won't be back for a while. Beth, get those newspapers off the table, Jill wants this cloth on there for lunch and, really, has anyone fed Cara this morning? You know she won't eat fruit salad, or those bran muffins." Mrs. Kuznicki sighs. "Nobody will eat those bran muffins. I don't know what Jill was thinking…"

"Well, *perch*," everyone in the living room hears Jill tell her mother, "they're *healthy*."

"They're disgusting," Beth informs her. "And don't talk to our mother like that."

"Clear the table so Mom can put the tablecloth on it, Beth," Jill snaps back, "and then go help Trick with the curtains, she's having a problem getting the ties back up or something. How are you coming with the place cards?" she calls as she makes her way into the dining room. "I told you not to leave them until the last minute, you're going to be at them all day now. Dad? Will you run out for ice? There's not enough left to ice the keg and then for lunch, too. Has anyone seen Deanie come in yet?"

Deanie imagines that all Jill wants is a whistle around her neck.

"In here," Deanie shouts in reply.

"Oh, this is just fine." Jill taps her toe when she enters the living room, the yellow legal pad in her hand bouncing with the rhythm, a pencil stuck behind her right ear. "I think you've all had enough dance practice by now. Chuck, you promised to mow the front lawn this morning, and you'd better get to it before it gets any hotter, and, Adam, the jewelry store is open by now so get moving if you want to have rings for tomorrow, and, oh, hi, Mike, Cecilia. Cecilia! Will you go up and help Madeline start to unpin her dress? Just halfway, I think, give us a little head start at detaching it from that cardboard form so nobody's crazed trying to figure out how to get her into it in the morning…"

"Mom…" Madeline's got one arm around her father's neck and she reaches the other out for Jill, lazily drawing her into their slow dance. "Remember what I told you when we started to plan this whole thing? It's a party. It's a *big* party, and I'm excited to have it, but it's just a party. Any two idiots can get married, idiots do it every day. It's the twenty-fifth anniversary that should really get this kind of royal treatment so stop acting like this is a coronation or you're not going to get to enjoy much of it."

Madeline has pulled Jill close to her, so Jill's back is to Deanie, but Deanie sees Jill give in, her shoulders relax, and nobody misses Jill tossing her yellow legal pad over her shoulder, letting Chuck rock them, his wife and his daughter, in the slow circle of his arms.

THE YOUNG WOMEN, Madeline and her friends, are heaping slabs of rye or whole wheat with chipped ham and Swiss cheese or roast beef and provolone, slathering on mayonnaise or mustard. Allison has taken charge of slicing tomatoes and onions and the girls are piling them on their sandwiches as fast as she can cut them. The young men, coaxed away from the hot sun and cool water of the pool are hardly less reticent,

atoning for the excesses of the previous evening with carbohy-
drates, their shorts dripping chlorinated water on the kitchen
tiles so Jill chases them with a mop, out to the deck to eat
their sandwiches.

"Pastrami," Deanie says, blissful that there is still some left
when it's her turn at the deli trays.

"I ordered extra, just for you," Jill tells her.

"I can't get good pastrami in Napa—what's up with that?
Any hot mustard?"

"In the fridge. On the door."

Deanie takes her pastrami on rye out to the deck, where
people are eating their lunches at every table, in every chair
save for one canvas recliner next to Madeline. "Perfect! I
haven't had any real chance to talk with you all week. Don't
go anywhere," Deanie tells the bride. She leaves her sandwich
plate on the seat of the empty chair and hurries to pour herself a paper cup of beer from the pitcher at one of the picnic
tables where Chas and the other young men are sitting. They
are confessing, the boyish brutes, to having indeed crossed
the border into New Jersey to try to get into the Boom Boom
Room after Chuck and Mr. Kuznicki and Mike Osic left
the bachelor party last night, but the bouncer at the Boom
Boom's door had required ID's of *everyone* in the group for
anyone to enter and George was still only twenty years old.
They'd all had to turn around and go back to the fire hall—
"Fifty dollars in cab fare for nothing!" Chas complains.

Jill scolds them, but with a smile, "See what happens to
you when you try to do the wrong thing? It costs you!"

Mary Golinski, Rachel and Angie, are sitting with
Mrs. Kuznicki who is shocked to hear that nail polish is not as
innocent as it is pretty. With Trick egging her on, she is digging for the details as though she's a reporter for *20/20*—"Do

you mean to tell me that the research about this has been out there for *twelve years* and not one cosmetics company has even tried to make a nail polish that's safe to use? I've never heard about this before, and I watch CNN. I read *Redbook* every month. Where did you get this information? Why doesn't anyone know about this but you?"

Rachel and Angie cite their sources, ticking off published reports on their fingers, but Deanie doesn't hear them, doesn't listen, only sees Trick engaged, lively, her hands drawn out from the deep side pockets of the wide cotton trousers she's got on today, arms expressive and unencumbered and free, free and unashamed as anyone's arms. As Allison's arms, gesturing to embellish a story she's telling Chuck and Mr. Kuznicki over across the pool, making them laugh. As Cara's arms, windmills of excitement as she runs to greet her father who has just arrived to have lunch with them all. As Mike Osic's arms as he demonstrates his golf swing to Beth over by Jill's brilliant rhododendrons.

Mike Osic lifts his arms and turns away from Beth to wallop another phantom ball across the lawn, and Beth seizes the opportunity to roll her eyes.

When Deanie returns to Madeline, she stretches out on the canvas with her Michelob in one hand and the sandwich in a plate on her lap. Madeline says, "I think if he was holding an actual golf club, Auntie Beth would yank it out of his hands and break it in two."

"Not the most patient person, Beth."

"I've gotten the golf demonstration. On the contrary, I think Beth is a saint."

"Mad"—Deanie speaks through a mouthful of pastrami, nodding to keep Madeline's attention until she swallows and can continue—"I know it's the day before your wedding, and you've probably been telling this story to everyone all week long and I'm the last person who's been able to corner you"— Madeline hands Deanie her own napkin, gesturing at some mustard on Deanie's upper lip—"Thank you. Look, do you have the inclination to explain one more time what this pro bono case of yours is all about? I've gotten little bits and pieces of it, but I need to hear the whole story, from the horse's mouth."

"Are you kidding?" Madeline tosses her head back on her chair, feigning a staggering astonishment. "Auntie Dean, I've copied you on every e-mail I've written about it since Tuesday. I thought you were never going to ask."

"Honey! I haven't checked my e-mail all week. I didn't know!"

"Jeez, I couldn't figure out why you of all people weren't interested."

"Oh, but I am. Of course I am!"

"Then listen up!" Madeline sits up, removes her own plate with its crusts of uneaten bread from her lap. She tucks her feet under her, getting comfortable. "Go ahead and eat your lunch"—she points at Deanie's pastrami—"I've got a lot of talking to do. All you have to do is listen.

"You know that one of the things I do is volunteer a few hours a week at my neighborhood's teen center"—Madeline pauses to let Deanie nod; Deanie has heard about this from Jill—"Yes, all right then. The center can't afford to pay a staff, and if there's no adult supervision they have to close the doors, so Adam and I go in on Wednesday nights. A couple of months ago we get there for our shift and there's a group of girls huddled in a corner of the kitchen area, and one of them is in just a fit of tears. Adam looks at me, like this is undeniably *my* thing to deal with, so I go over to them.

"There's five or six of them, fourteen and fifteen years old, and none of them are very friendly to me, at first. They don't want to let me into their circle. I have to stand there, kind of insisting to know what's wrong. See, these kids have a lot of issues, and not just with the world at large, with each other. It's important that supervisors know if someone's causing trouble, but I know the girl who's crying and she's not a troublemaker. I was thinking that one of the tougher kids had been bullying her, or there was a problem at home maybe. A lot of these kids have problems at home and they use the center as a sort of shelter.

"The other girls are very protective of the one who is crying, but the girl herself finally says, 'Just tell her. Everyone's gonna know anyway. Why should the nosy lady be any different?'

"Deanie, it turns out the girl is pregnant.

"I'm thinking, What am I supposed to do now that I know this?"

Deanie shakes her head, because she doesn't know either, and she's got a big bite of pastrami in her mouth.

"I've got all of these questions going around in my head— How pregnant are you? Who's the father? Was the sex even consensual? All of these questions, and advice to give her, too, legal advice, but, you know, even I figured out right away that's not this kid's priority..."

"And?" Deanie manages, because she's swallowed again.

"Fortunately, it was taking me a minute to decide what I wanted, or even needed to say first, and the girls started talking before I could open my big mouth. The girls filled me in without me having to ask a thing. The pregnant girl, Annalinda, is fifteen years old. She's five months pregnant. Or, she *thinks* she's about five months pregnant. The first three months it didn't occur to her that she might be pregnant—she's had sex only a couple of times, and her periods had never been very regular anyway, and her head is so full of ridiculous notions, like you can't get pregnant the first time you have sex, that it makes my head ache. Annalinda's finding out on the fly how a girl gets pregnant now that she already is. *Five months*, she *thinks*, and she's spent the last two months hiding it from her mother. Trying to work up the nerve to tell the father who, by the way, is no longer her boyfriend. Having her girlfriends hit her in the stomach..."

"Holy Mary, Mother of God," Deanie whispers, but as Mrs. Kuznicki would whisper it, not a curse but a prayer.

"Annalinda doesn't look five months pregnant to me. She's a tiny little thing and I think she'd be showing a lot more if she were that far along, but what do I know? I'm a lawyer, not a medical professional. I've never had a baby. I'm trying to remember what Beth looked like when she was five months along with Cara and I can't, so I'm thinking the best thing to do is get this girl to a doctor, get some facts in hand so she can think clearly about what she's going to do. Know what her options are for this pregnancy and learn how not to get pregnant again until that's what she wants to do. She's got to talk to someone who knows a lot more about this than I do."

"Right," Deanie says.

"Of course. Well, it comes out that Annalinda *has* talked to someone. Someone from a group that calls itself 'Pure Love.'"

"Ah-oh," Deanie breaths, wary now: "Is that one of those abstinence-only groups—True Love Waits Until After the Wedding to Get Busy?"

"Exactly," Madeline sighs. "It's one of those groups that sends what it calls 'teachers' all over the country, booking itself into high schools and staging sort of pep rallies for virginity, getting kids to sign pledges that they won't have intercourse until they're married. There was a rally like that at my high school when I was a junior"—Madeline shakes her head—"Mom wasn't going to let me go. I had to beg her. All of my friends were going and I really wanted to go along—it was a social event; I didn't want to miss out."

"I remember that."

"Of course you do. I came back from it insisting that everything you and Mom had told me about how to protect myself from getting pregnant, or getting a venereal disease, was wrong. What did you guys know about sex, right?"

"You were a little haughty for a week or so…"

"Oh, I was *so* jerked at Mom," Madeline laughs, remembering. "She made me promise that if she let me go to the rally I wouldn't sign anything. 'You can't make people wait until they get married to have sex! Not unless you want the average age of marriage to drop to eighteen! You've got college ahead of you, and you're talking about law school, Madeline—What? Are you going to wait to have sex until you're out of law school? Not very likely, and it's not healthy—no healthy person can wait to have sex until they're in their mid-twenties, for heaven's sake!'"

"If I'm remembering right, you were thinking about becoming a nun back then…"

"And *never* having sex," Madeline confirms. "But that's the point, isn't it? A person should have all of the information she needs to make her own personal decisions about what's healthy for her. I can't imagine anyone who would disagree that it's a good idea to wait until you're not only biologically ready to have sex, but emotionally capable of understanding what having sex will mean for you. As it was, I waited until I was twenty, and that was pretty much the outside limit for my personal health."

Deanie laughs. "But, sweetie, what does this have to do with your client? Annalinda?" she asks when she's recovered herself.

"'Pure Love,'" Madeline says. "'Pure Love,' like the group that came to my high school, doesn't give people the information they need to make healthy choices. All they talk about is the virtue of abstinence, which of itself, as we've just decided, isn't a bad thing. But for so many teenagers, 'Pure Love' is the only thing approaching sex ed that they're going to get. Schools don't have the money to provide their own, more comprehensive sex ed programs because, if they teach anything other than abstinence, they aren't eligible for government funding. Kids like Annalinda, who don't have the advantage I did of a mother and other grown-ups who'll give them the straight facts, have no way of knowing what to do when they get carried away in the heat of a hot opportunity. They let themselves get carried away because no one's helped them learn how to evaluate very real and very wonderful physical responses. Beyond telling them that they have to deny those responses until some unknowable future wedding date, these kids have nothing to go on. So I'm suing 'Pure Love'..."

Deanie is nodding, slowly. "But, Mad, I've read about this. It's not unusual for a kid to get caught up in the energy of a virginity rally, peer pressure, and sign her sex life away and then renege when the heat is on. You're suing 'Pure Love' on behalf of your client—but how can you hold 'Pure Love' responsible for your client breaking a pledge that wasn't worth the paper it was printed on in the first place? What's your legal angle?"

"I'm getting to that." Madeline untucks her feet, as if she's going to need to be more expansive as she explains this part. "What groups like 'Pure Love' do is more than simply withhold information about sex beyond abstinence. It's much more damaging than that, and I know this first hand, remember, because I've been to one of their rallies. They don't merely recommend abstinence; they try to remove any other human possibility. Not only don't they offer a contingency plan, they lie to kids so the kids believe they have no other option but abstinence. Case in point: when I asked Annalinda why she and her boyfriend didn't use a condom to prevent this pregnancy she just looked up at me and said, 'Why? He don't like the way they feel and they don't do no good anyway. Why bother?'

"Annalinda believed the 'Pure Love' people when they told her that the most inexpensive, accessible, reliable form of birth control available to her wouldn't do her any good anyway, so why bother with it?"

"And now she's pregnant."

"And I think that the 'Pure Love' groups, these people who rake in billions of tax dollars from the federal government for going around giving false information to teenagers, ought to pay for their lies. There ought to be repercussions to them for playing fast and loose with the truth.

"I've got everyone from condom manufacturers to family physicians to professional educators to clergy lined up to testify about things like the negligible failure rate of condoms, how undeniably effective they are in preventing pregnancy and the transmission of STDs. On the other hand,"—Madeline actually lets herself snicker—"I've got the 'Pure Love' brochure where it's written in black ink that 'Condoms don't work' and about twenty kids so far who went to the same rally that Annalinda attended who are willing to take the stand and tell how the rally leader stressed that point—condoms break and condoms slip and sperm can travel right through condoms, have you ever heard such garbage? This is the kind of disinformation that groups like 'Pure Love' spread routinely. 'Pure Love' spoon-fed Annalinda misinformation that directly resulted in her getting pregnant and I want 'Pure Love' to cough up the money their lie is going to cost her—her medical expenses as well as every penny it's going to take for her to raise the kid she's going to have because some fool told her not to bother with a condom."

Deanie is nodding furiously, not because she's got a mouthful of pastrami this time. This time she can't speak because she is astonished.

"I'm not done." Madeline wags a finger. "I want every group like 'Pure Love' to pay out to every kid who's suffered because of their lies. Every girl who's gotten pregnant. Every boy who's become a teenage father. Every kid who's contracted an STD because someone told him that using a condom wouldn't make any difference anyway. All the fifteen-year-olds who've screwed up their entire future just because they got carried away and screwed each other. Every kid who's got a screwed up life because Mom was still in high school and didn't have the wherewithal to take proper care of him. These abstinence-only people have institutionalized lying to our nation's teenagers"—Madeline clenches her fists—"so we have got to *break them*. You and I and the Pope and the Supreme Court can go round and round about the options that Annalinda may or may not have now that she's pregnant, but there's a good case to be made that she got pregnant because some people confuse being pro-life with being pro-stupid. Anti-information. They told her a lie and 'Thou shalt not bear false witness' is a Commandment, too; these people are trashing it."

Madeline's got her fingers locked together so tightly Deanie worries that they are going to start turning blue.

"I know it's a wild dream," Madeline says, making an effort to compose herself. Scooting herself back from the edge of her chair and shaking out her hands. "I don't know if I can win even this first case. But what I can do is put pressure on these groups. Hit them in their pocketbooks. Take the case to the media and expose their trash talk for what it is—and if people aren't moved by the faces and the stories of these kids who are made to suffer for the likes of 'Pure Love's' lies, maybe they'll be enraged by what it's costing them in tax dollars to have the highest rate of teen pregnancy in the industrialized world. Maybe all that will really ever move people is money and, if that's so, then I want some 'Pure Love' money for Annalinda and that baby she's going to have in a few months."

Deanie is nodding. Madeline's passion has made it hard to breathe, as if Deanie was the one who'd been speaking so fast and fervently. She has even started to sweat and she doesn't think it's entirely because of the blazing sun. "You keep on dreaming, Mad," Deanie says. "Dream big. If more people dreamed big and wild the way you do, we could save the world."

THE BAKULA HOUSEHOLD has quieted down since lunch. Jill has quieted down, the list of items on her legal pads checked and rechecked so even she can't find one more task to assign to anybody. The art major is in the dining room working diligently on the place cards and Mary, who unexpectedly knows a thing or two about calligraphy, is helping her. Chuck is riding the mower over the front lawn and Mr. Kuznicki is weed whacking around the flowerbeds. Mrs. Kuznicki is reading a Dr. Seuss book to Cara on a sofa in the living room, hoping she'll fall asleep—that a nap will keep her from being cranky through the rehearsal tonight. Trick and Beth are still trying to hang the curtain back up in the family room, Beth subdued by beer and still trying to boss the operation, Trick resuming the silent submission that even Deanie doesn't think is so strange anymore. Allison is sitting on the plaid sofa in there with them, fashioning bows from lengths of the tulle that had draped the deck the night of the bridal shower, securing the knots with tight, small stitches, readying them to hang on the ends of the pews in the church. The Osics have left to go to Bastioni's and pay for the rehearsal dinner, and most of the others have left, too—Chas and the groomsmen to pick up their tuxedos; Madeline's girlfriends out on a quest for plastic stemware and a bottle of good champagne to stock the back of the classic white Bentley, the rental of which is their wedding day gift to the newlyweds. The bride and groom have gone to meet with the photographer, a man known as much for the artistry of his work as for his petulance—he was the couple's enthusiastic choice and Jill has had to make the decision not to let herself be overwhelmed by tales of his hurtling lens caps at groomsmen who don't assume a pose as immediately as he decrees. The house is quiet, orderly, and the labor of its inhabitants is faithful; Jill has gone up to her bedroom to lie down for a while.

"Hey. Deanie?"

Deanie turns away from the dishwasher she is stacking, from the last of the lunch dishes in the sink. "Hey," she replies before it even registers that it is Rob Tedesco standing in the dining room archway. "Ohmigod!"

Rob looks—to Deanie's delight—really great. He's put on a few pounds over the years, as they all have, but his khaki pants still hang deliciously from angular hipbones. Deanie has such an abrupt vision of the boxer shorts underneath that she almost gasps; thankfully Rob puts down his travel bag and makes his way around the island to greet Deanie with a hug before any sound can escape.

Rob's embrace is sweet, and Deanie returns it smoothly though the conversation that follows is awkward for a few moments, a dredging of memory to decide when was the last time they saw each other, which Kuznicki-Bakula function last brought them together, Chas's high school graduation or Jill and Chuck's silver wedding anniversary? Rob doesn't make it to all of the affairs as Deanie does; he's had his own family affairs to attend, two kids, nearly nineteen years of marriage followed by a nasty divorce. It seems as if Rob is going to tell Deanie the reasons that his divorce was so nasty, so Deanie offers him lunch.

"A sandwich? You must be starved after the plane trip. And it's almost three o'clock in the afternoon."

"No, but I'd love a beer."

"Keg's right there." Deanie reaches into the cupboard over the sink to hand him a beer glass. When he turns around to pump the keg, Deanie watches the muscles working under his blue broadcloth shirt.

"WE DON'T DO that in *my* church," Father Cielinksi is saying. "No, no, no, the men do not stand at the altar waiting for the women to come down the aisle to them, like they're diners waiting for the meat platter, oh, no, no. Groom, groomsmen, who's the best man? Dad, that's right. All right, Dad is best man. Best man, groom, mother-of-groom, take groom's arm to walk him down the aisle, Adam, don't forget to kiss your mother before she takes her seat in the pew tomorrow. Now, ladies and gentlemen of the bridal party, come on, come on, pair up by height, line up, bridesmaids and their escorts, then matron of honor, Jill—oh, holy hell, Jill, Dad is best man so we're a man short, well, then, you'll just have to walk up the aisle solo, that's all right, hummm? Sure it is, now Cara, our little flower girl, honey, you'll be strewing the rose petals as you walk, one or two with each step, not entire handfuls, all right? It's only symbolic, after all, and bride and father, that's it, don't look so scared, Chuck, your daughter's finally making an honest man out of her live-in lover." Father Cielinksi chortles into the silence that greets his comment. "Oh, come *on*. As if we all don't know they're lovers—get a grip."

Deanie sees Madeline dig her fingernails into her father's arm.

"Ouch."

Madeline hisses under her breath. "Jeez, Dad, *Father Cielinksi*. Gram and Pop are right over there!"

"Go, go, go," Father Cielinksi is insisting, waving the procession down the aisle toward the altar. "Groomsmen line up to my right"—he gestures extravagantly with his right arm—"lovely ladies of the bridal party," he says and makes a matching gesture with his left arm.

Allison is attaching the tulle bows to the ends of every pew with satin ribbon. Rob is holding the fabric in place while she secures the knots and he smiles at Deanie as she makes her way around them to the altar.

"Pay attention," Father Cielinksi scolds her as he breezes past. "The faster we get through the rehearsal the faster we all get to Bastioni's. I'm simply *starving*."

Father Cielinksi, Deanie thinks unkindly, is as flamboyant as any reveler she's ever seen in the Castro. He spins himself into place on the altar so his skirts swirl around his ankles. Next to him, Father Paul, the parish's old priest, the sweet old man who Deanie is accustomed to seeing leading services in this church, looks absolutely dour.

Father Paul—who is called Father Paul because even the parish's oldest Poles can't wrap their tongues around all the consonants strung together in his last name—is taller than Father Cielinksi by a good seven inches, and outweighs him by at least fifty pounds, but he shrinks under the younger priest's direction. He's come out of retirement to help perform this wedding for the young woman to whom he has given the sacraments of baptism, first communion, and confirmation; Madeline made a special entreaty, and travel arrangements to get him here from his retirement home in Scranton and, even after all of that fuss, he seems content to let his replacement take the lead.

"Walk. Just *walk*, Madeline, slowly but only walking nonetheless," Father Cielinksi calls to her as Chuck leads her down the aisle, "none of that step/feet-together, step/feet-together nonsense, I never did understand that, that bridal shuffle thing. This is your wedding not a fashion show, although, sweetheart, you do look lovely. But just walk, all right?"

Madeline walks, slowly. Stately. Holding on to her father's arm and a half step behind him, to stay out of the way of his braces, which is the only reason she was doing anything like shuffling in the first place.

"That's right, m'dear," Father Cielinksi encourages as Chuck and Madeline draw close to him. "Kiss your father, and now, Dad, take Madeline's hand, that's right, and Mom,"— he crooks his finger at Cecelia Osic—"take Adam's hand and now Mom and Dad join your children's hands together. Give them to each other. Form this new family."

There is a moment of breathlessness in the church, utter silence as Madeline and Adam look at each other and realize that this is the first time they have been acknowledged as their own family unit, the two of them, alone and together, and it makes each of them smile and stand a little more erect.

And then Deanie's phone rings. The chords of the *Hallelujah* chorus seem to bounce in the holy quiet of Madeline's moment with her groom. To vibrate the richly stained glass windows.

"Fudge," Deanie scolds herself, hurrying from the altar toward the back of the church where she's left her purse, Father Cielinksi calling after her testily, "Oh, Handel, how marvelous. I didn't realize he was to be among tomorrow's musical selections."

BASTIONI'S BANQUET ROOM is aglow with candlelight. Clusters of votives surround the terra cotta cherubs on the tables, and fat, squat candles are tiered in the room's massive stone fireplace. The lights seem to flicker in time with the soft jazz playing in the background, making the room's stone walls feel warm and cozy. The aroma of the feast Lo has made for them wafts from nose to captivated nose. Scattered around the room, making four points of a circle around the dining tables, are food stations—a raw bar, a salad bar featuring greens as well as fruits and rounds of cheeses, a pasta station where Lo's assistant stands ready in front of two gas burners to make sauces at each guest's request, carbonara or vodka-tomato. Lo herself, buttoned into her pristine chef's jacket, stands by the base of the tavern's original staircase where prime rib sizzles under a heat lamp, sharpening her carving knife. Father Cielinksi leans over her cutting board, closing his eyes and inhaling dramatically. He reaches two fingers to pick a taste from the end of a roast, licking his fingers lavishly and murmuring his appreciation as he chews. He swallows and his hand moves over the roast for another nip and Lo says to him, "Father, I hope you're not thinking of touching my meat with those fingers now that you've had them in your mouth." Deanie winces when she hears Lo's gravelly words and everyone, including Father Cielinksi, his face indignant with innocence, pretends not to have heard.

"Allison!" Deanie is relieved to see Chas's girlfriend at the bar next to her, to have an excuse for an immediate diversion from Lo and the thieving priest, and she has been trying to waylay the girl all day now anyway. "Allison, I read the stories you dropped off for me."

Allison smiles and blinks, pleasure and anxiety. "And?"

"Honey, that's good stuff! Your characters are real people, and I want to follow them wherever they go, and I felt so satisfied at each ending. You know what you're doing. You're a writer."

Sometime during this short speech, Deanie doesn't know when, Allison has reached out and taken Deanie's hand to steady herself. Deanie realizes what she has said has landed on Allison's ears as a benediction. She feels Allison squeezing her fingers. "That's all I've ever wanted to be," she says.

The purity of Allison's wish makes Deanie dizzy. "Allison," she blurts out, now steadying herself, "would you like to come and work for me?"

Allison blinks again, this time in bewilderment.

"Just for the summer. My assistant, Layla, is up to her ears and we need someone for a few months to help us through the bottleneck. There won't be a great deal of creative work, a lot of typing and filing and organizing. That sort of thing." Deanie thinks. "On the other hand, you're a sure-footed writer, so the job could possibly become as creative as you yourself make it." Deanie smiles when she's through talking. She'd had no intention of asking Allison to come and work for her but, now that she has, it feels right.

"Yes!" Allison's fingers tighten on Deanie's. "Yes, of course! Thank you!" Deanie is concerned, for a moment, that Allison will start jumping up and down in glee. Instead, she becomes very serious. "Deanie, this is a tremendous opportunity for me. But, California? Where would I live while I'm there?"

Deanie winces, a small moue she hopes Allison doesn't see. The thought flits through her mind: *Fudge.* She had not thought through this offer before she made it and now she has no choice but to offer the girl a home as well as work. She has just invited one more person to populate the house where too many people already circle around her, require her attention and time and good humor.

Almost as immediately as it is completed, however, this thought is replaced by another one: Every time she goes back to Napa after a visit to Lenapi, it takes her a week to readjust to peace and quiet. After a visit in Jill's bursting, buzzing household, her own house feels empty and it takes her days to feel as if she's filling it up again. Both Layla and Mrs. Beech have complained in the past that whenever Deanie returns from a trip to Pennsylvania their lives become a whirlwind, Deanie whipping up out of thin air projects and problems for them to solve until she settles back down into her routine. Perhaps, Deanie thinks, after all of this wedding week's celebration, it will simply be too sad—too hard—to fill her house back up and for this reason, or for another reason she doesn't even know, she wants Allison as much as Allison wants this job.

Deanie takes Allison's hand in both of her own. "Why, you'll live with me, of course." Then she untangles her fingers so she can telephone Mrs. Beech and tell her to get the guest room ready.

THE BAR TONIGHT, probably because Jill isn't in charge of it, is a simple one. There is a lemony, grassy sauvignon blanc from California's Central Coast, and a fruity syrah from Sonoma, sodas for those who don't want wine and apple juice for Cara. "Does everyone have a glass of wine?" Madeline is asking, taping her spoon on a water goblet at her table. "Does everyone have something to drink? Get something to drink."

"Hold on."

"Almost."

"Where's my glass? I had a glass of white wine right here a minute ago."

There is a shift to the bar as the guests answer the bride, move to comply with Madeline's wishes. Deanie asks for a glass of syrah and gets out of their way.

"Got to go get my soda," Trick says to Lo, who she's been talking to since she walked into the banquet room, a conversation Deanie noticed and thought was out of the ordinary. Between Lo's bristly terseness and the reticence Trick seems to have taken up again, she can't imagine what they've been saying to each other. Deanie watches now as Trick takes her leave from Lo, swinging gaily from the newel post of the old staircase. "Jesus, Trick," Deanie hears Lo say, "that banister's been there for a hundred and fifty years, can you try not to rip it out today?"

Trick doesn't acknowledge Lo's comment, but Deanie sees the wind fail her, her shoulders fold, the way she slinks up to the bar to ask for a glass of Seven-up.

"Does everyone have a drink now?" Madeline asks, tapping again on the goblet.

The guests, forty or more, Deanie guesses, gather around the tables. Chuck and Father Paul are sitting next to each other at a table near the bar, Chuck's braces and Father Paul's walker leaning side-by-side against the wall. Mike Osic is sitting at Chuck's other side and Father Cielinksi, who has been nibbling at the cheese display, gathers his skirts up out of his way to hurry to join them.

When everyone's attention is focused, Madeline puts her hand on her soon-to-be-father-in-law's shoulder and sits down next to him, curling a leg under her girlishly, demure again now that she's circled the wagons for him.

"Friends," Mike Osic begins, "and family. Welcome. Your child's wedding is one of the most joyous, more *sobering*"—he winks pointedly at Adam—"events of any person's life. As Father Cielinksi pointed out at rehearsal, tomorrow is a day when we not only join together two people we already love, we witness the creation of something entirely new to the world—a new family. Until rehearsal tonight, the toast I was going to give at this dinner revolved around welcoming Madeline, who we know well and love dearly, to our family. I feel now that it's more appropriate to say to this young couple—Son, Madeline"—he turns to the bride and groom and lifts his glass of white wine to them—"I know I'm speaking for all of the parents here when I say that our pride in having raised such fine young people knows no limits. The love in your hearts, and the strength of your characters, give us the faith and confidence that your new family, this new part of the world that you will make together, will be as strong and loving as you are yourselves. My job tonight is to remind you that the families you came from will always be here to support you in times of sadness, and celebrate with you in times of joy, and then to step out of your way."

When Mike Osic is finished with his speech, there is not a dry eye in Bastioni's banquet room, least of all Deanie's. Beth touches her wine glass to Deanie's and whispers in her right ear, "Mike Osic has certainly redeemed himself for making me suffer through that demonstration of his golf swing this afternoon."

Rob, who is standing on Deanie's other side, leans in to her left ear and says, "I almost forgot the Crying Bridesmaid— are we in for a repeat performance this wedding too?" He pulls a crisp white linen handkerchief out of his back pocket and hands it to her.

Deanie snorts a laugh into Rob's hankie. "No, no. I'm much more mature now. I'm in much better control of myself." She says this believing that, after Mike Osic's toast, the party will begin and any further tear jerking won't take place until the wedding day itself. She believes she's safe for the time being.

She is wrong.

Mike Osic bends to hug Madeline, and then leans over his son to kiss him on top of his head—a kiss he lingers over for several seconds, his eyes closed, his mouth pressing on Adam's head, his nose lost in the deep brown mop of his son's hair. He lingers for a moment and then he grips his son's shoulder heartily and brings his own emotions back under control. He releases Adam's shoulder and stands again, raising his voice to regain the guests' attention. "Everyone. Everyone! Listen

up. Before Father Paul offers a prayer, Madeline has something she'd like to say."

Madeline rises, eager and shy. She is used to speaking in
public, of course, capturing the curiosity of an entire court-
room, arguing and objecting. Here, in Bastioni's banquet
room, she is less sure of herself, tempered not by the impor-
tance of what she has to say—she says important things every
day to her clients and colleagues and the judges who have
the last, binding word—it's the moment that has moved her,
the once-in-a-lifetime moment of speaking to a room full of
people who are beloved to her, on the eve of her wedding to
her beloved.

"Thank you," Madeline says to the man who will shortly
be her father-in-law, and then she looks around the room, at
the faces looking back at her with expectant smiles. "Thank
you all. Thank you all for being here. For coming long dis-
tances, or short ones, too, to be with Adam and me on our
wedding day."

Madeline looks at Adam, catches him beaming at her. It
helps her relax into the words she wants to say.

"The most important thing to us, as we planned what kind
of a wedding we were going to have, was that all of you would
be here. Father Paul. Father Paul has blessed every passage of
my life"—she turns to the elder priest—"and I am so grateful you're here to bless my marriage."

Father Paul's heavy eyelids blink slowly in acknowledgement. "There are some things that are simply tradition," he
laughs.

"Exactly," Madeline teases him back. "Adam and I decided
to honor a lot of traditions on our wedding day. It feels right
to us to make a procession down the aisle of the church,
and exchange vows in your company, and even to have a

silly-fancy cake to cut—to do the same things ourselves as our parents did on their wedding days and make our own link in the chain of memory."

Murmurs of approval float around the room, flicker and flare like the candles' light.

"One of the things we did that was a little untraditional," Madeline continues, "was the way in which we decided to make up our wedding party. I have to tell you, it all started when I asked Adam who he was going to choose to be his best man and he told me that his dad was the best man he knew. Our choices then became clear."

Madeline raises her glass of wine and uses it to gesture at Jill who is seated across from Father Paul. "Mom, my matron of honor." Madeline's eyes move around the room to locate Mrs. Kuznicki at a table, Cara curled up in her lap. "Gram. And Auntie Beth. Sister Mary. Auntie Trick. Auntie Dean." Madeline picks each of them out of the crowd, lifting her glass as she says each of their names. "You are the best women I know. Your love and your care, your grace and your wisdom, your strength and your humor have nourished me all of my life. Since I was a little girl, you are the people I've watched to figure out how to be a woman myself. I've followed your examples, and your advice, and I'm so proud and grateful to have all of you to walk behind at the church tomorrow."

There is no sound when Madeline finishes speaking. No one moves a glass to her lips. It takes several seconds, in fact, for anyone to resume breathing.

Then Father Paul puts the glass he's been holding up in acknowledgement of Madeline's toast back down on the table and begins to clap. Madeline blushes furiously—beautifully— as the rest of the people gathered in the room join with him. They clap and clap and smile and laugh and throw out cheers and toasts of their own—"To Marilyn," Vic shouts over the applause. "Woo hoo," Chas bellows and Beth, though the toast is for her, too, echoes, "Woo hoo!" "Jillie, Jillie, Jillie," Chuck chants likes he's at a football game spurring on the quarterback until Adam stands, his voice rising above all of the others: "To all of you, for whatever hand you had in making Madeline into the woman who wants to marry me! Tomorrow! Woo hoo!"

Then, at last, glasses are raised, and clinked, and drunk from, and the party begins.

Chapter Twenty

2004

*D*EANIE HAS BEEN IN AIRPORTS, ABOARD
planes, fumbling through customs and
following a snowstorm in to Pennsylvania for thirty-eight
hours. Straight. She has cramps in her legs, a crick in her
neck, and what feels like fur on her teeth. Jill is waiting for
her in the main lobby of Lenapi Hospital when she arrives.
"How is she?" Deanie asks. "*Where* is she?" she wants to know
as Jill leads her to a bank of elevators and pushes the button
for the I.C.U.

"She's stabilized. They're just waiting for a bed to open up
so they can move her to a regular room," Jill answers, dis-
pelling Deanie's alarm at being led to the Intensive Care
Unit, but not her general anxiety. Part of Deanie still doesn't
believe in the event that has made her gut wrench the whole
way back from Africa.

"I can't believe Trick would do this. It had to have been an accident."

Jill holds the elevator door open, looking at Deanie with a sort of slow, desperate burn.

"All right, all right," Deanie moans. She presses her fingers into her eyes and then uses them to brush her hair out of her face. She sees the greasy, disheveled mop on her head reflected in the elevator's aluminum panels and she doesn't care at all. "Why is she here, Jill? Why did she try to do this to herself? *Why?*"

THE ELEVATOR MOVES upward slowly, jolting at every floor.

"I don't know why," Jill says after a while.

After a while she adds, "I don't think Trick knows why. Or, if she does, she's not telling me. Maybe she's told her boys. You should have seen Nick and Cole. Of course they are wrecked by this. They're up there with her now. Oh, what does she think she's done to those boys now!"

On the fourth floor the elevator stops and its doors open to admit a harried nurse who turns to face away from Deanie and Jill as immediately as she enters the car. They wait until she gets off at five before they speak again.

"Jill?"

"What?"

"You need to forgive Trick for being a lousy mother. I don't think she had a real choice. She would have done things differently, she would have chosen differently herself. She was so young. And so sick, and she didn't even know. None of us knew."

"But we all know now, don't we?"

Deanie nods.

"Can we at least stop calling them 'boys'? They're in their mid-thirties now."

THE NURSES' STATION on the sixth floor I.C.U. is round, the patients' rooms pie-shaped cubicles surrounding this hub. The curtains are not completely drawn around Trick's bed and Jill and Deanie can see her sons standing to one side of it. They are tall men who look like their father, dark hair and flattened noses and kind brown eyes. Nick is leaning over his mother, holding a ball cap in one hand and with the other he is adjusting the blood pressure clamp that Trick says is pinching her finger. Cole is standing behind him, his hands in the back pockets of his jeans, a white felt cowboy hat on his head.

Only two people at a time are allowed to be in Trick's room, so Jill and Deanie wait by the nurses' station. While they wait Jill reaches into her out-sized purse and pulls out a miniature yellow legal pad with a pen clipped to it, and looks over the long list she's made there, adding to it, checking off other items. Jill isn't being efficient, Deanie knows, so much as she is occupying herself in a way that will bring her comfort in this terrible place. Jill's hands, Deanie notices, as she wields her pen, have grown thin. Her knuckles stretch the skin. Deanie can see the bones on the backs of her hands move as she writes, crosshatched with thick blue veins, dotted with pale brown spots that had not been there just a season ago. Her nails are unpolished, uneven, and her fingers are red, as if she's had them in a strong scrubbing solution without wearing rubber gloves.

Jill has been scrubbing, Deanie knows. Someone had to clean up Trick's bathroom, and Jill took the ugly job onto herself. She spared Trick's sons that horror. Spared Deanie.

Spared even the cleaning lady who comes in once a week to scrub Jill's own bathrooms. Deanie wishes she could take Jill's hands in her own. Hold them still and massage them with a soothing lotion that smells of sweetness, lavender or mint. Kiss them in gratitude. Paint them with henna in ancient designs so Jill will know how precious they are, the beauty they create.

Deanie wishes there was precedent in the American culture, a tradition, a ritual to perform to honor hands of love. She would right now throw her heart into such a performance and, perhaps, in the midst of the lovely duty, she would lose her own anger, the irritation with Jill that sits like a hard little pebble in her shoe, stopping her from taking confident steps, breaking her stride, making her limp. This irritation that Jill has lost faith in Trick, and for good reason, and now none of them, not Jill nor Deanie nor Trick herself, will ever be able to reclaim it.

Trick's sons put their arms around Deanie in shy, sorrowful welcome when they see her at the nurses' station. The words they say are few, and whispered—"Thank you for coming. It was a long way for you to get here." "Yeah, thanks." They are lost in a confusion of grief and fury, too, and someone has to take charge, so Jill goes over her list with them methodically—the disability claims that must be filed and the insurance paperwork that must be signed; the electrical bill that must be paid immediately so the heat at Trick's house isn't shut off and her pipes won't freeze; the toothbrush that must be purchased and brought to Trick, the first thing she's asked for, a good sign according to Jill, which makes Trick's sons smile, this slim evidence of recovery and these chores that will give them a part to play in it.

Jill assigns the day's tasks to Trick's sons and Deanie moves into the pie-shaped cubicle, to the bed, and takes Trick in her arms. Both of them sob dryly while they hold each other. It's frightening for Deanie to hold Trick, to feel her frailness, and it's frightening to step away from Trick, too, to look at her, the pale flesh and hollow eyes and the hair that seems too thin to cover her scalp. The bandages that wrap her wrists.

"I guess," Trick says, by way of thanking Deanie for being there, "I've really put a crimp in your travel plans. I guess I've really put a damper on everyone's plans."

Trick's voice, when she speaks, is soft. Hoarse. Her words as inappropriate as any others she has ever used to ask for forgiveness. And Jill has heard them, too. She has come into the room and put her big purse and her pen and her little yellow pad on Trick's tray table and she is standing there as if she has words of her own to say in reply but they are lost in the depths of the purse, or her stomach, or the emotions even stalwart Jill cannot, in this moment, wholly possess.

"Why?" Deanie says to Trick quietly. "Why?' she asks, not a demand but a plea.

Trick turns her head into her pillow. Wiggles the finger that is clamped in the pincers of the blood pressure monitor.

"Because," she says and Deanie and Jill both lean forward, imperceptibly, to hear her. "Because I am fifty-two years old and I have fucked up every one of those years. I have no real family. I can't keep a job. I hurt my friends… I figured I could either go on hurting people, or just get it over with all at once. One big hurt. Save everyone the trouble to come."

Trick's words touch Deanie. Stab her. She knows what it is to evaluate life at its midpoint. She knows the regrets that can chase after dreams in the night, even when those regrets don't involve lost children. Lost dignity. A life whose work has been sacrificed to the work of merely staying well. She knows that fifty-two is a dangerous place.

"Bullshit," Jill says.

Both Deanie and Trick look up at her.

"You did this because you stopped taking your pills again."

Jill, who takes pains to be kind, who is in possession of kindness, and heart, and herself, shakes her head and wags her finger. Her eyes don't blink, staring hard at Trick and then at Deanie and then at Trick again. Her mouth is set in a thin line between sorrow and cruelty.

"You did this because you stopped taking care of yourself," she says. "You stopped taking your pills, Trick. You can't do that. *You know you can't do that.* You know! And here is the bottom line—I'm telling you this because I love you. I love you so much that if I thought it would do any good I would slap you and slap you and slap you until I slapped it into your head once and for all: you can either pledge to your sons and to us and to yourself that you are going to take those pills every day for the rest of your life, or... Or..." Here Jill stops, struggling for a word, a phrase to convey the gravity of her despair. What at last comes out of her mouth is, "Or you will go through the rest of your life without ever getting your tit out of the wringer."

Chapter Twenty-one
Saturday

*T*HE GAUDY PINK AND ORANGE DRIVE-THRU sits on Lenapi's main downtown street, directly across from where the old Woolworth's used to be. Woolworth's red-and-gold sign is gone now, replaced by several less familiar logos as the big, old red brick building has been carved up to accommodate smaller business ventures—a dance studio, a computer repair shop, a rent-to-own furniture store. Only the furniture store has professionally executed signage, an awful purple plastic oblong that doesn't quite fit on the storefront, hanging over the tops of the old windows as if no one could be bothered to measure properly. The other businesses in the old Woolworth's announce themselves on sheets of plywood that have been lovingly, heartbreakingly, self-designed, hand painted in a corner of someone's garage;

couched optimism about their business' chances for success
has kept the owners from investing in signs that have a look
of permanence, of prosperity, a hedging of the bet that nearly
always certifies eventual doom.

Deanie tries but she can't remember what used to be on
the site where the drive-thru is now—perhaps the old haberdashery. Whatever old building it was it has been torn down
to make way for the new pink and orange one. Deanie is
tempted to pull the SUV through for a quick cup of coffee, restraining herself only with thoughts of the urn that is
most certainly waiting, steaming hot, on Jill's counter. She
is already later than she told Jill she would be, twenty minutes late; there isn't time for the drive-thru however much
there is need.

Coffee. Caffeine. Even with four Tylenol tablets working
their way through her system, toward the pain centers in her
head and her armpits, Deanie feels foggy. Unwell. Pissed off
with herself. She hasn't had a hangover since the tequila incident in 1982 and today, Madeline's wedding day, of all days
is not the day to screw up her track record. She remembers
being in Sal Turk's back room last night, the wedding party
crashing the teenagers' hangout, wanting, like the rest of the
revelers, to dance and Sal Turk's was the only game in Lenapi.
She remembers being disappointed that there was no live band
last night at Sal's, only a disc jockey, and someone—Beth?—
saying that, anyway, a disc jockey better suited their purposes:
they could ask him to play whatever good, old, familiar tunes
they wanted to dance to and they wouldn't have to suffer
through the homemade rhythms and melodies of some dippy,
hometown band practicing their original material in public.
She remembers doing the pony to *Mony Mony* with Jill, and
forming a high-kicking chorus line with Madeline and her

friends as Bob Seeger growled out, "Gimmie that old time rock and roll!" and shaking along with Tina Turner when Marilyn and Vic Kuznicki requested *Proud Mary*—"Our song," Mrs. Kuznicki laughed and, God knew, that was as much information as Deanie wanted to have about the matter.

She remembers someone—one of the boys? Josh, or George?—asking for the limbo, boys swinging their arms one way and their hips the other and singing, "Limbo limbo lim*bo*" in pathetic Rasta-accents, holding out the handle of an industrial mop one of them had fished out of Sal's broom closet. She remembers taking another surreptitious swallow from the flask Chas had stashed in the breast pocket of his jacket—Jack Daniels—and having a long debate with herself about whether the limbo was in any way actually Jamaican before Jill interrupted to pull her out on the dance floor. She remembers Jill throwing her arms over her head, bending deeply, shimmying under the mop handle and how she then threw back her own arms, well aware that of the two of them Jill had always been (and would always be) the better dancer and wondering why she was trying now not to let Jill get the better of her, go lower under the mop? She remembers, abruptly, that the third or fourth time she'd followed Jill through the limbo line she fell. Hit her head on Sal's concrete dance floor. Laughed and jumped right back up on her feet because the other dancers expressed immediate concern that she'd sustained an injury in the fall—they'd heard her head, they said, *crack*—and it makes her feel so foolish…

Oh, shit: she *remembers*.

Deanie groans. Waits for a traffic light at the end of Front Street to turn green. Squints in the sun and pushes her sunglasses more firmly against her nose. She is pleased that Madeline is going to have such a beautiful day for her wedding—"Happy the bride the sun shines on!"—but she wishes for just a little merciful cloud cover until she can get to Jill's, get a cup of coffee and a couple more Tylenol into her system, find out what was so all-fired important that it required this morning's summons to the Bakula house.

Her eyes start to tear in the sun and she squeezes them together, the better to filter out as much of the brilliant light as she can. She thinks, given the combination of her hangover and the irritation of the soapy residue still in her eyeballs and the stinging sun, she couldn't have put her contacts in even if she'd had all the time in the world. She resigns herself to squinting at everybody all day long. She looks at the traffic light, waiting for the green, through slits. Impatient, she shifts her eyes to the buildings on the corners, the white limestone that houses the Morning Star-Sentinel, the yellow granite pillars in front of Ty's dry cleaning shop, the sturdy stone of St. John's Lutheran Church, the red brick of the Elks Hall where, twenty-nine years and eleven months ago, Chuck and Jill celebrated their wedding.

The Elks had been, at the time, the only hall in town suitable for a wedding reception—the Farron House had been such an awful dump back then—and Deanie is pleased to see that the Elks is still a handsome building. Its bricks have been recently repointed, the white trim of its Federal façade freshly painted, the small lawn at its front is tidy and green. Through the two-story mullioned window over its double front doors she sees the crystal chandelier that still hangs there, gleaming in the sunlight. She remembers—a memory she hasn't dredged up since Chuck and Jill's wedding day— driving away from the Elks Hall with Rob Tedesco all those years ago and she remembers, unwillingly, that she drove away with him again last night.

"Where's Trick? I'm supposed to be driving her," Deanie remembers saying to Rob last night as they were leaving Sal Turk's, as she got into his car, as someone—Cecelia Osic?—thrust one of the terra cotta cherubs at her and told her to take it home as a favor.

"I took Trick home hours ago," Rob said, making room in the back seat of his car for the cherub, next to the cherub that Cecilia Osic had already insisted he take back at Bastioni's. "My God, is that woman carting these things all over town? Anyway, I don't think you're in any condition to drive anybody, Deanie."

"But, my car. I drove here tonight. I'll need my car tomorrow."

"Give me the keys, I'll get it back for you."

"How?"

"I'll drop you off at the hotel and then I'll walk back and get it."

"Really? Well, aren't you the hero, Rob."

Deanie had settled down then, into the passenger seat of Rob's red rental car, and they'd driven quietly for a block or more. She was amused, and a little moved, that after almost thirty years, she and Rob were once again leaving a wedding together. "Can you believe we're in our fifties now?" she had asked suddenly.

Rob had laughed. "All too well. Unfortunately, all too well."

"Oh, shut up."

In front of the Farron House Rob had gotten out of the car and come around to open Deanie's door for her. He handed her out of the car and let her cling to his arm on her way up the hotel's front steps.

"You'd better turn your engine off," Deanie told him when they got to the door, when she noticed it was still running at the curb.

"I'm going to go park it around back and then I'm going to go back for your car."

Deanie smiled and leaned into him. She spoke slowly, hoping she sounded light-hearted and flirtatious, trying not to slur her words, "Why don't you do those things after you come up to my room for a while?"

Rob, who hadn't been exactly smiling to start with, let himself frown. He pulled away from Deanie, a small, subtle step backwards but she knew to let go of his elbow. "Deanie…"

"Yes?" She stumbled on the hotel's top step, balancing herself by holding on to the porch's wrought iron railing, bracing herself to hear something she was not prepared to hear—Rob was seeing someone, or he was gay. Or he was impotent. Any of those things, she supposed, were possible but the bottom line was going to be that he was unable to take her up on her invitation to come up to her room for a while.

"Deanie," Rob continued. "It's one thing, don't you think, to have a one night stand when you're twenty-two. It's fun then. It's what you're supposed to do when you're young, sow your wild oats. It's a little pathetic to still be sowing them into your fifties."

Deanie was now the one to step away from him, suddenly sure-footed. Rob wasn't telling her he couldn't come up to her room, he was telling her he didn't *want* to.

"Don't get me wrong," Rob laughed, self-consciously, "I think you're even more attractive now than I thought you were when we were kids. You knock me out, if you want to know the truth. Which is why I can't sleep with you for just one night."

Deanie closed her eyes and gripped the porch rail. Felt the icy cold fingers of a headache massaging the back of her skull. Wondered if she'd remembered to pack aspirin.

"See," Rob went on like he was never going to shut up and go get her car, "I tried to have what Chuck and Jill have. A strong, happy marriage. I wanted that for myself but it didn't work out. I didn't get it. But I still want it. And I know you don't want it. You and I want very different lives. We're never going to be a couple. What's the point of one night of make-believe?"

Deanie nodded at him, though the motion made her head throb. "You're right," she told him. "You and I are very different people. See—now it's your turn to listen to me—making love with you wouldn't be make believe for me. I mean, first of all, there's a certain reality about the physical act. Beyond that there's the reality of pleasure given and received that would remain even after we'd gone back to different cities on different planes. There would be the reality that we would have *fun*. I'm sorry if you think that being in your fifties is some sort of cut-off age for fun. I feel really sorry for you, if you think that," she said to him, and then she pushed through the hotel doors and went up to her room.

Alone.

And she *had* felt deeply, condescendingly sorry for Rob. Right up until the moment this morning when she'd realized she couldn't get to Jill's house as quickly as Jill wanted her to because she didn't know where her SUV was parked. She called down to the front desk to ask them to ring Rob Tedesco's room. "Certainly, Ms. Morrow," the clerk replied and, then, just before she transferred the call, the clerk thought to add, "Mr. Tedesco left an envelope here for you last night. I think its keys? It's got 'Nineteen A' written across the front if it, that's a number for one of our parking spaces, anyway."

THE TRAFFIC LIGHT turns green and Deanie nearly squeals the tires, stepping irritably on the gas, pulling the SUV across the intersection and upsetting the cherub planter that Rob has, so thoughtfully, transferred to the floor in front of her passenger seat. The route she takes to Greentree Court does not have to take her past the old high school building, sheathed now in scaffolding so the construction crew can replace the old roof over the summer months, in time for a new crop of students to converge from elementary schools all over town in September, find each other and, in finding each other, come into friendships that will lead them through all of the life ahead of them. It doesn't have to take her past the first small house Chuck and Jill owned as a young married couple, its driveway crumbled now but just as steep, its front porch now screened-in so Deanie is unaccountably annoyed that she can't see the front door that was a portal during so much of her young adulthood, the entrance to what she had once considered home. It doesn't have to take her past the Kuznicki house with its squeaking screen door that she has banged through, she thinks, on more occasions than she has banged through any other door, the one house that has remained constant in her life experience; Mr. and Mrs. Kuznicki are out on its front porch as she passes. Mr. Kuznicki is sitting in a t-shirt and shorts on the wide glider nursing a mug of coffee and Mrs. Kuznicki is in a pink wrapper and slippers, watering the geraniums potted on the railing ledge. Deanie beeps and waves as she drives by. Her route doesn't have to take her by these places but the trip would not be shortened if she missed them, if she took, for instance, Clearview the whole way and passed by the old Victorian the Morrow family had once inhabited, places that contained other and less pleasant memories. Mrs. Kuznicki waves her watering can back at Deanie when she beeps, and Mr. Kuznicki salutes her with his coffee mug.

THE HOUSE ON Greentree Court is still quiet when Deanie arrives and lets herself in. It is still too early for anyone but the family to be stirring inside and they are all still upstairs, at their baths and showers. Deanie calls, "Good morning!" up the stairwell and makes her way quickly to the kitchen, the holy urn of caffeine, before anyone can call back down and waylay her. The coffee steams into her cup, black and strong, and Deanie sips at it gratefully, chooses a glazed donut from the excessive buffet set out on the counter—plates of pastries and sliced fruit, crispy bacon and sausage links, individual ramekins of baked eggs on hot plates. There is not, she notes, a single grain of confectioner's sugar anywhere to be seen; no one will have to wipe down the front of Adam's black tuxedo as, twenty-nine years and eleven months ago, she and Trick and Mrs. Kuznicki had had to fuss with Chuck's jacket, cleaning him up first with paper towels that only streaked the sugar, then with a dampened kitchen towel that picked up the streaks but left lint, finally blowing him dry with Jill's hair dryer and running a vacuum cleaner over his chest. Jill, Deanie smiles, has had the foresight to avoid that particular crisis.

"Dean?"

"Hey, Chas. Your mom called me to get here early. Is she coming down soon?"

Chas refills the cup of coffee he's carrying and shakes his head. "Not if you're lucky. Just a warning, but she's wound really tight this morning."

Deanie laughs. She had not expected less though she is as startled as Chas to hear Jill's primitive cry coming from the top of the stairs: "What are you doing down there, Chas! Roll out the carpet in the living room and put the furniture back where it's supposed to be, I can't believe you kids didn't have the sense to put that room back together before now. We're having wedding photos taken in there in less than an hour, and do something about the curtain in the family room. I don't hear you doing anything down there, Chas, and we have a wedding this morning!"

"What's wrong with the curtain?" Deanie asks as she and Chas jump to right the carpet and sofas in the front living room.

Chas shrugs his shoulders into unrolling the rug. "I don't know," he groans. "One of the tie-back things. Beth and Trick fudged with it all day yesterday. One of the little hooks that holds the tie-back came out of the wall and now the hole's too big and the hook keeps slipping out of it. I filled it with wood glue last night and even that didn't work."

"Duct tape," Deanie says as she slides an armchair back into its proper place.

Chas picks up one end of a sofa and waits for Deanie to lift the other. "Mom will kill us if we duct tape her woodwork."

Deanie hoists her end of the sofa. "Yes, but if we do it very cleverly, she won't know about it until after the wedding."

Chas laughs. Shakes his head. "Hey," he says, inching the sofa's feet back into old indentations in the carpet, "I hear you're taking Allison back to California with you."

Deanie smiles. She has to smile. If she doesn't put some effort into a positive expression the panic will show on her face. She, who can't even let housekeepers in to tidy up her hotel room, is taking on a roommate. Just last night a man refused to sleep with her because he knew that, while she might make room for him for one night in her bed, she will not make room for him in her life, and now she has agreed to let someone live with her. She is still not altogether comfortable with the prospect, the thoughtlessness with which she has backed herself into the arrangement and, on the other hand, there is a spontaneity about her invitation to Allison that she approves of, a quality of living with the opportunities of each moment that, it seems, she might have fleetingly captured for herself.

"It's just for three months," she says, shrugging at Chas. "And you'll come visit us, right?"

"Well, of course," Chas replies.

"Deanie!" Deanie and Chas's conversation is aborted by Jill's shriek. "I know you're down there! Are you ever going to come upstairs to talk to me!"

Chas raises his eyebrows, a comic show of tolerance for a mother who has gone infuriatingly, if not completely unaccountably, crazy. "Duct tape," Deanie reminds him, winking, and heads toward the second floor.

"Good morning," Chuck says to her on the stairs, hopping a step closer to plant a kiss on the cheek Deanie's raised to him. He's freshly showered, smelling of soap and Jill's kiwi-scented shampoo, wearing only his pajama bottoms. "She won't let me get dressed until I eat breakfast. Doesn't want me wrinkling my pants. I apologize."

"Oh, heavens, don't do that," Deanie tells him, taking in the naked torso, the muscles sculpted fine with years of using upper body strength to compensate for those things he can no longer do with his lower. "I think every woman should start her day looking at a pretty naked man."

"Jeez, Deanie," Chuck growls, blushing furiously as he passes her.

"'Morning, Auntie Dean," Madeline calls from the second-story landing. She is standing there in her bridal underpinnings, an ivory satin corset and stockings held in place with satin ribbons, Beth's blue garter around her upper right thigh and Adam's strand of pearls around her neck, her fuzzy yellow chenille bathrobe thrown over her shoulders in an attempt at modesty. She is standing in front of the full-length mirror in the hallway trying to fasten old-fashioned clip earrings onto her lobes. "Gram's pearls," she says. "She wore them for her wedding and they're my 'something old' and I can't get them to stay on."

Deanie leans into the embrace Madeline is reaching for. "You don't want them on until your hair and make-up are done anyway, do you? Wait until Mona gets here and has at you, and then I'll put them on for you later, OK?"

Madeline sighs, and laughs at herself. "I guess I'm nervous. Isn't that ridiculous?"

"It's your wedding day, Mad."

"That's why it's ridiculous to be nervous. It's absurd to be getting all undone about doing something I am longing to do. It's Mom," she confides, lowering her voice to a whisper, "making us all nuts. Go see if you can settle her down."

"OK. Yes, sure," Deanie says and heads toward the master bedroom, the direction in which Madeline is waggling one manicured forefinger, girding herself to scold Jill—to tell her to stop picking at her daughter and shrieking at her son and to let her husband get dressed if he wants to so they can all start enjoying this miraculous day. Deanie has worked up a good head of indignation in the short distance to Jill's bedroom door but when she finds her, standing over the sink in her bathroom, Deanie stops short.

Jill is in her underwear, dripping, and not only with the cold water she's got blasting full into the sink so she can splash it over herself. She looks up as Deanie enters. "I haven't had a hot flash in two years," she says desperately.

"Oh, honey."

Jill ducks her head into the sink, slapping the cold water down her back. "*Two years.* And, of course, today has to be the day the demon returns."

"Jill, sweetie. Here…" Deanie takes a cloth from the rack behind the bathtub and dampens it under the gushing faucet. "Try this," she says and lays it on the back of Jill's neck. "Doesn't that feel good?" she asks her friend, who is still hunched over the sink. "Breathe, too, Jill. You've got to breathe. Deep breaths."

Deanie can tell Jill is feeling relief. Her shoulders release as the cold cloth helps to cool the blood pulsing into her head. "Better?"

Jill grips the rim of the sink.

"Not better?'

"Trick called," Jill pants. "She says she's not coming to the wedding."

"What?"

"Will you go over to her place and see if you can talk to her and pull out whatever bug is up her ass before I have to tell Madeline and spoil her day?"

DEANIE TAKES A long leap over the missing step up to Trick's front porch and doesn't bother to knock before she pushes open the door. Inside, the air is thick with smoke, a Merit smoldering to its filter in an overflowing ashtray on the coffee table. The stink seems to penetrate directly through to the part of Deanie's head that hurts the most. Trick is lying on the sofa, her eyes closed, but her foot is *tunk, tunk, tunking* against an arm so Deanie knows she isn't asleep.

Deanie plants herself so she is standing over Trick's head, her legs rigid and her hands curled into fists, resting on her hips. "What is going on?"

Trick doesn't open her eyes to speak. "I'm not going to the wedding, that's all."

Deanie, who has never had Jill's gift for forcing people to conform to her will, feels herself deflate. "Why?" she asks, sounding even to herself as if she is whining the word. "Honey," she says, bending over to stub out the last of the life in the smoldering Merit butt, "*why*? What's wrong? Is it your meds? I know they make you groggy... Do you feel too groggy or sleepy or something? Is it your period? Do you still have cramps? Can I make you coffee?" Deanie asks this even as she sees the cup of it already on the coffee table, steam rising from its mouth so she knows it's fresh. "Maybe a bath to wake you up?" she asks weakly because she can see Trick is already bathed. Her hair is damp and her cheeks are shiny. The pads of her fingers are puckered and the aroma of Ivory soap rises up from the flannel robe Trick has wrapped around herself. Trick grunts, still without opening her eyes.

"All right, then, fine," Deanie says. Fresh throbbing in her head and the insistent ache in her armpits embolden her. "You explain to me why all of a sudden you've decided to throw a monkey wrench into Madeline's wedding plans. Explain that, please."

Trick grunts again. She *is* feeling groggy, disoriented, sorry for herself—none of which has anything at all to do with either her meds or her damned period—and she is angry, too, reminding herself to keep feeling the anger, how good it feels to be mad, how neatly the sensation of being pissed off penetrates the chemical haze and peels it back so she feels something more powerful than self-pity. She opens her eyes and glares up at Deanie. "You got good and drunk at the rehearsal dinner last night, didn't you?"

Deanie winces, unable to withhold a confession as she thinks anyone can probably see the punishing ache pulsating in her forehead. "So what?"

"Rob drove me home from Bastioni's. When you and all of the rest of them wanted to go out dancing and I wanted to go home, Rob drove me. I told him I'd just as soon walk, but he insisted."

Deanie cuts her eyes around Trick's dusty pink living room. "That's what you're upset about? That I couldn't drive you home last night?"

Trick laughs, a disgusted little *harrumph*. "Did you notice I wasn't at Sal Turk's? When you were dancing and carrying on, did you even notice I wasn't there? Or wonder where I went? Or how I got home?"

Deanie has to look away again. "And this is really why you're mad? You're going to punish Madeline because I got too drunk to drive you home?"

"No." Trick sits up abruptly, yanking the robe closed around her, stretching it over her knees. "I'm not 'punishing' anyone. I'm finally just allowing myself to realize I don't belong with you people."

Deanie staggers. She thinks she has to sit down. She flops on the end of the coffee table, facing Trick, and she can't stop herself from taking Trick's hands in hers even as Trick tries to shake them off. "What are you talking about? What? Are you really going to abandon us because I got drunk last night and..."

"Fuck you, Deanie." Trick bites her bottom lip. She thinks that she would like to cry—that if she hadn't forgotten how or if the medications would allow it, she would cry now and that would be a relief. Instead she lets her hands go limp—let Deanie hang on to the damned things if she wants to—and she tosses her head, thrusts her jaw defiantly and releases the grip her teeth have got on her lip so that she can speak. "I heard what Madeline said to you yesterday."

Deanie is bewildered. Madeline said a great many things to her over the course of the day yesterday.

"About fifteen-year-old girls getting pregnant and ruining their lives," Trick cries, exasperated when it's clear to her that Deanie really doesn't know what she is talking about. "Fifteen-year-old girls who get pregnant and ruin their lives, and ruin the lives of their children, too. Because that's what I've done, isn't it? That's what you all think I've done."

"Trick!"

"I had no business having those two babies. I was too young, and then I was too sick, and when I'm not sick, when

I'm on my meds like now, I'm only sick with regret for everything I put Nicky and Cole through, and the only thing I don't regret is that Dom took those boys away from me, that he wasn't too young and immature and stupid to do that even though I know everybody thinks I'm a rotten person for letting him, it was the best thing. It was the only thing!"

"We don't... We don't think that."

"I had no choice! I was sick. I'm glad Dom took the boys because what kind of life would they have had, growing up around a woman with her tit in a wringer all the time? And I love them! I wouldn't have been a bad mother if I hadn't been sick, because I love them! But I wasn't a bad mother only because I was too young, do you understand?"

Trick shakes her head hard. Mercilessly.

"I'm too confused. This is confusing! What I want to say, Deanie, is I know I'm not like you and Jill. I've let my life become a ruin, and you've tried to help me not to, but you couldn't and it's been a pain—*I've* been a pain—all along, for forty years I've just been along for the ride or, or, *worse*! I've just been a drag on both of you, and now Madeline wants to 'honor the women who raised her.' Deanie, I never did that! I couldn't even raise my own kids. What did I ever do for Madeline? I'm only included in the wedding party because I've been dragging behind you and Jill for forty years."

Deanie is crying by the time Trick stops speaking—fat, undignified tears leaking from each eye—and she is surprised that Trick is not. Trick's eyes are unfocused, a little wild, maybe, and bone dry.

"Is that what you think?" Deanie asks. She has the desperate impulse to scream, to do something abrupt and unpleasant to snap that wild look out of Trick's eyes. "Get up," she commands, standing herself. She has a death grip on Trick's hands so, while Trick resists, she has no choice but to give in. "Get up right now." Deanie pulls Trick away from the sofa, bullying her. Absolutely manhandling her. "Get upstairs and get your dress on. Get your shoes, and get the shawl Madeline gave you. We're going to Jill's right now and we're going to straighten this out and you're going to be in the wedding and don't even try telling me no."

JILL'S HOUSE IS controlled chaos, merry chaos, talking, jostling crowds of people and, even so, not everyone who is supposed to be here this morning has yet arrived. "Where's Jill?" Deanie shouts when she walks in the front door, at Allison who is standing over the ironing board pressing crisp seams into a pair of tuxedo pants.

"The last I saw of her she was in the kitchen, inspecting the groomsmen for wrinkles," Allison says, shrugging at the garment on the ironing board to indicate the result.

Deanie enters the kitchen through the dining room arch way, Trick submitting as meekly to the order to follow as she ever has to Jill's demands. Chuck and Mr. Kuznicki are standing beside the island, Chuck minus his trousers, his one mighty, shapely leg poking through the leg hole of a pair of blue boxer shorts. "You're seeing more of me than you ever thought possible today, Deanie," he laughs, dishing another bite of baked egg into his mouth.

Deanie doesn't even think to laugh back. "Where's Jill?" she asks again, but no one hears above the hubbub on the other side of the island: the young girls, Madeline's friends, all standing there with Beth, protesting when Beth tells them she isn't going to have any breakfast, that she *just* fits into her black satin dress, and the girls squeal in shrill disagreement,

"Auntie Beth, no, you look so beautiful!" and "You have such a womanly figure!" and "I wish I had curves like that!" Beth, amazed, asks, "Really? That's what you think?" She pats at the womanly curves she has always looked upon, privately, as simply *fat*. "Really?" she asks again, gauges the sincerity around her, then performs a quick inspection of Jill's buffet. She picks up a pastry, bites into it, getting Bavarian cream on the end of her nose and causing the girls to cheer.

The photographer out in the family room is calling out to the groom's family, arranging them in front of the bay window, the clean curtains, corralling the groomsmen, Josh and George and Mike Osic—who, Deanie sees, is also without his pants—"C'mon, Mike, I won't shoot below the waist until you get all of your tux back, all the men, line up at the window, just the men in the bridal party..." and Kelly Yocum, answering for the men, shouts out, "Wait, I don't have all of their boutonnières on them yet. Jesus!" Yelping as she punctures her finger with a straight pin, sticking the finger in her mouth to suck on it and staunch the blood so she won't get any on anyone's starched white shirt.

Cara in her gossamer dress, her hair gathered into two French braids and wound around her head and pinned there with two of Beth's rhinestone clips, is skipping between rooms, her basket of white rose petals hooked over her elbow, and she notes Deanie and Trick's entrance. Squeaking with glee, she runs to a long cardboard box that Kelly has placed on the plaid sofa, picking up two bouquets of white tulips trailing lavender ribbons and rushing headlong to deliver them to the bridesmaids who've just arrived. "Auntie Dean, Auntie Trick, these are your flowers! I get to give the flowers out to all the girls, Kelly said so! Here. Take your flowers and"—Cara squints her eyes and lowers her voice in fine imitation of her Bakula elders—"don't lose them before we get to the church."

"Thank you, honey," Deanie says, bending over to take both bouquets from the little girl. "Do you know where your Auntie Jill is?"

Cara nods sagely. "She went upstairs to try to get dressed again." The child adds, giggling, "She came down here to yell at Uncle Chuck about his pants *in her underwear!*"

"Her *slip*, Cara," Beth corrects, suddenly attuned, as if the sugar has helped her hearing. "She was in her slip, for fuck's sake, it wasn't as if she was running around in her bra and panties."

"C'mon," Deanie says to Trick, clutching both of the tulip bouquets in one hand and Trick's elbow in the other, pushing her ahead toward the stairs. "Jill," she calls as the two of them advance. "Jill, we're coming up. Trick and me."

"Oh, well, thank *God*," they hear Jill respond. "Trick's here."

"Here, J.R., cool yourself off with this."

Deanie and Trick arrive at the door of the master bedroom in time to see Mrs. Kuznicki hand Jill yet another cold washcloth. Jill stands in her slip and uses the cloth to wipe at her cleavage, her forearms, her armpits. "Fudge, fudge," she mutters, "oh, *fuck*, why can't I stop sweating!"

"You know what?" Mrs. Kuznicki asks her daughter. "If you'd only settle down a little, you'd stop flashing. You're the one who's working yourself up into this lather." She turns to Deanie and Trick. "You two deal with her. I need to go downstairs and see about Cara's hair. I don't like what Mona did with it," Mrs. Kuznicki confides on her way out of the room.

"Well, thank *God. Trick*," Jill says, as if she's accusing her of being the cause of the hot sweat pouring down her chest, flushing her cheeks crimson.

Trick closes her eyes and takes a step backward, ready to receive abuse or to bolt, it's not clear which, and Deanie tightens her hold on Trick's elbow. "We need to talk, Jill," she says. She tosses the tulip bouquets on top of Jill's dresser and takes Jill's elbow in the hand she has freed for this purpose, steering them both toward the unmade bed.

"What are you doing?" Jill is indignant. "My daughter's getting married in a few hours. I don't have time for nonsense."

"This isn't nonsense," Deanie assures her, giving them both a little shove so they plop down side by side on the rumpled sheets. "This is about our friend, Trick, whose needs, even at this pre-wedding moment, are slightly more urgent than yours, Jillie."

Jill looks back and forth, between Deanie and Trick, trying to decide with whom she is more furious. "Are you going to be in this wedding or not?" she demands of Trick.

"She is," Deanie answers for Trick. "Just as soon as you take a big, deep breath and do what your mother told you to do. Settle down. Settle down, it's a wedding not an audience with the pope and it'll hold for five minutes so you can tell Trick a story."

Jill, chastened, is still not in full possession of her enormous nervous energy. She actually makes the bed bounce as she insists, "*What story?*"

"One you've always told to everybody else but apparently never to Trick. The one where Trick and I arrive at the hospital after Chuck had his accident? Tell her *that* story, Jill, and don't condense. Tell her everything that happened."

Jill slaps the mattress, outraged. "Trick knows what happened that day! You both know! You were *there*, and why should we talk about that day *this morning*? Trick knows as well as you do that you two are the only reason I got through it."

Deanie nods reasonably. "Tell Trick again, Jillie. She forgot."

Chapter Twenty-two
1989

IT STARTED WITH A PHONE CALL. ONE HOT AUGUST morning at the innocent hour of eleven o'clock. Deanie was in Italy then, living in a small rented house in the heart of a village just north of Lucca. The house, both picturesque and medieval, had suited her for going on three years—it had a stone courtyard where she sat to work in mild weather, and to drink the strong local wines with lunch, and she had mastered the language well enough to no longer be merely a visitor among the villagers. She'd even made a few friends, though she was still considered a curiosity, the young American woman who wrote books few of them could read, and traveled frequently and, when she was in residence, took long, lone and energetic runs through the vineyards at the crack of dawn.

August was the month that her little Italian house suited her least, when the summer heat was at its annual peak. The dusty streets of the village and the twisted vines heavily pregnant with the year's harvest and the naturally cool stone floors of her home all seemed to steam and sweat like human creatures during these long miserable thirty days. Deanie had decided to forgo the last two hellish weeks of Tuscan summer and make an impulsive escape. She was packing her suitcase even before she'd decided on a destination—somewhere cool, and far away; perhaps a B&B somewhere on California's northern coast, some place in the world that intrigued her but where she had never been before. She was about to pick up her telephone, a heavy black plastic model that reminded her of the one that had been in her grandmother's kitchen when she was a child, call her travel agent, settle on the site of her August get-away, but the heavy black instrument rang of its own accord before she could lift the receiver.

Jill was on the other end of the line. Jill, her voice so thick with anguish that Deanie couldn't understand what she was saying. Jill making animal sounds. Jill screaming incoherently until Deanie screamed back, making Jill whimper and drop the phone.

Mrs. Kuznicki came on the line to explain that Deanie was needed in Pennsylvania.

IT STARTED WITH a phone call. Trick was in Texas, visiting her sons. The visit was ending the next day, and Trick was sad to be saying goodbye once again to the boys, but she was elated, too—the trip had been one of the most successful she had ever made to them. Dom and his new wife had allowed her stay in their home, doubling up the boys in

Nicky's room so Trick could have Cole's bed; there had been
no time wasted traveling between a motel or one of her brothers' houses before she could spend it with her boys. She'd
been on her meds for two months straight. Even Dom saw
how well and strong she was and had allowed her to borrow
his car and drive with their sons buckled in beside her. She'd
taken the boys—teenagers now, boys she didn't really know
anymore; Nicky could drive himself anywhere he wanted to
go—out for pizza, and to the movies, and to a speedway and
an amusement park and a rodeo and *the boys had wanted to
go with her.* There had been no cajoling, no bribery by Dom
on Trick's behalf to trick the boys into spending an afternoon
in her company. Granted, the activities she'd arranged, on
the advice of Dom's new wife, were ones that were innately
attractive to growing boys, but this was only an advantage
and not the reason her sons asked her every morning, over
her first cup of coffee, "Mom, where are you taking us today?
Can we spend the day with you again today, Mom? Mom, do
you have to go home on Friday, can't you stay another week?"

"Go ahead," Dom's new wife said to Trick, when they
were alone for a rare moment, dusk settling in, Dom still at
work and the boys in Nicky's room, Nick listening to music
through a headset and Cole in a chat room on the computer
Dom had just gotten for them to share. "Go ahead and call
the airlines. See what it would cost you to change your ticket
for next week."

The invitation was so unexpected Trick spilled the cup of
coffee she'd been drinking. It had been a blow when Dom had
told her that he was getting remarried and Trick wasn't sure
why; she harbored no hope that she and Dom would ever rec-
oncile and, except in a nostalgic sense, no desire either. Still,
she'd been wary of this woman, Naomi, jealous of her because

she was seven years younger than Trick, suspicious that she
would be a wonderful mother to the boys and usurp what little place Trick retained in their lives. That Naomi had turned
out to be Trick's advocate, even to the point of welcoming her
as a guest into her home, took Trick completely by surprise.

Surprise that delighted and humbled her.

"Are you sure, Naomi? I don't want to wear out my
welcome..."

"Trick, you're their mother. They love having you here. And,
anyway"—Naomi had actually winked in conspiracy—"it's
August. No school. If you weren't here with them think how
much trouble they could get in, with Dom and me both at
work most days. Consider that staying is doing me and Dom
a favor."

And, so, Trick and Naomi were waiting for the phone
to ring. For Dom to call with his final decision—would he
pay the fifty-dollar fee to change Trick's return trip ticket?
Dom was less enamored of the idea of extending Trick's visit
than the two women were, and he needed to debate it with
himself before he'd give his approval, and Trick wasn't sure
she should be hopeful that he would say yes because, when
Naomi had called Dom up at work to tell him of the plan, he
had grunted so loudly that even Trick had heard him. Trick
had not been able to choke down any of her meds since she'd
heard Dom grunt, heard his guttural, animal disapproval, and
she knew it was stupid stupid *stupid* not to take her meds now,
to stop them now, to think she would punish Dom for send-
ing her away by going crazy again, and yet the pills stuck in
her throat so not even two tumblers full of water could wash
them down. Her stomach was already in knots when the
phone rang. When Naomi handed the receiver to her there
was some confusion—"He wants to talk to me?"

"It isn't Dom."

"Who is it then?" Who would be calling here now, besides Dom, to tell her she had to go home? "Hello?"

"Trick, honey."

"Mrs. Kuznicki?"

"Trick, Jill asked me to call you. When are you coming back home? Because I think we need you here."

THE ACCIDENT HAD happened in the evening and it was already the second morning before Deanie and Trick arrived at the hospital. Not the Lenapi Hospital. A rescue team had spent two grueling hours trying to keep Chuck alive while all around him they cut and bent metal, extracting him from the mangled wreck that had once been his car, and airlifted him to a trauma center in Philadelphia. When she'd landed in Philly, Trick had made her way from her gate to the international terminal to meet Deanie, and Deanie had rented a car and they'd driven to the trauma center together though neither one of them would remember how they got there—how they came upon the directions to the place, who told them which roads to take and where to turn. Nor would they remember parking the rental car, or where they parked the rental car, or that they stopped in the main lobby of the Philadelphia hospital to ask how to get to the trauma wing. Instinct, intuitive knowledge, the intensity of their purpose, they would believe, moved them through the streets of Philadelphia, the halls of the imposing medical complex, toward Jill.

They found her in a small, corner waiting room on the fourteenth floor of the center, the top floor, the ceiling the only separation from the helipad where the EMTs had landed upon their arrival with Chuck. Every once in a while, in the course of the hours and days and weeks they would spend in that waiting room, they would hear the *whoop-whoop-whoop* of another helicopter coming in overhead for another landing and know they would have to include another anguished, anonymous family in the prayers—passionate and, soon, rote—in which Mrs. Kuznicki led them.

Jill was lying on her side on one of the room's orange vinyl sofas. She was wearing the same pair of white denim overall shorts she'd thrown on over a cotton pajama top the night the police had come to her door to tell her that her husband had been in a car wreck and was on his way, via helicopter, to this Philadelphia trauma center. Her wild curls sprouted from her head in great, unwashed kinks and knots. She wore no make-up, of course, and her skin was pale, shiny and clammy-looking. When Deanie, and then Trick bent to kiss her in greeting, they were startled by the heat coming off her cheek. She didn't sit up, or even speak when they greeted her, acknowledging their arrival only by pulling the red wool hospital blanket that was draped around her a little more snugly around her shoulders and sighing, a subtle settling to indicate that now all of her family were accounted for.

Now everyone who needed to be was with her, waiting.

Waiting.

Jill's colleagues and Chuck's; distant aunts and uncles and cousins from both sides of the family who Trick and Deanie could recall, vaguely, from one Kuznicki-Bakula function or another; Mrs. Kuznicki's friends from the LPGA and the CDA, Catholic Daughters come to wait, and to pray with the family for Chuck's intentions, that he would not be paralyzed, that he would not have suffered brain damage.

These were the concerns of Chuck's team of doctors—paralysis, brain damage. Should he live at all.

Trick and Deanie would ask later about the details of the accident; for now they had no need to know. For now it was enough to be in the waiting room, among the crowd of people gathered to wait with Jill; for being in the waiting room, at the hospital, meant that Chuck was still alive, and there was something hopeful to wait for.

Deanie took the last open seat in the waiting room, an inhospitably short length of cushion on the sofa opposite where Jill lay and Jill, in the only other moment of awareness she would have this hour, drew up her feet, slightly, to indicate that Trick could sit there, with her, in the space she'd made.

In the first half hour of waiting, the telephone, a chunky beige piece of plastic with no dial for outgoing calls that sat on a low table by Mrs. Kuznicki's turquoise chair, jangled maliciously. "Yes?" Mrs. Kuznicki answered it quickly. "No, Vic. No word yet. The surgeon told us he'd come right to us afterwards and he's not here yet so I guess Chuck is still in the operating room."

Trick and Deanie exchanged looks across the narrow waiting room; Chuck was in surgery. But Mrs. Kuznicki had told them both that Chuck was in surgery yesterday, right before they boarded their planes to come home. Could this still be the same operation?

They didn't ask.

At the start of the second full hour of waiting, Mrs. Kuznicki reached into her straw, basket-style handbag beneath her chair and fumbled her rosary beads out of it. *"Hail Mary, full of grace,"* she began, *"the Lord is with thee.*

Blessed art thou amongst women and blessed is the fruit of they womb, Jesus."

Jill shifted at her mother's words. She lowered her head, fishing under her heavy blanket, until her fingers closed around her own set of rosary beads. "*Holy Mary, Mother of God, pray for us sinners now and at the hour of our death. Amen,*" she joined her mother to recite, before they moved on to the next bead. "*Hail Mary, full of grace...*"

"*...the Lord is with thee...*"

One by one the others in the room took up the chant, passionate voices rising in rote, one of them professional, Father Paul who neither Trick nor Deanie had singled out among those gathered in the little corner room until they heard the rounded, stentorian voice, steady and strong, familiar to them from years of attending Mass and other church functions with the Kuznicki-Bakula clan, filling the ragged edges of everybody's soul with comfort and calm. Deanie joined in the intoning of the prayer, and Trick joined, and by the beginning of the third hour of waiting, at which time the rosary was completed, even the Protestants and the Jews and the one Buddhist in the room knew the prayers by heart as well as they knew the shared intentions of their hearts, their hearts that thrummed in time with Jill's heart, waiting.

Jill curled her fingers around the rosary beads and pressed them to her lips, kept them there, her eyes closed. In the hours and days and weeks ahead, Mrs. Kuznicki, who remained in that turquoise vinyl chair beside where Jill's head lay, would tell Trick and Deanie things about the accident—how it had happened (a drunk teenager running a red light), where it happened (at the turn into Shady Pines, when Chuck was on his way home from a fundraising dinner for the Lenapi Campus's women's basketball team). Mrs. Kuznicki would tell Trick and Deanie about the arrangements she and Mr. Kuznicki had hastily made for the care of their young grandchildren—Madeline, seven now, and Chas, just shy of five at the time—arrangements for the children's physical care (this morning at a hotel pool under the supervision of Mr. Kuznicki and Beth), and for their emotional care. How careful they all needed to be to tell the children only what was immediately necessary for them to know about their father's condition, a task generally left to Mrs. Kuznicki as no one else felt quite competent to toe the fine line she had drawn between hope and what the doctors considered real.

In the hours and days and weeks ahead, Deanie and Trick would find out that the teenager who'd drunk a six-pack-and-a-half of Stroh's Light and then run his 1974 third-hand huckleberry blue Ford 4x4 right into Chuck's six-year-old beige Dodge Omni had walked away from the scene of the accident without a scratch. They would find out that his parents were among the people gathered in the Kuznicki-Bakula waiting room at the Philadelphia trauma center. They would find out that he was one of the kids who'd hoped to have a place on Chuck's soccer team in the fall and that Jill could not care for the boy's future now but ended every prayer with a private plea that she would someday stop hating him.

"Are you thirsty, Jill?" Mrs. Kuznicki asked, moving forward in her chair and bending to retrieve the paper cup on the floor by Jill's head.

Jill nodded, pressing the beads onto her eyelids. She wasn't crying. None of them were. No one had yet found their way through shock to tears. Or, perhaps, the people in the waiting room wanted to weep but were not selfish enough to do so when Jill herself was gripping her equilibrium so ferociously. And maybe Jill was achieving this feat only because she had been sedated? Trick and Deanie glanced at each other, as if this possibility had struck them simultaneously, but they didn't ask.

"I'll go get her a drink, Mrs. Kuznicki," Trick said, rising to take the cup. "What is she drinking?" Trick asked, directing her question at Jill's mother, as if Jill were not in the same room, imposed in quite the same vigil.

"Cranberry juice and club soda," Mrs. Kuznicki said, but she held tight to the empty cup of it. "I have to get it. I know the right proportion. It's all she can keep down and it has to be mixed right." Mrs. Kuznicki spoke and her voice, normally as clear and direct at Father Paul's, seemed throaty, clogged, as if this mixture of cranberry juice and club soda, this important potion, was the thing that was at last going to make her tears begin.

Trick let go of the cup and returned quickly to her seat by Jill's feet, lest any action of hers, the fear—however unfounded—that she might swipe the cranberry juice cup from Mrs. Kuznicki's trembling hand, be the cause of pain. Trick looked to Deanie as she sat, twin scowls on their faces, worried but not surprised that watered down fruit juice was the only nourishment Jill had taken in nearly thirty-six hours. They scowled and shook their heads at each other, nearly missing Mrs. Kuznicki stumble as she hurried to leave the room. Father Paul caught her arm. "I'll walk with you to the cafeteria," he told her.

The tension in the room, riding high on the prayers, seemed to ease when the priest and Mrs. Kuznicki departed. There seemed to be, for a moment, the sound of breathing in the silent room, breathing resumed as people attended to needs removed from the wait—Trick reaching into her own handbag for a handful of pills, swallowing them dry, seeming to be accustomed to this; one of the men checking his watch; one of the women murmuring that she had to use the ladies room and giving up her seat. Even Jill, who was not, in essence, really in the waiting room at all, her energy or consciousness or maybe her very soul keeping the vigil somewhere nearer the doors to an operating room, sank deeper into the orange vinyl in some relief—perhaps an instant of fantasy: if she were not attended here by her mother and her priest there could be the chance that this was only a terrible dream.

Now, if the rest of them would only go away, she could wake up.

And, just at that moment, one by one, the people who were gathered in the room rose to leave.

Jill, enchanted, lifted herself to her elbow. Was her wish going to come true?

"Excuse me."

"Excuse me."

"Excuse me."

One by one the people made their way to the door, and out of it, around the surgeon who was standing in its frame. They made their excuses to the man in the gray-green scrubs, transparent blue booties over his shoes, a sweat-stained cotton cap on his head and a white mask dangling around his neck, removing themselves to afford Jill a privacy no one had even needed to request.

Trick gripped Jill's right foot in her hand. Deanie leaned toward her protectively.

"I need to speak with Mrs. Bakula," the surgeon told them and they rose now, too, in submission to the doctor.

"Where are you going?" The room was not yet empty. Many people turned to look toward Jill, wondering if she were speaking to them, but she was flailing out her left arm at Trick, her right at Deanie, fingers still curled around the rosary beads, claws now, as if she would dig them into Deanie and Trick if they tried to get away from her, too. "I need you to stay," she said, insistent, looking at them and not at the doctor who might be here to tell her the world had collapsed. "The rest of you go. Go. Deanie, sit down. Trick, sit."

They obeyed. All of them. Those whom Jill discourteously dismissed, and these two who Jill, in her customary blunt, efficient fashion, had retained.

The surgeon nodded, acceding to her wishes for this company, but Jill didn't see him do it. She wasn't going to see him. She had closed her eyes again, though now she was sitting up in the orange sofa, the red blanket tangled at her feet, around one goose-pimpled ankle. She clutched the hands she had finally caught in her own, Deanie's and Trick's. She didn't see the surgeon make his way to Mrs. Kuznicki's turquoise chair and sit, and spread his knees and rest his elbows on them wearily, rubbing the heels of his broad, freckled hands savagely into his sandy eyes.

"Mrs. Bakula?"

The surgeon waited while Jill swallowed, opened her black, river-stone eyes wide, and focused on him.

"Mrs. Bakula, your husband is stable," the surgeon said, words that might have been greeted with rejoicing but for the way his head dipped when he said them, the way his voice rose at the end of the sentence, depriving it of finality. "There is a complication. Your husband's left femoral artery, that's the one that runs from groin to foot"—the surgeon indicated the route on his own body—"was severed in the crash. We've done all that we can do to try to save his leg. We need to amputate. I need your permission to do the amputation."

Jill's gasp was inaudible. And yet you could have heard it on the other side of the world. And she hung on to her friends' hands so tightly it hurt them.

She was afraid to move. Afraid to nod in understanding, however murky, for fear the doctor would interpret the nod as the permission he came to her to seek. "His left leg?" was what she said, as if the answer to this question might be all the clarification she needed.

"His left leg," the surgeon confirmed.

And now Jill did nod, as if she couldn't help herself. "I mean… I mean, and what if you don't amputate?"

The surgeon bowed his head before he answered. "He will die."

Deanie and Trick felt Jill's fingers twitch. Contract. Sear their own with a flash of heat and then turn cool. Cold. To ice.

"But. He might die anyway." Jill spoke so softly that the three people in the room with her strained to hear.

"Yes." The surgeon allowed that this was correct. "He might die anyway. But he will die within the hour if we don't take the leg."

And still no tears from Jill. No whimper. No sound. Just those icy fingers that seemed melted now into Deanie's flesh, and Trick's, children's fingers stuck, on a dare, to an icy metal pole, too painful to remove and skin would likely be torn away, left behind on the unyielding metal, if you tried.

Jill was lost. Her body was in the waiting room, anchored there by Deanie and Trick. Her spirit was elsewhere. Considering. An athlete with but one leg. How could Chuck coach his soccer team, carry out the duties the campus was delegating to him as assistant athletic director, even if they hadn't officially given him the title yet? How would a one-legged man advocate for the state university's sports teams—what would potential donors at all of the fundraising events think of that?

What would Chuck think of himself?

Would he *want* to live? Crippled so?

Then, of course, he had to live—the young man who'd galloped on two fine, strong legs from his narrow dorm room bed to announce his love had to keep on living!

That vital, exuberant young man!

He shouldn't have to live without his leg.

What would she tell Chuck's mother? Call her up at the nursing home and hope to have caught her on a good day and tell her that his wife had given a doctor permission to cut off her son's leg? To mutilate her boy.

And, if he wasn't mutilated, within an hour he could be—not living. Children without a father and within an hour it could be her own children suffering the lack.

This was too much to consider! And there was too little time to wonder how any of these thoughts forced upon her could possibly be real. Madeline and Chas without their father! Madeline and Chas and Chuck's mother—and the boys on Chuck's soccer team. How would she tell them? Would *she* tell them? Who would tell them what had become of their coach?

These were the things that Jill considered. She did not think of herself. As a widow. She had little enough poise left without thinking of herself. One had to draw the line somewhere when one was asked to deal with the world collapsing. When one had to decide whether or not to allow someone else's leg to be cut off.

Deanie was lost. In the enormity of the decision lying upon Jill. It was too big to be anything more than a dream. If only Father Paul would lead Mrs. Kuznicki back into the room, right now—Deanie willed them to reenter the small, corner room with its ugly, vinyl furniture and the periodic *whoop-whoop-whoop* of another tragedy alighting on its rooftop—Father Paul could say some soothing words in his strong voice that would fix this problem. Mrs. Kuznicki could pray it away and no matter that, just minutes ago, in the midst of the interminable recitation of the rosary, Deanie had thought to herself, "Well, I suppose we might as well all sit here and say these same words over and over and over again because we can't do anything else for Chuck that's truly useful."

Trick was lost. For several seconds. *Tick, tick, tick—* Chuck's time ticking away.

The surgeon had his head bowed again, waiting patiently to be told to go back into the operating room. Or not.

Jill's eyes were crunched closed now, as if she were trying hard to remember something, where she put something, who might know where she last put this thing she was almost certain she'd lost. Deanie was staring, uselessly, out the window, onto a day no one had thought to notice was overcast and dreary, that overlooked nothing but a parking lost, consumed by one of her damned dreams, as if the circumstances that were laying over all of them were nothing more than a plot for one of her silly books and she could make it come out all right if she thought it through conclusively.

"Jill," Trick said, and she ripped her hand free from Jill's icy grasp.

"Jillie," Trick said, and slid to the floor so she was kneeling in front of her.

"Look at me," Trick said, and Jill did, with her large, black, vacant eyes.

"Really look. Please, try," Trick insisted, reaching up to take Jill by the shoulders, dislodging Deanie's grip on her other hand, shaking her, gently, until Jill's eyes were focused on her.

"Save your husband's life."

Jill blinked.

"The first thing," Trick said, "you have to do is save your husband's life."

Jill frowned.

"If this operation can save Chuck's life, there's really not a choice."

The clarity of Trick's words made Jill actually smile.

And made a knot of irritation form and lodge in her throat. It had been wrong of this surgeon to present his question about amputation as if there were a doubt of the answer. Wrong, and absurd and cruel to present a choice when there was no choice at all. The surgeon had confused her. Needlessly.

Jill swallowed, once. Twice. Before she could speak to the man who was waiting for her permission to salvage the fate of her beloved.

"Go," Jill ordered. "Go save his life. What are you waiting for? Go save his life!"

IN THE HOURS and days and weeks and months ahead, there was a steady stream of things to do to save Chuck's life, a list revised daily, often noting the same item day after day after day as Chuck's condition improved, did not improve, worsened, improved again. Paperwork that had to be filled out and filed so that Jill could be placed in one of the apartments the medical facility retained for the families of its long-term patients. A schedule that had to be drawn up so that at least one of them—Marilyn or Vic, Beth, Deanie or Trick—was always in Lenapi to care for Madeline and Chas, and at least one of them was always in Philadelphia with Jill, at the hospital, and then at the apartment with her when, after a solid month, Jill at last consented to leave Chuck's bedside and sleep at night. Someone had to drive Madeline and Chas to see their mother—if not yet their father—on weekends, and then drive them home. Someone had to bring fresh clothing for Jill to change into, and take her worn clothing away and launder it. They had to bring her face cream and lip balm to soothe the skin that was chapped and cracked with neglect and worry and urge her to put it on. They had to bring her a soft, chenille blanket to drape over herself in the little common waiting room when she was cold, which was often, so she wouldn't have to use the hospital's scratchy wool one. They had to bring her a liter bottle of gin to keep in the apartment and drink with the cranberry juice and club soda at night because, after the sedative that one of the doctor's had prescribed that first day wore off, Jill had refused more. She thought the drugs made her too fuzzy-headed to speak with the hospital staff, any one of whom might, at any time and with varying degrees of compassion, require her to make another life-altering decision. But she wasn't sleeping and she needed something to relax her at the end of a day and they all knew that gin would do the trick.

Five weeks after the amputation, Beth fished a right hightop sneaker out of Chuck's closet and made a special trip with her father to deliver it to Philadelphia, because the doctors recommended that Chuck's remaining foot needed the support. In the seventh week, when Chuck began to come out of his coma, he grew agitated upon each waking—reaching, searching, for his left leg—and he had to be told anew, every time, that it had been amputated to save his life. The pictures that Madeline and Chas drew for him had to be taped to the walls and the ceiling of his room, and the recording the kids had made for him had to be played continually during daylight hours in his room because he seemed, even within his deep sleeps, to recognize their voices and move the toe of the high-top sneaker in time with their words. In the eighth week a speech pathologist arrived in Chuck's room with a placemat-sized, laminated chart of letters that was to be held in front of Chuck to use to communicate, to spell out his words until the tracheal intubation was removed and he could try to speak to them again, and upon which he immediately spelled out "I feel like shit" and made everyone, even the speech pathologist, laugh.

Thank God.

There was laughter.

Saint Mona arrived to cut Chuck's hair again, and the boys on his soccer team arrived and made a circle around his bed and laid their hands on him, as his doctor had instructed, and said things like, "We miss you, Coach." "We're really doing really great for you this season and we need you back." "You gotta hurry up and get well, Coach." Rob Tedesco arrived and helped Vic Kuznicki build a ramp up the front steps of the Bakula house for Chuck's wheelchair, for the day when he would at last come home.

Since the task had been identified, clarified—the obvious priority that was not to grieve but to save Chuck's life—they went about the business of it efficiently, even cheerfully.

Chapter Twenty-three

HIGH NOON

THE ONLY TASK THAT REMAINED UNACCOM-
plished, all these many years later, though Jill
struggled with it and, sometimes, in moments just before
sleep or just upon waking, when her thoughts were cloudy
enough to grasp the slippery legalities that surrounded the
surgeon's question about saving her husband's life and made
such a question necessary, she came close to forgiving the
doctor who had made it seem, to an anguished and sedated
beloved, that there was any other course of action.

ALL THREE OF them—even, remarkably, Trick—are dabbing
at their eyes, trying to preserve their wedding day make up,
by the time Jill is finished telling the story.

"Why did we have to relive this story *this morning?*" Jill asks irritably, but she is laughing as well as crying into her wad of tissue. She knows. *She knows.*

"The two of you," Jill says, in wonder. "I would not have survived those days without the two of you. And maybe Chuck wouldn't have survived."

She looks at Trick when she says this. What she says is for Trick's benefit—Trick who needs to hear a story in which she is the heroine.

And it is for Deanie's benefit—Deanie who has been, she herself understands, annoyed with Jill for losing faith in Trick, for giving up on her stubborn sickness; Deanie who knows, *knows*, how they would all flounder even more than they already do without faith restored. Deanie who will not realize until much later this evening, until she has been on the dance floor doing the polka for a good hour or more, that all of her aches are cured.

Jill says this for her own benefit. She has stopped sweating. The beads of perspiration running down her chest have dried, and the hot red flush has faded from her cheeks. Today is not a crisis. It is a wedding day. And all of the people she loves are here—praise God—to celebrate it.

THE PROCESSION BEGINS. Bach. Music that oozes and aches joy.

The two priests wait at the altar. Father Cielinksi lifts his arms, not in blessing but to wiggle his cassock into its place on his shoulders, drawing the spectators' attention for a moment, bobbing his head and grinning as if his approval is the key to the whole magnificent event about to unfold. Father Paul stands beside him, his walker off to the side of the altar, just in case he requires it, but he is feeling strong on his feet this morning. His pleasure is the quiet sort; his smile small and steady.

Adam stands before the priest, having been brought down the aisle between both of his parents, pausing to kiss his mother as he handed her into her seat in the front pew, and to be wrapped in his father's arms for a long second before Mike Osic released him and took his own place at his son's side for the ceremony. The groom stands, turned expectantly to face the rear of the church, smiling, and shakes his head once, as if to clear it, settling into the glorious moment that has at long last arrived.

Deanie is the first of the bridesmaids poised to walk down the aisle, the tallest, paired with the tallest of the pretty groomsmen, Josh. She holds her bouquet of white tulips with her left hand and the arm Josh has offered to her with her right. She has promised herself that she will spend this day out of her head, out of her dreams, so that she will remember each moment as it happens, touches her, before it passes by. But there is a dream-like sheen to the air anyway—perhaps nothing more than the jewel-like sunlight shimmering through St. Boniface's beautiful stained glass—beams of light that distort what Deanie can see like a cloud of glitter. She knows she is smiling, feels herself walking, her feet moving slowly forward to the pace Josh is setting, though the sensation is more one of floating, her way smoothed and cushioned for having been a part of all that has come before, of this family, of this clan, of the possibility that this day has always awaited them and is here now because all of the love that has come before has allowed it. Deanie has been a part of teaching a child how to love, and the child is now a woman capable of bestowing her own infinite heart. Deanie is walking on air.

At the altar, Deanie and Josh separate, he to walk to his place at the far right of the chancel, she to hers on the left. As she turns she sees Allison among the celebrants, in the third row, and their eyes catch each other's. Allison is coming back to Napa with Deanie, to work with her and to live with her, to disrupt her life and, Deanie lets her smile grow more broad, open it up to possibilities not yet contemplated. Deanie winks at her, and Allison responds with a delicious shiver, a bright, silent giggle. Deanie's lavender shawl falls from her shoulders, to rest in the crooks of her elbows, and she lifts her attention to watch the others coming down the aisle after her.

Mary Golinski is next. Her modest black dress, in a wrinkle-resistant linen blend, skims her legs beneath her knees and is buttoned to the very top of its white lace collar. The shawl is also fastened around Mary's shoulders with a simple, old-fashioned stickpin, because she doesn't want to have to bother with the worry that it will fall off. Mary Golinski, nun poised to turn nail polish mogul, and yet the transition is not so extraordinary when you think about it: Mary Golinski will never polish her own fingernails, but if the stuff is bad for women who do polish, Mary Golinski will make sure they have a formula that isn't harmful to their health. It is a ministry, in its way. Rachel and Angie, seated a few seats behind Allison, on the bride's side, wave their fingers at their new business partner as she passes by. Mary Golinski nods her bouquet of tulips in their direction—acknowledging their greeting as well as pointing out, to Hubert who sits in a row just ahead of the girls, *These are the two young entrepreneurs I've been telling you about.* Deanie sees Hubert turn to get a look at the girls, the cosmetics visionaries whose new friendship promises Mary Golinski a community, small but of the sort her spirit had been in need of for many, many years; Deanie sees Hubert smile her approval, and she sees Mary's escort— Adam's older brother, if she's remembering correctly the clues she contrived to keep the identities of the grooms- men straight—pause, hold out his hand to Mary to help steady her as she takes the two steps into the chancel. Mary, whose knees have been no stiffer today than they usually are—and maybe less—still leans heavily on the young man, and mouths "thank you" before they part for their separate sides of the altar.

Beth follows Mary. Her great bosom and generous hips are straining the seams of her satin dress, as if she's been sewn into the garment. By the way she is walking it is evident that Beth sees the strain as an advantage, and she presses it, letting her hips sway and swivel as if they are mounted on greased fulcrums, movement not altogether appropriate for a stroll up a church aisle. Her smile, however, quivers between beatific and triumphant and Terry rises from his seat in the second pew and steps out into the aisle to get several good snapshots of his wife on his digital camera. Beth's escort, George, takes a step away from her so she can pose solo for her husband; there is a ripple of approval for Terry, a man demonstrating so freely his admiration for his wife, and then Terry steps out of their way so Beth and her groomsman can finish their walk to the end of the aisle.

Behind Beth is Trick. Trick in her teetering yellow stilet- tos, her shawl rakishly falling from one shoulder but not the other, her pretty face gaunt but pinked with excitement. Hap- piness. Her eyes skim the crowded pews, one side to the other, shyly, and yet it's easy for Deanie to see they are restless not with anxiety but wonder: *Here I am! Among all of these hon- orable women, I am here, too. And they tell me I deserve to be.*

Trick, it comes to Deanie stunningly, unexpectedly, maybe deserves to be in this procession most of all. For the rest of them, for Deanie and Beth and Mary Golinski, for Marilyn Kuznicki and for Jill, raising Madeline has been an almost involuntary act. They had simply lived their lives, in accommodation of a lovely new person, certainly, and with the greater and lesser adjustments in their schedules that nurturing the new person required, but they had never needed to will within themselves the strength to do it. To live the lives from which a child could be nourished. To struggle against their own body's chemistry for the peace of mind that allowed them to love themselves, let alone another person.

For winning this struggle, however intermittently, wasn't Trick a heroine?

And now she walks in the bridal party with shy confidence, her face still flushed with the color it had acquired as she'd arranged Madeline's veil in the vestibule, draping the creamy tulle around Madeline's bare shoulders and smoothing it with sure hands over the bow at the back waist of Madeline's wedding dress, chattering to Madeline about how, after the wedding, she was going to call up Dom in Texas and make arrangements to go see her grandchildren, she hadn't seen them in months and being around all of this family, well, it inspired her! And she was going to try to get to Napa, too, in July, when Jill and Chuck were out there for their anniversary; she had so many plans! So many plans she had to make, she said, and they filled up her heart, and Madeline was the one who'd started it all, started filling up her empty heart again by making her a part of this wedding day. And then Trick had run a palm over Madeline's veil, lightly, and stopped talking, at peace enough to know that no more needed to be said.

Now she walks with buoyancy up the aisle behind Beth, on the arm of her beefy, handsome escort, her fine heart—for the moment, and maybe longer—full.

The music swells as Marilyn Kuznicki begins her walk to the altar, a barely perceptible rise in volume, tempo—or perhaps it is that the organist simply adds one more note to the already striking and complex chord that accompanies Mrs. Kuznicki's first step. Mrs. Kuznicki, as Deanie has expected, wants to walk more quickly than the other bridesmaids—more quickly than Father Cielinksi has instructed them to walk—still a bit abashed at her extraordinary place in her granddaughter's wedding party. Her groomsman, Chas, places his right hand on top of his grandmother's, where she holds him at his elbow, to remind her gently of the pace. Mrs. Kuznicki grins at his touch, and more broadly than anyone has, in recent memory, seen her grin, releasing herself into the role Madeline has assigned to her. Even the shawl around her shoulders seems to relax, drape more fluidly around her strong, tiny body.

And then strong, tiny, practical Mrs. Kuznicki, newly discovered massage devotee and unexpected pinball wizard, catches her husband's eyes as he watches her advance. Vic Kuznicki's eyes, two black, moist river stones, lock on hers and the smiles they exchange are a physical conduit. They might as well have said it out loud, the thought that passes between them at this moment—*"Look at what we have done! Look at what has come since that spring day in 1954 when we made our own walk down the aisle. Could you have ever imagined we two could accomplish all of this!"* The whole congregation is grinning by the time Marilyn Kuznicki gets to the altar.

Jill follows her mother. Deanie feels a pang at her entrance, knowing as she does that this wedding, a beginning for Madeline and Adam, is a sort of a finale for Jill.

"But, don't you love what you do, Jill? What will you do if you retire?" Deanie had asked her several times over the course of the past week, once she found that retirement was Jill's true intention.

"Start on my second career," Jill had answered.

"And what will that be?" Deanie had demanded.

Jill had smiled, dreamily. "I don't know quite yet. I've got to close this chapter of my life before I can figure out how I want to begin the next one."

Jill, it seems to Deanie, is going to close the current chapter with style. She is meeting every eye anxious to meet hers on the way up the aisle with delight, throwing smiles, even using her bouquet of tulips once or twice to wave, pulling the lavender shawl that falls from her shoulder during this gesture back into place with a flourish.

Behind them all is Cara, in her gossamer dress, and she is clearly carried away by the energy that has preceded her down the aisle, the life force of so many delighted people. She is skipping, rather than walking as she has been instructed to do, strewing rose petals hither and thither from the basket she carries in the crook of her elbow. The congregation catches sight of the little girl and soft laughter ripples through the pews, encouraging Cara in her madcap princess mode, and Terry stands once again in the aisle to get a good picture, and then all of the people in all of the pews are standing, turning toward the double doors at the far end of the church where the bride is posed with her father.

THE WEDDING CEREMONY itself, it seems to Deanie, passes in a blur. It seems as if the day's main event passes too quickly though how that could ever be so is a mystery, it's a complete Catholic wedding ceremony, with a Mass and communion, and lasts more than an hour that can be recalled only as moments: the bride reaching up to touch her lips to her father's cheek for a lingering moment, Chuck bending to whisper something in his daughter's ear that makes a bubble of laughter escape from her lips right before they begin their walk up the aisle. Madeline handing Jill her bouquet, their eyes as entwined as their hands, before turning to her groom. The handsome couple touching their foreheads together, an unscripted instant as they meet on the altar, as if they need a moment to collect their joy before they gaze at each other. Father Paul asking, in his sweet, distinctive voice, "Who gives these young people to each other?" and Madeline's family and Adam's responding as if from one heart, "We do."

The readings, rendered in a bold voice by one of Madeline's girlfriends, making the declaration: "The greatest of these is love!" The achingly beautiful hymns—*Ave Maria* preformed by yet another gifted friend of the bridal couple, a young man with an otherworldly talent. A strand of Madeline's blonde hair falling free as Father Cielinksi pronounces her and Adam husband and wife, lifting her hand to brush it aside as she and Adam bend their heads toward each other, as they pause to behold each other's faces, lock the moment in memory before their first kiss as husband and wife. It all speeds by, in defiance of the months of planning that preceded it, and the bride and groom are leaving the church, trailing their attendants.

In the vestibule, the bridal party lines up to form a receiving line. Deanie makes a detour to the alcove near the green

marble baptismal font, to retrieve the basket Kelly has left
there at her instruction. She holds the basket against her hip,
looking for Angie or Rachel or any friend of the newlyweds
she can waylay to ask to pass out these favors to the guests
as they make their way through the line and gather on the
grassy lawn in front of the church.

"Deanie Morrow!" Sherry Platt sings, breaking from the
crowd toward Deanie. "How are you!"

"I am just fine, Sherry Platt!" Deanie laughs. "Hey, do you
think you could do me a favor? Pass one of these out to everyone on the lawn? We couldn't have rice, or birdseed, so these
are to use when Mad and Adam leave the church..."

"You just hand those right on over!" Sherry Platt takes the
basket from Deanie with plump hands, each finger sparkling
with a diamond or a ruby, fancier rings for today's formal
occasion than the rocks she'd had on when she and Deanie
first met. "I'll make sure every single person gets one," she
exclaims, seriously, the sort of guest honored to be asked to
perform a wedding task.

By the time Deanie returns to the bridal party, Heidi Jean
Welkins's ex-husband is making his way through the receiving line. It hadn't occurred to Deanie to ask which half of the
scandalous couple was going to be invited to this wedding,
seeing as how inviting both Heidi Jean and her ex would have
been asking for trouble, but it makes immediate sense that
Chuck's frequent golf partner would be given preference over
a friend from high school who Jill only ever sees anymore at
weddings and wakes. "Nice to see you," Deanie says, offering
her check for the kiss Heidi Jean's ex is leaning toward her to
bestow, and offering her hand to the woman who accompanies him, "I'm Deanie Morrow. Good to meet you."

"Deanie Morrow!" The woman laughs, and Deanie thinks that she's another fan surprised to find her favorite author at the Bakula wedding. "Deanie Morrow, don't you remember me? It's Amy Jenner. *Amy*. Amy Tanner?"

"Oh, my gosh!" Deanie laughs, too, at herself, hugging the old prom queen. Making a mental note to ask Jill if she knew Heidi Jean's ex-husband was bringing Heidi Jean's high school rival as his date. Marveling—and not incidentally—at the incest produced by the limited waters in a small town dating pool: "I used to be married to Stu Jenner—you remember him from school, don't you, Deanie? I think he even dated Jill for a little while? Anyway, we're divorced now..."

Jill keeps the receiving line moving too efficiently for Deanie to respond to Amy Jenner with more than acknowledgement—"Deanie," Jill asks, "you remember Stella Bruno and Madge Strunk?" Yes, the teacher who lives one cul-de-sac over from the Bakulas and her friend Madge who, Deanie seems to recall, is a teacher, too, or maybe a muckety-muck with the state teacher's union... "And Tip and Ellen Pomeroy?" Of course; he is the football coach, and Chuck's best friend, and she was at the bridal shower. "Rose Wild?" How could Deanie forget a woman with a name like that? Rose is a yoga instructor, and Deanie has always wondered if her beautiful name was bestowed or chosen—"Hi, Rose," Deanie says as the woman bends to kiss her in greeting. Then, almost before she can return the gesture, Rob Tedesco is in front of her, waiting to plant his own kiss on her cheek. "This can not be Deanie Morrow," he says to her gravely.

"Huh?"

"The Deanie Morrow I know would be a puddle of tears just about right now. Who is this dry-eyed creature I'm talking to?" He leans in conspiratorially. "What have you done with the Crying Bridesmaid?"

"Get out." Deanie pushes—but gently, playfully—against Rob's shoulders.

The church empties slowly for, no matter how many times Jill says, *Thank you for coming, I'll look forward to talking with you more at the reception*," guests feel the need to say one or two things more: how lovely the bride is, or how tasteful the flowers are, or how extraordinary is the make up of the bridal party. Finally Jill is able to shoo them all out, shoo the bridal party outside, too, ahead of the newly married couple. Deanie meets Sherry Platt at the bottom step, where Sherry has stationed herself to make certain no guest gets by without one of the little silver bells Deanie has commissioned her to pass out from the basket. Tiny silver bells, their clappers tinkling like stray crystal upon crystal among the guests milling on the church lawn, their tiny, heart-shaped handles threaded with lavender satin streamers. "Here you are," Sherry Platt is saying officiously as she hands one to each guest, "ring this when Maddie and Adam come out of the church. It's instead of rice."

Deanie has a moment of doubt. Are the bells—is her idea for the bells—hokey?

Will they make some hokey, tinny, anti-climactic sound?

Will two hundred people standing on the lawn struggling against the tiny clappers on the tiny instruments make a noise worthy of the day's celebration?

The wedding, as rapidly as it has passed by, has been chockfull of genuine moments—the bride and groom touching their foreheads together when they met at the altar; Deanie hoped the photographer had managed a shot of that!—and the day itself is glorious, perfect, the edges of a glinting sun softened by summer breezes that blow the streamers on the bells, dance them so they wind around arms and waists. The bells might come off as staged—after all, the bride and groom weren't really leaving the church, only making their way down its front steps to stand momentarily and signal to the guests that they could leave, go enjoy the open bar at the Farron House ballroom while the bridal party went back inside for pictures.

The bells feel suddenly gimmicky—small—to Deanie and she worries they are a bad idea and then there is no time to worry because the newlyweds have emerged and they are standing on the top step of the church, hand-in-hand, smiling out over their friends and family like royalty, absorbed in their benevolent power and in each other as they might never again be permitted to be—so self-satisfied, so delighted with themselves. So happy. And people are ringing the bells.

Lifting them up over their heads and jangling the clappers for all they are worth.

Filling the summer air with a sweet crystal-upon-crystal serenade that lifts on the breeze to the newlyweds.

And, in response, the newlyweds' mouths form their O of surprise. Laughter. They look at each other then raise their joined hands, stretch out their arms and, in this way, they descend the stairs, floating on the sound, falling from a star, the glassy sound holding them up like prayers.

Like love.

Like Chuck had once described the way that hands that were laid upon him while he was in the hospital had held him up. "The whole time I was in my coma—I think even when you all weren't actually in the room with me—I felt your hands and that's what kept me up, from crashing down into this dark, dank pit I felt like I was hovering over, your hands kept me floating in the place that was still light and warm."

As they were supposed to do, friends holding each other up for a lifetime, sometimes with love alone.

"What a terrific idea!" Jill squeals, hooking her arm through Deanie's. "What a great idea these bells are!" she says as the photographer hustles to capture pictures of the bridal couple—proof of what even he is aware is a gravity-defying descent, the couple in mid-air, mid-kiss. The bells finally stilled only as the people on the lawn join their hands to applaud.

"Great idea," Trick agrees, coming up beside Jill, letting Jill link her free arm through her elbow.

Jill sighs. "Madeline's married," she whispers. She tightens her hold on her friends.

"I need the bridal party and the immediate families back in the church for pictures now," the photographer announces. "Although, in this case, I think they're pretty much the same thing." He lets his camera dangle from his neck, raising his arms and pointing toward the church doors with extended forefingers, as if this gesture alone will herd his subjects back inside where no one is inclined to go. The sunshine is too brilliant. The sound of bells, tinkling intermittently on the breeze, in the hands of children still excited by their novelty, is too seductive. The bride and groom are giving each other yet another kiss and it is as impossible to stop watching them as it is to tear your eyes away from any beauty.

"*Really*," the photographer mutters, and he walks back into the church alone when no one follows.

Jill laughs, an abrupt, wicked little trill. "That poor man. Do you suppose if the mother of the bride goes after him, the rest will eventually follow?"

Deanie shrugs, in no hurry.

Trick says, "I suppose you could give it a try."

Jill nods. Turns her face to the sky for one more bright moment in the sun.

"Lord—" Trick staggers on her high yellow heels, rolls her eyes at Deanie. "I told you these were a little tight but I thought they'd be all right—my feet are killing me already."

Jill looks down at Trick's shoes. "How are you ever going to polka in those things?" she asks, and then a wild idea grabs hold of her. Her wide grin lets her friends know something is up. She uses the toe of her foot to peel off one sling-back, then the other, but neither Trick nor Deanie know what she's doing until she is suddenly three inches shorter.

Deanie's laughter is quick, and she is quick, too, to kick off her own pumps, and now both she and Jill are shorter, but only momentarily, than Trick. "What the hell," Trick says as she steps out of the yellow shoes.

"Now we'll be able to polka," Jill declares. Then she moves forward, holding fast where her arm is joined to Deanie's, and where her arm is joined to Trick's, and together they proceed.

About the Author

Cate Quintara has been a mom, a homemaker, a high
school English teacher, a community volunteer, and the joyful caretaker of lifelong friendships with the women who inspired this book. She has always wanted to be a writer and,
at 52, having lived a life rich with the extraordinary stories of
"ordinary" people, she has a wealth of material on which to
draw. *The Happy Party of Honorable Women* is her first novel.

Reading Group Questions
and Topics for Discussion

1. JILL, TRICK AND DEANIE have been best friends since they were twelve years old. What is the moment when they first bonded—when you first understood the bond they share?

2. *THE HAPPY PARTY OF HONORABLE WOMEN* is a book that is, in large part, about the joys and deep loyalties among a group of women friends. Discuss the nature of friendship among women—how friendship among women differs from friendship among men.

3. THERE IS A FLUIDITY of friendship in this novel; admiration and respect flow easily among the generations—from Madeline, the twenty-four-year-old bride, to her mother, grandmother, her favorite professor, her mother's friends, and even to young Cara, her five-year-old cousin. Discuss the value and inspiration you've found in your own intergenerational friendships.

4. TRICK SUFFERS FROM bipolar disorder. Discuss how this disorder can disrupt the life of the patient, and the patient's family—and if you agree with Deanie's conclusion that Trick really is a heroine for her ability to rise, however intermittently, above her struggle.

5. BOTH FAITH AND FRIENDSHIP play large roles in Jill's life, enabling her to transcend tragedy and forge a full life for herself and her family in its wake. Discuss the roles faith and friendship have played in your life, in buoying you through circumstances that, without these assets, would have been more difficult to overcome.

RECEIVE 10% OFF YOUR FUTURE WATER STREET PRESS E-BOOK PURCHASES.

Virgins & Martyrs
Hugh Mahoney
FICTION
Available Fall 2012

New Yorkers open their Sunday morning paper to find a photo of Virgil Quinn, teacher of history at St. Lucy's School for Boys, splashed all over the front page. How did he get there? Scandal, of course. Virgil has made enemies—the Cardinal of New York not the least among them. The Cardinal's research reveals that Virgil has lived many lives, all of them scandalous. Was he really a ranking nun in the Sisters of Mercy of Baton Rouge? Did he really walk the ramps of Seventh Avenue as the city's highest paid super-model? Just how did he come to know all those men whose names appear in his notorious (and deadly convenient) Black Books? *Virgins & Martyrs* is shrewd and malicious fun, a wicked commentary on love, life, gender and the history of our nation, a work in which the peripatetic and intrepid—yet all-too-human—Virgil Quinn lets no one off the hook.

Stalking Carlos Castaneda
Joan Wulfsohn
NONFICTION
Available Fall 2012

In 1972, professional dancer Joan Wulfsohn underwent a double mastectomy. And her soon-to-be-ex-husband abducted their three children and spirited them away to a foreign country. "I should have died," Joan writes. But she didn't. *Stalking Carlos Castaneda* chronicles her journey back to life by way of lessons learned from stunning transvestites and music hall dancers, teen porn stars, a brain damaged boy, Eastern holy men, Western supermodels and a certain aging sorcerer. It is the story of how one woman learned to live a magical life—bound not by spells and hexes but rather filled with wonder and transcendence.

The Muffia
Ann Royal Nicholas
FICTION
Available Fall 2012

Madelyn Scott-Crane is a smart, 42-year-old professional mediator and single mom who's having the best sex of her life—after twenty-two months of self-imposed abstinence—inspired by the ladies of her book club, The Muffia, and the Muff's latest racy read. But on their second date, as Maddie and her mysterious Israeli heartthrob, Udi, come together in orgasmic splendor that may or may not also be actual love, Udi collapses on top of her. Dead. When Udi's "friends"—who resemble large appliances— arrive to claim his body, the Muffs decide that Udi had secrets, and they need to know what those secrets were. That's when these well-read women put down their books and set out to expose the truth—whatever the dangerous truth might be. International intrigue combines with literary pursuits, lots of home-cooked food, and a little vibrator shopping.

Creole Son
Michael Llewellyn
FICTION
Available Fall 2012

In 1872, French painter Edgar Degas is disillusioned by a lackluster career and haunted by the Prussian siege of Paris and the bloodbath of the Commune. Seeking personal and professional rebirth, he journeys to New Orleans, birthplace of his Creole mother. He is horrified to learn he has exchanged one city in crisis for another—post-Civil War New Orleans is a corrupt town occupied by hostile Union troops and suffering under the heavy hand of Reconstruction. He is further shocked to find his family deeply involved in the violent struggle to reclaim political power at all costs.

Despite the chaos swirling around him, Degas sketches and paints with fervor and manages to reinvent himself and transition his style from neoclassical into the emerging world of Impressionism. He ultimately became one of the masters of the new movement, but how did New Orleans empower Degas to fulfill this destiny?

The answer may be found in the impeccably researched, richly imagined historical novel, *Creole Son*.

Go to www.waterstreetpressbooks.com
Use Coupon Code number 1005-12IBC